MAISEY YATES

One Night Charmer

HQN™

HQN™

ISBN-13: 978-0-373-78965-8

Recycling programs
for this product may
not exist in your area.

One Night Charmer

CONTENTS

ONE NIGHT CHARMER   7

HOMETOWN HEARTBREAKER   355

Dear Reader,

I'm so excited to welcome you back to Copper Ridge, Oregon, where the cowboys are hot and love happens when you least expect it.

Gruff, bearded bartender Ace Thompson was one of those characters that grabbed hold of me and wouldn't let go. I never intended for him to be a hero, but he kept showing up in everyone else's books and making a case for himself. When Sierra West, the rodeo princess of Copper Ridge, appeared for the first time in *Bad News Cowboy*, I knew she was the kind of woman who would drive a man like Ace crazy. Which was also how I knew they were destined to be together.

Sierra and the rest of the West family have been going through a shift thanks to old family secrets coming to light. I'm excited for you to learn more about the town's most prominent family in this story and in my upcoming Copper Ridge books, *Tough Luck Hero* and *Last Chance Rebel*, coming from HQN Books in July and September, and *Hold Me, Cowboy*, coming from Harlequin Desire in November.

I hope you enjoy getting to know the town's favorite bartender and fallen princess as much as I enjoyed finally giving them their story.

Happy reading!

Maisey

ONE NIGHT CHARMER

CHAPTER ONE

THERE WERE TWO PEOPLE in Copper Ridge, Oregon, who—between them—knew nearly every secret of every person in town. The first was Pastor John Thompson, who heard confessions of sin and listened to people pour out their hearts when they were going through trials and tribulations.

The second was Ace Thompson, owner of the most popular bar in town, son of the pastor, and probably the least likely to attend church on Sunday or any other day.

There was no question that his father knew a lot of secrets, though Ace was pretty certain he got the more honest version. His father spent time standing behind the pulpit; Ace stood behind a bar. And there he heard the deepest and darkest circumstances happening in the lives of other townspeople while never revealing any of his own. He supposed, pastor or bartender, that was kind of the perk.

They poured it all out for you, and you got to keep your secrets bottled up inside.

That was how Ace liked it. Every night of the week, he had the best seat in the house for whatever show Copper Ridge wanted to put on. And he didn't even have to pay for it.

And with his newest acquisition, the show was about to get a whole lot better.

"Really?" Jack Monaghan sat down at the bar, beer in hand, his arm around his new fiancée, Kate Garrett. "A mechanical bull?"

"Damn straight, Monaghan. This is a classy-ass establishment, after all."

"Seriously," Connor Garrett said, taking the seat next to Jack, followed by his wife Liss. "Where did you get that thing?"

"I traded for it. Guy down in Tolowa owed me some money and he didn't have it. So he said I could come by and look at his stash of trash. Lo and behold, I discovered Ferdinand over there."

"Congratulations," Kate said. "I didn't think anything could make this place more of a dive. I was wrong."

"You're a peach, Kate," Ace told her.

The woman smiled broadly and wrapped her arm around Jack, leaning in and resting her cheek on his shoulder.

"Can we get a round?" Connor asked.

"Yes, please," Liss said. "I have a one drink limit and we have a full two hours before I have to get back home."

"Eli and Sadie are on baby duty," Connor added.

Ace continued to listen to their conversation as he served up their usual brew, enjoying the happy tenor of the banter since the downers would probably be around later to dish out woe while he served up harder liquor.

The Garretts were good people. Always had been. Both before he had left Copper Ridge, and since he'd come back.

His focus was momentarily pulled away when the pretty blonde who'd been hanging out in the dining area all evening drinking with friends approached the aforementioned Ferdinand.

He hadn't had too many people ride the bull yet, and he had to admit, he was finding it a pretty damn enjoyable novelty.

The woman tossed her head, her tan cowboy hat staying in place while her curls went wild around her shoulders. She wrapped her hands around the harness on top of the mechanical creature and hoisted herself up. Her movements were unsteady, and he had a feeling, based on the amount of time the group had been here, and how many times the men in the group had come and gone from the bar, she was more than a little tipsy.

Best seat in the house. He always had the best seat in the house.

She glanced up as she situated herself and he got a good look at her face. There was a determined glint in her eyes, her brows locked together, her lips pursed into a tight circle. She wasn't just tipsy, she was pissed. Looking down at the bull like it was her own personal Everest and she was determined to conquer it along with her rage. He wondered what a bedazzled little thing like her had to be angry about. A missing lipstick, maybe. A pair of shoes that she really wanted unavailable in her size.

She nodded once, her expression growing even *more* determined as she signaled the employee Ace had operating the controls tonight.

Ace moved nearer to the bar, planting his hands flat on the surface. "This probably won't end well."

The patrons at the bar turned their heads toward the scene. And he noticed Jack's posture go rigid. "Is that—"

"Yes," Kate said.

The mechanical bull pitched forward and the petite blonde sitting on the top of it pitched right along with it. She managed to stay seated, but in Ace's opinion that was a miracle. The bull went back again, and the woman straightened, arching her back and thrusting her breasts forward, her head tilted upward, the overhead lighting bathing her pretty face in a golden glow. And for a moment, just a moment, she looked like a graceful, dirty angel getting into the rhythm of the kind of riding Ace preferred above anything else.

Then the great automated beast pitched forward again and the little blonde went over the top, down onto the mats underneath. There were howls from her so-called friends as they enjoyed her deposition just a little too much.

She stood on shaky legs and walked back over to the group, picking up a shot glass and tossing back another, her face twisted into an expression that suggested this was not typical behavior for her.

Kate frowned and got up from the stool, walking across the bar and making her way over to the other woman.

He had a feeling he should know the woman's name, had a feeling that he probably did somewhere in the back corner of his mind. He knew everyone. Which meant that he knew a lot *about* a lot of people, recognized nearly every face he passed on the street. He could usually place them with their most defining life moments, as those were the things that often spilled out on the bar top after a few shots too many.

But it didn't mean he could put a name to every face. Especially when that face was halfway across the room, shielded slightly by a hat.

"Who is that?" he asked.

"Sierra West," Jack said, something in his tone strange.

"Oh, right."

Ace knew the West family well enough, or rather, he

knew of them. Everyone did, though they were hardly the type to frequent his establishment. Sierra did, which would explain why she was familiar, though they never made much in the way of conversation. She was the type who was always absorbed in her friends or her cell phone when she came to place her order. No deep confessionals from Sierra over drinks.

He'd always found it a little strange she patronized his bar when the rest of the West family didn't.

Dive bars weren't really their thing.

He imagined mechanical bulls probably weren't, either. Judging not just by her pedigree, but by the poor performance.

"No cotillions going on tonight, I guess," Ace said.

Jack turned his head sharply, his expression dark. "What's that supposed to mean?"

"Nothing."

He didn't know why, but his statement had clearly offended Monaghan. Ace wasn't in the business of voicing his opinion. He was in the business of listening. Listening and serving. No one needed to know his take on a damn thing. They just wanted a sounding board to voice their own opinions and hear them echoed back.

Typically, he had no trouble with that. This had been a little slipup.

"She's not bad," Jack said.

Sierra was a friend of Jack's fiancée, that much was obvious. Kate was over there talking to the woman, her expression concerned. Sierra still looked mutinous. He was starting to wonder if she was mutinous toward the entire world, or something in particular.

"I'm sure she isn't." He wasn't sure of any such thing. In fact, if Ace knew one thing about the world and all the people in it, it was that there was a particular type who used their every advantage in life to take whatever they wanted whenever they wanted it, regardless of promises made. Whether they were words whispered in the dark or vows spoken in front of whole crowds of people.

He was a betting man. And he would lay odds that Sierra West was one of those people. She was the type. Rich, a big fish in the small pond of the community, and beautiful. That combination got you whatever you wanted. And when the option for *whatever you wanted* was available, very few people resisted it.

Hell, why would you? There were a host of things he would change if he had infinite money and power.

But just because he figured he'd be in the same boat if he were rich and almighty didn't mean he had to like it on other people.

Jack's defensiveness of Sierra made Ace a little bit suspicious. And he made a mental note to keep an eye on that situation. He didn't like to think that Jack would ever do anything to betray Kate. If for no other reason than that her older brothers would kill him dead without one shred of remorse between the two of them.

Hell, Ace would help. Kate was a nice girl, and up until she and Jack had gotten together, he would never have said Jack was a nice guy. A *good* guy, sure, but definitely not the kind of guy you would want messing around with your little sister.

He looked back over at Kate, who patted her friend on the shoulder before shaking her head and walking back toward the group. "She didn't want to come sit with us or anything," Kate told them, giving Jack a sideways look.

Now he wondered if she was an ex of Jack's. If she was, he also wondered why Kate was being so friendly to her.

Kate Garrett was good people, but even she had her limits, Ace was sure.

The Garrett-Monaghan group lingered at the bar for another couple of hours before they were replaced by another set of customers. Sierra's group thinned out a little bit, but didn't disperse completely. A couple of the guys were starting to get rowdy, and Ace was starting to think he was going to have to play the part of his own bouncer tonight. It wouldn't be the first time.

Fortunately, the rowdier members of the group slowly trickled outside. He watched as Sierra got up and made her way back to the bathroom, leaving a couple of girls—one of whom he assumed was the designated driver—sitting at the table.

The tab was caught up, so he didn't really care how it all went down. He wasn't a babysitter, after all.

He turned, grabbed a rag out of the bucket beneath the counter and started to wipe it down. When he looked up again, the girls who had been sitting at the table were gone, and Sierra West was standing in the center of the room looking around like she was lost.

Then she glanced in his direction, and her eyes lit up like a sinner looking at salvation.

Wrong guess, honey.

She wandered over to the bar, her feet unsteady. "Did you see where my friends went?"

She had that look about her. Like a lost baby deer. All wide, dewy eyes and unsteady limbs. And damned if she wasn't cute as hell.

"Out the door," he said, almost feeling sorry for her. Almost.

She wasn't the first pretty young drunk to get ditched in his bar by stupid friends. She was also exactly the kind of woman he avoided at all costs, no matter how cute or seemingly vulnerable she was.

"What?" She swayed slightly. "They weren't supposed to leave me."

She sounded mystified. Completely dumbfounded that anyone would ever leave her high and dry.

"I figured," he said. "Here's a tip, get better friends."

She frowned. "They're the best friends I have."

He snorted. "That's a sad story."

She held up her hand, the broad gesture out of place coming from such a refined creature. "Just a second."

"Sure."

She turned away, heading toward the door and out to the parking lot.

He swore. He didn't know if she had a car out there, or if she was intent on driving herself. But she was way too skunked to drive.

"Watch the place, Jenna," he said to one of the waitresses, who nodded and assumed a rather important-looking position with her hands flat on the bar and a rag in her hand, as though she were ready to wipe crumbs away with serious authority.

He rounded the counter and followed the same path Sierra had just taken out into the parking lot. He looked around for a moment and didn't see her. Then he looked down and there she was, sitting on the edge of the curb. "Everything okay?"

That was a stupid question, since he already knew the answer.

She lifted her head. "No."

He let out a long, drawn-out sigh. The problem was, he'd followed her out here. If he had just let her walk out the door, then nothing but the pine trees and the seagulls would have been responsible for her. But no, he'd had to follow. He'd been concerned about her driving. And now, he would have to follow through on that concern.

"You don't have a ride?"

She shook her head, looking miserable. "Everyone left me. Because they aren't nice. You're right. I do need better friends."

"Yes," he said, "you do. And let me go ahead and tell you right now, I won't be one of them. But as long as you don't live somewhere ridiculous like Portland, I can give you a ride home."

And this, right here, was the curse of owning a bar. Whether he should or not, he felt responsible in these situations. She was compromised, it was late, cabs were scarce in a town the size of Copper Ridge and she was alone. He could not let her meander her way back home. Not when he could easily see that she got there safely.

"A ride?" She frowned, her delicate features lit dramatically by the security light hanging on the front of the bar.

"I know your daddy probably told you not to take rides from strangers, but trust me, I'm the safest bet around. Unless you want to call someone." He checked his watch. "It's inching close to last call. I'm betting not very many people are going to come out right now."

She shook her head slowly. "Probably not."

He sighed heavily, reaching into his pocket and wrapping his fingers around his keys. "All right, come on. Get in the truck."

SIERRA LOOKED UP at her unlikely, bearded, plaid-clad savior. She knew who it was, of course. Ace Thompson was the owner of the bar, and she bought beer from him at least twice a month when she came out with her friends. They'd exchanged money and drinks across the counter more times than she could recall, but this was more words than she'd ever exchanged with him in her life.

She was angry at herself. For getting drunk. For going out with the biggest jerks in the local rodeo club. For getting on the back of a mechanical bull and opening herself up to their derision—because honestly, when you sat your drunk ass on a fake, bucking animal, you pretty much deserved it. And most of all, for sitting down in the parking lot acting like she was going to cry just because she had been ditched by said jerky friends.

Oh, and being *caught* at what was most definitely an epic low made it all even worse. Ace had almost certainly seen her inglorious dismount of the mechanical bull, then witnessed everyone leaving without her.

She'd been so sure today couldn't get any worse.

Tequila had proven her wrong.

"I'm fine," she said, and she could have bitten off her own tongue, because she wasn't fine. As much as she wanted to pretend she didn't need his help, she kind of did. Granted, she could call Madison or Colton. But if her sister had to drive all the way down to town from the family ranch she would probably kill Sierra. And if she called Colton's house his fiancée would probably kill Sierra.

Either way, that made for a dead Sierra.

She couldn't exactly call her father, since she wasn't speaking to him. Which, really, was the root of the evil that was today.

"Sure you are. *Most* girls who end up sitting on their ass at 1:00 a.m. in a parking lot are just fine."

She blinked, trying to bring his face into focus. He refused to be anything but a fuzzy blur. "I am."

For some reason, her stubbornness was on full display, and most definitely outweighing her common sense. That was probably related to the alcohol. And the fact that all of her restraint had been torn down hours ago. Sometime early this morning when she had screamed at her father and told him she never wanted to see him again, because she'd found out he was a liar. A cheater.

Right, so that was probably why she was feeling rebellious. Angry in general. But she probably shouldn't direct it at the person who was offering to give her a ride.

In spite of the fact that her brain had rationalized this course of action, her ass was still firmly planted on the ground.

"Don't make me ask you twice, Sierra. It's going to make me get real grumpy, and I don't think you'll like that." Ace shifted his stance, crossing his arms over his broad chest—she was pretty sure it was broad, either that or she was seeing double—and looked down at her.

She got to her wobbly feet, pitching slightly to the side before steadying herself. Her head was spinning, her stomach churning, and she was just mad. Because she felt like crap. Because she knew better than to drink like this, at least when she wasn't in the privacy of her own home.

"Which truck?" she asked, rubbing her forehead.

He jerked his head to the left. "This way."

He turned, not waiting for her, and began to walk across the parking lot. She followed as quickly as she could. Fortunately, the lot was mostly empty so she didn't have to watch much but the back of Ace as they made their way to the vehicle. It wasn't a new, flashy truck. It was old, but it was in good condition. Better than most she'd seen at such an advanced age. But then, as far as she knew Ace wasn't a rancher. He owned a bar, so it wasn't like his truck saw all that much action.

She stood in front of the passenger-side door for a long moment before realizing he was not coming around to open it for her. Her face heated as she jerked open the door for herself and climbed inside.

It had a bench seat. And she found herself clinging to the door, doing her best to keep the expansive seat between them as wide as possible. She was suddenly conscious of the fact that he was a very large man. Tall, broad, muscular. She'd known that, somewhere in the back of her mind she'd known that. But the way he filled up the cab of a truck containing just the two of them was much more significant than the way he filled the space in a vast and crowded bar.

He started the engine, saying nothing as he put the truck in Reverse and began to pull out of the lot. She looked straight ahead, clinging to the door handle, desperate to find something to say. The silence was oppressive, heavy around them. It made her feel twitchy, nervous. She always knew what to say. She was in command of every social situation she ever stepped into. People found her charming, and if they didn't, they never said otherwise. Because she was Sierra West, and her family name carried with it the burden of mandatory respect from the people of Copper Ridge.

Her father was one of the most esteemed horse breeders in the entire country, and it wasn't uncommon for his connections to bring people with big money into town, sometimes on a permanent basis. An entire culture of horsemanship had been built up because of her father, because of her sister Madison's dressage training. And in addition to that, her family made donations to the schools, to local charities…

And beneath all of that, what no one else knew was that her father was actually an awful human being.

That's not true. Jack Monaghan knows. His mother knows.

Her friend Kate knew, since she was engaged to Jack and all.

The secret was like a festering wound that had been tightly bandaged for years. But now the bandage was ripped off, and the wound was reopening, the truth of it slowly bleeding out around them, touching more and more people with each passing day.

She took a deep breath, trying to ease the pressure in her chest, trying to remove the weight that was sitting there.

"What's your sign?" Somehow, her fuzzy brain had retrieved that as a conversation starter. The moment the words left her mouth she wanted to stuff them back in and swallow them.

To her surprise, Ace laughed. "Caution."

"What?"

"I'm a caution sign, baby. Now where are we going?"

"I'm staying with my brother Colton. He has a ranch just outside of town. After the Farm and Garden. Not as far out as the Garretts, kind of by Aiden Crawford's place."

"Does he have an address?"

She blinked, shaking her head. "Right. 316 Highway 104."

"All right, I think I can figure that out."

"I can give you directions. Or you can map it on your phone."

He snorted. "Do I look like I'm carrying a smartphone?"

No, no he didn't. "Oh. A caution sign. Like on the road." Suddenly, the meaning of his comment washed over her. "I get it."

"Good job."

She sniffed. "You don't have to be mean. I'm drunk, not stupid." Actually, she was debating that last thing. Right now, she was heavily debating it. Most of her actions over the past twenty-four hours had been pretty freaking stupid. Apparently anger made her kind of dumb.

"This is a judgment-free zone, little girl," he said, making her feel smaller, sillier with that very reductive endearment. Was it even an endearment if it was reductive? She wasn't sure.

She was only pondering that because of the alcohol. She wasn't sure she would have noticed his phrasing at all if she'd been sober. A lot of men talked to her like that. *Baby doll. Pretty little thing.*

She didn't have trouble with men. Or, more to the point, she could have exactly the kind of trouble she wanted to with most any guy in town. She *didn't*, because she was a West, and she'd always been taught the importance of discretion in such matters. That truth had been hammered home when Madison had dealt with her own crazy scandal at seventeen.

Sierra'd had boyfriends at college, but, while she liked to engage in a little bit of flirtation with the men in town, she wasn't really one to follow through. In a place like Copper Ridge it was too easy to run into an ex at a stop sign, and she had never wanted to deal with that. Had never wanted to deal with bringing a guy home to her family. Too many expectations.

Which, given the recent revelations about her father, was a bit of a joke.

For all his talk about discretion he had apparently spread himself all over town. And he had a child with someone else. A child who was now a man. A man who had been in the bar tonight. A man who had just seen her go ass-over-head off a mechanical bull.

She'd totally lost the thread of the conversation, and her train of thought. Her head was starting to hurt. She knew that she was going to regret all of this in the morning, intensely. She was regretting it now, even with the comforting blanket of alcohol still somewhat wrapped around her.

Tomorrow was going to be a very particular kind of hell.

"I'm not a little girl," she said, because it was the only thing she could think of to say.

"Of course not," he replied, his tone placating.

She had known who Ace Thompson was for a long time. He was the guy that almost everyone in town had bought their very first beer from the moment they turned twenty-one. She was no exception. But she hadn't realized what a butt-head he was.

A hot one. He had dark hair, and a dark beard that was just a shade longer than stubble. It always made her wonder if it was intentional, or if he had just gone a few days without shaving. There was something about that, the careless presentation that still managed to make him look irresistible, that made her think of all the debauchery that occupied his time, and kept him too busy to shave.

"You don't have to sound so much like you're patronizing me," she said.

"But I am patronizing you."

She bristled. "I guess you've never had any crap happen in your life that makes you go out and get drunk and want to…"

"Ride a mechanical bull? Not specifically. But I've tried to drown my sorrows in a bottle of Jack a time or two."

"So, that's all this is." She sighed, looking out the window at the dark shapes of the pine trees, like a jagged spill of ink against the night sky. "Just one of those things."

"He wasn't good enough for you. It was him, not you. He looked like an ass in that popped collar anyway."

She let out a harsh breath that fogged the window and obscured her view. "It isn't about a guy."

"Honey, I don't really care what it's about. Guy, girl." He paused. "I'm actually more interested in the second option."

She turned toward him, barely able to make out the shape of his profile in the darkness. "Not a girl, either."

"Way to spoil a man's fantasies. Lucky for you, the only thing I'm really interested in is getting you home without you getting kidnapped and mangled by a drifter, okay? That's something I can't have happen on my watch. You can get drunk. You can make a fool of yourself riding a bull. I don't care. That's all part of how I get paid. What I don't need is some silly little rich kid getting herself killed trying to get home from the bar because she hangs out with a bunch of idiots who don't care about her safety. All right? That's as far as my good deed goes."

His words were harsh, exceptionally so, given her particularly raw state. She felt…bruised. Completely and righteously enraged. "You shouldn't have troubled yourself. In Copper Ridge the crime rate pretty much consists of kids throwing water balloons at shop windows."

"We have a police department for a reason, babe."

"Sierra," she said through gritted teeth. "My name is Sierra West. Not *babe*. Not *kid*. Definitely not *little girl*."

"Well, that puts me in my place."

"I haven't even begun to put you in your place." That was not as hard-core as it sounded in her head. She just sounded kind of pathetic. A little bit whiny. She was both of those things, but she would rather Ace Thompson didn't know that.

She was starting to bleed her issues all over the cab of the old truck in front of a man she barely knew.

Everything seemed to be falling apart.

She couldn't say anything else. If she did she would dissolve completely. Into a puddle of big, wimpy girl tears. She was better than this. She knew how to be better than this. She had been trained to keep a brave face on from birth. Where the hell was it now?

It wasn't his business what was happening with her family. She should have let him think her little mini-breakdown was about a guy.

In fact, she would retract her earlier statement. It was technically about a guy anyway. Her father. Jack Monaghan, the half brother she hadn't known she had…

"It's about a guy," she said, feeling her own subject change like a bad case of whiplash.

It was so strange to feel tongue-tied and clumsy around a man, around *anyone*. She didn't usually. She was going to put it down to her weird mood and the intoxication.

"I figured. Girls like you don't have a lot of problems bigger than that. Except maybe a broken nail."

Annoyance spiked through her. "Please. If I was the type to worry about a broken nail I would hardly have gotten onto the back of your mechanical bull. I might be spoiled, I'm not going to deny that. But I'm also a barrel racer. I've been riding horses since before I could walk. I don't exactly sit at home with my hair in curlers planning my next shopping spree."

He chuckled. A real laugh. "Point taken."

"Anyway. I'm just upset because… You know, sometimes people aren't what they seem to be. And then you just wonder… If you're a gigantic idiot. If you really shouldn't be allowed to cross the street by yourself because you can't tell that someone's a bad guy after spending… All that time with him… How can you ever be confident you know anyone?" Her throat tightened, emotion flooding her. She had no control right now, and she hated it. She was used to being able to put on a flawless show no matter what was going on inside of her.

She'd been dumped by her boyfriend junior year—her first boyfriend. First kiss, first *everything*—right before one of the big games in Autzen Stadium, and she'd managed to parade right in there with her group of girlfriends, a huge smile plastered on her face. She'd even done a little happy dance for the Jumbotron that had made it onto national TV. A big chipper eff-you to the man who'd broken things off with her.

She didn't let people see her sweat. She didn't let them see her cry. They thought her life was easier because she *let* them think so.

But it was all falling apart now.

"You can't ever totally know people," Ace said, something in his tone dark now. "People are liars. And they do what makes them happy. They serve themselves. So, of course they lie to you. For a month, for a year. They may not even know they're lying to you, not until something comes up that means they have to protect their own asses. They'll forget everything they ever told you to keep themselves happy. That's people. Sorry you're having to deal with it."

Ace's words were so hard, so desperately cynical. Not the kind of words she would ever have guessed would come from the friendly neighborhood bartender.

"So, you think that's everybody?"

"I can't test this theory on everybody. It's even tough to prove with one person. You would have to live with someone for a hell of a long time and never have it go to hell to prove otherwise. No one in my life has ever lasted that long."

Tears pricked the back of her eyes, and she felt like an even bigger idiot. Getting emotional not just for herself, but for some guy she didn't even know. "That's really sad."

"Not really. It's just life."

"So that means you don't even feel bad about it? About the fact that people are just a bunch of lying tool bags? I feel pretty bad about it."

"You'll get over it."

His words made her feel hollow. Not just her, the world around her. The ground. The sky. Like all the substance, the very foundation, was gone. "What if I don't?"

"Then it's going to be a hard road for you. Though you know what? It won't actually be that hard. You've got a lot of money to catch you when you fall. You've got your family."

Except she didn't. She had walked away. But he wouldn't understand that, and he wouldn't believe it.

Silence descended on the cab like a plague of locusts. Oppressive. Heavy. She wanted to think of something to say, and she didn't want to say anything to him ever

28 ONE NIGHT CHARMER

again. It was a minefield. He had all the wrong answers. Everything she didn't want to hear.

"Aren't bartenders supposed to be encouraging? Aren't you supposed to smile and nod and say what everybody needs you to say?"

After feeling like she would sit in resolute silence, the words came as a surprise even to her.

"Sorry. I'm out from behind the bar. You use me as a designated driver and you get my honest opinion. People tend not to like my opinions."

She didn't believe that was true. Trying to think back on every event she'd ever vaguely circled around him at, she really didn't believe it was true. If she was sorting through her thoughts correctly, he had a good reputation. He was a nice guy. He showed up at every charity event her family was ever involved in. He provided free drinks, in exchange for publicity of course, but still, he did it at considerable expense to himself.

She remembered about a year and a half ago when the community had come together to rebuild Connor Garrett's barn. Ace had been there then. Not just helping to rebuild, but providing refreshments.

He was usually smiling.

She wondered where that guy was now.

Maybe he just doesn't like giving people rides home at one in the morning.

That was fair. Anyone could be grumpy. She was most definitely off her game, so why shouldn't it be the same for him?

His life was so much simpler than hers anyway. What he had, he had *outright*, free and clear. He owned a bar, and it was his domain. He did what he wanted to with it. He was able to help people with it. He was high-profile in the community, but he had a certain measure of freedom with it. There was all kinds of acceptance for what he did, no matter what. He had a reputation for sleeping with anything that moved, but it didn't seem to damage him.

Yeah, he basically had it made. So for all he could say about the evils of people, she'd never seen any evidence that it had touched him.

And it made her think back to his earlier comment about her breaking a nail. How easy he seemed to think things were for her. How soft he seemed to think she was, and it made her angry. He didn't know. He had no idea.

He turned the truck onto a narrow, paved driveway, the one that led back to her brother's ranch.

If she was going to say the words that were bubbling up inside of her like boiling water, she had to say them now. And she wanted to. Maybe because she was feeling bold due to the alcohol. But maybe because it was just the right thing to say. Maybe because he needed to hear it.

"Things are easy for you, though," she said.

"Excuse me?"

"You said my road wouldn't be that hard, but you're the one who has it made. You're a man. A man everyone just kind of gives a pass to. It doesn't matter what you do. Everyone just kind of accepts it. You can say whatever you want. Like now. You're giving me a ride home, after being totally condescending. And you don't even care. Me? I have to watch what I say. I have to… I have to keep up appearances for the family name. You burned that bridge a long time ago. Aren't you like…a pastor's kid? And you own a bar now. But if anything, people just kind of laugh at it. How funny, your dad preaches sermons on Sunday to everyone who's hungover from being at Ace's place on Saturday night."

"You can stop talking now, Sierra West," he said, his tone deadly now. "You don't know what the hell you're talking about. You don't know my life."

"Maybe not. But you don't know mine. And you were more than ready to cast judgment on me, Mr. World-Weary, I-Know-People. You think you know me, but you don't. Maybe nobody does."

He laughed, and it grated against her skin. It was derisive. Unkind. "Trust me, baby, everybody thinks that. Everybody thinks they're so unknowable, so complicated. But they aren't. People are just people, you included. You don't have any hidden depth to awe and astound me."

"Stop the car," she ground out.

"We aren't there yet," he said, his voice hard.

"I don't care. We're in the driveway. I can walk to the top of it."

"Right. And I'm going to let you get eaten by a mountain lion now?"

"I'm not going to get eaten by a mountain lion."

"No, you're right. He probably won't eat you. He'll probably just gnaw on you for a while. But I think I'll go ahead and keep driving you so that doesn't happen, either. I'm not going to let anything happen to you."

She gritted her teeth. "Out of the goodness of your heart?"

"Hell, no. Because I don't want to deal with any of the fallout that would come from having you get gnawed on on my watch."

"Asshole."

"Well, now you know my secret."

"It's a poorly kept one. I just had to be around you for about five seconds and it became pretty clear."

"So we've established that I'm an asshole, and you're

a whiny rich girl. You're going to be very embarrassed by all of this tomorrow. I, on the other hand, won't."

That did it. Now she was just pissed. "Embarrassed? Why should I be embarrassed? You're the one who should be embarrassed."

"Why?" he asked.

Dammit. She didn't know why. She had said it, and it had felt strong, and kind of badass, but now she felt like it really wasn't. Especially since she didn't have anything to back it up.

"Because—" good one, Sierra "—because, you're just a bar owner. Serving alcohol and buying mechanical bulls for people to fall off. What is that?"

"Most of the town spends more than a bit of their free time at my humble establishment. And I seem to recall you spending money to ride good old Ferdinand, so I'm going to go ahead and say maybe you shouldn't throw stones from your glass house."

"Whatever. Other people grow up and move on from that kind of behavior. You wallow in it. And don't think I haven't heard plenty about your reputation with women. You're just one of those guys. An eternal…frat boy. You were probably hoping to get into my pants."

"I was very much not hoping for that."

"So you say."

He pulled the truck up to the front of her brother's vast log-cabin-style house. She could see that the porch light was on, probably out of consideration for her. Something Colton had done, she was certain, and not Natalie. Natalie would probably prefer that Sierra not be able to find her way to the front door in the dark.

Natalie wouldn't mind if Sierra was gnawed on by a mountain lion.

"I'm sexy," she said, opening the passenger door and stumbling out into the darkness. "And I know it." Dimly, she was aware that that was a song lyric, and she wasn't coming across very well.

"Keep telling yourself that, sweetheart," Ace said. "I'm sure some men will even believe you. And on that note, good night, Sierra West. It's been…interesting, but I think you'll understand when I say that I hope we don't have occasion to talk again."

She stood there for a moment, wondering why he wasn't pulling away before she realized she was still gripping the open passenger door, preventing him from doing just that.

"Same goes, Ace Thompson." She slammed the door shut. "Same goes."

CHAPTER TWO

ACE WALKED INTO the empty flour mill and looked around the open space. He had a cramp in his right hand that signified his ownership of the place, and he'd signed his name so many times that morning his signature had started to look like it wasn't even made of letters anymore.

But now it was official. The old mill that had been standing empty for years, a ghost waiting to be brought back to life. He stood, looking around at a whole lot of square feet of potential, and expense. The roof had a steep pitch, a mezzanine floor overlooking the vast, empty room. The large picture windows gave a stunning view of the steel-gray Pacific ocean and white-capped waves.

He'd gotten a killer deal on the place considering the location. Of course, it had been a killer deal since the building itself was little more than a gutted corpse lying on the beach. A giant-ass beached whale.

Call him Ishmael, and shit.

But he could see beyond all that. The bar did well enough that he could afford this investment. He could afford to expand. It was a strange thing, committing to that. Committing to moving forward. To really admitting that his life was in Copper Ridge now. That he owned bars. Or, in this case, a brewery.

He checked his watch. Jack Monaghan was supposed

to be here any minute, along with Eli Garrett. Ace had the money to put into this place, but he'd really like to kick it off with some investors.

The more interest he had from the community, the better off he'd be.

Buying his current bar had been more of a sure thing. Ted, the old owner, was retiring and that was going to leave a hole. Someone had been needed to step into that hole and fill it with booze.

Ace had been happy to oblige.

But this would be a new place in an old town. Another change to a landscape that had been pretty damn stagnant until recent years. And he had no idea if this was a change that would take, or if it would just get washed away with the next tide.

He turned a circle, his footsteps echoing off the high ceiling. It was easy for him to picture the place filled with chairs. Tables, the brewing equipment in the back. He was getting pretty good at making his own microbrews, and they were popular on tap over at his bar. He had done everything he could to test the venture and make sure it would be something that at least had a fighting chance. But like anything else it was impossible to guarantee.

Business ventures went to hell all the time. Business ventures. Careers. Marriage.

At least, that was his experience.

Still, he was starting to get itchy. He wanted more. Needed more. This was more.

He heard the door open behind him and he turned around just as Jack and Eli walked into the room.

"You made it."

"Yep." Jack paused, running his hand over one of the support beams. "I'm always interested in an investment opportunity. Contrary to popular belief, I'm not actually a dumbass."

"I know you aren't," Ace said, stuffing his hands in his pockets. "That's why I asked you to come out."

Of all the people in Copper Ridge, Ace had had the most contact post-high school with Jack. It still hadn't been much, but back when Ace was riding pro in the rodeo, he and Jack had crossed paths on a couple of occasions. Ace rode saddle bronc, and Jack had been a bull rider, but they'd made time for a beer or two on a few occasions.

But Ace had quit long before Jack, settling down in Texas for good, or so he'd imagined at the time.

Nothing could have been further from the truth.

Ultimately, Ace had made his way back to Copper Ridge permanently before Jack had to.

But he'd always gotten a sense that there was a lot more to the other man than he liked to let on. He related to that in some ways.

"I like a good investment, too," Eli said, moving deeper into the space. "But no one really doubts that."

Jack laughed. "That's for damn sure. We're all pretty sure you have the word *responsibility* tattooed on your ass."

"I don't," Eli said. "I don't have any tattoos."

"Of course not," Jack said.

"So," Ace said, eager to get things moving along. "This is the place. I plan on having a full restaurant menu, and a brewing facility. I'll be serving my own microbrews. Which I will also be selling over at the bar."

"Sounds like a great plan to me," Eli said. "What kind of food are you talking about?"

"More than hamburgers. I'm thinking we can get a

good assortment of seafood. I've already been talking to Ryan Masters about him supplying the restaurant with his catch of the day." Ace was pleased that this new venture gave him opportunity to work with local businesses. Ryan was the kind of guy Ace liked to do business with. Hardworking. Brought himself up from nothing. A guy very unlike the West family. Who he had no call to be thinking about now. "Not too fancy or anything but you know...the type of microbrew pub stuff that hipsters lose their minds over."

"Great idea, man," Jack said. "I'm in."

"That's it?" Ace asked. "You don't want to see any credentials, or spreadsheets, or anything."

"I wouldn't understand them if you showed them to me," Jack said. "I'm smart with my money. By which I mean I pay someone else to manage it."

"Well, sounds smart to me," Ace said.

"I'm in, too," Eli said. "I was telling Sadie all about it last night, and she was pretty excited. She would have come today if she had been able to get out of taking a group of people down to go whale watching. But this is exactly the kind of thing that's going to help bolster her business with the bed-and-breakfast, too. Tourism is really up and coming here, and I think we need more places like this."

"I'm surprised, Sheriff, that you'd want to invest in a place that encourages drinking."

"It's expensive drinking. Microbrews are pricey, right?" Eli asked.

"I guess so," he said.

"I like that. The cheaper the beer, the more people drink. Bring in some of that fancy-ass stuff and people have to think really hard before they go trying to get hammered on it."

Ace laughed. "True enough."

"Hey, before we head out," Jack said. "I did have a favor I wanted to ask you."

Oh, there was that other shoe dropping. Ace should have known it wouldn't be that simple. "What favor?"

"It's about Sierra West."

Ace thought back to last night, to the verbal sparring with that pretty blonde, who was a lot less pretty when she was running her mouth. "What about her?"

"She's going through some stuff. You could probably tell by her behavior last night."

"Not really. I run a bar. Her behavior seems run-of-the-mill to me. Actually, she was pretty tame. And I don't know her from a barnacle on the bottom of a fishing boat."

"Just trust me, she's going through some stuff. She kind of had a falling-out with her old man."

"Is that so?"

She'd said that all of her drama was over a man. He supposed that counted. It was difficult to imagine anyone opposing Nathan West. He was such an established figurehead in Copper Ridge, and as far as Ace had ever seen, a decent enough guy.

But hell, appearances didn't mean a damn thing, and he knew that better than most. Or maybe it was just Sierra throwing a tantrum because daddy wouldn't let her into her trust fund. Who knew.

"She needs work," Jack continued. "A job. But she hasn't had any luck finding one because she doesn't have any experience that extends beyond working at the family ranch."

"And how do you know all this?" Ace had observed there was something weird going on between Jack and the other woman last night, something about the way he watched her that went past casual interest.

But if there was anything shady going on he doubted that Jack would bring her up in front of Eli, considering Eli was Kate's older brother, and he wouldn't hesitate to cut off Jack's testicles and feed them to his cows should Jack ever do anything to hurt his sister.

They had only been together for a few months, but everyone in town knew that Jack belonged to Kate. Hell, they were already engaged. Which was really something, considering Jack had spent so many years avoiding commitment.

"Oh, you know, she's good friends with Kate," Jack said.

Ace knew there was more than that, but he could also see that Jack had no intention of sharing what more there was.

"So what are you trying to ask me, Monaghan?"

"I was hoping you'd give her a job."

"So, no one else in town will give her a job because she has no work experience, I just saw her drunk off her ass last night, and you want *me* to hire her?"

"The chicks in your place serve hamburgers. That's not exactly rocket science."

"Watch it, Monaghan, that's my livelihood."

"I know. Sorry. I'm not trying to be a dick. But it does come naturally."

"Sure. But I'm not sure I want a completely inexperienced cocktail waitress stumbling around the place messing up orders."

That was total crap. He'd hired people with a lot less

to go on. He'd hired a borderline drifter, Casey James, a few months ago just to help her get back on her feet. She'd ended up quitting when she'd fallen in love with Aiden Crawford, a local farmer. Working on her own land seemed to be more fulfilling than serving drinks. Which he understood, even if it had left him a little shorthanded.

But he wasn't admitting any of that.

"I'm helping you out by investing in this place. I'm taking a chance, and I think it's a good chance. Can you take a chance on her?"

He didn't want to. That was the simple truth. He so *violently* didn't want to that he didn't want to explore the reasoning. Because it was weird that he should care at all. She was rich, she was a spoiled brat. She had said some ridiculous stuff to him last night about him having it easy. But that shouldn't matter.

It wouldn't, if she wasn't such a pretty little thing.

He gritted his teeth, ignoring that internal voice. He didn't care if she was pretty. Pretty covered a lot of sins, but Jack had learned that early on. He spread his favors around fairly freely with women, he had no problem admitting that. But there was one type he always avoided.

Sierra West's type.

He also never screwed around with his staff.

If she was staff, that would put her in a double no-go zone. So, whether or not she was pretty should mean nothing. What she'd said to him last night shouldn't mean anything, either.

Still didn't want to hire her. She reminded him too much of another time in his life. Of another woman in his past. Women like her were poison in a good glass of wine.

You could drink the whole thing down before you realized you were already dead.

"I'm not running a charity. I don't give out first summer jobs to grown women who play like they're high school girls. If she wants a job, she needs to come and ask me for one."

Jack frowned. "Do you have something against her?"

"I wouldn't go so far as that. But I gave her a ride home last night, and she was in fine form. Like I said, I'm used to that kind of thing, but it doesn't mean I need to give that kind of thing a job. If she wants to come by the bar and apologize for her behavior and ask me directly for a job, then I'll consider it because you mentioned it."

"Fair enough," Jack said.

Eli had been silent through the whole exchange, and Ace took a moment to study the other man's expression. It was unreadable. Unhelpful.

"Is there anything else I should know?" Ace figured he should just go ahead and ask.

"Nope," Jack answered, shaking his head.

"Okay, then. Have her come down during the slow time. I'm assuming you're going to tell her she has a job interview."

Jack rubbed his hand over the back of his neck. "Kate probably will."

"However you want to work it out."

"Thanks. I do appreciate it, for what it's worth. From what... From what Kate has told me, Sierra's had a harder time than you might think."

"If she can deliver french fries to the appropriate table it doesn't much matter to me."

"Well, that part will be up to you. In the meantime, keep us posted on everything happening here."

"Sure," Ace said. "Did you want to help me pick out curtains?"

Eli broke his silence with a laugh. "I don't even want to pick out curtains for my own house."

"I suppose I'll have to hire someone. That's the problem with trying to open a place that sits a few notches higher on the restaurant scale than a dive bar. It means I have to cultivate tastes that rise above dive bar."

"If nothing else," Jack said, "there will be beer. Beyond that, I'm not sure you can really go wrong."

"True enough."

After that, Eli and Jack turned to go. And Ace tried not to think about all the ways this could absolutely go wrong. Sure things, in his experience, were never really sure things. Life had a way of going wrong in spectacular and unforeseen ways.

That was his only defense really. Expect an attack to come from somewhere, even if he couldn't figure out where it might come from.

At least he would have Sierra West's attempt at a job interview and humility to entertain him. Or she wouldn't show up at all.

Either way, he couldn't lose.

CHAPTER THREE

"Jack talked to Ace about getting you a job."

Sierra stared at the phone like it was a poisonous snake. Usually, she welcomed phone calls from friends. Particularly Kate. Right now, going through everything, Kate was her best bet for finding an emotional outlet for her pain.

The problem with her typical group of friends—beyond the fact that they had abandoned her at the bar last night—was that she felt obligated to protect her family secrets around them.

The other day, when she had overheard her father nearly bursting a blood vein screaming about Jack Monaghan going back on the deal they had struck years ago, she'd discovered that her entire existence was a carefully constructed facade.

Apparently Jack had confronted their father a few months ago, and now the secret was starting to leak out. In town, and now in their house.

The only reason she had spent many years thinking that her father was a decent person, a faithful husband, a loyal, giving human being, was that Jack had signed a gag order some seventeen years earlier.

In exchange, Jack had accepted a large sum of money. Jack had come and paid her father back, and had dissolved that bargain with that one simple action. There was no protection anymore. Jack could get a billboard and put it up in the center of town, proclaiming Nathan West to be the faithless scumbag he was. And then, it wouldn't only be her mother, her sister and her brother dealing with the fallout in a contained environment.

If that came out, who knew what else would come out? That was what terrified her the most. If people in town saw one person speaking out against Nathan West, how many others would come forward and reveal wrongs he'd committed against them? How bad was he?

It wasn't something she was ready to face. Whether or not that was fair, it was the truth.

But Kate knew. Because of her relationship with Jack she already knew the whole story, so while that made it difficult for her to deal with her friend in some ways, it also made it easier. She didn't have to explain her behavior last night. Didn't have to go through any awkward or dramatic confessions.

Of course, now she knew Kate's fiancé was Sierra's half-brother and it didn't make her feel too eager to go have dinner at their place.

But phone calls were fine.

This one, though, was a little bit confusing.

"Jack did what?"

"He talked to Ace this morning. He met with him about an investment opportunity, and they ended up discussing you. And the fact that you need a job."

Heat stung Sierra's cheeks. She *did* need a job, and until this past week she had not appreciated how difficult one might be to come by. There weren't a surplus of positions available for someone without a specific skill set. It was a small town, and most of the shops ran on a very small staff. People coming home from college for the summer had already secured positions at any place looking to hire extra employees to deal with the seasonal influx of tourists.

Sierra had always had a job. When she wanted one. All through school she'd known she would have a job waiting for her when she graduated. She'd been made office manager of the family ranch the moment she'd stepped off campus, because that was what her father had been grooming her for.

Colton had taken over West Construction, Maddy handled dressage lessons and horse training. Sierra had been slated for the business side of things.

Scheduling lessons, managing the horses that were boarded on the property, and the payments. Making sure feed was ordered, the farrier was scheduled to handle the horses' shoe needs.

Sure, nepotism had gotten her there, but she was good at her job.

But apparently if you took nepotism out of the equation she was like any other sad college graduate who was realizing her degree was barely worth the paper it was printed on.

Hey, at least she didn't have student loan debt.

"I can't imagine that Ace wants to give me a job."

"Why not?"

"Because. He gave me a ride home last night when I was drunk."

There was a brief moment of silence on the other end of the phone. "That shouldn't matter. He owns a bar. He understands how easy it is to overimbibe."

"How charming was I last night, Kate? You talked to me."

"Okay, you were kind of an ass."

Sierra frowned. "What did I say to you?"

"You said, 'Really, Kate? That hat with those boots?'"

"Did I?"

"Yes. It's okay, though. I knew you were drunk. If you were sober you wouldn't have said that to me in public."

Sierra grimaced. "I'm sorry."

"It's fine. And you were right." There was another slight pause. "My boots did not match my hat."

"You know that doesn't matter." Kate was one of the nicest people Sierra knew, and the idea of saying anything that might have hurt her made her heart crumble a little bit.

Okay, maybe she didn't have illegitimate children littering the countryside, but she had to wonder if in some way she was more like her father than she would care to be.

"Please don't feel guilty. Are you going to go talk to Ace about the job?"

She groaned. "He's mad at me."

"Why?"

"I didn't exactly tell him his hat didn't match his boots, but I wasn't all that nice to him, either." Not that he'd been Prince Charming himself.

"Well, that explains why he told Jack you had to come talk to him in person."

"Ugh."

"And why he said you had to apologize."

Sierra covered her eyes. "Serious ugh."

"I'm sorry, but you don't have better options, do you?"

"No."

"Then, much like my hat and boots, your resistance does not go with your situation."

Her friend was right. Sierra hated it, but her friend

was right. "Okay. When am I supposed to go talk to him and…apologize?"

"Anytime before things get busy."

Sierra supposed she should go as soon as possible. Like ripping off a Band-Aid. The very idea of working at Ace's filled her with a deep and abiding sense of nope. Everyone would think it was weird. There was no way around that. A West taking a job as a waitress in a bar was nothing if not conspicuous. But as Kate had reminded her, she was short on options. She couldn't live with Colton forever. And not just because his future wife breathed fire and left scorched earth in her rather petite wake.

Well, mainly because of that.

"So I guess that means I need to drive over there."

"Yes," Kate said, uncompromising.

Kate was like that.

Sierra sort of wished they could meet up for coffee. But she was afraid that would force her to confront Jack, or interact with him in some way, and she really wasn't ready to deal with him.

"Okay. I'll go."

"I'll check in with you."

"I have no doubt you will."

Sierra hung up the phone and looked up just as Colton walked into the room. "Something going on?" he asked.

"Just…still on the job hunt."

"Honestly, Sierra, if we had a position available in the office at the construction firm I would give it to you. But I can't justify the expense of adding an employee that we don't need. If I'm going to give you charity, it just makes more sense to have you stay here rent-free."

"I know. And I completely understand that. Anyway,

I don't feel like it should have to be charity for someone to give me a job. I'm not completely inept."

"You're not inept at all." He opened the fridge and started rummaging for something, pulling out a pitcher of orange juice a moment later. "Where are you job hunting?"

"I'm going down to talk to Ace Thompson, actually."

"Not about a job," came a shrill voice from the next room.

"Yes," Sierra said, "about a job."

That was Natalie's cue to walk in. Or rather slide in like an eel cutting through the water. Natalie was sleek, her blond hair ruthlessly tamed back into a bun, her figure ruthlessly trimmed by years of eating little more than salads.

Sierra had no patience for that kind of thing. You could try to make them cute by putting them in Mason jars, but they were still salads, and she still wanted a hamburger and french fries on the side.

"But how is that going to look?" Natalie asked.

It was on the tip of Sierra's tongue to say that Natalie couldn't have it both ways. She couldn't have Sierra out of the house and able to support herself and worry about what kind of job she ended up with. But Colton had instructed her to be sensitive to Natalie, because she was stressed with the wedding getting so close. He assured Sierra that Natalie wasn't usually so high-strung.

Sierra didn't believe that. What she did believe was that her future sister-in-law was beautiful, and suitable by the standards the West family used to measure suitability. She had a feeling her older brother was thinking with his trust fund and his trouser brain.

She also hoped that he was making sure there was a prenup.

"I don't know, Natalie, probably not as bad as if I end up taking a job at The Naughty Mermaid," Sierra said, naming the strip club on the outskirts of town.

"That isn't true," Natalie countered, "because no one could say anything about it without admitting they were there and bringing flack back onto themselves. The same can't be said for Ace's."

"Your concern is touching," Sierra said.

"I am concerned," Natalie said, gliding to the fridge and taking out some kind of preprepared breakfast smoothie. "Our wedding is only a few months away. Your family is on the verge of a meltdown. One of my bridesmaids has decided to run against my father for mayor. And everything just needs to calm down until after I say I do."

"Natalie." Colton's tone was patient. "Everything's going to be fine."

"You don't know that," Natalie said. "Because, I bet you also didn't think your father had a secret bastard."

Sierra gritted her teeth. "Don't talk about him like that," she said, not entirely sure why she felt protective of Jack.

"That's enough," Colton said. "Of course you should go ahead and apply for Ace's. If you have an in there, take it. Making an honest living is hardly going to disgrace anyone or anything."

"People are going to wonder about your family's finances." Natalie clearly wasn't ready to let the subject drop.

"Who cares? They're still going to come to the wedding. There's a free steak dinner. I know, because I'm paying for it. They won't care whether I paid with cash or credit. Everything will go off without a hitch. And I'm sure people will be so thankful to your father for hosting such a delightful event that they'll vote for him without batting an eye. They won't even read Lydia's name on the ballot. Why would they? He's been the mayor forever."

Natalie seemed somewhat mollified by this. "You make it sound like it might not be so bad."

"You're marrying me. How bad could it be?"

Sierra noticed that Natalie seemed to deflect that. But she did turn her cheek and allow Colton to bend and give her a kiss. "All right," she said, looking at Sierra. "I guess it's okay."

Again, Sierra had to grit her teeth and hold back her commentary. "Great. Well, I'll let you know how it goes." She was suddenly in a huge hurry to get down to Ace's. Mainly because she really needed to get away from Natalie. And honestly, away from Colton when he was with her.

He wasn't totally whipped or anything, but he spent way too much time placating her and managing her for Sierra's tastes. She didn't like to imagine that the entire rest of her brother's life would be spent with a woman who was little more than a temperamental cat in human form. She was constantly needing to be scratched behind the ears and petted in all the right places or she would bite you on the hand.

"I'll see you both later," Sierra said, walking out of the kitchen into the front porch before realizing she was wearing jeans and a T-shirt, with her hair in two braids, because she couldn't be bothered to deal with the mess falling asleep on it loose had left it in last night.

She wasn't exactly dressed for a job interview. But

she supposed this was close enough to what she would be wearing if she actually worked in the bar.

Except she would probably have to show a little more cleavage.

She was pretty sure that's how jobs like this worked.

She heard the door open behind her and turned to see Colton standing there, his arms crossed over his chest. "Are you sure you want to do this?"

"I don't know. But I kind of have to." And if she felt a little spurred on by her future sister-in-law's controlling attitude, well, that wasn't so bad, she supposed. "Hopefully I'll end up with a better job someday, but the reality is I need to do something."

"You could go back home."

She made a scoffing sound. "No, thanks."

"He was your dad for twenty-five years, Sierra, and you were fine living there, and fine taking his money. The only thing that's changed is that now you know."

Sierra's throat tightened. "I know. I've only known about Jack and all this other stuff for a couple of days. And you would think twenty-five years would be so much bigger than two days, Colton, you really would. But it's not. Not for me. This is the biggest, ugliest two days I have ever lived through. I can't ignore what I know. I can't go back. Not now."

"He's our father."

"Right. And you need his influence to keep your business running smoothly. And you need to not create a huge rift because you're having a gigantic wedding and Natalie will completely melt down if you cut ties now, especially since she's half marrying you for your last name."

Colton's expression turned stormy, his brows locking together. She looked at his eyes, that bright blue color so striking and unique with his dark hair. It struck her then, how similar his features were to Jack's. It hit her so hard it took her breath away.

"You might want to retract the assertion that my fiancée is only marrying me for my name."

"I said it was *half* of why," Sierra said, not backing down.

"You're a little butt-head, you know that?"

"Ouch. A butt-head? That cut deep, Colton. Right where it hurts most."

"You'll be fine."

"I'm sure Natalie cares about you." She wasn't really. But, she didn't want to hurt her brother. Even if she did think Natalie was a social-climbing weasel, desperately trying to sink her little claws into Colton so she could use him as a rung on her ascent to the top.

"It's fine. I'm not an idiot, Sierra. I do understand that if I was a nobody she never would have pursued a relationship with me. Well, she wouldn't be marrying me anyway. But that's the way relationships work. It's not all attraction, or mushy feelings. You pick the person that fits into your life the best. The person that supports your ambitions. I support hers, she supports mine. It's not a bad thing."

It was on the tip of her tongue to tell him that it would be a bad thing to meet an untimely death at the hands of his wife's nasty weasel claws, should he ever disappoint her in any way, or should their family scandal grow any vaster.

"You're not really selling me on the institution, Colton, I have to say."

"Just wait until your quarter-life crisis is over. You'll feel differently."

He turned and walked back into the house, and Sierra made her way over to her truck. She opened the door and got inside, jamming the keys into the ignition, the engine roaring to life. She loved her truck. Cherry red and perfect, with feathers hanging off the rearview mirror and a hookup for her phone so she could play all of her favorite country music.

But it wasn't really her truck. The thought struck her numb as she put the vehicle in Reverse and began to pull out of the driveway. Her phone wasn't hers, either. Not really. Neither was the music on it.

That realization stopped the little moment of happy she'd experienced upon getting into the truck. And it weighed her down on the drive back into town, toward Ace's.

It also reinforced what she was about to do.

Ask for a job. Apologize.

Another thought hit her as she pulled into the parking lot, putting her truck in Park and killing the engine. She wasn't sure if she'd ever apologized to anyone before in her life. That couldn't be right. Surely, she'd apologized at some point. To someone. For something.

But she couldn't think of an example. She could remember fights with friends blowing over with some laughter and a whole lot of hand waving and such, but she couldn't recall any of them apologizing to each other sincerely.

She blinked, shoving that uncomfortable thought to the side. She climbed out of the truck—not *her* truck—and made her way into the bar before she could think things through too deeply. She needed to just get this over with. Like ripping off a Band-Aid, she reminded herself.

Ripping off an Ace bandage.

She smiled faintly at her own joke as she ventured deeper into the empty dining area, looking around the space. It was clean, but that was about all she could say for it. She wasn't a huge fan of the Western decor that clashed with the more nautical elements. There was half a fishing boat mounted to the wall with nets and those weird little glass balls that appeared all the time in oceanic themed decor. She had no idea what they were. Or what they were for.

Lately, Ace had certainly been upping the Western angle. The addition of the bull, and a new little bar seating area that had stools made out of barrels. Even though it wasn't her personal taste, she realized that it was an accurate representation of the town. This was where the fishermen came to drink when they came in off the water, where the ranchers came to relax after they were finished with a hard day's work.

It was a cross section of the community, right here in one location. And even if she wouldn't put a fishing boat or bar stools in her bedroom, she could appreciate them here.

The door to the kitchen swung open and Ace walked through it, wiping his hands on a rag. Her eyes were drawn to the shifting of his forearm muscles, and then the rather firm grip he had as he chucked the rag onto the counter. She looked up, hoping to distract herself from her illicit hand-related thoughts. It didn't really help. Because from there, she ended up with illicit thoughts about his square jawline, partly disguised, but not completely, by his dark stubble. And from there those thoughts went to his lips. She knew from experience that they smiled easily, that they were shaped nicely, and that when he looked at her, they seemed to get a little sterner.

His eyebrows also seemed to turn sterner when they focused in her direction. Strong, dark eyebrows that were attractive in a way that eyebrows had no right to be. For heaven's sake.

Apparently, even sober, Ace had an effect on her. Strange, because she couldn't recall him ever affecting her before last night.

She blamed the emotionally compromised landscape inside her. Severely shifted, rerouted and in general destroyed by all the revelations that had crashed through her like a flash flood recently.

"Hi," she said, slowly approaching the counter.

"What can I do for you?" he asked. He smiled. Effortless. Friendly. As though he had not given her a ride home last night when she'd been drunk. As though they hadn't said anything offensive to each other while he'd been giving her a ride home when she was drunk.

"I came to… Jack said—well, Kate called. Kate Garrett. And she said that you might have a job for me."

"I have a server position available," he said, crossing his arms over his broad chest.

She took another moment to check out his muscles. She hadn't decided to check him out, so much as she'd been held captive by an involuntary urge. She wasn't sure how she felt about that. About any of this. Maybe it was all a displacement activity to offset how uncomfortable she was. Being here. About to ask for work. About to beg forgiveness.

"I thought… I thought that maybe…"

"Are you about to ask me if I can donate a kidney, or something?"

She blinked. "No. Why would I want your kidney?"

"I don't know. I don't know your life. I don't know

your medical history. But you're acting like you have something serious to ask me when I was pretty sure you just came to find out about the server position. So maybe stop looking at me like you'd rather be anywhere—including the deepest pit of hell—other than here."

She could feel her temper starting to warm up. This was hard. Coming here, humbling herself. Okay, she hadn't exactly humbled herself yet. But she was about to. "I just… I need a place to work. Because I had a falling-out with my father, and I'm not living with my parents anymore. But that also means that not only do I need a place to stay, I need a new job, because my job as an office manager type person was at the ranch. The family ranch…" She was the opposite of eloquent right now, and she knew it. What was it about this guy that made her so tongue-tied? It wasn't the guy. It was just the situation. Bolstered by that, she took a deep breath and pressed on. "Please."

"I'm sorry about the situation with your dad," he said, not sounding it at all. But he said sorry so easily. Maybe it would be easy for her, as well. "But I'm not really sure if you'd be a good fit for the bar."

"What? My excellent mechanical bull riding skills didn't convince you?"

"That's about all you have going for you, from where I'm standing."

"Ace," she said, trying again. "I was…not myself last night."

"Uppity, kinda snotty. Seems to me like it was probably you."

She gritted her teeth, wanting so badly to tear a strip off him with a very sharp word. But that would run counter to her objective. "I was rude."

"And?"

She looked up, curling her fingers into fists, digging her nails into her skin. "Drunk."

"Anything else, little girl?"

He was going to make sure this killed her. Now, if it did kill her, she wouldn't need a job. She would just need a house to haunt. Maybe she would haunt his ass. "I'm sorry," she said, the words pulled from her as grudgingly as any words ever were.

"Now, that wasn't so hard, was it?"

"Borderline impossible," she said. "Can I have the job?"

"Have you ever waited tables?"

"Of course I've never waited tables," she said, belatedly realizing that that was just the sort of attitude he had an issue with. "Because I've never had the opportunity," she added, trying to make the words perky.

"You don't want to do this," he said, resting his hands flat on the bar, flexing his fingers in a way that sent a strange sensation down her spine. "I know you don't. You know you don't. Let's not play games."

"I've looked for work everywhere else in town. I haven't been able to find it. I'm not an idiot. I have a degree in business from the University of Oregon. I know that I worked for my father, but I did my job well. If you know anything about Nathan West, then you know he didn't give me anything just because I was related to him."

A fact that was driven home by the discovery that Jack was one of their siblings. Their father had given him nothing, less than nothing. A onetime payout to disappear. He certainly hadn't been made a part of the family dynasty. Then there was Gage. Her oldest brother. She didn't know all of the circumstances surrounding his leaving. She'd been too young to fully grasp the situation at the time. But she knew it wasn't because her father was a loving, forgiving man. "I'm not useless. I'm competitive. I've done pretty well with my barrel racing, and you might not take something like that seriously, but it takes a lot of grit. A lot of work."

"I know it does," Ace said, a strange look in his eye. "I don't run a charity, I run a business. I don't like to hire people that don't have experience. But if you really want a job, you've got one. On a trial basis. You have three weeks to prove to me you can do this. But if you mess up too many orders, or spit in anyone's food because they make you mad, or mouth off to any of my customers, you're done."

She waited to feel some sense of triumph. Some sense of relief. Instead, she felt nothing more than a grim determination and a sinking feeling in the pit of her stomach.

Because now it was real. There was no going back. No crawling back to the West ranch with her tail between her legs, begging her father's forgiveness, even though he'd been the one who was wrong.

"Sure."

"That's it?"

"Thank you?"

He chuckled, that same dark sound she'd first heard last night. There was something strange in his happy sounds, his happy expressions. An undertone that didn't quite match. Of course, she didn't have time to try to figure out why his expressions didn't seem to match his deeper emotions. She could barely sort that crap out for herself. "You don't have to sound so excited."

"Sorry." That was easier. "Excitement has been a little bit hard to come by these days."

"Now that," he said, "I do relate to."

"What do you suggest for that?"

He lifted a shoulder. "I don't know. Fake it 'til you make it? Drink it 'til you think it?"

"Great. I will…use my employee discount to help with that."

"There's no employee discount."

"What?"

"No drinking on the job, either. Working at a bar isn't actually any fun. Except the part where you're sober while everyone else is drunk. That is actually pretty funny."

"Is it?"

"Hilarious. In fact, last night, some little blonde girl got up on that mechanical bull and fell on her face."

Sierra gritted her teeth. "Ha-ha."

"You start tomorrow."

"I do? What if I have plans?"

He shrugged. "Cancel them. Or quit now."

She blinked. She couldn't quite work out what was happening between herself and Ace. There was something. Something that wasn't neutral. On her end, it was that weird moment where she suddenly thought his hands looked capable. Of all kinds of things. Like pushing a strand of hair out of her face or deadlifting a fallen tree. With him…who knew? It wasn't really a friendly feeling she got from him.

"I'll be here. Just name the time."

"Be here at five. Be ready to work."

CHAPTER FOUR

SIERRA WEST WAS a problem. A bejeweled, bouncy problem.

She'd shown up to work on time, which had kind of pissed Ace off, because he'd been looking for an excuse to fire her out of the gate, and that had been taken from him. But she'd shown up wearing a pair of shorts that looked painted onto the skin they covered. And they didn't cover much. Instead, they did a good job of displaying a lot of smooth, tanned leg. He wondered how the hell she had a tan.

This was the Oregon coast. In late February. It wasn't all that sunny.

Maybe she went to one of those fake-and-bake tanning beds. His ex had been a big fan of those. It was how she kept her warm orange glow all year-round. Either that, or sucking the blood of virgins. He wouldn't really put anything past her.

He studied Sierra, who was talking to a table full of men who were absolutely thrilled with his new hiring choice.

She didn't look like the type to go lie in a tanning bed. He wasn't sure why. She probably went and lay out back in the yard, in that private, gated ranch she and her family lived at. She probably lay out in a hot-pink bikini. She maybe even took the top off to avoid a suntan line.

He gritted his teeth and turned his focus to wiping

down the counter. It was clean. But cleaning an already clean counter was better than thinking about Sierra West topless. He really needed to deal with these inconvenient fantasies. Get laid. With someone else.

He looked around the bar, and for some reason, didn't see any appealing prospects. Not because there weren't beautiful women here. There were. It was just, for some reason they didn't really register to his body.

Funny, usually his body wasn't all that picky. He didn't do relationships. He did satisfying evenings. Which left his options pretty wide-open. His type was female. Thin, curvy, blonde, brunette, pale, dark... Didn't much matter to him. Women were a glorious creation. One he preferred in his bed, and nowhere else in his home.

In fact, he had a bedroom up above the bar, so that he never actually had to have women in his home at all.

There was a time when his own behavior would've shocked him. Or it would've shocked the boy he'd been. But he could barely remember that time.

Now, the most shocking thing was that he wanted one woman specifically.

Yeah, Sierra West was a problem.

She turned away from the table, her walk particularly bouncy in those little cowgirl boots as she made her way back to the kitchen. Everything on her bounced. Her hair. Her ass.

Damn, some other woman needed to start looking good.

She disappeared into the kitchen for a moment, then reappeared a second later. "I think I got everyone for now," she said.

She was looking at him expectantly, blue-eyed and far too innocent. "Is there anything else I can do?"

"I'm not going to hold your hand, little girl," he said.

That was unnecessary, and he knew it. But he didn't particularly care. With most employees, he would be happy to show them what to do next. He would even be happy that they'd asked what they could do. But he wasn't happy about her asking, because it meant he had to interact with her, and he didn't want to interact with her.

He supposed it wasn't her fault that she was far too pretty for her own good. But he was going to hold it against her anyway. Because he was never going to hold her against him, and that was the source of a lot of problems.

The trouble was that he was out of practice with self-denial. He'd spent the past decade indulging himself whenever he wanted to.

When he'd turned away from the teachings of his father, he'd turned away hard. Then life had gone and kicked him in the balls, and made him question every damn thing he'd ever done. Every decision he'd ever made. It had made him question why he'd ever practiced restraint of any kind. Why he'd so firmly believed that self-denial, the greater good, morality and a host of other things would lead him down a smooth path in life.

No. He'd spent a lot of years doing the right thing. Being a good man. The better man.

It hadn't gotten him anywhere in the end. So when he'd broken free of his marriage, when he'd finally left it all behind, left it all as dust and rubble in his past, he'd set his foot on the road to hell, and figured he'd better make the journey there pretty spectacular.

And he had.

When he'd decided to go for a life of debauchery and sin, he hadn't gone halfway.

That made it difficult when he actually wanted to employ a little bit of abstinence. He didn't know how.

These days, he only knew how to do three things really well.

He knew how to make drinks, he knew how to drink drinks and he knew how to screw. He did all those things as often as he could, and whenever he felt like it.

He hadn't anticipated the effect trying to resist a woman he was attracted to might have on him. He'd figured it wouldn't have an effect at all. But then, he didn't typically try to resist women he was attracted to. Because he wasn't usually attracted to spoiled little rich girls who also happened to work for him.

"You need to keep an eye on everyone, and make sure they don't need anything else," he said finally.

"Right."

But she looked surprised by the directive. "You've been to restaurants before, right? I know you have. You come here."

"Yes."

"What does a server do? They make sure you have french fries, all the drinks that you need, and they do a little tap dance if you require it. So make sure no one needs french fries. Or a tap dance."

"No one here has ever done a tap dance for me."

"Have you ever asked them to?"

"Why would I ask someone to tap dance for me?"

"I don't know. Hopefully, for your sake, no one wants you to tap dance tonight."

She rolled her eyes and tossed her hair, the blond curls bouncing again, the glittery shadow on her lids twinkling beneath the light. She was a human glitter bomb. Which, in his opinion, had no place outside of a strip club. Or the rodeo arena.

She definitely looked like a rodeo queen. That thought did a little bit to quench the heat that had settled in the pit of his stomach. He'd made the mistake of getting involved with a rodeo queen once before. He knew how that ended.

"So then should I just hover around the tables like a fly, waiting for french fry shortages or demands of dancing?"

"You could fold bar towels."

"There," she said, planting her hand on her hip and cocking it out to the side. He might have noticed the dramatic curve of her waist down to that very sassy hip, only because he was human. "Now, Ace, was that so difficult?"

"You seem to be having a hard time remembering that I'm your boss, little girl."

"Do you call all your employees little girl?"

"Only when they act like one."

"I'm going to go fold bar towels." She turned on her heel and started to saunter back into the kitchen, then paused and turned back around. "Where are the bar towels?"

He smiled, as slow and lazy as possible, because he knew it would make her mad. "Under the bar."

Her cheeks flushed slightly, a sweet little rosy color that made her look a lot more innocent than he was certain she was. She tossed that golden mane again and sauntered to the bar, bending down and pulling out the stack of unfolded white towels.

Those little shorts of hers rode up high, revealing the sweet curve of her ass. Were his scruples so easily discarded? He only had maybe two of them. You would think he could cling to them a little bit tighter.

She placed them on the back counter, and began to fold them clumsily.

He let out a heavy sigh. "That isn't how you do it."

He crossed the space between them, coming to stand beside her, taking one of the towels off the top and spreading it on the empty bar in front of him. He held the edges tight, before folding one half toward the green line that ran down the center. "This. You do it like this."

"There's a specific system for folding towels?"

"Of course there's a system. If there aren't systems, the whole damn world falls apart."

"Because of a breakdown in bar towel folding?"

He snorted, folding the other side of the towel in tightly and smoothing the fabric flat with his hands before folding it in half again. "Like this," he said, setting it off to the side. "Keep it compact. Keep it clean."

"You do keep the place awfully clean. I've noticed." She copied his movements, dainty hands sliding over the terry cloth. He tried not to imagine them sliding over his skin.

Restraint was a damned nightmare.

This, he remembered from his high school years. The more he had to think about not doing something, the more he obsessed about it. Abstinence in deed led to anything but in thought.

You thought so much about not doing something that it took over your life anyway.

But it had been pressed upon him from an early age that he had to be an example. His father was pastor of the largest church in Copper Ridge, after all. It wasn't all bad. He'd believed in his father's lessons. Back then, he'd believed that virtue was its own reward. He'd felt a kind of confidence, a direction that accompanied that belief. He had known who he was.

Then it had all bitten him spectacularly in the ass, and he'd turned away, hard and sharp. Now, he was firmly out of practice.

She matched his movements precisely, producing a very nicely folded towel. Which kind of irritated him. Not that he thought it was going to take her a whole lot of time to learn how to do such a simple task. But he wanted to cling to his irritation, and to his completely unfair thought that this job would be beyond her somehow. He wanted to hold on to his prejudice.

He had earned that prejudice.

"There," she said, smoothing it down flat and placing it in a stack with the other towel. "I think I've got it. You don't have to supervise me."

"Good. Because I don't have time."

"You're very busy," she said, something in her tone irking him. He was certain it was designed to do that.

"I am. I have an entire bar to run. A lot depends on my presence."

She lifted a pretty, bare shoulder. He swore that it had glitter on it, too. "It is your place. Your name is on the sign."

"I'm also working out logistics for opening a new brewery." He didn't know why he'd told her that.

Actually, he did know why. There was clearly something in him—a part of him that wouldn't die—that still wanted people like her—people who were born into a certain level of privilege—to understand that he was important, too.

"In Copper Ridge?" she asked, her tone genuinely interested.

"Yeah. In the old flour mill building, down by the beach."

"That sounds nice. Is it going to be fancy?"

"*My* kind of fancy."

"What's your kind of fancy?"

"You put french fries on a plate instead of in a basket."

She laughed. Unsurprisingly, her laugh sparkled, too. "Maybe because it's by the ocean you can get a mechanical dolphin for people to ride."

"A mechanical dolphin?"

"Yeah. To keep with the theme."

"No one rides dolphins."

"They would if they could."

She placed another towel on the growing stack and smiled at him. All he could think was that he would like to eat her up. Which was inappropriate in every way, all things considered.

"Why don't you go check on a table," he said, his words coming out more harshly than he intended.

She shrunk back slightly, looking like a wounded puppy. He didn't feel bad about it. He didn't. "Okay. I will finish folding when I get back."

"If you see something that needs doing, do it. That's all I ask."

He did not watch her go out into the dining room. He turned away, heading back toward his office, away from the bar, away from the kitchen. He had stuff to get done and he was not going to allow Sierra West to distract him any longer.

HER FEET HURT LIKE a son of a bitch. Tonight had been, without a doubt, one of the longest nights on record. And it wasn't over yet.

She worked hard at the family ranch. But mainly, she

managed the office. When she went out and practiced barrel racing, she was on her horse. It definitely worked her muscles, but it also fed her soul.

Right now, she was pretty sure her soul was leaking out the bottom of her feet, which she had certainly worn a hole through walking around the dining area of the bar.

Being a waitress—it turned out—was exactly as little fun as it had always appeared to be.

She supposed some people might enjoy it. They might enjoy interacting with tables full of people and making runs between the kitchen, the bar and the dining area. She, it turned out, did not.

Also, she had discovered that men were slightly different with her when she was serving them drinks, versus when she was drinking near them. Sure, they still flirted with her. But there was a different tone. It was stickier. It left a film over her skin, and she didn't like it.

"You're a precious, precious blossom, Sierra," she muttered to herself as she bent to clear glasses off one of the tables that had just been vacated, before straightening and looking back over at the bar.

Chad, Leslie and Elyssa, the friends she'd been here with just the other night, were half draped over it. They didn't usually hang out right at the bar, but Leslie had just broken up with her boyfriend and it looked like she was thinking of testing her odds with Ace.

She was grinning and giggling and working the duck face like she was trying to take a selfie, not talk to a guy.

Ace, for his part, didn't seem disinterested. He was smiling. Smiling in a way he certainly hadn't smiled at Sierra. That just wasn't fair. Leslie was not less of a spoiled brat than she was. He should be mean to her, too.

But he wasn't being mean. He was being…charming. When he handed her drink over the counter his lips curved up into a half smile that made Sierra's stomach flip from all the way across the room. His dark eyes were glittering with intent. Wicked intent, even. Sierra could imagine that any woman on the receiving end of Ace's attention would feel like the only woman in the room. Maybe even in the world.

Of course, he didn't give her that kind of attention. He always acted like he wanted to stick her in the corner and cover her with a blanket so he could pretend she wasn't there.

She realized she'd been standing there, frozen and staring, for way too long. She mobilized. Holding tight to her bin of dishes, she walked quickly back toward the kitchen, her focus fixed straight ahead.

"Sierra?"

She turned at the sound of an incredulous voice, just in time to see Elyssa and Chad walking toward her. Leslie was still on her bar stool giggling loudly at something Ace said.

"Are you...working here?" Chad asked, his lip curling up into a borderline sneer.

"Yes," she said, steeling herself as she propped the bin on her hip. "I am working here. Since I'm not working with my dad anymore I needed to get another job."

Elyssa frowned. "But...at the bar?"

"All the glamorous positions at high rises were filled. Also, in another town. I had to take what I could get."

Elyssa scoffed. "Come on. Couldn't your brother help you? This is...beneath you, honestly."

Sierra bristled. "Why? It's fine for you to come drink here but it's not good for me to work here? Leslie can sit over there flirting her tits off with the man who owns the place but *this* is beneath me?"

"That's different," Chad said. "I'd do a waitress, but I wouldn't wait a table."

Sierra felt like she was having an out of body experience. Like she was witnessing this exchange from high above the bar. And with that distance came clarity. These people were terrible. They had also been her friends for a long time. And she couldn't say she wouldn't have felt the same way a few months ago if one of them had gotten a job here.

She wasn't even hurt. Or embarrassed. She was mad. Not even at them, but at herself. For all the coasting she'd done for so many years. For doing the schooling her father had wanted her to do, taking the job he'd created for her, having the friends that were convenient for her to have.

Suddenly, she didn't feel tired anymore. She felt energized. Empowered. Standing there in front of her former friends she felt separate and different. And like she might be more herself than she'd ever been before.

"You're an asshole, Chad," she said, her tone crisp. "I mean, do you hear yourself? Do you ever stop and listen to the words that come out of your mouth?" She knew he didn't. Because she never had, either. "You think you're above any of this? Trust me, you're one parental crisis away from being here. Except I don't think you have it in you to work this hard. You think you're too good for a job like this? You aren't good enough."

She continued on past them toward the kitchen.

"Wow, Sierra." Elyssa's voice stopped Sierra in her tracks. "Just wait till the town sees you like this."

Sierra shot her former friend one last furious glance.

"I'm not worried about that. In fact, I'm looking for-ward to it."

She glanced over at Ace, who was still flirting with Leslie, and then barged into the kitchen, angrily deposit-ing the bin of dirty dishes by the sink. She wasn't going to let them make her feel ashamed. She hadn't sunk to anything.

She was rising to the occasion.

She'd be damned if she felt embarrassed about that.

She spent the rest of the shift working as hard and furiously as possible. As if she could prove the world wrong right here in this bar, as long as she was the best waitress she could be.

Anger fueled her for a while, but that ran out quickly enough, leaving her drained and a bit less full of purpose than she'd been a few hours earlier.

She looked up at the clock on the wall and every-thing inside of her sagged. It was just after two thirty in the morning. She stayed out late often enough, but not usually this late. And definitely not usually schlepping drinks and hamburgers.

She wrinkled her nose. That was what she smelled like. Beef, bacon, french fries and exhaustion. It was in her skin.

Suddenly, she felt very small, and very persecuted.

She dragged herself back into the kitchen, setting the dishes on the edge of the sink. At least she didn't have to wash those. That made her feel slightly less persecuted.

She walked back out into the dining area, untying her apron and setting it on top of the bar.

"That isn't where that goes," Ace said, suddenly ap-pearing out of his office like a flannel, bearded vapor.

"You certainly have a lot of systems," she told him,

rubbing her temples before snatching the apron back up. "Where exactly do I put it?"

"I'll take it," he said, reaching his hand out.

His shirtsleeves were pushed up to his elbows, revealing those muscular forearms that her body seemed to be kind of obsessed with.

She tried to think back to her last boyfriend. Had she ever noticed Mark's forearms? What had they looked like? Had they been hairy? They must not have been, because she hadn't really noticed. Anyway, he had lighter hair. She made a mental note to go look at a picture of Mark and see if his forearms were spectacular, and if she was suddenly just now into forearms, and hadn't been back then.

"Why don't you let me take it," she said, snatching the apron back. "I'm going to need to know where it goes."

"You're stubborn," he said. "You know that?"

"Thanks to you, I do." She smiled so wide it made her cheeks ache.

"Come back here with me." He opened the door into the kitchen, which was empty now. "Didn't you get your own apron when you came this afternoon?"

"No, I traded with one of the other girls."

"Okay," he said, gesturing to a back wall. "You hang them up here."

She followed his directions, hanging the little black apron on the hook and turning back to face him. "Don't you have a manager who normally trains new staff?" It occurred to her then that it was kind of funny that the guy who owned the place was taking so much time to show her what to do. Of course, she was asking a lot of questions. But still, he never referred her to anyone else.

"No. Not really. This is my place. My name is on the sign, as you mentioned earlier."

"Sure. But when you open the new place you're not going to be able to be tending bar at both. You're going to have to delegate."

"Did you say you have a business degree?"

She nodded. "Yes."

"Yeah, that kind of thing sounds about like something someone who has taken a class might say."

Heat fired through her veins, blood boiling into her cheeks. "Right, let me guess, you went to the school of hard knocks. You're all street smart instead of actual smart."

"I can't imagine why no one else wanted to give you a job." He turned away from her, walking out of the kitchen, and she scurried after him.

"What do you mean? I did great work tonight."

"You were rude to the customers."

She burst out of the kitchen, breathing hard. "To who? The jackasses who accosted me? They're my...well, they were my friends. And they were being horrible. How did you see that anyway? You were busy staring down Leslie's shirt."

"No," he corrected her. "I made Leslie feel like I wanted to look down her shirt since that was how she wanted to feel. She went through a breakup. She needed a boost. I gave it."

"Wow. A full-service kind of guy."

"That's customer service. I treat everyone better than they deserve to be treated. It's why they come back."

"You don't treat me that way."

"You aren't my customer. And that's the second thing

I was going to mention to you. I'm your boss. You need to remember that."

"Well, it isn't like you're being very nice to me."

"Nope." He turned back to face her, his hands stuffed in his pockets.

That was when she realized that no one else was here. They were completely alone in the dining area, possibly completely alone in the building. Which shouldn't matter. It wasn't like he was going to do anything to her. He was angry, that much was clear, but he wasn't going to hurt her.

That isn't what you're worried about.

No. Maybe it wasn't.

"Why?"

"Why what?" he asked, placing his hands on his narrow hips.

"Why aren't you nice to me? I mean, other than the fact that I kind of said some stupid things when I was drunk, which I apologized for, you don't really have a reason to hate me."

He let out a hard breath, rolling his dark eyes. "That's where you're wrong. I know you, Sierra West. Probably better than you know yourself."

"Beg to differ. We don't know each other."

"No, but I know your type. You're spoiled. But you don't even realize how spoiled you are. Because you've never actually experienced life without privilege. How would you know the remarkable pieces of your existence? You don't know how anyone else lives. Everything you've ever needed has been put directly in front of you. You've never even had to reach for it. You're so proud of that college degree, you think it makes you better than me. You think it makes you smarter than me. But you didn't have to work for it. You didn't have to pay for it. You're not in debt over it. You didn't have to scramble to find a job after you graduated, so in the end, you've never even had to use that piece of paper.

"You think you're too good for this job," he continued, "you think you're too good for this bar. You've manipulated every boyfriend you've ever had with your good looks and your charm, with that little bit of superiority you feel. You do it without even trying."

His words were rapid-fire, like high-velocity gunfire from an automatic rifle. They hit their marks hard, and they left a lot of damage.

Mostly because he was saying things that she'd been grappling with herself over the past few days. He was drawing back the curtain on the facade of her life. Tearing down pieces of the walls that she wasn't ready to look behind yet. Parts that concerned herself, and not simply the sins of her father.

The little things that were starting to gnaw at her. Innocuous things. Like getting into her truck. Like realizing she'd never apologized before.

She was raw enough, certain enough that what he was saying had truth to it without him actually saying it.

"Oh, congratulations, you read the rich girl stereotype handbook," she returned, infusing her words with as much bite as she could manage. She might suspect that he had the right end of the stick, but she was never going to let him see that. Because he didn't say these things to help her, he said them to hurt her. He didn't deserve validation. Not from her. Maybe this would be the end of her career as a waitress. But as far as she was concerned he could suck it. "Sadly for you, I read the disaffected hipster bartender handbook. You're so over life. Money is so mainstream. And so is Coors Light. But of course, you want your business to be successful, and you actually need money to live. So you don't hate it nearly as much as you pretend."

She took a step toward him, her breathing labored. "You act like you have some big, deep wound that makes you inaccessible to the rest of us mortals, while you remind me and everyone else that we aren't really special. You think *you're* special, don't you, Ace? You're certainly more special than me." She took another step toward him, and another, and she extended her hand, poking him in the chest. "So complicated and manly. How can a feather-headed little lady like myself ever truly understand you?"

Much to her surprise, he laughed. His lips curving up into a half smile, something dark, dangerous, glinting in his eyes. "Don't be fooled by the flannel, babe. I'm not a hipster. I'm not that complicated, either. I work, I eat, I sleep and I fuck. End of story."

His words sent a searing rash of heat burning through her veins. She didn't know why but hearing that word on his lips made her feel things. All kinds of things.

She hung out with plenty of guys who dropped F bombs like they didn't mean a thing. She'd been known to do the same herself in the right company.

But when they did it, it was a silly kids' game. A bid to spit out the most naughty words in the fewest sentences.

It wasn't like that now. The way he used it...it forced her to see it. Something raw, rough and untamed. Something harder, deeper than she'd ever known before. With that one word he made every other man she'd ever known into a boy, and he made sex something unknown and forbidden, something she was sure she'd barely scratched the surface of.

And they were fighting. Something that should underscore how much she didn't like him. Something that should douse the heat that shimmered between them. Because fighting was not hot. At least, historically, fighting had not been hot. With him, it was.

If that wasn't some kind of freaky weird magic she didn't know what was.

She was breathing hard, and she knew he would be able to tell. If there was anything worse than feeling this strange, errant attraction, it was the fact that it was so completely transparent. She took another step toward him, reached out, her fingertips brushing the collar of his shirt.

Her whole face was hot. Her body was hot. Everything was hot. He really needed to adjust the temperature in here. Or find some way not to be attractive when he was being such a dick.

"Was that supposed to shock me?" she asked.

He leaned in, his face inches from hers. "It did, didn't it?"

She squared her stance, her breasts nearly brushing his chest. "Do I look like I'm shocked to you?"

"You look like something, that's for sure," he said, dark eyes raking over her body. "But let me tell you something, Sierra. I'm not that hard up. You want me, that much is obvious. It isn't like I haven't noticed you're a pretty little thing. But things come too easily to you. You think you can manipulate me like you're used to doing? You're out of luck. You need to learn to ask for what you want. If you want me, you're going to have to ask. You're going to have to beg."

That should not turn her on. Absolutely not at all. His words should have been like a bucket of cold water over her head. It should not have been gasoline on a lit match. She took a step back, stumbling a bit, knowing she was doing a terrible job of maintaining her composure.

Somehow, in all of this, with him, she did not have her usual command of herself, of the situation. Was that because of all this stuff with her father? The major revelations and changes that had rocked her existence? Or was it just Ace? She couldn't decide which disturbed her more.

All of it. All of it was disturbing.

She snorted, straightening the hem on her black tank top, even though it didn't need straightening. "I'm afraid you have the wrong end of the stick, *babe*," she said, repeating his earlier endearment back to him. "Maybe other women routinely lose their alcohol-ridden minds over you, but I'm not going to be one of them. All I want from you is a paycheck."

"Then why are your cheeks so pink?" he asked, reaching out, dragging his thumb over her cheekbone.

She shivered, a flash of lightning shooting down the center of her bones. It rocked her, rattled her, shook her to her core. It was unlike anything she'd ever experienced before. The problem with Ace was that he was different. He was nothing like those boys she had dated in the past. The silly frat bros who were barely edging into their twenties and were more interested in the care and keeping of their own biceps than they were in dealing with a girlfriend.

They were shallow, silly, they didn't have the kind of intensity Ace radiated without even trying. Of course, she wasn't entirely certain that was a negative. She wasn't sure she liked Ace's intensity. But it touched her. Deep, way down deep, in places no one had ever touched before.

With nothing more than a look and a brush of his thumb against her cheek.

It was problematic if nothing else. And she had enough problematic without adding him to the mix.

"Pure, unmitigated fury," she said, taking a step away from him. "That makes my cheeks pink without any kind of maidenly excitement, or whatever it is you're imagining I feel for you. News flash, not maidenly. Not excited."

"I'll try not to lose any sleep over that. Be here tomorrow, five thirty."

"I'll be here. And I'll work hard for you, I swear it. By the end of the three weeks you're not going to be able to deny me the job, Ace Thompson. I'll wait tables, pour drinks, do dishes and mop floors. I'll do all that with a smile on my face. But I will never beg. You have a good night, now."

Heart pounding so hard she thought it might beat its way straight through her chest, she turned from him and walked out of the bar.

What had happened in there was nothing. Just her extended bout of celibacy beginning to show. It had been a while since she'd broken up with Mark. Closing in on a year and a half. And even then they'd been hit and miss since he'd lived and worked in Portland and she'd been in Copper Ridge. So yeah, tonight's bout of hormones was perfectly understandable.

The fact of the matter was, with everything happening in her family, and her having this job, she really didn't have the energy to go looking for another relationship.

You don't actually need a relationship.

That was true. But she'd never really been a random hookup girl. Her relationships had never been intense, but they had been monogamous, and pretty long-lasting.

When they died, they always died natural deaths. In the case of her and Mark it was all long-distance stuff. She was never going to move to the city to be with him, he was never going to come to Copper Ridge to be with her. And once they'd both realized that, there hadn't seemed to be much point in continuing on.

She was regretting that now. Because a well-worn relationship would have been nice right about now. She could have driven up to Portland for a while, spent a few nights with him. She could have distracted herself.

She wondered, for a moment, if it was worth calling Mark up to see if he was still single. To see if he wanted her to come visit.

Except she had a job now, so she couldn't just take off and go wherever she wanted to.

And the bigger problem was, she didn't want to. Because she didn't want Mark.

She let out a long breath, then inhaled deeply, taking in the scent of salt and pine. She was attracted to Ace. That didn't mean she *wanted* him. Not in a serious, real way. She had one shot at this job. If she could prove that she could do it, then maybe other people in town would take her more seriously. Maybe they would hire her. If she was ever going to be self-sufficient here, then she needed to get some job experience that extended beyond the West family ranch, and she knew it. Moreover, at this point it was about pride. Ace didn't think she could do this. All of those rejected job applications meant that most people in town didn't think she could do this. They might like her, they might respect her family name, but they didn't think she was capable of being anything more than the daughter of Nathan West.

Suddenly, she felt like she was standing on the edge

of a hole. A void containing all of her achievements. Or rather, not containing them. She wondered if she had any. She'd gone to college, but her father had paid for it. She'd gotten a job only because it was assured due to her family connections.

She put her hand on the handle of the truck door that wasn't hers.

She gritted her teeth, tears stinging her eyes, determination lashing her like a whip. The bottom line was, whatever she felt for Ace shouldn't matter. Because it wasn't as important as her future. She was going to prove to him that she could do this job, and that she could do it on her own merit. She wasn't going to let anyone make her feel ashamed.

She wasn't going to play these games with Ace, wasn't going to let him touch her again. Wasn't going to allow herself to touch him.

She was a waitress right now. And that meant that she was determined to be the best damn waitress in all of Copper Ridge.

CHAPTER FIVE

IT WAS JUST about noon by the time Ace got himself out of the house and to the grocery store. He had a few hours before he was going to check in at the bar and he needed to get some things for his house that extended beyond beer and ranch dip. Like, chips for the ranch dip.

He walked slowly through the store aisles, basket in hand as he perused the shelves. He stopped, turning toward the produce, toward the heads of lettuce stacked all bright green and pointless. He supposed he should probably eat vegetables. Going to the store was always weird. Because he saw things in it that were reflective of a life he could hardly remember anymore.

Liar. You remember it perfectly.

For a while, he'd lived in a house that was well stocked with this kind of healthy stuff. Salad and tomatoes, and all manner of stuff that was good for you but tasted like dirt. He supposed that had also been true of his childhood home. His mom had always had things like that around the house, but he'd figured when he grew up he wouldn't have to eat it anymore.

At that stage of his life, he hadn't factored a wife into the equation.

He turned away from the lettuce. He didn't have a wife anymore. Therefore, he didn't have salad.

"Ace?"

He turned around, the impact of recognition hitting him like a punch to the gut when he saw the person behind him. "Hayley," he said, shock being worn away by a rush of guilt the moment he spoke his little sister's name.

"I haven't seen you in… It's been way too long."

"You know where I work," he said.

She smiled. "You know where I work, too."

"Not really interested in paying the church a visit," he said, shoving one hand into his pocket, tightening his grip on his basket with the other.

"Well, I don't drink."

"We serve hamburgers."

"I know. We should get together, is my point. And not to fight about places neither of us really want to go."

Hayley was nine years younger than he was, a late-in-life surprise for his parents who had long given up hope on ever having another child. She had been nine when he'd left Copper Ridge for Texas, seventeen when he'd come back.

He had been distant from his family all those years he'd spent away, sporadic phone calls his only real contact. He had always stopped in to visit when the rodeo had passed nearby, but when he'd settled in Austin with Denise his life had just wrapped itself around her, and it had become impossible to do anything but pour himself into that relationship.

"How have you been?" he asked.

She lifted her shoulder, a half smile curving her lips. In some ways, she looked sixteen, instead of twenty-six. Either that or she looked closer to sixty-five. Her dark hair lay flat and limp against her head, restrained by a headband. She was wearing a dark blue sweater set and a long skirt. She was every church secretary stereotype imaginable. Though he supposed he was every stereo-type of a pastor's son.

"Fine," she said, "nothing really new."

"Mom and Dad?" That stab of guilt went deeper, drawing blood inside.

"Also fine." She looked down. "Well, Dad had a bit of a health scare. A little chest pain. But everything was okay. They're just having him monitor his cholesterol, and all that."

He thought about his dad, tall, lean. He had a hard time imagining the older man might have issues with his heart. It worried him. It also made him think twice about the lettuce.

"He didn't have a heart attack?"

Hayley shook her head. "No. Like I said, he's fine. Ace, if anything serious happened, you know I would call you."

And he knew that he should call them and try to get updates more often. He should go over for dinner more often than every few months. But what was he supposed to tell them about his life? His father wouldn't even go into the bar because of appearances in the small town. Hayley and his mother basically had the same policy. And he couldn't even get upset about that because he had been well aware of how they would feel about him running a bar before he had ever done it. To their credit, no one ever made him feel guilty about his choice; they asked him about how things were going, expressed interest in the place. They just didn't come in.

There were no relationships for him to tell them about. He was hardly going to confess to the endless array of women whose names he couldn't even remember that passed through his bed on any given weekend.

That was the real problem. Sometimes it was just hard to sit across from his father and look him in the eye.

"Good to see you," he said, reaching out and pulling his sister in for a hug. He should have done that right at the first. There was something wrong with him that he hadn't thought to hug her until now.

But that was hardly a revelation.

"Good to see you, too," she said, her voice muffled against his shoulder.

He released his hold on her. "Tell Mom and Dad I said hi. If anything… If they need help with anything around the house, see that you give me a call."

"Usually, the youth group takes care of any work that Dad needs around the house. They do a good job of saying thank you for everything he does."

Hayley was too sweet to imply that they had to do it because Ace didn't, but it hit him that way anyway. And fair enough.

"Still. He can call me."

"I'll tell him." She rocked back on her heels, holding onto her basket with both hands, awkwardness that should never exist between siblings settling between them. "Well, I have to go. I'm just on lunch break."

"See you around, kiddo." The old nickname didn't help ease any of the weirdness between them.

She ducked her head, turning away and walking over towards the checkout lines, and Ace continued to stroll down the aisles. He did not get lettuce. He waited to pay for his various assortment of frozen dinners until he was sure that Hayley was gone, which was a jackass move, but he was kind of a jackass.

He walked out of the grocery store, loading up his truck and pausing for a moment, looking across the cracked, mostly empty parking lot and toward the mountain view beyond. It was a strange thing, realizing that the near decade spent away, and the decade he'd been back home had changed him into the kind of person who would never fit into his own family. It was his own decisions that had done that. That had reshaped him in such a way that sitting down at the dinner table he'd grown up eating around now felt nearly impossible.

Of course, the fact that he lived in Copper Ridge meant that he had to contend with running into his family at the grocery store. It meant that he felt guilty for not coming over more often, even if coming over only resulted in him sitting there feeling too large in his seat. As though he were being held beneath the magnifying glass, his every sin conspicuous in the eyes of his parents.

He could have stayed away. When he had left Austin, there had been no real reason to come back to Copper Ridge. Except that it was home. Home in a way no other place ever had been.

It was the kind of place that got underneath your skin. He hadn't truly noticed it until he left. Until he'd spent years traveling across the country on the rodeo circuit, until he had settled in Texas, making plans on the Lone Star State being his permanent home.

But the need for mountains was in his blood. Pine trees and sharp salt air that burrowed beneath your skin. That made every breath taken in any other place taste wrong somehow.

So that was why he had come back. It was why he was here now. It was why he stayed.

Even though when he'd rolled back into town all those years ago, it hadn't felt quite like he'd imagined. Sure, the air was the same. The main street was the same. Most of the people were the same.

But he was different. He supposed that made everything else feel a little different, too.

You can't go home again, and all that stuff.

He got into his truck, starting the engine. He had to stop back home, deposit his supplies, and then make his way over to the bar. Where he was sure to have another uncomfortable encounter. With a woman he felt decidedly unbrotherly toward.

He thought back to last night. To his close encounter with Sierra.

She wouldn't beg. That was the thing. That was why he'd said that. To make it easy to keep his hands off her.

When she had closed the distance between them last night, when those delicate fingers brushed against the collar of his shirt, he had been certain of one thing. He wanted her. More than he could remember wanting any woman in recent years.

In fact, there had only ever been one woman like that in his memory. Only one woman he had ever lost his control with. One woman he had abandoned good sense to have.

And that had ended in a fiery crash of doom that had destroyed him and everything around it.

She wouldn't beg. So he wouldn't touch her. It was that simple.

And maybe tonight he would find another woman to take home. Someone who would help him take the edge off of this need, this arousal.

That was a much better thought than his family and Sierra combined.

He would focus on that, and forget the rest. He was

good at forgetting the bad things. Everyone needed to have their strengths.

He cranked up the radio, turning up the country station. And he looked out the window at the view, that cleansing, perfect view. Misty clouds dropping low over the pine trees, casting everything in a muted shade of gray that extended down to the ocean, liquid fog stretching as far as the eye could see.

For a few blissful moments, there was nothing except the song on the radio, and that view.

And he definitely did not think about Sierra West.

SIERRA WAS KICKING ASS and taking names tonight. Well, she was kicking metaphorical ass and taking orders for food and drink. But in her world right now, it amounted to the same thing.

Everything felt a little more familiar tonight, and she didn't feel quite so much like she was flailing around in the dark as she completed her tasks. And whenever she found herself not busy with customers, she went and folded bar towels. Because she knew how to do that. She also didn't ask Ace for help.

After last night, she didn't know how to deal with him. Well, really, she didn't know how to deal with herself. When it came to Ace she was in a whole seascape of uncharted water. But at least she felt like she had some guideposts here in the bar.

She proudly delivered another order back to the kitchen, then set about to straightening up while she waited exactly five minutes to go check on her last table. She was determined to do an excellent job. And she was doing an excellent job.

She wasn't a stranger to trying hard. She didn't half-ass her horse riding. She took barrel racing seriously. Mostly because if she didn't, she knew she could wind up flat on her back on the ground in the arena, getting trampled by her own steed. But she was starting to realize that life was a whole lot more like barrel racing than she had initially given it credit for.

And lo, she had been trampled by the steed.

But she was getting back up. That was important. If she was sticking with the horse analogies, then it meant that when you got thrown off life, you just had to get back on. She frowned. Well, she wasn't exactly getting right back on. That implied going back to doing the same thing. She was changing things. Everything. She was after some kind of ownership in her daily existence. Because before this she'd had none. Everything belonged to her father, to the West family.

Well, she was going to get some things that belonged to her. Starting with this work experience.

She turned back around with her stack of folded bar towels, ready to put them under the counter, and paused when she saw her sister, Madison, standing there. "Maddy. What are you doing here?"

"Colton told me you were here." Madison wrinkled her nose, tucking a strand of light brown hair behind her ear. "He said you had a job."

"Yes." She was still clutching the stack of towels. "This is my job."

"You're a…barmaid?"

"I'm not a barmaid. It's not like I'm wearing lederhosen."

"I don't think you have to wear lederhosen to be a barmaid." Madison held on to her purse, clutching it tightly in front of her, as though she was afraid if she released her hold on it she might have to touch something else. As though the place might infect her. "I think you just have to be a maid. Who works at a bar."

"I'm serving tables."

"You could just come home."

Oh, there was the bottom line. "No, *Madison*," she said, emphasizing her sister's full name, which she rarely used, "I can't. And you of all people should understand why."

Madison's expression turned to stone. "Whatever I've been through in the past isn't really about this. I know that finding out about Dad hurt. It hurts me. Finding out that Jack is related to us, that he spent all of his life with nothing so the dick could protect his reputation… I don't like it. And my staying is not an endorsement. But my life is at the ranch. I don't see the point in burning everything down because of Dad. Mom is in the car…"

Sierra's heart twisted. "How is she?"

"I think not as surprised as the rest of us. Upset. But you know she isn't going to do anything."

Her throat tightened. "I just can't. I'm not upset at you, or Mom, or Colton for not… I just can't."

"Why? I mean, honestly, you're right. If anyone was going to leave because of this, you would think it would be me. Cheating married men are basically my least favorite. But my business is tied to the West family ranch, and to Dad's name. And I can't just overlook everything that he's done for us because of a mistake he made over thirty years ago. It's a mistake that's older than we are, Sierra. We've never known him before the mistake."

"You keep calling it a mistake. But a mistake is something that happens once. And you don't mean to do it.

Every year, every birthday, he ignored Jack. And he kept on doing it year after year—"

"Don't tell me you have warm fuzzy feelings for Jack Monaghan," Madison said.

"Why shouldn't I?"

"He was fine without involving himself in our business from where I'm standing. Anyway, I just don't believe that's the primary problem you have with Dad."

"I don't know. I don't really know how I feel about Jack. That's true enough. But… I'm a West. That's what I am. My name is everything to me. It got me everywhere I've ever gone in life. But it isn't what I thought it was. This whole reputation that Dad has constructed… How many lies is it built out of?"

Madison's green eyes softened. "I know. I know that's hard. But does it matter? Dad loves you. He loves us."

"And he doesn't love his other son. He…he sold him. Traded him for a spotless reputation. I understand why Mom can't leave him. But I wish she would. I wish she would ask for better."

"It isn't that simple. Do you honestly think at this point being a sixty-year-old divorcée is better for Mom than just sticking it out with him? Colton is getting married. There will be grandchildren. She needs her marriage for everything she does, for everything she loves. She could let go of it because of pride but then…what would she have?"

"I guess she might have to be a barmaid," Sierra said.

"I wish you would reconsider. I miss you. You could move out of the main house and come live in my little villa. You wouldn't even have to pass Dad coming and going."

"Maddy…I love you. And I miss you. I'm sorry I haven't

seen you since I left. I'm not mad at you for staying, I'm
really not."

"I'm not mad at you for leaving. I just wish I could
understand. Why all this… I mean, if you're going to be
upset anyway, why not be upset…not working in a bar?"

"I have to prove this to myself, Maddy. I have to find
a way to be something other than a West. I have to do it
now. And I should have done it a long time ago."

"I like hiding behind the name, personally," Madison
said. "I tried to step out from Dad's shadow once. Now I
have a scandal and a ruined career to my name. All before I turned eighteen. Yay me."

"None of that crap with David was your fault." Just
thinking about that time in Madison's life made Sierra
angry all over again. "He lied to you. People are assholes
so they blamed the actions of a thirty-five-year-old man
on a seventeen-year-old girl. This isn't that. I'm twenty-
five. I need to… I need to figure myself out."

"I'm twenty-seven and I still haven't done that."

"The dressage lessons, and training and all that…that's
your world. It's who you are. I just manage the office.
I got a business degree so I could do that. I don't know
if I care about business. Not that I regret my education
but… I really wanted to barrel race. To travel with the
rodeo. But that wasn't in the plan, so I didn't. You would
be leaving something that matters to you if you left the
ranch. I'm not. I don't know what matters to me anymore.
I don't know if I want to go hard-core after racing. I don't
know how I want to earn a living. I don't even know how
I would decorate my room if it were up to me and not
Mom's designer." She let out a long, slow breath. "I think
I should figure all that out, don't you?"

"I guess. And I'd better leave you to it. I would stay for a drink, but…Mom."

Sierra smiled. "You wouldn't stay. You hate places like this. You'd rather be at a vineyard having chardonnay."

"Silly." Madison winked. "I like Shiraz better."

"We'll do something fancy with my first paycheck. Like wine and appetizers at Beaches. Or, if I make crappy tips tonight, diet soda and Tic Tacs at Colton's."

Her sister laughed. "Right. Well, maybe we'll land in the middle with Perrier and fish and chips? Dare to dream?"

"Depends on how much I wiggle my hips when I clear out the tables, I suppose."

Madison leaned in, still careful not to touch the counter. "I'll call you. I hope you're keeping garlic under your pillow."

"Why?"

"To ward off Natalie, the undead fiancée."

"Ha. No. No garlic. I hung a crucifix on my door, though. That seemed to do it."

"Good."

"If I get infected, promise you'll kill me."

"I promise. Because I love you."

"I love you, too," Sierra said, her heart tightening a little.

Madison turned away, offering a small wave as she waded through the crowd at the bar and walked out the door. Sierra looked out at all the people, all the orders she had to fulfill. Well, she'd chosen this now. So she was going to wait some damn tables.

Tonight's shift went much faster. She didn't have any unpleasant encounters with people she knew. In fact, most people she recognized had been nice to her, if a little concerned-looking at seeing her so out of context.

But by the end of the night she wasn't as ready to fall into a heap on the floor. She actually felt energized, even though it was well past time for her coach to turn into a pumpkin. She might actually get used to this.

Maybe waiting tables was like training for a marathon. You could work up to it. Or maybe she was on some weird high that would end tomorrow when she had to roll out of bed feeling like crumpled newspaper wrapped around chewed-up gum.

The bar was empty, most of the employees heading out. And she was lingering. Because Ace wasn't anywhere to be seen and she didn't want to leave before she was in his eye line. She wouldn't let him accuse her of slacking off or leaving early or…going out to get emergency eyeliner or whatever BS he would try to pull to both compromise her job and mock her *poor little rich girl* status.

She wasn't going to give him an opening. She had performed perfectly tonight, and she was not going to give him a chance to say otherwise. He wanted her to fail. She had no idea why he seemed so invested in her failure, even as he had her here on staff. Honestly, it didn't make sense.

But, regardless of what she had said the other night, she actually hadn't ever read the hipster bartender handbook. So the workings of his brain truly were a secret. And she was content to keep it that way.

She walked by his office somewhat conspicuously, hoping that the sound of her footsteps would make him open the door. Nothing.

She paced in front of the door again, making sure to stomp a little bit louder this time. Still nothing.

She let out an exasperated sigh, then turned to face the door, raising her hand, getting ready to knock. As she was about to bring it down, the door swung open, and there was Ace. Looking as cranky and attractive as he always did. His dark hair was disheveled, the stubble on his jaw looking all rakish and sexy.

She supposed he didn't always look cranky. He didn't scowl like this when he was dealing with women in the bar. That seemed to be reserved for her.

She wondered if she should feel special.

"Hi," she said.

"Yes?"

"I just wanted you to know that I'm going to leave now, because everything is clean."

"Okay. Go. You don't have to check in with me, no one else does."

"I didn't figure you would trust that I hadn't knocked off work early and had a couple of the other employees carry me out of here on a rickshaw."

He leaned against the doorjamb, rubbing his forehead with his hand. "I don't think that. Anyway, you can go." He turned, preparing to go back into his office.

"Are you staying?" She had no idea why she was asking. She should be leaving as quickly as possible. Staying was like willingly putting her foot into a badger trap. "Because it's awfully late to be doing things in the office." Foot. Trap.

"Oh, I'm not working. I'm just watching porn."

"What kind?" *What kind? Really?*

He turned toward her again, treating her to a lopsided smile that was a whole lot more interesting than it had any right to be. "The kind with spreadsheets. And fabric swatches." At her blank look, he shrugged. "Actually, it's just some planning that I'm doing for the new brewery I'm opening."

"Okay, that makes a lot more sense than the porn thing."

His smile broadened, and she felt compelled to return it. "I guess that depends on what you're into."

"Not spreadsheets. But you do you."

"I really hate this, actually. Especially all the decorating stuff. It all looks the same to me. There aren't any curtains in here. Most of the decor was in place when I took over. This is kind of all new. Plus, the brewery is supposed to be a little more upscale. Meanwhile, I'm not all that upscale."

"You're not?" she asked, planting her hand on her hip.

He was making her smile. And she realized now that the gesture was a little bit flirtatious. She wasn't sure she cared.

You should. You're supposed to be proving that you're a good waitress, not that you're good at picking up guys.

She dropped her hand back to her side.

"Do you think I could use flannel upholstery on the furniture? The curtains, too?"

"Why not? Maybe you could go with the whole lumberjack theme. Individual fireplaces by the tables, people could chop their own wood. It would be cozy."

"I think you might be overtired."

"I'll bet you are, too," she said, not quite sure why she cared, only that she did.

"Sure. But I'm basically running two businesses right now. And one is a little bit of a problem child."

"I can help you with that," she said. And as soon as

the words slipped out, she realized she should. She had done a good job waiting tables today, but she wasn't exactly going to win an award for it. It was also a skill a lot of people could hone, possibly faster than she could. But there were a few skills in life she knew she'd honed to perfection. Event planning, interior design. She was such a cliché. She blamed her mother. Or had her mother to thank. She wasn't sure which. "I mean, my mother hosts a lot of charity events, and I've spent a lot of time helping with menus, and wine lists. Decorations… Anyway, I'm just saying this type of planning isn't hard for me. It's something I actually know how to do. So if you ever get tired of hanging out in your office until three in the morning, I'm on hand."

"You have experience with all of that?"

"Yes, I do. And you can pay me minimum wage to help."

"But you won't make tips like you do here."

She didn't even have to weigh that. She would take less money to do something that made better use of her skills. She was willing to do her best at waitressing, but managing a project like this and helping with decor sounded much more appealing than spending all night on her feet. "That's okay."

He shook his head. "No, it isn't. I'll pay you more than minimum wage to help."

She eyed him skeptically. "And why exactly would you do that?"

"Because it would save me having to hire someone, and I guarantee you that it would be more expensive to hire a professional than to pay you minimum wage plus whatever tips you make in an evening."

"My tips are pretty good. I don't know if you can afford me."

"I have a feeling I can swing it. So, what hours are you interested in working? Do you want to trade shifts?"

"Honestly? I don't really have anything else going on right now. So, if you want to tackle this tomorrow, and I can still come in to work…"

"I don't want to work you to death."

She snorted. "I'm not as delicate as you seem to think I am. I already told you, I'm a barrel racer. Not just some pansy-ass rich girl."

"If you're sure. Why don't you meet me out at my place tomorrow."

She ignored the little thrill that went through her at the thought of being at his place with him, alone. It seemed so much more intimate than being here with him. A lot more dangerous. "Directions?"

He reached into his back pocket, pulling out his wallet and producing a business card. Then he took a pen out of his pocket and scribbled something on the back of the card. "Why don't you put this in your smartphone?"

"Do I look like someone who has a smartphone?" she asked, paraphrasing their earlier conversation from the night he'd driven her home.

"Absolutely."

"Fair enough. Because I do." She took the card from his hand and looked at the back, where he had written his address. "Well, should be easy enough to find. What time do you want me to come over?"

"How about noon? I'm not really human before then. Sometimes I'm not even awake."

It struck her then, what strange hours a bartender must keep. She was slowly acclimating to the later nights, but she wondered what it must be like to live the way Ace did. He wasn't really beholden to anybody. He could stay in the office until three in the morning if he wanted to, and then get up at noon, because why not? His entire life centered around what happened after 5:00 p.m.

She wondered what that must be like. To answer to no one, not even the clock in the way regular people did. No wonder he was kind of an ass. He wasn't used to making concessions for anyone or anything.

She wasn't sure if she envied him or not. Mostly because she wasn't sure if she lived by someone else's rules or her own. Which was really stupid, when she thought about it. But it all went back to what she had been saying to Madison earlier. She just didn't know what she wanted.

She felt like she was floating. She was just going to blame that on how late it was.

"Okay," she said, tapping the edge of the doorjamb. "See you tomorrow."

"See you tomorrow."

It was strange, how familiar those words were becoming. How familiar it was to hear them back.

She blinked, released her hold on the doorjamb and waved faintly while she turned and began to walk out of the bar.

Tomorrow would present a new opportunity to show him that she could do this job. This job, and more. And that was the only reason her stomach turned over when she thought about it. The only reason.

CHAPTER SIX

SIERRA WASN'T ENTIRELY certain what she had been anticipating when she pulled up to Ace's house. But it wasn't what she saw. The large, craftsman-style house with the expansive porch and the red door was absolutely not what she expected from someone like Ace.

She wasn't sure what a taciturn house would look like, but she had imagined his was taciturn. Not…homey. Certainly not immaculate and well kept. Which was silly, because for all that his bar wasn't fancy, it was clean. So she should have expected his home to be the same.

She parked the truck and got out, walking toward that red front door that made a mockery of everything she'd thought about him. "Or it's just a door."

She scuffed her boot through the gravel in the driveway, leaving a pale line in the dust. She glanced around. It looked like there was a barn down the path that led away from the house. She squinted in that direction, wondering what was in there. Horses?

Horses were her weakness.

She shook her head and walked up the steps to the porch. She paused at the front door, swallowing hard before gathering her courage to knock. For some reason, no matter how often she saw him, an encounter with Ace felt like a whole event.

She could hear his footsteps as he approached the

door, each one leaching a little more moisture from her throat, leaving it dry as sandpaper by the time the door swung open.

And…oh dear Lord.

He was wearing that typical lumberjack uniform of his. Flannel with well-fitted jeans. But his shirt was tucked in, and he had on a belt with a big buckle. And he was wearing a hat. A cowboy hat.

She was so done. She was a sucker for a cowboy, always had been. But put her favorite-least-favorite bartender in a cowboy hat and all the blood in her body rushed to her extremities.

"Good morning," she said. "Afternoon, I mean. Noon?"

"Morning to me," he said, stepping away from the doorway and back into the house. "You want some coffee?"

He disappeared without waiting for her answer. Or maybe he'd seen it in the glint in her eyes at the prospect of caffeine. After he retreated, she continued to stand there on his surprisingly homey porch, unsure of what she was supposed to do.

She poked her head in the doorway and blinked. The rest of the house was not as the porch had her believing. It was…pretty, sure. The natural wood beams and large windows gave the place a rustic charm, but it was… empty.

Well, not empty empty, but it contained little more than a couch and a large, rough-hewn table that looked like he'd straight up carved it out of a log. There were no photographs on the walls, no art, no mirrors.

There were empty beer bottles, standing sentry on every available surface like empty vases waiting for a daisy.

Unsurprisingly there were no daisies anywhere.

Ace returned a moment later, holding two coffee mugs in his hand. They didn't match. One was black with a chip around the rim, and the other was shaped more like a soup bowl.

"I will take the industrial-sized one." She reached out, flexing her fingers.

"Ladies' choice," he said, extending the mug in her direction.

"The lady chooses to have a tankard." She wrapped her fingers around her bowl-o'-coffee and lifted it to her lips, looking around the sparse room. "I see what you mean about not being very big into decorating."

"It's serviceable." His gaze followed her own, clearly taking stock of his surroundings.

"Yeah." She cleared her throat. "Anyway. You have swatches and samples and things?"

"You sound way too excited about that."

"I am. Fabric choices get me hot under the collar."

He laughed. "Excellent. This is my new strategy with women. Come back to my place and look at my flannel."

"That would…" She looked him over and tried not to let her mind go to very bad places. Like what it might be like to look beneath his flannel. "Work. That would probably work."

"Okay," he said, walking across the room and heading over toward the couch, toward that big, striking table. "This is what I have."

There was a stack of fabric samples on the table. Little square pieces of different material attached to cardboard. She walked over to them, crossing her arms and studying all the options. "Okay, what vibe are you going for?"

"Is there a particular fabric that says *I want to spend my money on the most expensive alcohol in this place*?"

She laughed, looking down. "I'll tell you right now," she said, reaching for one of the samples, "it isn't this." She ran a finger along the red-and-white checked fabric. "Unless you're going for overpriced picnic by the sea."

"Not so much. Look, I'm not a frilly guy. So this is all kind of beyond me. I sort of know what I want it to be."

She looked around the room again. "Simple."

"Yeah."

"I like your coffee table," she said. "I don't see why you can't go with something like that. Handmade furniture with some softer details."

"What do you mean by softer details?"

"Lace. Lace with natural wood would actually be really nice."

"I'm not... Lace?"

"Yes, lace. Unless you're serving no one but lumberjacks you're going to have to have something pretty. But I do think that we should do something with the rest of things that you like."

He snorted, sitting down on the couch, propping his foot up on the coffee table they were currently discussing. "There's only one way I like lace."

"And that is?"

"As women's panties."

Heat shot down her spine like a lightning bolt. "Well, you are not using my panties for your curtains. But I assure you that lace has other uses. Picture it. We can do tables made with natural wood, I bet we can coordinate with some people in town. Who all have you helped out, Ace?"

"I'm not sure I know what you mean." He rubbed his chin, the sound of his palm scraping over his stubble making her shiver a little. She held more tightly to her coffee, hoping that its warmth would erase the chill, or whatever it was, that had just raced through her.

"I know we don't know each other that well, but I see you at a lot of different functions. And even when you aren't there, your drinks are there. I know that you donated beer and soda for Connor Garrett's barn raising. You also provide drinks every year for the Fourth of July barbecue. I think there are a lot of people who'd be willing to return the favor, people whose skills you could make use of. Your brewery would be a showcase for local talent. And I'm not suggesting you go around asking people to give things to you, but I think you could probably get some handcrafted furniture for decent pricing."

He clasped his hands and raised his arms, placing them behind his head. "That isn't a terrible idea."

"Please, you have to be more careful, Ace. You're going to inflate my ego beyond all recognition."

"Then you'll be insufferable."

"Absolutely." She rubbed her hands together. "I'm already planning on the best method to make your life a living nightmare."

"Suggesting I use lace curtains in my brewery is actually a good place to start."

"Don't be a drama queen, Ace. Nobody likes that. Or so I'm told. Frequently."

"Somehow that doesn't surprise me. But I actually like the idea about using local furniture, art, whenever we can. Because if the point is to give tourists a great place to get a sense of Copper Ridge, then that's what we need to do."

"I imagine you're not going to have any trouble getting local distribution for your beer, either."

He straightened, then stood, making a very male noise

that seemed...gratuitous. Like he was just stretching noisily to remind her that he was a man and she was...vulnerable to his powers of testosterone. "I imagine not."

"Your excitement is catching," she said, treating him to her fakest smile.

"Sorry," he said. "I'm not your sorority sister."

"I was not in a sorority."

"Well, there you go. Busting stereotypes all over the place."

She lifted the coffee mug to her lips, taking another sip. "Absolutely to change the subject, because the one we are currently on basically amounts to you being an ass... What's in your barn?"

"Is that a double entendre?"

She made a face. "No, what could that even mean?"

"Well—"

"No. Please don't tell me what it could mean."

"I didn't take you for a prude, Sierra," he said, his voice suddenly getting warm, thick. Certainly not the sort of tone he should be using with her, since he didn't like her, and she was a waitress. His waitress. His waitress that he didn't like.

"I hide my Puritanical streak underneath my short shorts."

"Is that what the kids are calling it these days?"

Her throat tightened, her whole body getting tingly. "We shouldn't do this."

"What?"

He looked innocent. Which really wasn't a great or authentic look on him. "We shouldn't banter."

"A little banter isn't going to hurt."

"Banter is dangerous. Especially good banter."

"Maybe. But it won't go anywhere, because you're the one who has to beg."

She nearly choked on her tongue. "Well, I'm not going to. I was trying to change the subject. A gentleman wouldn't stop me from doing so."

"I never said I was a gentleman."

"Clearly."

"And we actually did change the subject."

"But you commandeered my subject change. You didn't answer my question."

He sighed. "I have a few horses."

"Okay. How do you keep horses and sleep until noon?" she asked.

"Well, I pay a couple of kids to come by and feed them in the morning before school. Seriously. I stay up too late to get up in time to take care of them. But, I do like to ride when I have days off."

He had a cowboy hat. And horses. He was quickly becoming Sierra brand kryptonite.

Except for the part where he was a giant jerk, and her boss.

"Like, do you trail ride or..."

"Sometimes."

"Does your family own horses?" Her own behavior mystified her. She shouldn't be trying to get to know him. She should be sticking to the script. If she was going to be here, then they needed to be menu planning, or discussing wall sconces, or something. They did not need to be discussing his horses, or his background in horsemanship.

"No. They don't. I got into riding when I took a job at a ranch mucking stalls. One of the guys was an old, retired rodeo cowboy. And, since I was sixteen, I thought riding bucking broncos sounded like a great idea."

"You didn't, did you?"

He nodded slowly, touching the end of his hat. "Yes ma'am. Once upon a time, I was a rodeo cowboy."

ACE HAD NO IDEA why he was telling Sierra all of this. He didn't like to talk about his past. Didn't like to talk about the decade he'd spent away from Copper Ridge. Because it led into dangerous, murky territory that he barely allowed himself to think about, much less have a conversation about.

"I didn't know that. I guess, I thought you'd been running the bar forever. Or maybe that you worked at the bar. But, I would've been, you know, not legal drinking age when the bar actually changed its name to Ace's."

"Are you calling me old?"

"Well, you're older than me."

"Not that much," he said, sounding slightly perturbed.

"How long have you had the bar?"

"About seven years."

"Yeah," she said, scrunching her nose. "I was only eighteen when you took over then."

"Ouch."

He was suddenly very conscious of the decade that stood between his and Sierra's ages. Of course, he had always known that he was older than her, he didn't need to tally up the years to figure that out. She was shiny. Sparkly. Regardless of whatever was going on with her father, she retained the kind of innocence that was difficult to keep into your thirties.

"Oh, come on. Men get better with age. Women just start shedding their sequins."

"Bullshit. Fashion magazines might want you to believe that, but trust me when I tell you I've had some of the best nights of my life with women over the age of forty."

He had said that to get a response out of her. What he hadn't anticipated was the response it would elicit in him when her cheeks turned a deeper shade of rose. "I only wanted to know about your horse riding, Ace, not about the other kinds of riding you do." Her tone was biting, dry. She was not as unaffected as she was trying to pretend.

Which was good, because he wasn't unaffected at all.

She had to beg. Thank God for that edict. Because it was the only thing stopping him from grabbing her and pulling her flush against his body, backing her up against a wall, bending her over some furniture.

He'd made a rule, and he would damn well stick to it. He wasn't completely beyond the pale. He wasn't unable to control himself. He was not that far gone.

You are.

Maybe he was. But in this, he wouldn't be. He would stand strong.

Yeah, that's a real moral high ground, Thompson. You won't touch her unless she begs you for it. And if she does, you know you will.

"It's been said I have no shame," he said. "It's probably true."

"Oh, I would say more than probably."

"Do you want to see the horses?" He wasn't really sure what either of them was doing. They could act as irritated with each other as they wanted, and they probably were that irritated with each other, but they were also coming up with excuses to stay in each other's company.

Probably because she had the nicest rack he'd seen in

a while, and he really liked looking at her ass when she walked. He was that basic.

"Yes," she said, a wealth of subtext beneath the agreement.

Or maybe there wasn't. Maybe she just wanted to see the horses. Maybe he was a pervert.

"You said you barrel race," he said, heading toward the front door, hoping some of the fresh air would dispel some of the tension between them. "You doing much of it now?"

"No," she said, walking onto the porch just ahead of him, taking the steps two at a time down to the driveway. And yeah, he watched her ass.

"Why not?"

"My horse is at my dad's house."

"And you aren't."

She looked over her shoulder, her blond curls bouncing. She was eternally bouncy, even when she was annoyed. "Right. Because, massive falling-out."

"So you said. So what happened? He cancel your credit card?"

"Do you honestly think that's the only thing I could possibly worry about? My fingernails, a credit card. Some rich bitch must've screwed you over good."

That stopped him in his tracks. "Why would you say that?"

"Come on. You didn't just wake up one morning deciding that girls like me are ridiculous. Someone taught you. I'm rich, but I'm not stupid. You're right, my life has been pretty easy. And a lot of people are nice to me because of where I come from. A lot of it's fake, and I'm aware of that. But being wealthy doesn't automatically mean people are nice to you. A lot of people resent you for it. You think you're the first person to hate me on sight? I already told you, you aren't that original."

He wasn't in the mood to talk about Denise. But then, he never was. Still, the path of least resistance in this case was to tell just enough of the story to satisfy her curiosity. "My ex-wife."

That stopped her in her tracks. "You were married?"

"Yeah. For a couple of years." Three years. Closer to four. He remembered every single one, because it was easy to mark them with Callie's age.

He gritted his teeth.

"To a rich girl. Who had daddy and credit card issues, I take it?"

"Pretty much."

"Predictable."

"You keep saying I am."

"It has nothing to do with a slashed credit card," she said. "I don't... My father isn't who I thought he was."

"I know how that goes."

"Your ex-wife?"

He stuffed his hands in his pockets and nodded, bringing himself into step with her. "The very same."

"You know what it's like. And you know that sometimes you have to leave."

Except he wouldn't have left. "That's true," he said, even though in his case it absolutely wasn't.

"It was pretty bad," she said, kicking a rock.

"Are you going to hint around about it, or are you going to tell me?"

"Why would I tell you?"

He treated her to his best smile, the kind that got him laid more often than not. "Because I'm the bartender. Everyone tells me their secrets."

"When they're drunk. I'm not drunk. Unless you spiked my coffee."

"I don't give out free alcohol. Plus, I don't let my employees drink on the job. You are technically on the job." Which he said more as a reminder to himself. Because he also didn't allow himself to check out his employees' asses.

"I don't think I can tell you."

"Why not?"

"Because," she said, "you hate me. Why should I trust you with my secrets?"

"I don't hate you."

He didn't like her. Not beyond the look of her anyway. But he'd hired her, and he was taking her to see his horses. So, obviously he didn't hate her.

"Well," she said, "you are not Team Sierra."

"In fairness, if I'm team anything, I'm probably just Team Tits and Beer."

"They appreciate your support, I'm sure. Not enough love happening for boobs and brew."

"I have all the love in the world."

She upped her pace, walking a few steps ahead of him. "My dad had an affair."

"That sucks." It did. He could barely have a conversation with his dad these days, mostly because he didn't know how to talk to him. Didn't know how to pick the undesirable words out of his vocabulary anymore, didn't know what topics to bring up. His dad had no idea what Ace served at his bar, but in fairness, Ace had no idea what his father's latest sermon was about.

Or any of his sermons for the past seventeen years.

"Yeah. It sucks," she said. She stopped, turning to face him. "It really sucks."

"Were you close to him?"

"I don't know. It's kind of hard to be close to my dad. Which I guess is kind of a red flag when you think about it. But…" She paused, angling toward the mountains. She closed her eyes for a second, the breeze catching hold of her hair and tangling it around her face. "He was my hero."

She opened her eyes, turning back to Ace. "I don't suppose he can be that anymore. And I don't know how to talk to him when he's something else. He was Superman. To me. He couldn't do anything wrong. I remember hugging his leg because it was the only thing I could reach. And even though I grew, he stayed this giant. Really, he's just a man. And I… I don't really know how to deal with that."

He tried to imagine that there was a bar top between them, and a little more alcohol on her end. And then he tried to figure out what he would say in that situation. Well, he probably wouldn't say much of anything. He would just nod and pour another drink. But that wasn't an option here.

Apparently, he counted on alcohol being a crutch even when he wasn't the one drinking it.

"People surprise you," he said finally. "In terrible ways." He'd said as much to her the night he'd driven her home. That people were liars and couldn't be trusted. A grim life motto, maybe, but it kept him grounded.

"Thanks, Ace. I feel like I should really get that put on a T-shirt."

"Don't put it on a T-shirt. You can't read it when you're wearing it. Maybe mount it to the wall."

"I'll keep that under advisement."

They approached the barn and he pulled the door open,

the motion kicking up a cloud of dust and the scent of hay. It was a good smell to him. A strong one. One that rooted him back to a simpler time in his life. Before marriages and custody battles and breweries.

When he'd loved to ride, and that was all he'd needed.

There had been a whole lot of clarity in the ring. Other people might find it crazy. That he'd found a kind of calm on the back of a bucking bronco, but he had. Pounding hooves, flying dirt and people cheering faded into one indistinct blur, until it shrank, receding into total silence.

One wrong move on his end or the horse's made the difference between glory and getting your ass stomped into cowboy dust beneath angry hooves.

That had been the clearest he'd ever thought. His body, his brain…his soul—if he had one—all worked together in those moments. One unified machine. It was something he could never go back to, because the man that had saddled up for the rodeo back then was a completely different man.

He had to settle for flashes of memory that broke through him sometimes, clean and bright like lightning, on the heels of a tailwind carrying the smell of dirt and hay.

They walked into the barn and Sierra followed him. The expression on her face was what he imagined it might look like to bring a woman into a castle or something. Apparently, a barn was a castle to Sierra. Of course, for a woman like Sierra West, raised in a ranch positioned high above the town, luxury was an everyday kind of thing. He wondered if that allowed her to see the beauty in dirt and hay and horses just a little bit clearer.

He gritted his teeth, not liking his line of thinking. It was giving her a little more credit than he wanted to give. He didn't need to give her credit. Theirs was nothing more than a boss-employee relationship. Banter notwithstanding.

"What are their names?" she asked, walking in front of the stalls that contained his three horses.

"Whiskey, Tango, Foxtrot."

"That's random."

"Not really." He waited for the meaning to hit her. He waited until it was clear that it wouldn't. "WTF."

She whipped her head around, looking at him, her eyes wide, her mouth open. "That is a very…internet-oriented joke. I thought you didn't own a smartphone."

"I know my way around the World Wide Web, Sierra. It has porn."

"Ah, yes. We're back to that."

"I'm a simple man. With simple needs."

"I seem to recall you reciting a list," she said, turning back toward the horses.

"I probably did. That sounds like me."

She put her delicate fingers through the slats on the stall, reaching out and stroking Whiskey's nose. "This is simple," she said, her words an interesting echo of his earlier thoughts. "I like this. Horses aren't lying assholes. That really helps with the simplicity."

He crossed the barn, coming to stand beside her, leaning up against the wall. "No. They can be assholes, certainly. But they can't lie."

"I prefer an asshole to a liar. And I'm not sure I would have said that a few weeks ago. But it's how I feel now."

"Well, then, I suppose that's why you're working at my bar and not living with your family. Because I'm one of those things, but not the other."

She smiled, ducking her head, a lock of blond hair falling into her face. He wanted to brush it back. Then tilt her face upward and take a taste of that perfectly edible mouth of hers. If he did that, they couldn't talk anymore. He wouldn't be tempted to spill any more secrets about his marriage. She wouldn't feel compelled to keep untangling the mystery that was her father and all of his lies.

He wouldn't, though. That was just another fantasy, twisting around the familiar barn smell and the rodeo memories.

A bunch of things he couldn't have.

"You wouldn't consider yourself a liar?" she asked.

"No."

"I think you were right that night in your truck. Everybody lies. Little ones. The kind that you tell quickly to convenience yourself. To keep from getting in trouble. The kind that grow more elaborate the more you have to water them and feed them and care for them to keep people from finding out about the first seed."

"Do you think that's what your father did?"

"Maybe. But then, maybe I'm just justifying."

"I can't say as I blame you."

"You don't know…"

"Right. I can't possibly know your pain, and all that."

She shifted, crossing her arms, resting her hip against the wall. "I'm sorry. That isn't what I meant."

"That's okay. But I'm serious. When I say everyone lies…I guess my parents are exempt. My dad is great." He cleared his throat. "He's… He doesn't get mad easily. He always tells the truth, even when it's painful. He's been loyal to his wife for forty years."

"Your dad is the pastor at Copper Ridge Baptist. Right?"

"The very same. I guess not everyone connects us.

Thompson is a common enough last name, and I was gone for a long time. Then I came back and opened a bar. And I don't exactly make a habit out of going to church."

"I suppose you don't."

"Not really my scene."

"They have some dim views on drunken debauchery, so I can see why." She smiled again, but this time there was something complicated in it. She looked at him, looked at him like she was trying to unravel *his* mysteries now.

"Don't," he said.

"What?"

"I already told you, I'm not a liar. So don't look at me like you think I might be interesting. Or complicated. I have secrets, but I'm not a mystery. You're not going to scratch beneath a layer and find something worth having."

"I didn't say I was looking."

"You look at me like that… Yeah, I think you were looking."

She pushed away from the wall, a crease appearing between her brows. "It isn't your layers I was checking out. I promise."

"So it was just my body?"

"Don't pretend that you haven't checked out mine."

"Are you ready to beg yet, Sierra?"

He hated himself for asking that question. For being the one to bring it up again. He hated his voice for sounding so raw, so rough. It was supposed to be simple, it was supposed to be easy. Because he had declared that she had to make the move. But that wasn't stopping him from bringing it up as often as possible.

Stupid restraint. He blamed that. He blamed the com-

plicated bullshit of testosterone that seemed to like nothing better than mixing anger with desire. He blamed
anger for making desire so much better. Anger that had
originated with Denise, so he blamed her, too. Most of
all, he blamed Sierra, for being so blonde and bouncy.

For being some kind of reimagined fifteen-year-old
fantasy that he couldn't seem to shake. He knew better.
Sure, back when he'd been young and dumb, something
about the soft, glittery rodeo queen thing had fired up his
libido like nothing else. But back then he'd been exist-
ing in a world full of men, and dirt, and tobacco. And
the shiny, sparkling women who stood in opposition to
that presented a temptation he hadn't been able to turn
away from.

He knew how that ended now.

*But you're not stupid enough to think that Sierra is
Denise.*

No, he wasn't. He was also smart enough to know that
there were a lot of women out there. So avoiding one type
wasn't the end of the world.

His dick seemed to think that it was.

"You seem awfully invested in my hypothetical begging."

He was. He couldn't deny it. If she did, he would break
every rule he'd laid out since he had left Austin. Smash
them to pieces and barely even feel bad about it.

"Just reminding you to be careful. If you don't want
me to answer the question in your eyes, don't ask it so
loudly."

"What question do you think I'm asking?" she asked,
angling toward him.

She was supposed to back down. She was supposed

to be intimidated by all of this. She was supposed to slap him, call him a name and flounce away.

But there was a grit to Sierra; there was the fact that her spine was shot through with steel. Those things made her unpredictable. And made her so much more than the fragile rich girl he constantly accused her of being.

And he had to keep up those accusations. Without them it would be too easy to forget. Too easy to forget and kiss the hell out of her the way he had been imagining doing for the past week.

He reached out, grabbing hold of her chin and gripping it tightly. Desire and anger were quickly becoming identical twins that he could hardly tell apart. "You know. Don't play the part of innocent. It doesn't suit you. It doesn't suit either of us."

"Then stop. Say it," she said, blue eyes meeting his. "Tell me what you want. Tell me exactly what you think I want. Tell me what you want me to beg for. Because you bring it up often enough that we both know you wish I would." She angled toward him, her full breasts brushing against his chest. Desire burned through him like a shot of whiskey down his throat. Exhilarating, painful. "How am I ever supposed to beg if I'm not sure what you think I should be begging for?"

He turned, backing her up against the wall of the barn, closing the distance between them as he wrapped his arm around her slender waist and pulled her tightly to his body. They were both breathing hard, her eyes glittering with that same mix of anger and lust roaring through him. Apparently testosterone didn't have the monopoly on that one.

"You don't want to take a guess?" he asked, lifting

his hand and tracing the outline of her full lower lip with his thumb.

Her lips parted and she moved, her teeth grazing the edge of his thumb lightly. "Do you want to lose a finger?"

He chuckled, dropping his hand down to his side. At least this was comfortable, in that it was so uncomfortable it made him want to peel off his clothes to escape the heat and to ease the tension that was arcing between them like an electrical storm. It was more comfortable than talking about his divorce. Than talking about her father. More comfortable than remembering the rodeo and getting her mixed up in those strange, calming memories that belonged to him and only to him and didn't need another person in them.

It was wrong. But it was easy. Which was pretty much the story of the past nine years.

And she deserves to get caught up in that?

Great, now his conscience decided to speak up. Right when he didn't want it.

He released his hold on her, backing away. She just stood there, as if she was still being pinned against the wall, her hands at her sides, her expression all wide-eyed and openmouthed and full of emotion he didn't want to try to decode, because he wasn't in the business of decoding female emotion.

"Not interested in losing a finger," he said.

She closed her eyes, resting her head against the wall. "Please don't fire me," she said.

"It would be a pretty dick move for me to fire you when I was the one who started that."

"I was complicit."

"I'm not going to fire you," he said, gritting his teeth. Mostly because firing her would be giving in to temptation. Firing her would be proof that he couldn't handle what was happening between them. It was just a little bit of attraction. Not for the first time, he considered that he needed to find another woman to expend his pent-up sexual energy on.

Just the thought made him feel like someone was grabbing hold of his stomach and twisting it tight. He didn't like the thought. Not simply because he couldn't imagine being attracted to anyone other than Sierra right now, but because he wasn't sure quite when he had started thinking about women and sex like that. And when it had stopped registering that he did. The only reason he felt anything about it now was because she was looking at him. Still looking at him like she was trying to figure him out.

"Well, good," she said, sounding anything but happy. "I think we're done here."

"Sure." She reached up, tucking that strand of hair behind her ear that he had been fantasizing about earlier. "I'm going to go ahead and research a few options for you. Furniture. Curtains. Things like that. I'm going to try to go through as many local businesses as possible, and I'll make sure they know it's for you."

"Good. Because I'm so charming that I know we'll get some good deals," he said drily.

"You're charming with other people. That will have to do. Actually, it works out, because I can't make things out of wood. And I can't really make curtains or anything, either. So, be nice to other people. You don't really need to be nice to me."

"Have I ever been very nice to you?" he asked.

She tapped her palm over the top of her other closed

fist. "Intermittently. You gave me a job. So you aren't really a total troll to me."

"Just a partial troll."

"Serves me right for crossing over your bridge."

"Does that make you a billy goat?" The absurdity of the conversation had him tempted to smile. She was a witch. There was no other explanation for how she'd made him hard as a rock a moment ago, and pissed enough to punch a hole in the barn wall, and had him laughing now.

"Stubborn as hell and ready to head-butt you? Yeah, I'd say that sounds about right."

"Why don't you clip-clop back across my bridge until your shift tonight," he said, his stomach and everything else tightening up when her blue eyes met his.

"Sure. I'll clip-clop away. I won't be your problem again until tonight."

She turned away from him and started to walk away, shoving her hands down into the back pockets of her jeans.

Well, that didn't help anything. She was drawing his eyes right to where they shouldn't be. Not that there was much she could have done to have him not check her out while she walked away.

"Hey," he said.

She stopped and turned. "What? Just *hey*? Not *hey you*? How will I know if I'm special?"

"I don't think we should do work over here anymore." He felt like he was channeling youth group meetings past. Words like *accountability* and *appearances* floated around his mind like screeching buzzards, looming over the diminished carcass of his self-control. "For professionalism and...stuff, I think we should keep meetings confined to the bar."

She looked up, then at him, then nodded slowly. "Okay."

"We'll still discuss the drinks menu and things. And you can still work on this project—the decor and all. But we'll confer there."

"That sounds good. I want to get along with you, Ace. I'm sorry your ex-wife was an evil bitch. But I'm not her."

"I know," he said.

That made him feel like an ass, because of course he knew that, but he sure as hell hadn't been acting like that was the case.

"All right, then. I'll go off and do things. Things you can presume are non-evil bitchy." Then she turned away from him and bounced off. Again with the bouncing.

Sierra West was a problem. But one he was determined to get a firm handle on.

CHAPTER SEVEN

"STILL WAITRESSING?" COLTON asked, when Sierra came downstairs in her unofficial uniform of shorts and a black tank top.

It got really hot in the bar, and even though February evenings in Copper Ridge were cold, she was sweaty after running back and forth between the kitchen and the tables.

In some ways, it made her miss her office job. She did primarily paperwork for the West ranch and physical activity was a choice she made. Now it was part of what she had to do to get paid.

And okay, she felt a little like the jackass Ace assumed she was. She'd never given a lot of thought to his kind of work. Only that she'd assumed certain people—not her—did it. And that they did it because it was easy.

Yeah, well. She felt asstastic about all that now. It wasn't easy. It was damn sweaty and hard. And it didn't pay that much along with it.

The hard work was what made her feel hot. Completely the hard work. Not Ace. Ace and his dark, watchful gaze that made her feel like he could see straight beneath her tank top.

Just thinking about it now made her breasts feel heavy and her stomach tight. She frowned. She needed to get a grip. He was hot, but there were a lot of hot men. There was no use turning into a big fluttery hormone over the least suitable one around.

"Yes. Still waitressing," she said, walking into the kitchen and picking up the sweater she'd left draped over the counter last night. She wasn't hot and sweaty yet. "It's my job." She jerked open the fridge and pulled out a can of diet soda.

Living with Colton was fine, maneuvering around Natalie aside. His place was a little more rustic than her parents', but it was big and provided them all with plenty of space.

He had a couple of workers who came and took care of his livestock, but it was nothing half so chaotic as the daily bustle of the West ranch.

The problem was that she had to deal with her well-meaning, but overprotective older brother being all up in her grill.

"Maddy said she talked to you about moving back," Colton mentioned, just a little too casually.

"Yeah, well, Maddy is meddlesome. With good intentions out the wazoo. But it's just not something I can do right now."

He sighed and rubbed the back of his neck, the lines on his forehead looking more pronounced than she'd ever noticed before. She had a feeling she knew why. Like maybe, impending weddings that were more of a nightmare than a fantasy.

But she doubted saying *Hey you look old, is it that harpy you're engaged to?* would go over well.

"I don't mind having you here," he said. "I just think maybe it's shortsighted to cut Dad off like this."

"It's not shortsighted. Shortsighted was him cheating on Mom. It was keeping Jack a secret and hurting him and…" She blinked. "I can't get upset about this right now because my mascara will run."

"Well, we don't want that." Colton moved closer, then reached out and pulled her in for a hug. "I'm sorry," he said. "I know you think I'm not supporting you. You probably think you're alone in taking a stand against injustice. But I…"

"You can't cut Dad off right now."

"Maybe not ever," he said. "I'm the only son left." He released his hold on her and took a step back. "I know you blame the wedding and Natalie. They factor, but… not much. When Gage left he basically blew a bomb up in the middle of the family and I swore I would never do something like that. I swore that I would make things work, not run when things got hard. Someone had to."

The mention of Gage made her eyes feel dry and prickly. She had long given up crying when she thought of her older brother. There was no use mourning someone who was still alive and who could choose to come back to you if they wanted.

She hadn't fully appreciated what his absence meant to Colton until this moment. Colton was the oldest sibling still around. The only son that remained. Everything—the eventual ownership of the ranch, the construction business, and all the pressure that went with it—that their father had intended for Gage would have transferred to Colton in Nathan West's mind.

And all of that had been put on Colton when he was only sixteen.

She had been a kid when Gage left. The majority of her life had been spent with the hole he left behind. It was difficult to remember what things had been like before it was there. Difficult to remember a time when it hadn't existed. But Colton remembered. Madison also, to a certain degree. But no one better than Colton.

"I know how hard it was on Mom for the family to splinter apart like it did," he said, as though he was reading her mind. "And whether or not Dad is actually a decent human being, losing Gage hurt him. Having his oldest son walk away from everything he built wounded him deep. Things are broken, Sierra. They have been for a lot of years. But I don't see how walking away from the family now will fix anything."

"Maybe I'm not trying to fix things for anyone else," she told him, feeling like the world's most terrible person. "Maybe I just need to fix things for me."

"You have the luxury of doing that," he said, his blue eyes level with hers.

"Because no one has any expectations of me?"

He let out an exasperated sigh. "You said it, Sierra, not me. But the fact is that's true enough. You don't have half the expectation put on you that I do. And Madison is still trying to atone for a sin that wasn't even her doing. She brings it on herself, but she's not going to change the way she's dealing with it. You have a smaller piece in the business. It's easier for you to separate yourself. Maybe you think that Dad doesn't care about you as much. But from where I'm standing, I would say that you're a lot more special to Dad than you know. Can you imagine him allowing Maddy or me to get involved in the rodeo? To spend all that time *wasting* time? He indulges you. That's fine. But don't mistake the lack of pressure for a lack of caring."

"Way to make me feel like an ass, Colton," she said, running her hand over the top of her tied-back hair.

"That isn't my intention. I know…I know you have to do this."

"You guys are acting like I'm selling all of my earthly possessions and signing up to go on a space station. I'm working at a bar. I moved away from Mom and Dad's property. That isn't exactly Mars."

"Good point."

"It's not that big of a deal."

He laughed. "I guess I just never pictured you waiting tables."

"Why does everyone think I'm a terrible fit for a waitress? It isn't like I don't work hard. Working with horses is damn hard work. So is organizing the records for the ranch, and the schedules and all the paperwork. I mean, maybe it's different than construction, Colton, but it's very hard work."

"I know my way around a horse, Sierra. And I know that's hard work. But it's different."

"Am I too good to be doing this? Is that what you're trying to say?"

She didn't know why, but the idea of giving in and quitting now filled her with absolute panic. She felt… she felt so connected to the bar. And she felt committed to seeing this through.

The job, she reiterated firmly to herself. Not whatever this intense connection was with Ace. Though, even as she thought it, she knew it was a lie.

There was something about being with him that infuriated her. And exhilarated her in equal measure. Something that made her feel reckless and alive.

As if she was in danger of being caught up in something bigger than she was.

That should make her want to run away. Should make

her want to wave her white flag in surrender and accept Colton's offer to pay her way.

But God help her, she didn't want to. She wanted to stay on the edge of it. Perilously balancing between giving in and resisting.

It was the closest to barrel racing she could get without a horse.

"You're a West, Sierra."

"Who couldn't get a job apart from her father's charity. Obviously I'm not too good for this. Obviously, no one actually thinks I can do it."

"I just think you shouldn't have to."

"I think everything you're saying is probably really sweet. But right now I'm just kind of irritated. And I have to go to work. Because I show up to my shift on time."

"I'm rooting for you. That's the bottom line. Whatever you think, whatever I say that hits you the wrong way. I'm rooting for you, Sierra."

"Root a little softer from the sidelines, asshole."

He snorted. "I deserve that."

"You do. But even though you're a little overbearing sometimes, I really appreciate you letting me stay here. If it weren't for you I'd still be at Mom and Dad's and it just isn't the place for me right now."

He smiled at that. "That's what big brothers are for. Helping out while giving you hell."

She laughed. "Come get a beer from me anytime."

"I might take you up on that."

"You have to pay."

"What kind of garbage is that?"

"I am a laborer, Colton. I deserve my wage."

"All right. Go off and earn it, then."

She walked out the front door and stood on the porch

for a moment, letting the salt air drift across her face. She hadn't realized how warm her cheeks were until the cool ocean breeze touched her skin. She knew that Colton loved her, and that he was well-meaning. But it didn't mean she wasn't a little bit pissed off.

She felt guilty. Because so much of what he'd said was true. And she did kind of have to admit he had a point—their father loved her very much. Even if it was in a different way than he demonstrated for Colton and Madison.

But it was so hard to reconcile that man with the man she'd seen a few weeks ago in her parents' home. Ranting. Nearly unhinged.

The news of Jack being his illegitimate child had apparently filtered down to the country club he was a member of, and it had been the talk of the men—and the women.

Her poor, fragile mother had been subjected to cruel commentary from women who were meant to be her friends, and then her father—who should have hung his head in shame—did nothing but rant about how it was all Jack's fault for going back on their agreement.

That overheard argument changed everything for Sierra. Destroyed the illusions she'd built up around her family.

Someday, she would find some balance in all of this. Maybe when she was stronger she would be able to figure out a way to accommodate Jack. To give him a position in her life, and still maintain some kind of relationship with her father.

But there was no way to do any of that as long as she leaned against her family. She was going to stand tall, on her own.

And if it started with waiting tables, that was fine with her.

A LOT OF WAITRESSES had come through Ace's bar. A lot of pretty ones. And he was human, so he had taken the occasional moment to sit back and admire their earthly charms. Because he was a dude, and when there was a beautiful woman in front of him he was hard-pressed to do anything else. Hell, he didn't want to do anything else.

But they didn't distract him. None of them had ever challenged his no-banging-the-staff rule. But he could barely keep his eyes off of Sierra for more than a few minutes at a time. Every time he looked out into the dining room there she was, bouncing. Smiling. In general acting like she was completely oblivious to his presence while he was in no way oblivious to hers.

He had watched her deliver hamburgers all night, barely able to concentrate on what he was doing, barely able to concentrate on what his customers were telling him. If she had been any other woman he might have thought that all of the persistent springing and flicking of hair and effortless smiles were performance art for him. But this was just her. It was just who she was. A sparkling, effortless creature who should seem ridiculous, impractical and silly. She did. She honestly did. It was just that he also found her captivating.

She was like a lure. Twisting around beneath the surface of the waves and capturing the sun. And she sure as hell had a hook buried in her. Still, he was the dumbass salmon swimming right toward her.

You don't have to swim toward her.

No, he did not.

That was the point of enforcing a strict rule about where they met. About firmly putting her in the box of employee. That was, at the beginning of the night, why he had decided to keep a close eye on her work. Because if he saw her as a waitress, then maybe his body would recognize that she was a waitress. His waitress, who he paid. Which meant he couldn't touch her. Ever. Apparently, his loathing of rich women was not going to keep him away from her. It was not going to kill the lust that overtook him every time he looked her direction.

The last buffer was that he signed her paychecks.

So he needed to internalize that buffer. He wasn't sure if you internalized buffers, but he was going to try.

The dining area was starting to empty; the last call bell had rung already. He should send Sierra home. He should tell her to knock off early, honestly, since there wasn't that much to clean. The first part of the day was slow enough that if there wasn't a thorough cleaning done at closing, it could easily be done at opening.

She walked across the bar, headed toward him. There was nothing ambiguous about it. Her blue eyes were locked with his, a sassy little smile curving her lips. "Did you want to take some time to go over the menu for the new place?"

"This late?"

"I'm acclimating. I'm becoming a creature of the night."

"Have you grown any fangs yet?"

She lifted her top lip and slid her tongue beneath one of her teeth, testing it gingerly. "Doesn't seem like it."

His brain had stopped working around the time he started following the motion of her tongue. Because he could easily imagine it on his skin. All over his body. And that fantasy, so strong, so real, was his cue to send her on her way.

But he didn't.

"Well, let me know if you suffer a severe case of bloodlust later. I'll find you a small rodent."

"What, you don't want the privilege of being my first victim?"

"Already had all the blood sucked out of me, babe," he said. "Divorce is a bitch."

He hadn't meant to bring his marriage up. He almost never did. Before Sierra had come into his life he had gone a long time without ever mentioning it. But for some reason the past seemed very close to the surface when she was around. Probably because of the little ways she reminded him of Denise. Though that was a disservice to Sierra. The similarities were skin deep, and he knew that. At least, he knew it now.

"Ouch. I bet. Did she get all of your earthly possessions?"

Her question, innocent, *light*, hit a wound that was low, and deep. One that would never heal. No matter how much time passed. He gritted his teeth, unwilling to say anything else. Because it was one thing to talk about his marriage, and another to talk about everything that had happened during the dissolution of it. It was something he wasn't willing to do. Not with her, not with anyone.

"Something like that," he said. Well, that had doused his arousal.

Sierra frowned. "I'm sorry. I shouldn't have made a joke."

He shrugged. "I made one first."

"Sure. But it's one thing to joke about our own pain. It's something else entirely when someone else grabs hold of it and handles it insensitively."

"Well, I would hate for you to handle me…insensitively," he said, deliberately making his tone provocative.

Because he would rather pull it into this uncomfortable space than back to where they had just been. Where she hit close to the bone, close to the nerve.

"Yeah," she said, looking away. "So...the menu?"

"You sure you want to do that?"

"I have nothing but time." She smiled, her whole face brightening. "Besides, if we discuss menu stuff tonight, then that means we can sample some of the items."

"I should have known the possibility of wine tasting might excite you."

"I was born with a refined palate," she said. "Part of my pedigree."

"It just so happens that I have some bottles back in my office that I've been meaning to sample. To see what I want to put in the brewery."

"What about your beer?"

"I have some of that if you're interested."

She spread her hands wide. "I'm interested in it all. I'm getting paid to drink."

"Are you finagling yourself into an overtime shift?"

She lifted her shoulder. "I have been known to finagle."

"If I'd been aware that you were a known finagler I might not have hired you."

She tapped her chin with her forefinger. "Sorry, did I not put that on my résumé?"

"You didn't give me a résumé."

She wrinkled her nose. "Really? That's so unprofessional of me."

"I have a feeling we're about to get drunk at work. So let's save conversations of professionalism for later."

He walked back into his office and grabbed hold of the bottles of wine that had been sent over by the local vineyards. Sierra was right, a lot of businesses had been very supportive when they had found out about his new venture. And of course, the different vineyards wanted their wines on the list. In reality, he didn't see why he couldn't showcase some from each, but he needed to find a way to make a selection that was manageable and economical.

When he came back into the dining room, it was completely empty, the rest of the employees gone, the lights low. Sierra was standing there, her hands behind her back. The corners of her lips were turned up into an impish smile, her eyes glittering in the dim light. She looked like she had been caught doing something naughty. Or perhaps he was just projecting.

Either way, he was in trouble.

He was being an idiot. He had made the mandate about not meeting at his place anymore to keep them out of potentially sexual situations. And here they were. Alone in the empty bar, about ready to start drinking.

And he wasn't going to turn back. Not now. Maybe nothing would happen. Maybe he would keep his distance.

Adrenaline twisted his stomach tight, his heart pounding heavily. He knew this kind of excitement. It was the way that he'd felt before he'd gone out into the arena back when he'd been in the rodeo. There was nothing else like it. That sense of inevitability about what was going to come. Knowing that he was throwing himself headlong into a dangerous, unstable situation, and knowing just as strongly that he wasn't going to turn back.

Whether he would triumph or fall flat on his ass, he didn't know. But the gate was about to open either way.

"I have red, white and some other stuff I know nothing about."

Sierra wandered over to the bar and sat down on one of the stools, draping her arm over the counter, her foot propped up on one of the slats beneath the stool. "What pairs best with exhaustion and identity crisis?"

"Anything. As long as you have enough." He walked behind the bar, taking a position across from her as though she were a customer and this were normal in any way.

"You look like you have enough."

"You're actually going to have to take it easy. Because we have wine, and I wanted to try some of the beer. Also, we're going to sample some whiskey."

She laughed. "Is this work or a frat party?"

"I don't know, you tell me."

"I have a lot more experience with frat parties than I do with jobs." She smiled, the expression wry. "I suppose I can see why you, and Colton, and Madison think that I'm crazy."

"I never said you were crazy," he said, setting a glass down in front of her. "I said I didn't think you could do it."

"Fine. Colton and Madison think I'm crazy."

"That's what siblings are for. To keep your self-esteem in check." He poured a healthy measure of wine into her glass. "And, I can tell you from experience that older siblings worry about everything their younger siblings do. My sister is the secretary at my dad's church. I don't think she's ever set one foot out of line, and I spent about eight years living away from Copper Ridge. Away from her. Still, I worry. I think sometimes *worry* sounds an awful lot like being an ass."

She let out a heavy sigh and lifted the glass to her

lips. "Well, it definitely manifested itself that way with Colton."

He poured himself some wine and took a taste just as she did. He grimaced. "So, this isn't really my thing. What do you think?"

"I'm not going to talk about it being full-bodied or complex or anything. I think it would be a good all-purpose choice for red meat."

"Well, there will be red meat. I'm firmly pro-steak."

"A fact I can attest to since my work clothes smell permanently of hamburger." She took another sip of the wine. "Yes, it is very good. Make a note of this one."

"Ready for the next one?"

"Don't we need something for a palate cleanser?"

He chuckled. "Sure, let me get you a Wet-Nap. You can rub it across your tongue."

"That is disgusting. Just give me more wine."

He reached beneath the bar and pulled out another glass, this time pouring a measure of white wine into it. Some for her, some for him. "This is supposed to be a dessert wine. What the hell does that mean? Do you have it for dessert, or are you having it with dessert?"

"Well, both. It's with dessert, *part* of dessert."

"I prefer milk with my dessert."

She snorted into the glass, splashing some wine over the side. "Okay, I didn't expect that."

"You drink milk with chocolate, Sierra. It's a fundamental fact of life. Cake is better with milk. Anyone who says otherwise is just pretentious."

"Or doesn't want to drink a giant glass of udder juice."

"Now who's being disgusting? I thought you were a lady."

"News flash, sometimes ladies are disgusting. But

usually daintily so." She flashed him a broad smile and batted her lashes. Then she took a sip of the wine, sliding her tongue over her lips, the action sending a slug of heat down to his stomach and beyond.

"What do you think?"

"Sweet. A lot of apricot."

"Is that good or bad?"

She wrinkled her nose. "Not to my taste."

"Well, we have another dessert wine here," he said, "from Grassroots Winery." He got out new glasses and poured the new wine in. "It's a rosé."

"Do you know what that means?"

"Clearly it means it's pink."

"Yes. It will match the lace curtains."

He lifted the glass to his lips. "I might agree to lace curtains, but they will not be pink." He took a sip of the wine. "Okay, I like the pink one."

Sierra took a taste, too. "Yes, indeed. Very good. Mark this one down for your list."

They kept on going like that, through the wine, and then the beer. It didn't take long for a pleasant haze to build up around his vision. He felt a little more relaxed. A lot more relaxed. It made him wonder why he had been so uptight around Sierra up until this moment.

Sobriety.

Right.

Whatever. Sobriety was obnoxious. It made him think. It made him worry. He couldn't muster up enough memories about his past to bring worry into the present. That was why he was so uptight around Sierra. Because of everything that had happened in the past. Because of one rich rodeo queen who had taken his heart and used it as a chew toy. Even that didn't hurt as much right now.

"Whiskey," Sierra said, the word more a command than a request.

"Are you sure we should keep tasting?"

"We're past the point of driving home anyway," she said, staring down into the bottom of her empty glass. "Which I perhaps should have thought of before I agreed to a 3:00 a.m. adult beverage tasting."

He swore. He hadn't been thinking, either. Well, he had been, but he had been thinking with the brain below his belt. With the aid of alcohol he could be honest with himself. He had known that he was putting them in a compromising position, he had known that their resistance would be down. And he had decided to go ahead with all this anyway.

"We might as well keep going, then," he decided, adding to the line of glasses already on the bar. "Okay, this is really expensive. But you know I want to have the option."

"Sure. Fanciness options." She gave him a thumbs-up. "Super important."

"Are you mocking me?"

"Probably," she said, smiling at him, this one a little lazier than the last. "You kind of like it, admit it. You push me on purpose, and I push you back. Everything feels a little bit electric. It kind of builds. Like foreplay."

The words shot to his gut, burning hotter than a shot of whiskey ever could. "You think it's like that?"

She flipped her hair over her shoulder. "I think it's possibly what we've been doing this whole time." Her whole face turned red. "Sorry, that was the wine. It makes me honest. Which is too bad, because I prefer games."

His teeth were locked together so tightly he was afraid he might shatter them. But then, if you could die from sexual frustration he had much bigger problems than cracked teeth. He was so hard he thought he was going to bust through his jeans.

He poured the whiskey, knowing it was a bad idea. He did it anyway. Because that was the theme of the night. "You like games?"

"Sure," she said, "because they don't feel real. They don't feel hard. Anyway, I much prefer presenting an idea of who I am as opposed to showing people who I really am. Which has actually been the hardest part about working for you. I actually have to try. To do that I have to care, and I have to show that I care. I don't like that. But when you have the whole town watching you…"

"Yeah, I know something about that."

"Do you?"

"My dad is a pastor. It's a small town. People at the church… They expect a certain thing for me. Hell, people outside of the church expect a certain thing for me. They know who I am. Who I was. And I'm either some kind of cautionary tale that they whisper about behind their hands, and confirmation that there's no point to what my father does, because even I couldn't continue to follow his teaching. Or I'm a disappointment."

She frowned, tilting her head to the side, the expression on her face shifting to one of deep pity. Like she was looking at a scraggly, orphaned puppy or something. "Does your dad think you're a disappointment?"

Ace shook his head slowly. "He doesn't seem to. I don't think he can really support me. But he's less judgmental than some of the people around town, that's for sure."

"I think you've done some pretty amazing things. I mean, making this place such a huge success. It used to be that only old fishermen came here. Now almost everyone does."

"How do you know this was where all the old fishermen used to drink? As you pointed out, you were a kid when I bought the place."

"I don't know. It's something my dad used to say when we'd drive by when I was a kid."

He laughed. "Sounds about right. And thank you for not judging me," he added with mock sincerity.

"You judged *me*," she said, sounding slightly petulant now. Which should not be cute at all, but it was.

"Yes," he said. "But I'm mostly over it now."

She looked down, dragging her fingertip over the top of the bar. It was like she'd struck a match on his cock. When she looked back up, there was no pity on her face. "I think you have to act like you don't like me because if you started being nice you might do something crazy. It's the same reason we argue."

"The foreplay again?" he asked, his chest tight, a ball of fire lodged there, keeping him from breathing.

"Yeah, exactly. Except we're not using it to build up to anything. We're trying to keep it from exploding. I think we both know that if we stop talking for two seconds we'll be screwing instead."

The crude word on her delicate lips lingered in the air, scorched across his skin. He pushed the whiskey to the side, pressing his hands flat on the bar top. "You think so?"

She took a small sip of the whiskey, then set the glass down, curling her fingers around the glass. She looked up at him and slid the edge of her tongue across her lips, taking in every last drop of alcohol left there. "I do," she said, the words hushed. "Granted, I don't have a lot of experience with the F word."

Lightning streaked down his spine. "You don't?"

"I'm not a virgin or anything. It's just that, you know college guys. They act like a quarterback running for a touchdown. Funny thing about that, only one person is left standing in the end zone doing a stupid dance."

"Is that code?"

"I've never had an orgasm with a guy. Not that I've slept with that many. Two. But." Her whole face turned as pink as the wine they'd had earlier. "I mean, I like sex. It's nice. I like men's bodies. And…like, not being alone. I shouldn't have told you that. It's just that I'm still talking to keep from…"

He didn't let her finish the sentence. He leaned across the bar, extending his hand, wrapping it firmly around the back of her neck and cupping her head, and drawing her forward. Then he pressed his lips to hers.

CHAPTER EIGHT

THANK GOD.

That was the closest to a prayer he'd gotten in a long time. And he supposed there was an element of sacrilege to it. But it was all he could think as those soft lips finally touched his. He growled, parting her lips effortlessly with the tip of his tongue, allowing himself access to everything he'd denied himself for the past week. Everything he had *poorly* denied himself. Holding out for a week wasn't a lot to be proud of.

But he didn't want to be proud. He wanted to come.

With her. That was essential. Because no matter how many times he had thought he should over the past week, he had not found another woman. He didn't want another woman.

He tightened his hold on her, curling his fingers around her hair. She whimpered, opening her mouth wider to him. And he tasted her deeply. Satisfying a mystery that felt like it was older than time. She tasted like burgeoning spring, and wine. New, a little bit fancier than what he was usually allowed.

The bar stood between them like a chastity belt that the buzz of the alcohol was working very hard to unlock. He planted his foot on the bottom shelf, keeping his hand firmly fixed on the back of her head as he took a step up, before putting his knee down on the top of the bar, drawing his other leg up along with him. Only then did he release his hold on her head, taking both hands and grabbing hold of her waist, lifting her up onto the bar with him, drawing her onto his lap.

She whimpered, pressing her hands to his chest, curling her fingers around the fabric of his T-shirt. "We should probably talk about this," he said, pressing a kiss to her neck as he slid his hands down her waist, grabbing hold of the hem of her T-shirt. "But I don't want to talk." He wrenched the top over her head, tossing it on to the floor.

"No," she said, her voice breathless, "there has been way too much talking."

"And the minute we stop, look what happens."

"Sorry," she said, sliding her hands down his chest, then beneath the edge of his shirt. "Not sorry."

"How drunk are you?" he asked, reaching down and grabbing hold of her wrist, keeping her wandering hands still.

"Pleasantly buzzed. Not really all that drunk."

"Then why haven't we done this before?" His own voice sounded thick and intoxicated. Everything seemed hazy around the edges, with only Sierra in focus.

He didn't mind. Not a damn bit.

He lifted his head, watching as she chewed on her lip, her eyes darting back and forth. "Because we're stupid when we're sober?" she suggested.

"Not good enough."

"I want this," she said. "I wanted it before I ever had a drink. There's a reason that I stayed. There's a reason that I keep pushing you. Yes, this might be pushing things faster. But I don't care. I was being honest when I told you I've never...you know...*climaxed* with a man. But,

I can't honestly remember wanting a man the way that I want you. And it isn't because I like you. I don't like you."

"That's…nice."

"What I mean is this has nothing to do with a crush, or feelings. And you aren't suitable. Like, you aren't a boyfriend that my dad would ever approve of. I don't even want a boyfriend. I don't want you to be my boyfriend."

"Am I part of a rebellion against your father?"

She squinted. "Would you care if you were?"

"Hell, no."

Then he released his hold on her wrist and she continued in her exploration, her delicate fingers traveling up the ridges of his ab muscles. Her soft lips were parted, rounded into a perfect little O.

"Oh, baby," he said, his voice rough, "I'm gonna make you scream later."

"I hope not too much later."

"Not at all," he said, unfastening her bra as she pushed his shirt up over his head. Their movements were a little clumsy, but that only made it hotter. Because they were both desperate. Desperate for this. All of it.

He took a moment to admire all the bare skin she had on display. "Damn," he said, the word as reverent as a curse had ever been.

She was perfect. But then, he had known that before he ever took her top off. Not because of a particular shape to her body, the size of her breasts, the color of her nipples, although that was all good. He had already known she would be perfect. For the past week she'd been a specific craving for something he had never tasted before. But now that he was here, now that he was indulging in it, it was everything he'd needed and more.

He wrapped his hands around her slim waist, sliding

them upward before teasing the underside of her breasts
with his thumbs, just teasing the edges of her tightened
nipples enough to make her gasp.

They were the same pale pink as her lips. And they
reminded him of that sweet rosy wine. He looked to the
side, saw that there was just a little bit lingering in the
bottom of one of the glasses. "This was my favorite," he
said, picking it up, examining the rosy liquid inside. "I
think I'd like to try it again."

He tipped the glass, spilling it over her pale skin, the
wine pouring over her tempting curves, trails of sweet
temptation swirling around all that pink, perfect beauty.

He lowered his head, leaning in, drawing the tip of
his tongue across her skin, taking a slow, indulgent sip
of wine straight from her body.

She tasted better than any of the alcohol that had
passed his lips during their sampling. He was determined
to take more than a sample of her. He was going to indulge himself completely. Because why not. He had lost.
Restraint had lost. Being a decent human being had lost.
He was never very good at it anyway.

He was good at *this*. True to his word, drunk or sober,
he was good at this. No, he could never give her anything
beyond this moment, beyond this little bit of satisfaction
for them both. But what he would give wasn't nothing.
That was for damn sure.

She said she had never come with a man before. Which
meant she had only ever done it by herself. It was far
too easy to picture those long slender fingers between
her own legs, stroking herself, bringing herself pleasure.

He bit back a curse, lowering his head, his hands shaking. Dammit, what was wrong with him? He didn't lose
control like this.

But you're committing to losing control tonight. Might as well embrace it.

Still, it didn't matter how tempting an image that created in his mind's eye. He wanted more for her than that. He was going to give her more.

Even as the thought crossed his mind he realized it was a dumbass justification for what he was doing. To pretend that he had some kind of altruistic motivation for sliding his tongue across her beautiful, perfect skin. To pretend he was being a hero for stripping her clothes off and laying her down on top of the bar.

He nearly laughed out loud. He wasn't a hero.

He was nothing more than a damned lecherous villain. And these might as well be the railroad tracks he was laying her across.

He ignored that, too. Which was easy to do with his head fuzzy, and the arousal in his body sharp as a knife.

He lowered his head, closing his lips around her nipple and taking it into his mouth. He sucked hard, gratified by the low, throaty sound she made as he did. He allowed his teeth to graze her sensitive skin, just enough. Just enough to let her know who was in charge. He could tell that she liked that. Could tell by the way she wiggled against him. By the little begging sounds she made in the back of her throat.

He put his hands on the clasp on her shorts. It was one of those weird-ass metal clasps that wasn't super intuitive. But, in his day, he'd seen about every kind of woman's garment there was, and removed most of them.

He tugged the shorts down over her hips and she wiggled slightly, aiding him as he slipped them down her legs and threw them off the bar. That left her in nothing more than a pair of simple, black panties. Cotton, nothing spectacular. But, for a woman as beautiful as Sierra he felt like sexy underwear would be overkill. At least, from where he was at right now.

His restraint was at an all-time low. Black cotton was likely the only thing that stood between him and total insanity.

He drew his fingertips slowly down her rib cage, across her stomach, teasing the line where fabric met skin. She let her head fall back, her elbows resting on the bar, her back arched, thrusting her breasts into greater prominence.

He had the very distinctly unromantic thought that she looked a lot like those girls pervy country boys put on the mud flaps of their truck.

He was not going to say that out loud. He had enough sense left to reason that out, at least.

Instead, he dipped a fingertip beneath the fabric. "Good?"

She bit her lip, nodding her head.

He took that as an invitation to continue. His breath hissed through his teeth as his fingers came into contact with the wet heat between her thighs.

His mind was a total blank as he felt the evidence of her desire for him beneath his fingertips. Maybe he should feel guilty for this. She was his employee. She was under duress. Except, this did not feel like duress. And he did not feel guilty.

She parted her thighs, letting them fall open as he explored her deeper, sliding his finger deep inside of her as he drew his thumb across her clit. He felt her entire body shake beneath his touch. Her lips parted, her lids heavy as she watched him touch her. Her breath was coming in short, hard pants, a dark flushing creeping up her neck.

"There's nothing wrong with you," he said, his voice low and gravelly. "It was them. I hope you know that, Sierra. You're perfect. And if those bastards didn't know how to touch you right, if they didn't care to learn how to touch you, then they never deserved to be with you in the first place. You're a gift." He increased the rhythm of his movements, the pressure. He could feel her internal muscles tightening around his finger, could feel her getting closer to the edge. She shook her head, her blond curls cascading around her shoulders, but he kept going. Because he knew this was the point where you had to keep going, or you wouldn't reach the end. She wouldn't reach the end.

"You don't know what this is like? Do you? To have all of this out of your control. To have someone else bringing you pleasure. You're used to getting it for yourself. Does this scare you, baby?"

She nodded, her chest rising and falling rapidly with the force of her breathing.

"Don't be afraid of me. I just want to make you feel good."

The words tasted strange on his lips. Not exactly a lie, but not strictly the truth. He wanted to make himself feel good. He wanted it all. He wanted her pleasure, he wanted her ecstasy. He was going to take it.

Yeah, he was a selfish bastard. In this moment, it had very little to do with her.

He added a second finger to the first, stretching her gently as he continued to stroke her clit.

She reached out, grabbing hold of his wrist with both hands, wrapping her fingers tightly around him, squeezing him as she went hurtling over the edge into oblivion. She let out a low, rough growl, and he could feel pleasure moving through her in wave after wave, her internal muscles pulsing hard around him as she came.

"There," he said, his voice sounding like a stranger's. Too rough. Too soft. "Now you can't say you've never had an orgasm with a man before."

She was breathing hard, the hair around her face damp from sweat, her cheeks flushed. "It's your turn," she said, the words shaky.

"Hell, yeah it is." He leaned back, undoing the buckle on his jeans and shrugging them off along with his underwear and boots, kicking them down to the floor with the rest of their clothes.

He grabbed her panties, drawing them down her legs, leaning in and pressing a kiss to her stomach before lowering his head just a little more to get a taste of just how badly she wanted him.

She gasped, working her fingers through her hair. "Ace," she gasped. "I can't. Not again. Not so soon."

He pressed a kiss to that most intimate part of her before raising his head. "You can. And you will. But no, not like this. Not today. Or at least, not right now. I'm pretty generous in bed, but I have my limits."

"We're on a counter," she said, the words dazed, breathy.

"Well, you'll have to tell me if I'm good on counter." He moved up, kissing her stomach, the curve of her breast. Then he kissed her lips, deeply, sliding his tongue against hers as he braced his hands on either side of her arms, positioning himself between her legs and testing the slick entrance to her body with the head of his cock.

"Tell me you want this," he said, his voice low, strained.

"Yes. Yes, I want it." The last word was a whimper,

her fingernails digging into his back, her petite frame arching beneath him.

"I said I'd make you beg," he rasped, his voice strained. "I think this is the time."

"Bastard," she panted.

"Do you want it?"

He could tell she was considering telling him to go to hell. Then he rocked his hips forward, teasing them both.

"Please," she said. "Please, Ace."

And then his restraint was gone.

He lowered his head, kissing her neck and pressing more deeply inside of her as she urged him on.

He had the brief thought that he was forgetting something. That he'd skipped a step somewhere along the way. But he couldn't think. The alcohol, combined with the intensity of being inside her body, took everything over in a flash of brilliant light.

There was nothing but her. Nothing but this.

She gasped as he began to fill her, stretch her slowly.

He gritted his teeth, closing his eyes as he tried to catch his breath. Tried to deal with the rush of blood in his ears, drowning out everything else. She was tight. So tight. Perfect.

He had to fight with everything he had in him to keep from coming right away. She was so hot. So perfect. And when he flexed his hips forward, seating himself deeply, perfectly inside of her, he nearly lost it altogether.

Complete the ride, cowboy.

He pulled away from her before thrusting back inside, gratified by the throaty sound of pleasure she made as he made contact with that sensitive bundle of nerves. Then repeated again, and again. Each and every movement drawing them closer toward ecstasy. Toward completion.

But he found he wasn't really in a hurry. He wanted to delay it. Wanted to prolong it for as long as possible. Because this, *she*, was everything. The journey mattered more than the destination, and he couldn't recall ever having thought about that before.

She gripped his shoulders, her nails digging into his skin as he established a hot and heavy rhythm, pounding them both to oblivion.

She buried her head in his neck, her lips pressed against his skin. He rocked against her and she shuddered, another release crashing over her. And once it did, he couldn't hold back his own.

It was like an explosion going off behind his eyes, bursting down through his stomach, a release that threatened to destroy everything.

It was pleasure. Pure and simple. And complicated, too. Destructive, renewing.

It was the best damn sex of his life.

When it was over, he lay there, his forehead resting against her chest, his breathing slowly coming back to normal.

And then, he realized he was bare-ass naked on his own bar at four in the morning with a woman whose paychecks he signed.

Dammit.

SIERRA HAD NO IDEA what had just happened. Well, she knew exactly what had just happened, she just wasn't sure why.

You aren't?

She was lying to herself. Big-time. She knew what had happened, as sure as she knew they'd been leading up to this from that first night in his truck.

As sure as she knew she'd pushed him at every turn so that he would keep on pushing back. So that he would keep talking to her, looking at her, tempting her.

She had never done anything like this before. She waited three dates to let guys even get to second base. And she made sure she was in a relationship with someone before she ever let him make it all the way home.

But then, she'd never felt like this before. Had never wanted like this before. She had definitely never had an orgasm like that before.

One thing was for sure—though it had been ill-advised, it had been very, very good.

But the haze from the alcohol and her orgasm was starting to dissipate, and in its place came a hard slap from reality.

A ball of panic started to form in her chest, a looming cloud of doom overhead. This was wrong. It was so wrong, no matter how good it had felt.

He was her boss. And she had…

"I can't… I can't breathe," she said.

"Sorry," he said, rolling to the side, his withdrawal feeling more like a loss than it should. Feeling deeper than skin and sex and pleasure.

It wasn't his weight that had made it hard to breathe. Suddenly, everything felt overwhelming. This had been wrong on so many levels she couldn't even sort through them all.

What had she done?

She didn't blame him, not at all. She had wanted it, big-time, and as for the drinking, he'd been just as impaired as she had. But she had not thought this through. Or thought at all.

"I don't. I didn't mean for it… This wasn't my plan," she stuttered.

She was so angry. Mostly with herself. Because she had been determined to do this waitressing job well. Determined to make it on her own merits. Now she'd slept with her boss. So now, no one, including Ace—including *herself*—was ever going to believe that she had kept her job on her own.

She was so angry at herself, and yet, it was difficult to be angry when she felt so good.

He was right, she could no longer say that she had never had an orgasm with a man. Not only had she had an orgasm with a man, he had effectively proven that she was multi-orgasmic. Who knew?

She was a jumbled up mess. And alcohol was only partly to blame.

"I'm sorry," she said.

"Why are you apologizing?" he asked, getting down from the bar and bending to pick up his jeans.

She watched him while he did, completely captivated by the sight of him. He was the *most* gorgeous man she had ever seen. Possibly because he was the most man she had ever been with. Ace was tall, broad, with well-defined muscles and the perfect amount of hair sprinkled across his chest, across his stomach. Not to mention the most important piece of his male anatomy. That was impressive. The most impressive she had ever seen.

She felt her face getting hot.

She was trying to apologize for jumping on him, trying to chastise herself for her behavior, and she was checking him out while doing both.

"I just don't want you to think that I did that because I wanted the job."

He frowned. "Well, I don't want you to think that you needed to do it to keep the job." He pulled his pants on, and she moved her focus up to his chest.

"I don't think that."

"Good," he said, tugging his black shirt over his head, covering up all his pretty muscles.

She was sober now. Her orgasms had effectively broken through the alcohol haze. She could see things too clearly now. The bar. The empty dining room. Her panties on the bar.

Dammit.

She reached out and snagged them, stepping into them. She felt hideously self-conscious dressing in front of him. But then, dressing in front of someone was always worse than undressing in front of them.

When you were taking clothes off you were turned on at least.

This was just awkward.

It was so quiet in the empty room. She could hear the faint sound of the waves crashing against the shore outside.

"I…"

"There's a bed upstairs," he said. "You can go sleep up there. I'm going to bunk down in my office."

"There's a…bed?"

"And a bathroom."

Oh, crap. That was where he normally took women.

She closed her eyes, trying to deal with the rockslide of jealousy that tumbled through. "Fresh sheets on the bed?" she asked, clipped.

"Yeah," he said, not even bothering to ask why she'd questioned this.

They both knew.

"I don't really want to put you out," she said. Except that was a lie, because she kind of did want to put him out. She didn't want to sleep on the couch in his office after having transformative sex on the bar. The gentlemanly thing for him to do was to take the couch. And in return, the ladylike thing for her to do was to protest, at least once. Her mother would be so proud.

No, actually her mother wouldn't be proud about any of this.

"You're not putting me out. It's almost the butt crack of dawn and I'm drunk and… It's not like I'm going to have any problems sleeping."

His words hung strangely in the air between them. Of course he wouldn't have any trouble sleeping, he had just been given the world's best sleeping pill. But then, so had she.

Suddenly, she felt incredibly exhausted. Everything in her life felt like it had been turned over onto its side and rummaged through. She was *so tired* of feeling like everything was being rummaged through.

"Okay. If you say so." She really wasn't going to argue too much, because she didn't want to. Because she just wanted to go to sleep. And she didn't care if that meant sleeping in Ace's love nest. Anyway, she was one of his conquests, so she supposed she belonged in that little above-the-bar bedroom.

"I'll walk you up," he said, making his way toward her, his expression strangely blank.

"You don't have to," she said, but her protest was half-hearted, and he didn't listen anyway. She didn't mind.

They walked quietly to the back of the bar. There was a door there, one she'd never really stopped and looked at before. It opened up to a flight of stairs and he led the way to the top, where there was another door. "Here we are," he said, making no move to enter.

"Great," she said, swallowing hard. "That's...great."

Except it wasn't really that great. She was going to have to sleep in her shorts. She didn't have a toothbrush. And everything felt weird and wrong.

She almost wanted to ask him to stay with her, but he hadn't mentioned that and she didn't want to be the one to bring it up. It would be needy and clingy. She felt a little needy and clingy but she would be damned if she showed him that. She didn't have a whole lot of pride left after tonight's incident. She would cling to what she did have.

"Good night, then," he said, nodding once and turning away from her, starting back down the stairs.

"Yeah," she said.

She realized it was more like *good morning*, but she wasn't sure she had that kind of salutation in her. She wasn't sure she had much of anything left in her.

She walked into the bedroom and closed the door behind her, staring at the neatly made bed. Then she crossed the space and flopped down on top of it. She didn't care why it was here, she didn't care what he typically used it for. All she cared about was going to sleep and forgetting that the past hour had ever happened.

Difficult to do when her skin still burned with his touch and her body still burned from the memory of her release.

Difficult to do when the past few hours had been some of the best and hottest of her life.

If only she could erase the terrible feeling that came after. But she couldn't.

Dammit.

CHAPTER NINE

IT WAS MIDMORNING by the time she got back to Colton's house, and she was hoping that he hadn't noticed she hadn't come home last night. Maybe he would just think she had left for work before him.

Except, when she pulled in the driveway, his truck was there.

She cursed.

As owner of the construction company, he often did work at home unless he had to be out on a job site, so it wasn't too unusual for him to be around at odd hours of the day. But she had lived in hope.

Her new hope would have to be that he hadn't looked out the window yet to discover her truck wasn't there, and never had been.

She walked up the steps to the front porch and crept into the house, through the entry and past the living room. Sadly, he was there, sitting on the couch, his arms draped across the back.

"Just getting in?" he asked.

"Would you believe I got up early and went and had breakfast and am now coming back from breakfast?"

"I might have if you hadn't asked me if I would believe it or not."

"Well, that's inconvenient," she said.

"Sneaking in usually is."

"You speak from experience?"

"Yeah. I mean, not in recent years, but still. I recommend climbing in and out of your bedroom window if you really want to escape detection."

"I'll remember that next time." Not that there would be a next time. She started to edge out of the room.

"Care to share with the class?" he asked.

"I'm wandering into your house at the wrong side of a.m., wearing the same clothes I was wearing last night. Undoubtedly, my makeup has slid several inches down my face and my hair may—in fact—contain a live ferret. I am the very embodiment of the walk of shame, Colton. I don't think you want me to share with the class."

He frowned. "I don't want you to be going all wild just because you're rebelling against stupid mistakes Dad made. Don't go making your own."

She frowned. "I'm not sixteen. That's ridiculous. I'm not going off the rails."

"This looks…derailed, a little."

She met his gaze and arched a brow. "Did you honestly think that I was a virgin or something?"

He put his hands up. "Honest to God, Sierra, in my mind you're still about thirteen. So in my mind you remain pretty untouched. Let's not have a discussion that would disillusion me on that score."

"Sorry to be the bearer of disillusionment. I need to go stand under hot water for about an hour," she said, wearily beginning to climb the stairs that led up to her bedroom.

"Are you okay?"

She turned and shot him a deadly look. "If you don't want details, then don't question me. Or I will start relaying details that will scorch your ears."

"Okay," he said, his expression one of horror. "I'm not questioning you. But I do need to make sure I don't have to kick any ass. So just tell me that no one hurt you in any way."

She thought back to last night, to Ace, and how damn hot it had all been. "No one hurt me. No ass needs to be kicked. I was complicit in the debauchery."

She sighed heavily and continued on her way up the stairs. She walked down the hall, making her way into her room and pawing through her things to try and find an outfit that would make her feel slightly more human.

Something cute and soft, and not crumpled from the night before. From being worn during a long shift, then being carelessly discarded on the floor. Something that maybe didn't smell like beer and french fry grease.

She found a flowing top, a pair of black leggings and fresh underwear. She carted everything into the bathroom with her, turning on the water and stripping off her old, stale clothes. She shimmied around outside the shower, trying to keep warm until the water got to a semi-reasonable temperature. Then she stepped inside, lowering her head as the water heated up, pouring down over her skin.

Last night had happened. There was no point in regretting it. She squeezed some soap onto a loofah and began to drag it across her skin, ignoring the fact that the faint scrape of the material reminded her a bit of the way Ace's beard had felt.

The thought made her whole body feel like it was melting.

No. She was not going to obsess. There was nothing between them. Nothing but some strange pent-up sexual aggression that was tied up in a whole lot of weird, negative feelings. So she wasn't going to waste any time thinking about him. She wasn't going to worry about what any of it meant, because it didn't mean anything. She wasn't going to act like it was the end of the world. It wasn't. So, they'd had sex. Adults had sex.

Sure, in her experience casual sex wasn't really a thing, but it was for a lot of people. Clearly it was for Ace.

She didn't think this was a habit she was going to get into, but she wasn't going to waste a whole bunch of time beating herself up about it.

She gritted her teeth as she continued to clean her skin, wishing that she could replace the memories of his touch with the scratch of the sponge. Wishing that she could wash it all away. Not because she felt dirty. But because everything felt too significant. Too large.

She thought of the way he had touched her, teased her, thought about how it had felt when he had finally slid inside of her.

Her internal muscles clenched tight and she squeezed her eyes shut, ashamed that just the thought of it brought her so close to climax again.

He was great at what he did, she couldn't deny that. There was a reason that women lined up to experience a little bit of what he brought to the table, that was for sure.

Her mind went completely blank as she thought about that moment again. That first moment when he had slid inside of her.

Her stomach sank at the memory. Something gnawing at the back of her brain. But she couldn't quite think of what it might be. It was all fuzzy. She had been just tipsy enough that a lot of details seemed to blur together.

Some things were sharp, brilliantly so.

The way his hands had felt on her skin, the rough feel of his fingertips. The heat of his kiss.

The fact that she'd ended up begging him, just like he'd said she would.

Her own voice echoed in her mind. That soft, needy word. *Please*.

She'd never been desperate like that before. Had never begged a man to make love with her.

It made her whole face hot.

That wasn't it though. She felt like there was something else. Something she wanted to remember. But she was just sleep deprived enough this morning that things weren't becoming any clearer. And the more time passed, the more it almost seemed like a dream she'd had, rather than anything real that had happened.

A really, really good dream.

She shut the water off ferociously and got out of the shower, dragging the towel over her skin. She wasn't being gentle with herself. But she didn't care. She didn't deserve gentle. She was kind of an idiot. And she really, really wanted to punish herself sufficiently enough so that she wouldn't go allowing the memories of pleasure to confuse her. To trick her into thinking this was something she should do again. Because she absolutely should not. Not. Not at all.

She dressed quickly, then grabbed her purse from where she had discarded it on the floor, digging for her phone. She pulled up the work schedule that Ace had sent to her earlier. And she swore. She was on an early shift today. Restocking the bar and doing other before-opening projects. Which meant she had to go back in to work in about an hour. Life was cruel. Her boss was cruel.

She thought of last night again and shivered. He was cruel, but also very talented.

No. She was not allowed to think that way. She was not allowed to think of any of this that way. She was not allowed to get lost in the memories of how good it had felt. That was shallow, it was counter to what she was attempting to do with her life, and it was the path to madness and all of that.

One of the things that made her so angry about her father's decisions, about everything that had happened with the affair, with Jack, was the way he had completely tried to erase the consequences of what he'd done. In Sierra's mind, if you screwed up you had to own it. Well, last night she had screwed up, there were no two ways about it. But it was a new day. She had a job to do. She had a shift to get to. And she was determined to see it through.

ACE HAD FORGOTTEN he had made the dumbass move of scheduling Sierra for an early shift today. Obviously, he had created the schedule before he had screwed her brains out in the bar last night.

When she walked in wearing an outfit that covered a lot more skin than normal, looking pale and tired, damp blond hair pulled back into a bun, his entire body seized up tight. It was only the two of them in the bar right now; no one else would be coming in for another hour. He had a feeling that he had subconsciously made the decision to schedule her for this shift. Well, also, there were likely a lot of other employees who hadn't been available to do it. Maybe. Or, his subconscious was a sick bastard who had been chomping at the bit for another chance to be alone with her. Even though he was supposed to be *avoiding* being alone with her.

Yeah, that sounded like his subconscious.

"Hi," she mumbled, barely meeting his gaze as she walked over to the counter. "So, what exactly are we doing today?"

"Just figuring out what needs to be restocked up here, then going down to the basement to get it. Here's a check-list," he said, sliding a square piece of paper with a list of different ingredients across the bar. "See the number next to each item? That's how many there should be. If there aren't enough, write how many you need in the box next to it. Then you go down to the basement and find what you need."

"I can do that," she said, her voice muted.

He bent down, picking up a milk crate that was on the floor by his feet and setting it on the counter. "When you go down to the basement to get things, go ahead and put them in here. It will make for fewer trips."

"Okay," she said, nodding.

She was wearing some kind of delicate-looking top that he thought might snag easily on the edges of the milk crate. It was pretty impractical for the kind of work they were doing. And before they had slept together, he prob-ably would have called her on that. But, it was different now. Dammit all.

It shouldn't be. He should treat her exactly the same as he had before. But he couldn't. Because now if he said anything to her about what she was wearing it would seem like he was being needlessly assy. Or worse, a little too interested in her appearance.

This was why you didn't sleep with your employees.

Sierra quickly went to work, going through the fridge and making sure the various bottles of soda and beer that they didn't serve on tap were available, rummaging through the other fridge that contained a small amount of dairy products.

And Ace did his best to concentrate on the list they had begun building last night that would start to form the menu he would offer at his brewery.

Sierra went in and out a few times, each time returning from the basement with a crateful of different things. They didn't talk. It was better that way.

Finally, after about three trips, he sensed her getting twitchy with the silence. She was flicking her hair while she moved things around, making broad gestures as she moved empty bottles into the recycle bin and shuffled items around on the shelves.

Finally she cleared her throat.

"What?" he asked.

"Nothing," she said, squatting down and rummaging through the bottom shelf. "I was just wondering what you were working on. If it was the wine list."

"Yeah. The menu in general. I've been checking out what different restaurants and breweries serve in the other towns up and down the coast. I want this place to be different than anything in Copper Ridge, but I need to make sure it's appealing."

"Right. That makes sense," she said.

It took a moment for him to understand what she was doing, but suddenly, it hit him. She was trying to get them back on track. Discussing the relevant things. Dealing with their work, rather than getting caught up in the sexual tension between them. Rather than dissecting and examining what had happened between them last night.

She was a smart little thing.

"I know that I want some kind of fish and chips. Because no matter how fancy the restaurant, that's what people want when they come to the coast. And you have to have a hamburger."

She nodded thoughtfully. "Definitely. I think that a catch of the day like you were discussing with Ryan Masters is probably also a good way to go."

"Yeah." He rubbed the back of his neck. "That seems like it might be hard to plan for."

She shook her head. "Not exactly. If you have a chef's choice item where your chef is free to try to create something around a particular fish that is available in a specific season, people can have what's fresh and what's good. A rotating special basically."

"Right. That makes sense."

"And any kind of ahi tuna platter. Appetizers, rolls..."

"That's the stuff you basically serve raw, isn't it?"

"Yes," she said, laughing. "It doesn't sound like you're very impressed with that."

"I have no desire to eat my fish rare."

"Yes, but a lot of your customers will."

She stood up, brushing her hands over her thighs. "I think what people really want, especially when they go to a brewery that has an emphasis on small batches and local flavors, and its location, is to really accentuate the natural resources you have available. That's what they're looking for in their brewery experience."

"You're just saying this because you're some kind of Eugene hipster."

"Now you're calling me a hipster? I mean, yeah, I absorbed a lot of that eating food in Eugene. You can't deny that they're a little more of a food city than we are."

"Well, what isn't?"

"Tourism is just starting to pick up here, so things aren't really settled. We get to choose what Copper Ridge becomes, and I think that's kind of exciting. You're on the forefront of that."

"Kind of ironic since I'm not exactly pro development."

"You want it to stay the same?"

"Kind of. I mean, I have a lot of respect for what the town is. I don't exactly want it to change too drastically."

She nodded thoughtfully. "That makes sense. But it doesn't have to. Catering to the tourism industry isn't about changing it, it's about highlighting all of the wonderful assets. It's about making sure that other people know why we love this place. And that supports everyone who lives here."

She wrinkled her brow. "It's interesting, and I never really thought about it before. My dad does bring a lot of people into Copper Ridge when they come to look at horses for purchase, or for possible studs for breeding. But it's a certain type of person. It doesn't necessarily benefit every business at every level. But if broader tourism becomes more of a thing then we'll have people with all budgets visiting town. And the really great thing about that is it opens up the opportunity to have all different kinds of businesses see an increase in their profits. Your bar will have more visitors, the little crab shack down the street will have more visitors. And your new brewery will be popular, too. It's all about having variety."

"You really are kind of something," Ace said, marveling at her.

Her cheeks turned pink and he tried not to analyze the warm feeling that created in his gut.

There was a lot more to Sierra than he had originally imagined. Yes, he had known that she had some kind of a degree, and that she was theoretically not stupid. Still, so much of him had dismissed the knowledge. Thinking that because her education had come from her father's bank account, that her first job had come from her connection to him, it didn't really count for much. But he could see that Sierra had a good head on her shoulders in her own right.

He was even sure that he wasn't just being mentally charitable to her because they'd had sex. That was how convincing her little speech had been. He felt a little more like a tool, though. Because obviously all of his bad feelings about her were completely unfair. They were based on his own issues.

He had superimposed the face of another woman onto her from the moment she had walked in. Putting all of his negative feelings for Denise, and for the dissolution of their marriage, on to Sierra, just because they had a common background.

He was a dick. And he'd allowed all of that pent-up frustration to turn into some kind of weird sexual tension, which he had acted on when she had been pretty vulnerable.

He owed her an apology.

He remembered when she'd first walked into the bar asking for a job, and how he'd embarrassed her by forcing out an *I'm sorry*. He was a dick, but he'd be damned if he was so big a dick he couldn't admit when he'd done wrong.

Denise had beaten a hell of a lot of his goodness out of him. Had squeezed his money and his morals right out along with the rest. But there was something good left. He was sure.

"You're doing a really great job of ignoring everything that happened between us last night," he said, "and believe me, a huge part of me would like to keep on ignoring it. But I feel like I owe you an apology."

She ducked her head, but not before he could see that her cheeks were bright red. "For what? The screaming orgasms?"

"Yeah." His throat felt tight, his skin prickly and hot beneath the surface.

"Why? I think we both got everything out of it that we wanted."

"I've just been kind of an asshole to you. Let's not pretend otherwise."

She blinked, crossing her arms. "I wasn't going to argue."

"Well, good. Don't argue. I haven't been nice to you. I'm going to be honest and say that I really only helped you because of Jack Monaghan. He promised to invest in my brewery if I helped you out and I agreed. But I didn't really want you here, and I treated you like I wanted you gone. That was unacceptable. You've done good work. You helped me out. And I have a feeling that the way I treated you kind of contributed to last night's explosion."

She frowned. "Well, I guess that could be true. It was a lot of…fireworks. And feelings."

"Right."

She cleared her throat again. "It kind of makes sense that it happened. Just kind of built up so much that it had to…go somewhere."

"Right."

For some reason, it was all he could really think to say. Probably because in the middle of him trying to be contrite about what happened, he kept seeing flashes of what had passed between them last night, and it was scrambling his brain. And making him hard. All over again.

It was difficult to learn from mistakes when the result of the mistake had been so momentarily rewarding.

"So, I think we can both agree that it shouldn't happen again," he said, immediately wanting to punch his
own face for saying it.

His cock didn't agree that it shouldn't happen again.
His cock thought it should happen again right now. And
then again. And again thereafter. It had been the best sex
of his life. Mind-blowing, teeth-busting, backbreaking
sex. And he was telling her it had been a onetime thing.

Why the hell had his conscience shown up to the party
now?

He *hated* that bastard.

"I agree," she said, her words landing hard and solid
down in his gut.

"Great. We're on the same page."

"We are. That's good."

"Really good."

"I don't see any reason we can't act normal around
each other. Or maybe we shouldn't act normal. Normal
for the two of us is kind of mean. Maybe we should act
like we're just getting to know each other now."

He found himself nodding, even though he wasn't sure
he agreed. Then he extended his hand, trying not to feel
foolish. "I think that's a great idea," he said. "I'm Ace
Thompson. I'm happy to have you working for me."

His hand was just kind of hanging there. It was such
a stupid thing, shaking hands with a woman you'd had
sex with. She seemed to think so, too, because she was
just looking at him.

But finally, she stuck out her own and curled her fingers around his. "Sierra West. Thank you for hiring me.
I will do my very best to do a great job for you."

It was just a handshake. But it felt like touching lightning. Her soft skin against his was everything he remembered it could be and more. He wanted to strip her clothes off again. To bend down and kiss those sweet lips. To taste her a little more deeply between her legs. But he didn't do any of that. Instead, he released his hold on her hand and shoved his hands in his pockets, keeping them trapped so that he didn't get carried away.

"I guess I'd better go finish stocking," she said.

"Yeah. I appreciate it. And the menu help. And the commentary on tourism and businesses. And I'm being serious. I'm not being ironic."

She smiled, a genuine smile, the kind he so rarely earned from her. "You're welcome. I actually find it really interesting. So anything you need. Anything at all, with the business, just let me know."

"I will."

She turned, milk crate in her arms, and bounced away from him. They might have started over, but his body remembered everything that had come before.

And she still fucking bounced.

CHAPTER TEN

IN THE THREE WEEKS since Sierra had started over with Ace, things had been a little bit tense, but more or less friendlier than she had thought they could be.

So there was that.

Sure, she lay awake at night imagining what it would be like to have him kiss her again. To have him touch her again, but otherwise, it was fine.

Completely fine. She was fine, they were fine. Everyone was fine. And if she had been avoiding Madison so her sister wouldn't immediately guess that something was up, it was only because she didn't really want to talk about it, because she was doing such a good job of forgetting it. So, if Madison wanted details, Sierra doubted she would even be able to recall them.

She was super Zen like that.

But after dodging calls for a few days, and returning texts with sullen, one-word replies, her ability to avoid Madison had come to an end. She'd received a shrill call rightfully scolding her for the avoidance, and avoidance had become much more suspicious than the alternative. So she had agreed to meet her sister at Beaches for a light lunch. Since she wasn't paying rent or anything, her waitress's salary was more than enough for her to have a fancy little lunch. She inwardly sighed. That was something she was going to have to deal with eventually. The fact that she was still sponging off of Colton. It wasn't really going to be independence until she figured that out.

She adjusted her purse on her shoulder and walked into the white two-story building that overlooked the sea. The structure was old, and drafty thanks to the floor-to-ceiling windows that overlooked the waves across the street, with ample outdoor seating for days when it didn't seem like it would drizzle. Today was a little bit drizzly, though Sierra honestly didn't mind.

The mist and the gray was all a part of the charm of Copper Ridge. As was the way that it mixed in with the deep green of the trees and swirled around the base of the mountains as they rose above, their sharp peaks touching the cloudy sky.

She liked the way the air smelled when it was like this. The way the ocean seemed to float up and mix with the breeze, settling over her skin.

She could easily understand why not everyone could live in a place that had so many moments of gray. But there was something about it that touched her soul.

She let those calming thoughts wash through her as she walked deeper into the restaurant and started scanning the tables for Madison.

Thinking about Ace right before she sat down with Madison was a recipe for insanity. So, she wasn't going to think of him. She was going to think of mist, and the sea, and the salmon salad she was about to eat.

Salmon salad was a very happy thought. She would probably get clam chowder to go with it.

Yet more happy thoughts.

She saw her sister sitting at a table in the middle of the room. She was scanning the room, looking for Sierra. There was something strangely heartwarming about that.

"Hey," Madison said, "I was starting to think that you were dead, or avoiding me. Or avoiding me by being dead."

"Neither one," Sierra said, sitting in the chair across from Madison and tapping the front of her menu. "I've just been really busy. I mean, I guess it really changes things when you don't work in the same place as your sister anymore."

"Yes, we did used to be on the same campus, so to speak."

"How are...things?"

"I have a student that I would like to do bodily harm to. She does not know how to handle her horse, and she doesn't seem interested in learning. She's going to give that animal bad habits, and then punish her for them. I'm not super thrilled. I might have to drop her."

"Oh, sorry, Maddy, that's rough." Madison took her dressage training very seriously, and she was intense about the treatment and care of the animals she came into contact with. It was a much easier subject for Sierra than all of the stuff happening in her world, and her sister was passionate about it.

Madison lifted her shoulder. "I don't really mind being the bad guy. I'm kind of past caring whether or not people like me."

Sierra knew that wasn't true, but she appreciated that her sister firmly believed it. She also knew that Madison was a lot more sensitive than she let on.

"And... Everything else?"

"Mom is going to give herself some kind of medical event trying to keep track of the details for Colton and Natalie's wedding."

"They have months until the big event. And isn't Natalie handling most of that?" This was just giving her another reason to feel irritated at her future sister-in-law.

"She is. Trust me. Natalie is a lot of things, but able to let go of details is not one of them. So she's killing herself trying to figure out all of the minutia for the event, which I am convinced is a Cirque du Soleil performance, and not a wedding. Mom is going crazy trying to think of things that Natalie hasn't thought of, even though there aren't any things. So she's adding things."

"What?"

"She was asking me how much I thought it would be to get ahold of some live doves."

"Please tell me she was joking."

"Not joking, but under the influence of Valium."

Sierra's stomach sank. "So she's…about the same."

"Yeah. Honestly, I think she just blocks out Dad's bad behavior. I think she's been doing it for years. I don't really know if she ever believed he was faithful. I don't know if she ever thought that she had a perfect marriage. I just think she's very good at pretending the problems aren't there. I think she excels at putting her head in the sand and keeping things the way that she wants. I mean, it's kind of strange. To be able to believe firmly that you have the life you want even when you don't."

"Sure, but a lot of us don't want to live in Narnia. We want to live in the real world."

"I don't know. I would take Narnia. Maybe I could get myself a castle."

"You would have to fight in battles."

Madison laughed and lifted her glass of water to her lips. "I've already fought a few."

The server came by and took their order—they both got the same thing—and after that they fell into easier conversation, avoiding talking about the state of their family. They kept it to celebrity gossip and whether or not they thought neon nail polish was a trend that had any staying power.

"So how are things going with your boss?" Madison asked just as Sierra was taking one of her last bites of salad.

"Fine," she said, which wasn't really a lie. But she had a feeling she looked like she was lying. If only because she was holding back a wealth of information.

"Uh-huh. Is it just me, or is he really hot?"

Sierra froze. Full-on, deer-in-the-headlights froze. "Yeah, sure, he's hot. If you like older, cranky men."

"I don't," Madison said. "Anymore."

"I know. So why do you think I do?"

"I didn't say you like him, I didn't say I liked him, I just think he's hot. There are two different things at play here."

"Yes, then. He is," Sierra conceded.

"But he's cranky?"

Sierra let out a harsh breath and put her fork down. "He's not really. I mean, he can be. He was. But he's better now."

"He was cranky with you?" Madison was leading the conversation. Sierra could sense it. But she didn't know how not to be led. The only option was avoidance and that would be suspicious, too. "Surprising. I've always heard he was…uh…good with women."

She waved a hand. "It has something to do with his ex-wife. I guess I remind him of her, lucky me."

Madison frowned. "That's dodgy."

"Yeah." Of course, none of that would have been a

problem if they weren't also attracted to each other, but she wasn't going to say anything to Madison about that.

"But he's been nicer to you lately?"

Had he been nice? He'd been more than nice. She thought of how he'd touched her. How he'd kissed her. Madison's words brought their late night in the bar back into hot, sweaty focus in Sierra's mind. "Yeah," she said.

Dammit. She was bright red.

Madison's eyes narrowed. "This is why you're avoiding me, isn't it?"

"No," Sierra said, her face turning even redder. She could tell she was glowing, because her cheeks were so hot she was sure she was radiating warmth like a furnace. Not only that, she could feel a smile tugging at the corners of her lips. She was the world's worst liar. For some reason, every time she lied it made her grin, a kind of borderline grimace that was blatant advertisement of the fact that she was uncomfortable.

"What happened?"

"Nothing."

"You're a liar. You are a liar who lies," Madison said. "You're the color of that cherry tomato you left on your plate, and you look like you want to slide underneath the table."

"How do you do this?" Sierra asked. "I didn't say anything. It was just an innocuous conversation."

"I'm your older sister. I'm magic. Evil magic."

"You're terrible. And inconvenient."

"You're not the first person to say that to me. And I'm unrepentant. Tell me your sexual shame."

"I don't… I don't have sexual shame."

Madison let out an exasperated sigh. "Do I have to

drag this from you piece by piece or are you going to come clean?"

"If I make you drag it from me will you get bored?"

"No. There is zero percent chance of me getting bored. This is the most interesting thing I've had to focus on for weeks. I haven't had you to hang out with or talk to, there are mind-numbing wedding incidents happening all around me, and I don't have a love life of my own. So. There is no chance that I will be bored. I will needle you until you break. And when I break you, I will break you into the tiniest pieces imaginable."

"Fine. There's a little something."

"Little?" Madison asked, arching a brow. "That doesn't sound very promising."

"*That* wasn't little. I meant the…that was big. I don't… Something happened and it was good."

"I knew it," Madison all but crowed. "Tell me now."

Sierra frowned. "You can ask nicely."

"I'm not going to. I don't care for your delicate sensibilities, or niceties. I care for details."

"We might have…" Sierra let out a harsh breath. "We had sex."

Madison slapped a hand on the table. "I *knew* it."

"How?"

"I have a sense for these things. You've been avoiding me. And you don't do that. So, I knew there was something you didn't want me to know."

"Okay, fine." She growled. "It happened. It happened once. It isn't going to happen again. Because he's my boss."

"Right, your boss who was angry at you because you reminded him of his ex-wife. Is that why he had sex with you? Is he hung up on her?"

Her stomach twisted and went into a free fall. "I don't… think so."

"Well, I hope not. But if it only happened once I guess it doesn't really matter."

"It matters for my pride. The thought of being some kind of weird ex-wife security blanket isn't a very good one."

She thought back to that night. To the way he had talked to her. They had talked about the fact that she'd never been able to orgasm with a partner before, and he had set about to right that wrong.

He had done it spectacularly.

She couldn't believe that he had been thinking of someone else the whole time. Not when what they had done was so specific to the two of them.

"Well, whatever, that doesn't matter. He didn't take advantage of you?"

"No," she said, feeling defensive of him for some reason.

"Well, I have to do the big sister thing. He didn't hurt you, you had safe sex…"

Suddenly, the little thought that had been chewing at the back of her mind on and off for a few weeks hit her in the side of the head like an anvil.

"No," she said, feeling all of the color that had flooded her face earlier drain away.

"What?"

"Oh, *no*."

"What?"

"We didn't use a condom."

Horrified silence settled between them. The world's worst after-dinner treat.

Then Madison mobilized.

"But that's fine," she said, her words rushed. "That doesn't mean anything's wrong. I mean, it's not super smart, but just talk to him about, you know, his health and safety and things. And make sure that you don't need to get tested. I'm sure it's fine. It isn't like you're late or anything."

The other anvil dropped. Straight on her head.

"Oh, no," she moaned, reaching down to the floor by her chair and rifling through her purse, pulling out her phone. Madison wasn't talking anymore. She wasn't offering any platitudes, wasn't telling her everything would be okay anymore. Which sucked. Because Sierra really needed her to tell her it was okay.

Except, they both knew it might not be.

She pulled out her calendar and looked for the little markers she used to indicate the starting point for her period. "I'm not *very* late," she said.

Madison screwed up her face. "How late is not very late?"

"Only like a day."

Her whole face relaxed. "That's not late at all. I mean, a day could be anything."

Except they both knew that a day a few weeks after you had unprotected sex was a little more terrifying than a day under any other circumstances.

"I could just wait and see what happens," Sierra said.

"Yeah. There's no point panicking over a day."

"No. No point at all." Sierra bent down, picked up her purse and gathered it to her chest. "Well, I have to go buy a pregnancy test."

"I'll go with you," Madison said, popping up out of her chair. "I'll just get the check."

Another panicky thought occurred to her. "Where am
I going to buy a pregnancy test? People here *know* me."

"We'll go to Tolowa. There's no reason to do it here.
Are you parked in a timed space?"

"No, I'm parked in the lot by the beach."

"Great. I'm going to drive you out of town. And then
we can go back to my place and you can take the test."

Sierra bit her lip. "I'm not going to be able to wait."

"Okay, fine, we don't have to wait, we'll use a public
restroom. But let's just go."

Sierra felt like the world was muffled around her, like
she was underwater. Like she might pass out and dry-
drown right there on the floor in the restaurant. Which
would create even more gossip than if Sierra West bought
a pregnancy test in town, in front of God and everybody.

Madison somehow managed to keep her cool and pay
the check. Which kind of irritated Sierra, since she had
fully intended on paying for her own, and if Madison paid
for hers, then indirectly, her father was kind of paying
for it. She imagined living in Colton's house was much
the same. Though Colton had his own money, his own
business.

Still, it had been funded originally by her father.

*You're still driving the truck he bought you, and using
the phone he bought you, and you might be pregnant, so
maybe chill.*

Too bad for her, there was no chilling. It was a twenty-
minute drive from the city center of Copper Ridge to
the larger town of Tolowa a little bit to the south. Sierra
rarely had occasion to go there. But when people in town
needed to shop at a big box store, that was the place to
go. They had more fast food, more chains of every kind.
It was less homegrown and artisanal. It was practical.

And right now, the size was practical because she wouldn't know every third person in town.

"Let's just go to Freddie's," Madison said. "I know they have them. And the bathrooms will be nice enough."

"Okay," Sierra said, curling her fingers around her seat, tapping her foot impatiently. Madison found a parking space toward the front of the store and she pulled in. Both of them got out quickly, without talking.

They hurried into the store through the automatic doors, rushing past the sales tables positioned at the front, making their way to an aisle Sierra had never needed to venture into before.

They both stood there, in the same pose, their arms curved tight around their bodies, hands gripping their elbows. This was the weirdest, scariest thing Sierra had ever done. But having Madison right with her made it bearable at least. "Why the hell are there so many different kinds of these things?"

"Search me."

Sierra turned to her sister. "Have you ever taken one?"

"I took about five of them after I broke up with David. I wasn't late or anything, I was just afraid. After I found out about everything. About what a liar he was, I knew I couldn't be with him. I was so desperate to get away and I was scared... I mean it would figure, right? I'd get pregnant and not be able to get rid of him."

Sierra scanned the shelves. "Why did you take *five*?"

"When I want cheese, I want a platter. To make sure that all of my cheese needs are met. I wasn't going to be less thorough with something like that. It was kind of a pregnancy test sampler. To make sure that everything was right. I mean, I wanted a second, third and fourth opinion."

Fear curled itself around Sierra's stomach. "How many should I buy?"

"Maybe two. Don't go crazy like I did. I mean, I was a lot younger than you are, so crazy was par for the course."

Sierra sighed. "Maybe digital and... Is it analog? Do you call it analog when it's a pregnancy test?"

Madison scoffed. "Who cares? Just take them." She took a couple of tests off the shelf and thrust them into Sierra's arms. "I can't wait anymore."

"*You* can't wait? You're not the one who might actually be pregnant."

Her sister laughed. "Nope. No chance of that. Anyway, I doubt you are, either. So, let's just pay for the tests and you can go take them."

Madison led the charge across the store and over to the checkout. They opted for self-checkout. Which really was a gift she had never truly appreciated before she'd had to buy such sensitive material.

Sierra held the small plastic shopping bag to her chest as they walked across the store and into the restroom. It was empty, thankfully. She disappeared into the stall and began to tear at the pink packaging. The thick foil wrapper that the test itself was contained in was impossible for her to tear open. She ended up digging in her purse and pulling out her truck keys, stabbing at the packaging until she managed to tear it enough to rip the rest open.

She read the instructions three or four times before commencing to follow them.

"Is it done?"

"No, Madison, you have to wait."

"How long?" her sister asked. Sierra could hear her jingling on the other side of the stall door. Probably hopping up and down in place nervously, her jewelry and car keys clattering together.

"Eleven million years. Or, maybe three to five minutes? I don't know. Does it really matter? Time is relative. And right now it's relatively torturous."

She looked back down at the little white sticks sitting on top of the toilet paper dispensers. Mocking her with their blank screens.

Slowly, she saw a pink line begin to fade in on one. Her throat dry. One was okay. One was safe.

Then another line started to fill in, a faint blush at first that turned into an angry slash across the white background. That was two. Two lines. Then she looked down at the digital one, sitting there, mocking her with a word that was already echoing in her brain.

Pregnant.

"Oh, dammit," she said, sitting back down on the closed toilet.

"What?"

"Just…"

The stall door jiggled, and Madison curled her fingers around the top of the door, tugging hard. "Let me in."

"No," Sierra said, her voice shaky.

She stood up, her hands trembling as she collected the pregnancy tests and threw them into the trash. Then she pulled on the toilet paper roll, collecting far too much toilet paper for her purposes, and dabbed at dry eyes. She wasn't crying. She kept expecting to. So she kept pressing the toilet paper against her tear ducts.

Her throat was dry. Her eyes were dry.

As though all the life was being drained out of her.

Was this some kind of weird pregnancy symptom? Did you have pregnancy symptoms after only a couple of weeks? She had no idea. She didn't know anything about this kind of thing. She didn't really want to know anything about this kind of thing.

She twisted the lock on the door and opened it. Madison all but tumbled into the stall. "What?"

"It's not…negative," she said, pushing past her sister and heading toward the mirror.

She looked like death. Completely white, her lips a strange bluish color.

"Oh. And it's… It's his?"

She turned around and faced Madison. "Yes. There aren't any other candidates."

Madison held up her hands. "Not judging. Just checking."

"I broke up with Mark more than a year ago. And this is not my usual modus operandi. It was just a stupid thing. Just a stupid, onetime thing."

She looked down at her stomach, which appeared exactly the same as it had three weeks ago. She poked it with her forefinger. "So, seriously… I can't… I can't believe there's anything in there."

Madison stared at her. "I keep thinking you're expecting wisdom from me."

Sierra looked up, meeting her sister's eyes. "You're two years older than me."

"But I've never been pregnant. I have no idea what to tell you."

"I don't know. Something supportive?"

"I'll stand by you no matter what," Madison said, nodding.

"Thanks." Sierra turned around to face the mirror again, turning on the faucet and splashing some cold water on her wrists. Then she splashed some on her face.

"I'm never going to be able to eat salmon salad again. I'm going to have post-traumatic stress associated with that salad."

"The salad isn't what got you pregnant."

"Fine. I'll never be able to look at a penis again."

Madison frowned. "*That* I am familiar with."

"I know."

Madison reached out and wrapped her arms around Sierra's shoulders, then pulled her in for a hug. They both wobbled before Sierra regained her balance and settled into her sister's hold. "This is really awful," Sierra said, feeling sorrier and sorrier for herself with each passing moment.

"It is. What are you going to do?"

Sierra took a step back from Madison, scrubbing her hand over her eyes. "I… I'm going to deal with it."

"Okay. What does that mean?"

She didn't know what it meant. She felt…uncertain and terrified and so very tempted to just make it all go away. Before anyone knew.

Her throat tightened, her muscles tensing. It was a galling thing, to understand her father. To have that sudden, strong impulse to hide it all no matter what.

She had options. She could even…disappear from town for nine months and give the baby up for adoption.

There was no shame in that, she knew.

But could she do that to Ace? Could she give up his child without ever giving him a chance to decide?

But if she did that it would mean no confrontation. It would mean her baby could have a normal family.

And when it came to Ace, there would be no reckoning of any kind.

That was so, so tempting.

A while ago, a month ago, it was what she would have done. Games and hiding, because that was what she did. Keeping people at a distance, avoiding anything hard.

It wasn't her anymore.

"I mean…" She took a deep breath, clarity coming to her in small increments. "I made a mistake. And I have to face up to that. I have to deal with it."

"You mean you're going to have a baby?"

The sentence wrapped itself around Sierra's throat and threatened to strangle her. "I guess so."

"Really?" Madison asked, her expression concerned. "And you'll keep it?"

"I think I will."

"You really want to do this?" Madison pressed.

"I *am* doing it. It's too late for regrets now. At least, for me. I'm not going to be like Dad. I did this. It's a result of my actions. At the very least, I can't hide the baby from Ace."

Through all of the panic, all of the pain, her chest burned with one thought. She wasn't going to sweep everything under the rug to make her life easier. It was exactly why she had left her parents' house. It was why she had to separate herself from her family. Because she couldn't condone the way her father had handled things with Jack.

She'd been so hard on her dad in part because she believed so firmly you had to own up to your own mistakes. Now she had to prove how deeply she believed that.

She had to figure out who she was. Had to learn to stand on her own two feet.

Well, this was going to test her ability to do that.

Madison let the silence stand between them for a

while. Then finally, she spoke again. "Do you want me to help you with Mom and Dad?"

That made Sierra feel like she had been kicked in the head. "I don't... I don't think I want to tell Mom and Dad yet. It's really early. Anything could happen. At least, I've heard people say that in movies, so I'm pretty sure it's true."

"Yeah. That's true. I think."

"So, we don't need to worry about them. Yet. Maybe at all."

Sierra swallowed hard.

"And your boss?"

"Yeah, him I will have to tell. Not just because I might have to take time off for morning sickness, but because it is his baby."

Madison forced a smile that looked more like a grimace. "Okay. Do you want me to go with you?"

Sierra shook her head. "No, I'm going to have to tell him on my own. He's really not terrible. He's actually been really nice lately. I'm pretty positive he won't want an audience. And I'm sure that he won't...freak out."

"Are you *sure*?"

"Well, no. Because I have a feeling that I'm about two seconds away from completely freaking out."

Madison wrapped her arm around Sierra's shoulders and started to lead her from the bathroom. "Come on. Let's go back to Copper Ridge. I'm driving, so you can freak out in the car."

"I will take you up on that."

CHAPTER ELEVEN

THERE WAS SOMETHING different about the way Sierra walked in at the start of her shift. It took a few steps for Ace to realize just what it was.

She wasn't bouncing.

She crossed the room, her hands locked in front of her, her lips pressed into a flat line. "Can I talk to you?"

"Sure," he said, crossing his arms over his chest and leaning back against the edge of the bar.

She looked around, her expression shifted. "Not here."

"Do you need help burying a body? Because I'm not that involved of a boss."

"I'm serious," she said, closing her eyes. "I need to talk to you in your office."

His stomach twisted, his heart pounding a dull rhythm in his chest. Because there was something about all of this, all of this great seriousness that seemed a little bit too familiar. That picked hard at the thing he had been trying to ignore for the past few weeks. But he wasn't going to guess.

In spite of that resolution, his brain was trying to do a lot of guessing as they walked through the bar area, past the other employees and into his office. He shut the door behind them, and she turned the lock.

For one, strange fraction of a second he thought maybe she was going to try and seduce him again. Well, she wouldn't have to *try* and seduce him, he was seduced already. He was just doing a better job at holding himself back from acting on it.

If she took a step toward him, he knew that all of his restraint would be gone.

But she didn't look like a woman with seduction on her mind. She didn't look like a woman with anything happy on her mind at all.

"Is everything okay?" he asked, possibly the stupidest question in existence. Clearly, things were not okay.

"Not really."

The back and forth was starting to irritate him. "Are you going to tell me what's going on?"

She took a deep breath, looking up at the ceiling. "I'm pregnant."

The words just about knocked him back on his ass. He had wanted her to hurry up and spit it out. But, now he sort of wished she would suck it back in. Wished that he had time to prepare. Except there was no preparing for news like this. It wasn't the first time a nervous woman had stood in front of him and told him that she was pregnant.

His stomach pitched. He was... Well, he didn't know what he was. Because the one, dominating emotion that poured through him—unfiltered, unchecked—was pure, blinding rage.

"Are you sure it's mine?" he asked, his tone fierce.

He had never asked Denise. Never. Because why on earth would he ever ask his girlfriend, the only woman he had ever slept with, if the baby she was carrying was actually his? No, he had done the right thing immediately. He had gone to her father and he had asked for her hand in marriage. Had bought a ring with what little money he had.

And then everything had gone to hell.

And it was going there again.

"Yes," she said, drawing back as though he had slapped her. "I'm completely sure. There hasn't been anyone else for a long time. I told you that."

"I'm just supposed to believe everything you say?"

"Why would I lie to you? Do you think I want a piece of your bar empire?"

"I don't know. I've been lied to before."

"Oh, this is about your ex-wife."

"Not exactly," he said. He was lying.

"You need to tell me what it is about, then."

He felt like someone had reached into his chest and grabbed hold of his heart, squeezing it tight. He couldn't be numb, not to this. Of all the things life could throw at him…this was the one he hadn't built up enough defenses to withstand.

He took a deep breath, rubbing his hand over his face. "I'll tell you one thing. We're going to make absolutely sure that this is my baby. And you're going to marry me."

OF ALL THE REACTIONS Sierra had imagined, none of them had been the world's angriest marriage proposal. Was it even a proposal? It was more of a demand.

She hadn't expected the anger at all.

He didn't seem shocked, not like she did. He was just…mad.

"I'm going to pretend that you didn't say that," she said, taking a step away from Ace.

"Why, exactly?"

"Because I'm not sure how I feel about the father of my hypothetical baby being *crazy*."

"The baby isn't hypothetical. And there is nothing

crazy about getting married when there's a child involved."

"I'm like less than three weeks pregnant. At this point, it's pretty hypothetical. And a lot of people have kids and don't get married."

"Not me."

"Well, fine. Great for you. But also, *me*. I'm not just going to marry you because we're having a baby. That's going to cause more trouble than staying apart."

"Never. Leaving anyone without full protection isn't okay with me. Divorce and separation cause more trouble than marriage ever could."

She was suddenly very conscious of their age gap. Of all the extra living he'd done that she hadn't scratched the surface of. All the extra years he'd spent being kicked around by life. She was sort of just getting to all that. To the pain. To losing what you thought you'd had. But he was…he was a veteran. And she knew no matter how crazy it all seemed, he was speaking from the kind of experience she hadn't had the chance to collect yet.

"I know you had a bad experience," she said, "but because of that I think you should realize the importance of being absolutely certain that you're marrying the right person for the right reasons."

"No. What my divorce taught me was that a man in my position has a lot less rights than he should. I lost one child, Sierra, I'm not losing another one."

Sierra felt like she'd been kicked in the chest by a bronc. "What?"

"Do you want to know why I'm so bitter about my divorce? It has nothing to do with not being with my wife anymore. She can rot for all I care. I wouldn't sleep with her again if my dick was going to fall off if I didn't. No.

I'm not bitter because I'm not with her. I'm not bitter because she left me. I'm bitter because she set out to hurt me in the way that she knew would cut deepest. And she was damn successful."

"You have a child?"

He rubbed a hand over his face, shaking his head. "Not really."

"You're going to have to just tell me. You have to explain all of this to me, because I'm catching a bunch of the baggage that you're carrying around right now. At least let me know what's in the bag."

He sat down on his desk, gripping the edge tight. "I got married the first time because Denise told me she was pregnant. I was living in Texas at the time, competing in the rodeo. Denise was one of the rodeo queens. I had lived in Copper Ridge most of my life, and my dad is the pastor, as you know. That meant that I behaved a certain way when I was here. And I behaved…less that way when I was gone. She was the first woman I was ever with. So when she came to me and she said she was pregnant I never questioned it. Not for one second. Never questioned her. I just asked her to marry me."

"Okay, so as of right now, all I see is you repeating the same mistakes you already made."

"The problem is, we were never compatible. I didn't realize that because I was blinded by the fact that sex was fun, and she was the only person I had ever had it with. We *really* discovered that incompatibility once we were married. Throw a baby into the mix, then a toddler, and you realize just how unfit the two of you are. We were young. And we made a lot of mistakes. But Callie never felt like a mistake. Ever. She was the prettiest little girl I ever saw. All blond curls and bright blue eyes. When she called me daddy, nothing else seemed that bad." A muscle in Ace's jaw jumped, his hands curled into fists.

His tone was flat when he talked, something in his eyes flat, too. She could sense that flatness was only on the surface. But it was covering up a wealth of pain.

"I loved that little girl, Sierra. You have to understand. They grab a hold of you, in ways that you don't realize they will. I never spent much time around kids. I never cared much about them one way or the other. I didn't even think they were particularly cute. But let me tell you, *my* daughter... They don't make anything else that cute in the whole world."

My daughter. Sierra put her hand down flat on the back of the chair by his desk, bracing herself. "What happened?"

"Denise decided she didn't want to be with me anymore. You see, the problem with being with a guy like me is that her daddy still had to bankroll her lifestyle. I wasn't rich. And I wasn't going to be rich. She encouraged me to quit riding in the rodeo, because it wasn't like I was making big bucks. I had to get a job at her father's ranch. That was fine. But it was very clear that she was married to one of the ranch hands, not to a ranch owner. Eventually, she told me she was leaving me. For the guy she had been dating just before the two of us had gotten together. And that's when things went to hell."

"Help me understand," she said, her heart squeezing tight.

She wasn't sure how she had gone from being completely enraged at him to feeling unchecked sympathy. But even without him finishing the story she felt hollow inside. Like she could taste the devastation pouring from him.

"When we went to court about the divorce, she filed

for full custody of Callie. I was livid. I couldn't believe she would pull something like that on me. And when it was looking like things were going to go my way, she brought out a new piece of information. She wasn't totally sure that Callie was mine. Now, I think I still might have ended up with custody except... Well, it turned out that the ex-boyfriend—the man she was now engaged to marry—was actually Callie's father. She got paternity testing done and she proved it."

"I... How can that matter? I mean, if she thought you were the father..."

"In an ideal world, sure. Or, *my* ideal world. But I didn't have the money or the reputation that she did. That her family name did."

As the possessor of an important name about town, that made her feel sick with shame. As if her every possible advantage because of her personal connections—and anyone it might have hurt—were suddenly written right across her skin for him to read.

It certainly made his issues with her a bit clearer.

"I guess the judge wasn't impressed with you being a ranch hand, either?" she asked softly.

"Not particularly." He took a deep breath, then let it out slowly. "She went to family court, managed to get a hearing date changed without notifying me. You can do that, apparently. And because I wasn't there, I essentially waived my parental rights. With everything taken into consideration, the fact that the biological father was present and wanted to be in his daughter's life, the fact that the two of them were getting married... The court sided with Denise. I lost custody. I fought it. I fought it for as long as I could. I spent all my money—as little as

there was—I lived in Texas for another two years, just to
try to get a judge to let me back into my daughter's life."

He looked up at the ceiling and for just one moment,
Sierra saw the raw, open pain in his eyes. A window into
that deep, private wound he carried with him. The story
behind all of his behavior. His treatment of her. She felt
like a voyeur for having witnessed it. And yet, she was
glad she had seen it.

"Callie wouldn't even know me now. That's the worst
part. I fought it for two years, and I never got to see her
all that time. Just a couple of times. Here and there. About
six months after our divorce was final, Denise married
Callie's father. Then they all lived together and...I was
confusing her. Denise liked to tell me that. I was getting
in the way of their *real* family. I was a mistake she'd
made. They were family."

"Ace... I don't know what to say."

"There isn't anything to say. It sucks." He shook his
head. "I'm glad, so glad, that she's alive. That she's safe.
That she's happy. A lot of people lose kids in more trau-
matic ways than I did. She has a home, and a mother and
father. I'm grateful for that in some ways, no matter how
angry I am at them. But some days I don't feel grateful.
Some days I'm just pissed. Those wounds don't heal."
He clenched his teeth together, his dark eyes hard. "I will
never stop missing her."

She felt completely unequal to the task of dealing with
all of this. She felt like...well, she felt like what she was.
A spoiled twenty-five-year-old who'd flounced away
from her family to go and find herself. It had seemed
noble at first. Right and principled and all manner of
other things. But now it felt so small.

Small and insignificant as an accomplishment when

rolled out next to his. This man who had spent everything for the love of a child. "Of course you won't. No father would."

For a moment, just one moment, she thought maybe he would keep the walls down. Thought maybe he would soften a little.

But then his eyes hardened, and any vulnerability she'd thought she'd seen was gone. "You're going to marry me. Because I will be damned if I'm ever in a position where I will be blindsided again. I will not lose another child, Sierra, do you understand me? The minute that baby's born, I need proof that it's mine. And if she is..."

"Marriage didn't protect you before, Ace," she said, feeling like she was rubbing salt across a raw wound. She felt unkind. She felt downright evil. But she had to do it. Because she had to think of herself, too. "What makes you think it would protect you this time?"

"Oh, I damn well know there's no real protection. But I'll take every legal claim I have. And if you refuse to marry me when it comes time to do a custody agreement I'll make sure they know that you, with your waitress's salary, who refuses to take money from her mom and dad, wouldn't marry me."

Any sympathy she'd just felt for him evaporated in a hot rush of anger. "You're not seriously suggesting you would try to take the baby from me?"

"I will not lose custody again," he said. "I'm not the powerless ranch hand that I was. I'm not a West, but I have my own assets. I have my own money. I'll throw that around if I have to."

"The baby is yours. I have no intention of ever keeping him or her from you."

"And I don't trust that. I just don't. I can't. I have nothing in me to trust the word of anyone when it comes to something like this. The only person I can trust is myself."

"That just isn't going to work for me."

"I don't think I asked you, princess."

"You can't force me to marry you, Ace Thompson. We need to be adults and work something out."

He stepped behind his desk and leaned forward, planted his hands flat on the top, like he did when they stood out in the dining area. Him behind the bar. He really liked to have things between them. "All right, how about this? You come live with me, and when the baby is born, we get married."

"There was not even a little bit of compromise in that. In fact, there was just some additional crazy."

"There's nothing crazy about it to me. A child needs a mother and a father. And to not have their father ripped out of their life."

She threw her arms wide. "I would never do that."

"Right. And I think you should maybe understand why I can't just take you at your word."

"Counteroffer," she said, not quite able to believe that she was having this conversation with him. Contending with the emotions that had swamped her during his confession about his child. Still reeling from the fact that she was actually having a baby. "We work on a way to figure out how we can co-parent our child without drama. If we never have a romantic relationship of any kind, then we're not going to have some dramatic divorce."

"You're going to want to get married at some point," he said. "And when the time comes you may decide you don't want to deal with a third wheel."

"I wouldn't. I would never, ever take my child away from his father."

"You say that now—"

"I would say it forever. Do you know the real reason I'm not speaking to *my* father?"

"An affair," he said, rocking back on his heels and stuffing his hands in his pockets.

"But there was more. I know you were confused by the fact that Jack Monaghan was lobbying for you to take me on here at the bar."

"Yeah, I was worried that something might be happening between the two of you and I might have to kill Monaghan for hurting Kate Garrett. Or at least watch for witnesses while Eli and Connor took turns dealing with him."

"Well, Jack and I do have a connection. But it isn't the one you were thinking." She took a deep breath. She was committed to this now. To letting someone else in on the horrible, devastating secret. "Jack is my half brother, Ace. My father kept him a secret. My father paid Jack off. Made him sign an agreement keeping their relationship a secret. My father made Jack feel like he was worthless. Like he was dirty and shameful." Her voice trembled, all of the pent-up rage she felt over the revelation about her half brother, all the fear she'd experienced in the hours since she'd taken the pregnancy test, roaring through her like a thunderstorm over the ocean. "He took Jack's birthright from him. Took his siblings, his right to the West family ranch. All of these things that I have simply because my father had me with my mother instead of someone else, he denied Jack. I could never do that. I will never do that."

She could see some of the anger drain from him. The

crease between his brows softened, the set of his jaw releasing a bit. Maybe now he believed her. Maybe now he understood.

Or maybe he was just shocked, processing the potential ramifications of that revelation. Well, he could join the club. She was still processing the ramifications.

"I'm so angry at him," she said. "For doing that to Jack. For forcing him to grow up the way that he did. We were all… We had everything. A beautiful house, education. The luxury to pursue whatever we wanted. And Jack…he lived in a trailer. And everybody treated him like there was something wrong with him. Like he had done something bad to be born not knowing his father."

She shook her head. "I would never, ever hurt our child by denying him or her access to you. I think the reason people do use their children like pawns is because they want to hurt each other. Because love goes wrong, and then when they separate they want to inflict pain. I think my father was angry at Jack's mother for making him want someone that he saw as beneath him. I think that's why he treated them so badly. I think he took it out on Jack. I think that's what your wife was doing to you. She wanted to hurt you because your…love went wrong. So let's just skip the love part. Let's skip marriage. If we're just two acquaintances who work at getting to know each other so that we can give our child the best life possible… I think in the end it will be better."

"That sounds like some kind of New Age ridiculousness to me."

"Maybe. But it makes more sense than the two of us getting married. We can't have a conversation without yelling at each other. We can use this one as exhibit A."

"Like you said—" he tipped his chin up, crossing his

arms over his broad chest "—the only reason we have so much trouble dealing with each other is because what we really want to do is tear each other's clothes off. That isn't going to make for a very healthy parenting relationship, either."

Heat rushed through her, and she had to marvel at the degree to which Ace had cast a spell over her body. Here she was, arguing custody arrangements and marriage with the man who had knocked her up, and he was right. Really, she just wished that she could tear his clothes off. "Well, we need to get over that. Not encourage it."

"Okay, I'll make you a deal. If we can figure out a way to deal with each other platonically over the next few months, then I will see how I feel about your co-parenting idea."

She sighed. "That is completely noncommittal, stubborn and not all that giving."

"It's all I have."

"Okay… What's the flip side?"

"If we can't, then you marry me."

She crossed her arms, her stance mirroring his own. "You can't make me marry you."

"And you won't be able to keep your hands off me."

She laughed. "Honey, I'm pregnant. This may be my first rodeo, so to speak, but I guarantee you that in a few weeks about the only thing I will want to get my hands on is a cheeseburger."

"I'd be willing to bet money that you and I will end up naked again."

"I'll take that bet."

"Well, look at it this way, if I win, we both win," he said.

She gritted her teeth. "You're not winning. So I'd let go of that right now."

"I'm going to need you to move onto my property."

"Excuse me?" she asked, the subject change giving her whiplash.

"I want to keep you close. And I want to take care of you. It makes sense. The original house that came with my land is still in great condition. I had it all fixed up when I moved in. Because I lived there while I had my house built. We won't be living together, you'll just be close."

"It seems unnecessary."

"You're living with your brother, so refusal seems unnecessary, too."

She threw her hands up in the air. "All of this seems unnecessary."

"All of it?"

"I am... I have always been very responsible. I don't sleep with men until I'm good and ready. And when I have a boyfriend I get on the pill, and I make him use condoms every time. I always have. I've only been with two men aside from you. I had long-term relationships with them. I don't...have unprotected sex with strangers on countertops."

He rubbed his chin slowly, his palm scraping across his whiskers, his dark eyes heated. His response was slow in coming, as deliberate as the slide of his hand across his face. Making her imagine touching him. Kissing him.

Bastard.

"Except that you *do* have sex with strange men on countertops," he said, finally.

"Did. Once. And now I'm dealing with the world's most long-running consequence."

"It's an age-old consequence," he said. "You play, you pay."

A sudden thought occurred to her, and her stomach sank. "How many women have you gotten pregnant? Because, judging by this little conversation we had about your family history and now this, it seems like you get yourself in this situation a lot."

He frowned, his dark brows locking together. "Do I have more than one ex-wife?"

"Not that I know of," she said.

"Then I think it's safe to say I don't make a habit out of this. First of all, Callie wasn't actually mine, but I can't deny I felt like the possibility was there. Then, after Denise, I was very careful. I have been very careful."

"Until me," she said, feeling annoyed and persecuted all at the same time. He was some kind of legendary sex god, who was apparently also super into safe sex. But he had failed her.

You failed yourself. You can't pawn it off on him.
You failed each other.

"Exactly," he said. "Which is why I don't have a very big amount of confidence in the two of us keeping our hands off of each other in the future. The fact that both of us acted so out of character says something."

"So, we were trying to deal with it by…acting out?"

He shrugged. "Maybe. But the fact remains we're in this situation. We have to deal with it. You're moving in with me. That's final."

His words skittered down her spine, ricocheting around inside of her. She should be hideously offended by them. They were commanding, and ridiculous, and all of this was a bit patriarchal. But then, something inside of her gloried in it.

Because this man was her child's father.

She thought back to her own father. To his casual disinterest. To what he'd done to Jack.

But this was a man who would hold on to any child of his. Who had gone broke trying to keep his visitation rights. Who carried the pain over the loss of his daughter still.

This was a man that she could trust with her child.

Now her heart was another matter. Her heart was staying out of this.

"Fine. I'll move to your property," she said. "But nothing is going to happen between us. I'm more than happy to work out some kind of an arrangement."

"Great."

"But I mean it, Ace. Nothing is going to happen between us," she reiterated.

"Of course not."

"I don't like your tone."

"You never do, Sierra. You never do."

"When do you want me to—"

"As soon as possible."

"I guess I need to talk to my brother."

"What are the odds he comes after me with a shotgun?"

"High. Very high. But I think if I deal with him, maybe I can save your balls."

"I'm not very happy with my balls right now, so I may just let it happen."

For some reason, that made her laugh. Possibly because the entire situation was just so ridiculous she couldn't even believe she was standing here. There was a surreal quality to the past three hours. She felt like she was in a haze. Like she had to be dreaming. And so there really was nothing to do but laugh.

"What? You think the idea of me being separated from my balls is funny?"

She laughed harder, doubling over. The tears that had been conspicuously absent in the cramped bathroom stall were now streaming down her face. "Yes," she said, waving her hand. "It's all funny." She straightened up, drawing her fingers beneath her eyes and wiping the tears away. "The idea of you sacrificing your balls for their bad behavior. The word *balls*. It's all so funny."

"I'm glad you see some humor in it."

"Well, it's that or have a nervous breakdown," she said, sighing. "So I guess I'll take this."

"Do you have furniture or anything?"

"Not really," she said.

"Well, we'll see if I have any in storage. Because we're going to have to get something in that house."

"Is there at least a bed?"

"Yes, a bed, a couch. But I don't have dishes in it or anything."

She had no way of getting them. Well, she had a little bit of money from her job. And she supposed if she was getting herself into yet another position where she didn't have to pay rent, she might well be able to buy some small things for her little house. But it struck her then, how perilously close she was to needing charity.

"I'll figure it out," she said.

"All right. But the beauty of it is we'll be figuring it out together."

"I'm not really sure how great that will be," she said, forcing a smile. "But I guess we'll find out."

He nodded, his expression grim. "I guess we will."

CHAPTER TWELVE

"I'M MOVING OUT."

Sierra knew that pronouncement would be met with interrogation. She was prepared for it. Well, as prepared as she could be, considering the fact that the only answers she could possibly provide for her older brother were unpleasant, embarrassing and potentially problematic.

She wasn't ready for her parents to know about the baby. Really, she wasn't ready for Colton to know about the baby. Come to think of it, she hadn't exactly been ready for Ace to know about the baby.

She wasn't entirely sure *she* was ready to know about the baby.

But she did. So, Ace did. And a part of the deal was she would move onto his property for a while. So Colton had to know, too.

Unless he didn't press for answers, but she had a feeling that the odds of that were almost nonexistent.

"When?" he asked, leaning back in his seat on the porch swing.

She had chosen to ambush him after work, hoping that he would be too tired to try and get details. It was a nice evening, the sun touching the tip of the mountains and spilling rose gold over the tops of the trees.

He had a beer in hand, and—until she had spoken at

least—an easy smile on his lips. So maybe this wouldn't be so bad.

Maybe.

"As soon as possible," she said, fixing her eyes on the flowery wreath on the front door—courtesy of Natalie, she assumed.

"Meaning what?" he asked, lifting the beer bottle to his lips and taking a sip.

"I guess, as soon as I can pack my bags. It isn't like I have a whole passel of worldly possessions squirreled away in your house."

He stared at her for a moment. She raised her brows and lifted her hands. He stared back. She said nothing because there was nothing to say that she wanted to deal with at the moment.

And he just kept staring. Then he sighed heavily, setting his beer bottle down on the porch by his feet. "Okay, Sierra. I am trying to be patient here, but clearly you're not going to just give me the reason you've decided to move out. Did something happen with Natalie?"

She was a little surprised that Colton was so willing to acknowledge that his fiancée might have driven her away. "No, it doesn't have anything to do with Natalie."

"Good. I know that things aren't always easy between the two of you. But you have to understand that it's just the stress of the wedding. Plus the fact that her best friend is running against her father in the mayoral election. I'm not feeling very happy with Lydia at the moment."

Sierra cringed. "Are you ever happy with Lydia?"

He made a scoffing sound. "Why would you say that? She's…uptight and irritating, sure, but until she started running against Natalie's father I didn't have anything against her."

Sierra disagreed, since she'd heard Colton make disparaging remarks about Lydia Carpenter on more than one occasion, but she wasn't going to press the issue. "Well, it would have been nice for her to wait on announcing her candidacy until after the wedding. Although I'm not entirely sure that election timelines consulted your event planner on the subject."

"Much to Natalie's chagrin, not nearly enough people have consulted our event coordinator on their comings and goings."

Sierra laughed uneasily. "Yeah, well. Life goes on and all. Even around the wedding of the century."

"Wedding of the century?" he asked, brows arched.

"Well, as far as Copper Ridge is concerned. It's basically a royal wedding."

"Don't say that in front of Mom or I'll end up leaving the country club in a carriage."

She scrunched her face up. "Heaven forfend."

"Things will calm down. And so will Natalie. I swear, when she's not dealing with wedding fever she is a pretty pleasant woman."

Sierra didn't think *pretty pleasant* was good enough for her brother, and she really didn't see why he was settling for a marriage that would be—at best—mediocre.

But then, look at his example. Their parents' marriage was such a mess. Even before the revelations about Jack had come out, it was clear it hadn't been a functional relationship.

She imagined Colton was taking on whatever he felt he could handle. It didn't mean she had to approve. "Well, I hope you find her pleasant. Since you're marrying her."

"And you're sidestepping the issue. Why are you moving out?"

Sierra sucked in a sharp breath and started counting yellow flowers on the wreath while she tried to figure out what to say next. One thing was certain: if she didn't tell Colton the whole story, Madison wouldn't. Because Madison was her sister, and as much as they both loved their brother, the bond of sisterhood won out above all else.

So, she could lie to Colton if she wanted to. Could hang on to her secret just a little bit longer.

The thought made her feel shaky.

There had been enough lying.

It hit her then that *this* was how it started. The temptation to make your life easier just because you didn't want to face the consequences.

She was ashamed, in that moment, that she had already been tempted to go the route of her father. To deny the existence of her own baby simply because she didn't want to deal with Colton's reaction.

No. She wasn't going to do that. She was responsible for this, and she was going to take responsibility.

She swallowed hard, then wrenched her eyes away from the wreath, forcing herself to look at her brother. "Well, I'm kinda moving in with someone? Only, not really."

Colton frowned. "Uh-huh."

"I mean, it's a man. But, I'm not moving into his house."

His frown deepened. "Uh-huh."

"I'll just be on his property. It isn't sexual." Colton's brows shot upward. "Well, it *was* sexual. Once."

"Hold it right there."

"I'm trying to explain," she said.

Colton stood. "Is there any part of this explanation

that will make me not want to go punch some guy in the junk?"

"No. Anyway, I haven't even gotten to the part of the story that will really make you want to junk punch him."

Colton's eyes narrowed. "Sierra, what's going on?"

"Well," she said, smiling, trying to force a smile on to her brother's face, too. "You know Ace Thompson."

"Hell yeah, I know Ace Thompson," Colton responded, not smiling. "He's your boss. And he's older than I am."

She waved her hand. "You make it sound like he's aged. He's not. He's in a perfectly reasonable age group for me."

"I don't like where this is going."

"I know you don't," she said, sounding weary. "So I might as well tell you the rest. I'm pregnant."

The string of expletives that came out of her brother's mouth was so creative she didn't know whether to be offended, or to congratulate him.

She winced. "I knew you weren't going to be happy."

"A baby? You're a kid. How are you going to handle a baby?"

"Okay, slow your roll, mister. I am not a kid and I'm not too young. I'm twenty-five."

"*Not too young.* If you don't think it's young, that just proves my point. Because you're still too young to have any idea how young that is."

She knew she was going to have to let him have his moment, even though it was annoying. She didn't really feel like he was entitled to have a freak-out when she was the one who should be curled up on the floor, but she knew he'd have one.

Anyway, in some ways it was nice to have her brother

do the freaking out for her. She was the one who had to survive this day, this change, this future. She couldn't afford to lose her mind.

"You don't make any sense," she said, grabbing hold of the bridge of her nose.

"No, Sierra, *this* doesn't make any sense. You go to work for this guy, and the next thing I know you're pregnant with his baby? Actually, even more disturbing, moving in with him. I was with Natalie for two years before she moved in here. We were engaged before she moved in."

"She's also not pregnant."

At the mention of the word the color drained slightly from Colton's face. "No," he said, "she's not."

"You're one hundred percent sure?" she asked, wondering for a moment if the reaction was just to dealing with her news, or if he had some doubts.

"Yes," he said, his teeth set on edge.

"Well, I guess you can't really be one hundred percent sure…"

"I sure as hell can, since we have been sleeping in separate bedrooms for the last couple of weeks, because she likes the idea of abstaining before the wedding."

Sierra nearly swallowed her tongue. "Too much information!"

"Quid pro quo," he said, his tone hard, "because I'm privy to the fact that you had a one-night stand with the town bartender."

"Why do you have to say it like that? You make it sound like it was…dirty or something."

"Are you trying to tell me it isn't?"

She gritted her teeth, and tried hard to keep the annoyance off her face. She was not going to let him get to her.

Instead, she allowed one corner of her mouth to lift upward. "Well, now that you mention it, it was pretty dirty."

He held up a hand. "Stop."

"Don't be a jerk or I'll retaliate accordingly."

"Obviously," he said, gesturing broadly, "you need somebody to be a little bit more of a jerk. Because then maybe you would have made better choices."

"Look, I'm not going to claim this was some kind of complicated matter of the heart, but trust me when I say the loins want what the loins want," she said. "And I'm sure you know what I mean by that."

He sighed, the long, slow breath seeming to take a good portion of the anger out of him. He let his hands fall down to his sides. "I don't know why I'm bothering to argue with you about something that isn't up for debate. It isn't like you can go back in time."

"Exactly," she said.

She looked down at her hands and began to pick at her fingernails. "I just want to do the right thing. I don't know if a relationship with him is in the future. In fact, I'm sure that it isn't. But I do need to get to know the father of my baby, and work out the simplest way for us to share custody."

She purposefully pushed Ace's angry words from earlier today out of her mind. She wasn't going to think about that. Wasn't going to think about his commands and promises and intent. About that hastily issued marriage proposal.

Marriage *demand*, more like.

"You know you can stay here," Colton said. "Don't feel like you have to jump into anything. Even though I'm an ass, I'm here for you."

"I know. Except this is something that Ace and I need to work out."

He pushed his hand back through his hair. "I don't like this at all. This you-growing-up thing. I'm afraid you're going to get yourself hurt. That your life is going to be difficult now and I... I don't want that for you, Sierra."

"Well, look at it this way, this is kind of the worst-case scenario. And I'm pretty much living it already. What else is there to worry about? I mean, maybe a drug problem, except I'm pregnant. So I'm not even going to be drinking anymore."

"Don't joke," he said, sounding even wearier than she felt. "It has been one hell of a weird few weeks and it just got weirder. There's no insane scenario you could suggest that I wouldn't believe was entirely possible right about now."

"I guess. But look, this is why I wanted to tell you. And this is why I want things to work out with Ace. I mean, not *work out*, work out with him, I just mean I need things to be civil. I'm not going to do to this baby what Dad did to Jack. I'm not going to hide."

Colton breathed in deeply, leaning up against the side of the house. "So, are you going to tell Mom and Dad?"

"Oh, hell no. I'm going to hide it from them."

In spite of himself, he laughed. "How long do you think you can get away with that?"

"I don't know. Celebrities seem to hide baby bumps pretty effectively. I thought I'd invest in a lot of baggy tops."

"Uh-huh."

"Don't *uh-huh* me! You don't know what it's like. You're all perfect and stuff. You never make mistakes. The rest of us are a damn disaster."

"You're not a disaster. And you just said you weren't going to hide things anymore."

"I meant more in the general sense. The overall sense. With people that I trust, and who don't terrify me."

"Is that where I went wrong? I don't terrify you enough? Were you not as afraid of my wrath as you should have been?"

She lifted her shoulder. "It's difficult to say. Actually mostly because I wasn't thinking about you at all when this stuff with Ace went down."

"Okay, well, fair enough."

"Sorry the world doesn't revolve around you." She took a step forward, stretching her arms out. Colton returned the favor, pulling her in. She rested her head on his chest, wishing suddenly that she were a little girl again, and a bit of affection from her older brother was all it took to eradicate any fear or uncertainty she might be experiencing. "I love you," she said. "I'm really sorry to add all this to the craziness."

He released his hold on her. "This isn't about me. It's about you. But…still I think it would be best if we didn't tell Natalie right now."

Sierra frowned. "You would keep a secret from your fiancée?"

"If I had to. I mean, it's for her mental health. And, as a result, mine. Trust me. She and Mom are going nuts planning this thing."

"I know. Madison told me."

"Does Maddy know about the baby?"

She nodded. "Yes. She was there when I figured it out."

He nodded. "Well, thanks for telling me. I guess. I'm

glad that I know what's going on in your life. I just wish it were something a little easier for me to fix."

"Yeah, life was easier when you could fix things for me."

He forced a smile. "No kidding."

"Except back then you would have gotten in trouble for swearing in front of me," she said.

"Yeah, Mom would have yelled at me, and probably cussed at me while she did."

Sierra laughed. "That sounds about right."

Those memories seemed so easy now. Part of a simpler time. Of course, while she had been living it, it hadn't seemed particularly simple. She had never felt like her life was easy. But she was starting to see how easy it had been. She hadn't really appreciated it until it was gone.

She was such an idiot.

"If you need to borrow my truck," he said, "I suppose that's what older brothers are for."

She smiled. "I have my own truck. Anyway, I have, like, a few duffel bags full of clothes and that's it. I left everything else at Mom and Dad's. I don't have much. I guess that has to change, too." She had a sudden, sobering thought. "I'm going to need a bunch of stuff for a baby. Oh, dammit. I'm really not ready to be this much of a grown-up."

Colton looked stricken for a second. "Hell, I'm not sure *I'm* ready to be this much of a grown-up. I'm definitely not ready for you to be one."

"Is that so?"

"Nothing, and I mean nothing, makes me feel older than realizing how old you are. Throwing in the fact you're going to be a mom..."

Her insides crumpled. An intense, and not entirely

unpleasant sensation overwhelmed her and she swayed slightly. "Oh, my," she said, putting her hand flat on her stomach. "A mom. I didn't… I guess I'm going to be a mom." She squeezed her eyes shut tight. "Things can still go wrong," she said. And she wasn't sure whether it was a prayer for them to be okay, or for it all to go away.

"Sure. That's life, I guess. It could always go wrong. But things could go right, too. I don't really have any wisdom for you. Except if I know one thing about you, Sierra West, it's that you are the strongest woman I know. You might even be the strongest of all of us."

"Me?"

"Yes, you. You're standing up for what you believe in. You told Dad just what you think of him. You left when it was hard. Not when it was easy, like Gage. Not just for yourself."

"Gage is kind of an easy target at this point," she said, feeling a bit badly how often and how easily they maligned their long-lost brother.

"Well, he's not here to deflect the shots."

"Fair enough."

They stood there, just staring at each other for a moment. She felt it then. The passing of time. How much things had changed. The fact that they were going to change even more. Her entire life had become a spin-off of the life she'd been living before. And this was just one more spin-off into a different direction. She had no idea how this had become her world. No idea at all.

But it wasn't going to become any less surreal standing there on her brother's porch. She needed to make arrangements for the move. Needed to get her things packed.

And then she was going to have to go to work.

CHAPTER THIRTEEN

Sierra had texted Ace late the night before to let him know that she would be by his place early the next morning. No sleeping until noon, the very short message had read.

Well, he wasn't sleeping at all right now, much less until noon.

The revelation about the baby had just about knocked him on his ass. But once he had regained his composure, he had found a single-minded focus. This was his second chance. He was going to be a father again.

He walked out onto the front porch and stared out across his property, and at the pastures beyond the grove of trees in the front. At the mountains past that, pale blue sentries standing guard over the perimeter. He had never stopped being a father, he supposed. Whether or not she was with him, Callie was his daughter. But he was ready to have another child in his life. He felt that, so intensely, so fiercely, it had shocked him.

Because when he had left Texas and any hope of re-claiming his daughter behind, he had thought he'd left any desire to ever have family again.

Apparently not. Apparently that desire still existed in him. Fierce. Almost overwhelming. He leaned against the railing, pressing down on his forearms until they ached. Sierra was going to see things his way, eventually. He would be damned if he had one more broken family. That certainty was another thing that surprised him.

If he had been given a quiz only twenty-four hours ago he would have said emphatically that he had no desire to get married ever again. After all, in recent years he would never have classified himself as a traditional man.

Sure, when Denise had come to him to say she was pregnant, he had acted like every good pastor's son would.

Because he had been a good pastor's son, and he'd had to make things right. They had fornicated and all of that, so he had been honor bound to make an honest woman out of her. So he had.

Now that he had spent the past few years almost making a career out of fornicating, he saw things a little bit differently.

Or he'd supposed he did. Because the minute Sierra had told him about the baby, he had known there was only one choice.

Yes, but that's to protect you and the baby.

Sure, but also, he couldn't exactly imagine leaving Sierra West an unwed mother. The town would crucify him.

There were a lot of reasons they had to get married. And she would come around to his way of thinking soon enough. She wasn't thinking clearly about the stigma, he figured as much. Because, sure, it was tempting to believe that they lived in the twenty-first century and people were more modern about these kinds of things. But while that might be true in the wider world, it was definitely different in a small town like this. Or maybe things were different. Maybe people simply wore their opinions a little more transparently. And it would be especially brutal when everybody knew your name. That was the truth of the matter for both of them. Everyone knew him either as the bartender or the pastor's son. Everyone knew Sierra West, golden girl of Copper Ridge.

If they didn't take control of the rumor mill, it would grind them up and bake them into bread.

But she would come around. She had to.

He heard the rumble of an engine and he looked down the longer driveway, just in time to see the hood of a cherry-red pickup barreling his direction. Behind the wheel was that bouncy blonde who had turned his bar, and his life, on its axis. Sierra West was trouble, he had known it from the beginning. He just hadn't realized how much trouble she would be.

She pulled up to the front of the house and killed the engine, getting out and stepping down from the oversize vehicle. She was a funny little thing with her gigantic truck. Another one of those rich cowgirl things he had a tendency to be hard on. A big old truck purchased by Daddy, to pull some tricked-out horse trailer full of pink tack.

But his judgmental view of her wasn't exactly going to be helpful to his cause. So he was going to have to knock it off at some point.

"You came," he said. "And here I half expected you to scamper off into the mountains."

"Nah," she said, wrinkling her nose. "I'm not one for scampering."

"Are you sure? You seem exactly like the type who would scamper."

She crossed her arms and tilted her head to the side, cocking her hip out. "Oh, really? And why exactly is that?"

"Because you're small. And you have the kind of

bounce in your step that would lend itself to a scamper if the need ever presented itself."

She nodded, blond hair spilling forward like a river of gold. "I see. Well, it's not an unadorable attribute, I will admit."

"You yourself are not unadorable," he said.

He was gratified when her cheeks turned pink. That was when he realized just how he had to play this.

If he wanted this arrangement with her to work, he definitely needed to be a little nicer. He knew how to flirt. He knew how to be *nice*. All of that came easy. At least, on a casual day-to-day basis with people he interacted with on a surface level.

Sure, things had been more challenging with Sierra from the get-go, but that was only because he had been fighting the urge to strip her clothes off of her and satisfy his burning lust.

But his lust was satisfied. Curiosity dealt with. At this point, it should be easy. He should just treat her like he would any other woman he was trying to get into bed. Only, with her, instead of being after sex, he was after a marriage license. The very thought made him sick to his stomach. But he was going to have to get over it.

"That's very nice of you," she said, looking at him suspiciously. "Are you afraid I'll get all emotional and cry if you're mean to me?"

"Not an unfounded fear."

"Right, because you've been through this before."

He nodded slowly. "I guess I have. But it doesn't really feel like it. That was thirteen years ago."

He didn't like thinking about how long ago that was. Because then he had to come to terms with the fact that the girl he still thought of as his daughter was a teenager now. A teenager he never got to see. It brought into sharp relief all of those missing years. Yeah, it was better not to think of it at all. "Besides, I hear every pregnancy is different."

"Great. So, neither of us really knows what we're doing."

"I would say that's an understatement."

"You could lie a little bit. You can tell me you're an unofficial expert on women and pregnancy and childbirth."

"Sorry," he said, knowing he didn't sound it. "I forgot to tell you that I'm not just a bartender. I moonlight as an ob/gyn."

"Oh my gosh, that would be the world's worst pickup line."

"I'm above cheap lines like that, Sierra West. I am much smoother. As you well know."

She cleared her throat. "Okay, that I do know is true."

"A little too smooth for both of us, it turns out."

She wandered to the back of her truck and opened the tailgate. "I don't know. Why are we crediting all of this to your skills? Maybe I'm the one who's smooth."

He leaned against the bed of the pickup. "You think so?"

"Maybe I'm the one who seduced you." She planted her hands on the open tailgate, looking up at him, a little bit of glitter back in her blue eyes.

Right now, it was almost easy to believe that she wasn't moving in with him because she was having his baby. It was almost easy to believe they were just having a normal conversation, like any other they'd had for the past few weeks. Entertainment mixed with tension and a hint of unease. The kind that was electrifying. As exciting as it was terrifying.

But that would have only been possible three weeks ago. Before they had actually had sex. Before she had found out she was pregnant with his baby. Before they had made mistakes that had irrevocably changed the course of their lives.

So no, this was not a normal moment.

"I guess we'll never know," he said. "Want to give me your stuff?" He rounded to the back of the pickup truck and saw that the bed was empty other than two large bags with *Sierra* embroidered across the side in pink. "Is this it?"

She nodded. "Yes, and just so you know I've had those bags since I was twelve."

"Hey, I'm not judging." Though he kind of had been.

She shoved her hands in her pockets. "I left a lot of my clothes and things at my parents' house when I moved out. I mean, my dad bought most of it, and even though it's mine, I didn't feel right about taking any of it. It just felt weird. It all feels weird. And obviously I took my truck, and my phone, but I didn't really know how to get by without them. I'm able to pay my phone bill..."

"Look, I know that I made you feel like you had to justify everything to me. Because I was a prick. But you don't have to explain yourself. I'm sorry that I put you in the position where you felt like you had to."

"Have you been body snatched?" she asked, tilting her head to the side.

"Not that I'm aware of. But then, would I tell you if I had been?"

"Yeah, you've definitely been body snatched. You're being a lot nicer."

"Again, just trying to avoid the tears of a pregnant woman."

Or he was trying to change the dynamic between them so she wouldn't act like marriage was tantamount to getting thrown into a rabid badger den. But he wasn't going to cop to that. Not while he was still a rabid badger in her eyes.

She reached into the back of the truck and grabbed one of her duffel bags. He took it from her, then picked up the other one. "I'm going to make myself useful. You don't carry anything. You're in a delicate condition and all that."

She snorted. "Is that so?"

"Yes."

"Okay, if that means you're going to carry my stuff for me, that's fine. I can't drink, so there had better be other perks."

"If memory serves, there aren't that many."

She winced. "Well, that sucks. I've never done anything for nine months," she said, following him as they began to walk in the direction of the original house. "I've never even kept a hairstyle for that long. And I have to be pregnant for nine months? About the only thing I've ever made that serious a commitment to is barrel racing."

"I wish I could tell you it wouldn't be a big deal."

She crunched her nose up. "But experience tells you differently?"

He winced. "Sorry."

"That's okay. Actually, it isn't. But what can you do?"

"I mean, the good thing about you moving in with me is that I'll be here to take care of you."

"You're acting like I'm suddenly made out of cotton candy. I'm not going to melt in the rain."

They continued down the wooded path that led to the small house, the trees growing thicker, closing in on the pathway. He hadn't been out this way in a while, so it was a little wild and overgrown. Eventually, he would need to widen everything so that she could drive right up to the front.

But then, if he had his way, she would be living in his house before it got to the point where she needed shorter walks.

"I know that," he said, "but you don't know how your morning sickness is going to be. I know some women can barely get out of bed all day. Someone is going to have to take care of you."

"Well, I just can't be that sick," she said, sounding obstinate. "I have work. At the bar. I can't just…"

"Honey, I own the bar, and I'm the father of the baby. I think I can cut you some slack."

She stopped, stamping her booted foot and turning to face him. "No! That's exactly what's wrong with all of this. I was supposed to be doing this myself. Earning things on my own merit. And you know what? I'm not. Jack got me a job in the first place, then we were attracted to each other, then we slept with each other, now I'm having your baby. So, tell me what part of this is my own merit?"

Ace's heart twisted. She made it pretty easy to feel things for her. Things other than anger and suspicion. Not that he was ready to let go of the latter entirely, for his own safety, but there was something vulnerable about Sierra. Something different. Different not just from Denise, but from every woman he'd ever met.

"You're a damn fine waitress, Sierra West," he said. "And not only that, you helped me with my brewery in ways that I couldn't have ever known to ask for. You suggested things that I never would have thought of. You've been invaluable. And yeah, I know in the beginning I was skeptical about the kind of job you would do. Yes, it took Jack's recommendation to get me to hire you. But I was wrong. Everyone who didn't hire you is wrong. Obviously, your dad's ranch was in good hands when you were managing it. Nepotism be damned."

Her throat worked as she swallowed hard, blinking rapidly, as though trying to hold tears at bay.

He hadn't been lying about wanting to avoid tears. It looked like he might have failed. He hadn't gotten to know a woman well enough to be responsible for any tears in recent years. A little laughter, a little screaming—the fun kind—and that was it.

This was a little bit deeper, a little more real than he was used to dealing with.

She looked at him, her cheeks waxen, her eyes glassy. "Sometimes you aren't that bad."

Then she turned away quickly and started down the path again. And he followed, like she might be the one who knew where she was going. The path only went one direction, so he figured it was self-explanatory enough. He had the idea she needed to feel like she was in charge of something.

"I'm not an ogre," he said, "I promise. In spite of the way we started out together."

"Well, I figured you couldn't be as bad with every woman as you were with me. After all, you have a reputation."

"Do I?" He was vaguely aware of that, but of course, no other women had never said anything quite like that. So he was curious about what exactly his reputation might be.

"Oh, yes. You're a notorious manwhore and seducer."

"I don't know that I'm much of the seducer. It never seems like it's that much work."

"I suppose I can't really disprove that, I guess. I didn't really make you work for it."

"Not exactly."

"Well, you didn't exactly make me work for it, either," she said.

"Fair enough."

She stopped walking when the house came into view. "This is…"

"A lot smaller than you're used to, I imagine."

"I've been living in a bedroom in my brother's house. I think you might have an inflated idea of where I'm coming from."

He walked past her, up the steps that led to the modest porch. "Well, I have been to your family ranch for various special events. Even if you aren't coming directly from there, I know where you're coming from."

He set the bags down on the ground and reached into his pocket, pulling out a set of keys. "These are for you," he said. "You can have all the privacy you need. This is your place."

He extended his hand, holding out the keys to her. Slowly, she took them, her fingertips brushing his as she did. It was a small bit of contact. The kind that he took for granted every night of the week as he passed drinks over the bar. But this was different. It was Sierra. And touching her was never simple. It was never anything less than a lightning storm coursing under his skin.

He was going to have to get a handle on that.

"Thanks for this. If you don't mind, I think I need some time alone."

"Not a problem," he said. "If you need anything, you have my number."

He turned and left her standing there. It was fine with him if she needed a little space. It would give him time to plan his next move.

ACE WASN'T WRONG. The house really was a lot smaller than what she was used to. But it was empty. She had filled the small closet in the bedroom with all of her clothes. And it was a good thing she hadn't brought anything from her parents' house, since just this sampling filled up the space.

But as for the rest of the house? He hadn't been exaggerating when he'd said there was a couch and a bed. A very small bed in the room she had chosen, covered with a threadbare quilt that was clean if a little bit musty. There was a small living area with a woodstove and an aggressively plain brown couch. There were no curtains in the windows, lace or otherwise, and there was no table to sit at. Which was fine, because there were no dishes to eat out of.

She had always had things. Her entire life had been filled with them. But more and more she was beginning to realize how much of that had nothing at all to do with her. The ornate dining set she had eaten most of her meals out of all of her life belonged to her parents. The beautiful canopy bed that she had spent her nights in starting from childhood had belonged to her parents.

The matching living room set that she had plopped down on every day after school wasn't hers, either.

The dorm where she had spent her college years had been well stocked, mostly because her mother had arranged for it to be.

Even going to Colton's house after leaving her parents had been less jarring than this, because it had been filled with her brother's earthly possessions. There wasn't much here beyond earthly dust.

The reality was, Sierra didn't have all that much.

She put her hand on her stomach. Well, she had this

new development. And she did have money. Some. Saved up from her waitressing job, and some from when she had been working at her father's. Since she didn't have to pay rent she could easily fill the place up with better and brighter things.

She would get things. It wouldn't stay all bleak and empty like this. And, she wouldn't allow herself to sit around and feel desolate about what she didn't have. She would be fine. Yes, it was a change. Her entire life was in flux. She wasn't about to fall apart over the fact that she didn't have a set of dishes.

Well, she had been about to fall apart over that, but she wasn't going to let herself.

She would get new dishes, dammit. Her first dishes. The first dishes to actually belong to her. She would figure out how to deal with all of this Ace stuff, claim her independence, and possibly some furniture.

She was getting thrust into adulthood in kind of a rough and unforgiving way. But she was twenty-five. It was time.

She took a deep breath and surveyed the small space. The square little kitchen and living room area, the cracked cement floor underfoot, the large picture window that looked out into the forest that surrounded the undeveloped portions of Ace's property.

Well, since she had the day off she was going to go out and go shopping. There was no point sitting in an empty house, so she wasn't going to do it. The thought made her smile. She had control. She had resources.

She was going to use them.

CHAPTER FOURTEEN

BY THE TIME Sierra pulled back into Ace's driveway, it was nearly dark outside. She hadn't expected him to be there. She had expected that he would have gone out to the bar already, but much to her surprise, his beat-up blue pickup truck was sitting there, right in front of his house.

There was a horse trailer hitched up to the back, though it didn't look like it had any horses in it.

She pulled up alongside of it and put her truck in Park before turning the engine off. She opened the door and got out, nearly falling over when she about ran into Ace. "You scared me!"

He smiled. "Sorry. I didn't mean to."

"Then why were you playing the part of stealth panther?"

"Stealth panther? I like that. I wasn't trying to be stealthy. But I do want to show you something."

She looked into the back of her truck, at all of the white shopping bags lined up in it. "Well, I have some things to take back to the house."

"In a minute."

"Hey," she said, starting after him as he began to walk toward the barn. "Why exactly do you get to set a time frame?"

"Because, I'm the one that has a surprise."

"It better not be a clown."

"Why would it be a clown?"

She lifted her shoulder. "Because that would be an-other strange and unsettling surprise in a week of strange and unsettling surprises. I thought there might be a theme."

"No clowns."

"Is it circus-related at all?"

He laughed. "No. But I'm going to make note of this little bit of paranoia."

"Don't do that! I have revealed my soft white under-belly to you. You can't take advantage of that."

"Oh, sweetheart, I can and I will." He paused, turn-ing and treating her to a wicked smile.

Her stomach tumbled down into her boots. Somehow, in all of the drama of the past few days she had forgot-ten that she was in this situation because of her devas-tating attraction to this man. It had been easy to forget, all things considered. But she remembered now. Oh boy, did she remember.

She took a deep breath, trying to clear all the fuzz from her mind. Ace-induced fuzz. "I expected better of you."

"That was your first mistake."

"You could work to better yourself now."

"I've done nothing but make efforts to worsen my-self for the past decade, I don't see why I would change course now."

She cleared her throat. "I can think of one."

A heavy, thick silence fell between them. It irritated her. She wanted to go back to before. To being teased. To feeling all fluttery over his smile.

Suddenly, she was angry about all of it. About the fact that she'd spent weeks resisting this beautiful man. About the fact that she'd waited to give in until she'd been desperate enough to forget birth control.

About the fact she had to resist him now because things were complicated and they had a bet with marriage or sanity as the ultimate endgame and that meant no butterflies, no lust and no kissing.

She should have spent every moment from the first time she'd seen him kissing him, because maybe then she wouldn't feel quite so deprived now.

Either way, the opportunity was lost forever now. They had gone from strangers with growing attraction between them to expectant parents who were still basically strangers, and who now had a whole heap of baggage to deal with.

So, the attraction was a not happening thing.

"How far is it to your surprise?" she asked.

"Just to the barn."

They walked the rest of the way in silence and Sierra did her best not to think too deeply. Instead, she closed her eyes and took a breath of the fresh air, letting the cool breeze whip across her face. It was beautiful here at Ace's. It would feel like home easily, quickly. It was exactly the kind of environment she had grown up in. Okay, so it wasn't as plush or as overstated, but it smelled like salt, and pine, and horses. Those were all the things she liked best.

Eventually, they would have to work out some kind of rent situation. She couldn't continue living here and paying nothing. It didn't feel right. But also, she didn't know if moving away from the property—at least when their child was a baby—would be the best plan. No, living right on the same piece of land seemed like it would be a wonderful compromise for shared custody. That way, neither of them would feel as if they were missing anything.

Well, you'll only have your child part of the time.

That made her stomach sink. But if she and Ace never became bitter exes, it wouldn't be the same as it was for most people in her situation. It could be completely workable. There would be no reason for them to have separate birthday parties for their child. No reason to have separate Christmases. They would share it altogether.

Right. And someday, Ace's wife and the rest of his children are just going to be thrilled that the woman he had a one-night stand with and his child are crashing all of their family get-togethers.

She gritted her teeth, setting her chin. Well, whoever the woman was, she would have to get used to that. Just as the man she eventually married would have to deal with the fact that Ace was in her life.

It would work.

Anyway, eventual spouses were not her top concern right now. It was just getting through this. Navigating the day-to-day changes and strangeness that were coming out of this circumstance. She would worry about the rest when she actually came to it.

The doors to the barn were already open, and she followed Ace inside, and down the row of stalls.

"I called your sister this afternoon."

"My sister?" she asked, upping her pace.

"Yes. She helped make all this possible."

"What?"

He stopped in front of the stall at the end of the road, wrapping his fingers around the bars. "Say hi to Lemon Drop."

Her heart slammed against her breastbone, her stomach twisting up. "Lemon Drop. You went and got my horse for me?"

"Yeah. Madison was happy to help."

"Was she?"

"Yes. In fact, she said it made the entire situation a little less upsetting."

"What situation? Us having a baby?"

He smiled, leaning back against the stall door and crossing his arms over his broad chest. "She thinks I'm nice."

"That's only because she had about one conversation with you."

"I went and got your horse for you."

She smiled at him, if a little begrudgingly, and turned toward the stall. Her heart—it turned out—might be made of cotton candy now. Because it completely melted at the sight of Lemon Drop. Her beautiful palomino that she had figured she wouldn't get to ride anymore. At least, not until she worked things out with her parents. And since she had no idea when that might be, she had no idea when she might be back in the saddle again.

She supposed she could have arranged to have the horse brought to Colton's house herself. But she had been so caught up in keeping the job at the bar, and in general dealing with the emotional trauma of her life, that she hadn't really thought it was in her horse's best interest.

But she could not be sorry that Ace had brought her here.

"I'm going to increase the pay for the kids who take care of my horses already. That way, you don't have to worry about her being taken care of. Or her getting ridden enough. I imagine you won't be riding because of the pregnancy."

Sierra had no idea. None of her friends had had babies yet. And she had been so far off from this place in her mind that she hadn't collected any information on the subject. "I guess I'm going to have to talk to a doctor about that. I really don't know."

"Well, either way, you don't have to worry about it now. But I thought you might want your horse close. And," he said, moving away from the stall and heading toward the back door of the stable, "I'm not done."

"What more can there possibly be?"

"Come out to the arena." He opened the door that led out back behind the stalls and she followed him through it, stopping dead in her tracks when she saw the covered arena. He had set up a barrel racing course inside of it.

Now she really was afraid she would cry. She didn't really know how to handle this newer, nicer Ace.

"I might not get to use it for a million years."

"Or nine months."

"Same thing. Anyway, it will be way longer than nine months. Do you honestly think I am getting straight back into the saddle after I push something the size of an... Well, the size of the baby out from... There."

He winced. "Okay. Well, this will be available for you whenever you decide you're ready."

"This is... I really can't think of anything else that would have made me feel more at home. Thank you."

She swallowed hard, her throat suddenly feeling dry and prickly. It was a little too early for her to be having hormone fluctuations. Which meant she was just having feelings. She preferred the idea of hormone fluctuations.

"I want you to feel at home here."

She scuffed her toe through the dirt, leaving the deep groove behind. "I appreciate that. Really. I think that living here after the baby is born is probably the best decision."

"I agree," he said. There was a note of something triumphant in his voice and she felt the need to issue a correction.

"So you can be around our child. Not for any other reason."

He lifted his shoulder. "Okay."

He was being far too casual and she didn't trust it. Not at all. "That's it?"

"We have an agreement. I don't see any need to harp on my view of things. I think you're well aware of it."

"I don't trust any of this," she said, gesturing to the barrels.

"Are you looking a gift horse in the mouth? Because you aren't supposed to do that."

She sighed. "Well, I'm doing a lot of things I'm not supposed to do lately, aren't I?"

"I assume you're referring to the pregnancy."

"Mostly the events leading up to it."

He raised a brow, shoving his hands deep in his pockets. He looked… He looked almost boyish, mischievous right now. And most definitely irresistible. How annoying. "I wish I could say I'm sorry about that."

"You're kind of impossible."

"But nice," he pointed out. "A little bit ago you said I was nice."

"Right. That was before I realized there were ulterior motives at play."

"You are too suspicious." He turned and started to head back toward the barn. "You want help unloading all your stuff?"

She thought about it for a second. She should do her

best to get rid of him. Obviously, her resistance to him was at some kind of a low, so she should get back to her little house, and get some space. But she really did want help.

"If you don't mind," she said.

"Of course I don't mind."

She made a face at his retreating back as she followed him back to the stalls and to where they had parked their trucks. He didn't mind because he was being sneaky. He was trying to bring her around to his crazy, marriage-minded way of thinking. But she was not that easy. She would not be bought with a horse and a barrel racing course. Though she imagined that people had been bought for a lot less. Succumbing because of a pony really was not the worst thing. There was a little bit of pride left in it, at least.

"I bought a lot of stuff," she said.

He approached the back of the truck and leaned over the edge of the tailgate. "No kidding."

She took a moment to admire... Well, everything about him. His broad shoulders, his narrow waist, the way the battered denim clung to his butt. In his standard uniform of flannel shirt and faded jeans he was hotter than any guy in a suit she had ever seen.

He bent forward, reaching in to the bed of the truck and pulling out five bags, looping handles over his forearm. Then he bent forward again, grabbing more.

"You aren't trying to get them all, are you?"

"Of course I am. We don't need to take two trips."

"I have dishes in there. They're only wrapped in paper."

"I'll be careful."

"You had better. Because those contain all my earthly possessions."

"What all did you get?"

She watched him continue to load up his arms. She gave up the idea of scolding him. Pretty soon, he had everything from the truck hanging from his arms, the bags dangling from fingertips to elbows.

"Things. For the house. It was as empty as you said it was, and I figured that I would fill it up."

She had bought two sets of dishes for the kitchen, towels for the bathroom, soap dispensers, towel racks and a lot of other things. She had left the acquisition of any furniture for another day. She had also passed on any baby supplies. Even though walking by the aisle had made her chest seize up and her throat nearly close. She had intended to walk through and see what kind of things there were.

But she had decided against it. She didn't want to end up having an emotional moment in the middle of the store. And anyway, she was so early in her pregnancy. She had nearly had a crisis then and there. Because maybe it was too early to be making any of these changes. Maybe she should have waited to move on to Ace's property. Maybe she should have at least gone to the doctor first.

But it was too late for second thoughts. And too early to be looking at baby supplies.

They walked quickly down the path and she rushed to open the door for him. He walked inside, carefully depositing the bags on the couch, and on the floor in front of it.

"You're going to need a dining table and chairs."

She nodded. "Among other things. But I'll cross that

bridge when I come to it. For now, I don't mind eating cereal sitting over here on the couch."

"You're also always welcome over at my house for meals. I've been a bachelor for a long time, I imagine I cook a lot more than you do."

That was something else that hadn't occurred to her. She didn't know how to cook. She was such an idiot. New things kept coming up, pretty much on the hour, that made her feel helpless. It made her feel like she had no idea what she was doing with her life.

When she'd been in college she'd had a meal plan, and otherwise she and her friends had simply gone out. When she lived at home, their housekeeper cooked. And at Colton's the situation was the same. While she knew, logically, she no longer had a housekeeper, apparently the implications of that had yet to sink in.

"Probably." She admitted that slightly grudgingly.

"The invitation is open. I don't want you to starve."

"I hear I'm eating for two now. Or, one and a grain of rice."

A strange expression passed over his face, like a sneaker wave had overtaken him on the shore, leaving him shocked, shaken. "True enough. Okay, I suppose I'll leave you to it."

She nodded. "Okay."

For some reason, she didn't want him to leave. Because at least he was experiencing the same strange mix of emotions that she was. At least he was knocked off-kilter, too. She hadn't fully appreciated that until this moment. He had felt like the commander, the one who was steering this crazy ship. Only now did she realize he was just as lost as she was. Just as at the mercy of the storm as she was. He was just handling it differently.

But she had a feeling if he stayed she would want to get closer to him. Want to touch him. Want for him to take her into his arms. And really, that was why she was in this situation in the first place. The fact that she found him more or less irresistible.

Adding to that, now she wanted to lean on his strength.

But she couldn't do that. She had to learn to stand on her own.

"Thank you," she said, finally. "For all of this." *Except for the ultimatum.* But she didn't voice that last part out loud.

"You're welcome. Thank you for not scampering off into the hills."

She lifted her shoulders. "I guess it's the least I could do."

"Right."

He just stood there, and so did she. She didn't know what to do. Didn't know how to deal with him now. "If you need any more help on the brewery plans, I am more than happy to pitch in. Hell, it's my child support now."

He chuckled. "I suppose it is."

He was being too nice. She was deeply suspicious of it. He should have at least given her side eye for that comment. She had to remember that even though they were in the same boat, he was intent on manipulating the boat.

"Well," she said, "good night."

He nodded once. "Good night."

Then he turned and walked out of the little house, leaving her there surrounded by the results of her shopping spree. She sighed heavily, suddenly feeling way too tired to unpack anything. Suddenly feeling so exhausted she wasn't even sure she could continue to stand, much less put all of the dishes and various other things away.

She wandered down the short hallway and into the little bedroom, staring at the small bed in the corner. She
had a strong sense of déjà vu. Of that night she had had
sex with Ace and he had taken her up to the room above
the bar. Standing in front of that bed and feeling that
same sense of being outside her body, outside of reality.

She moved over to the bed and sat on the edge, her
heart pounding heavily. She didn't know how she had
ended up here. She lay down slowly, stretching her arms
out to the side, her head tilted back, her eyes closed.

When she opened her eyes again it was because of
the sound of thunder rumbling in the distance. She must
have fallen asleep. She didn't know for how long. She
could hear rain pounding on the roof of the small house,
could hear a small, tinny sound coming from a different
room. Probably a leak in the roof hitting a pan that was
strategically positioned beneath it.

For a few moments, she wasn't entirely sure where she
was. But then she remembered. This was her new house.
She was living on Ace Thompson's property, because
she was having his baby and they were going to try and
figure out exactly how to handle things between them.

She sat bolt upright, her heart struggling to free itself
from her chest.

Adrenaline poured through her veins, terror. She was
having a baby. She had no idea how she had been so eff-
ing calm through all of this. Through these past couple
days of making major life decisions and changes.

She had been shocked when she found out, yes, but she
hadn't panicked. Right now, she was panicking.

She put her hand on her chest, felt her heart raging beneath her fingertips. How was she going to do this? How
was she supposed to raise a baby? She couldn't even raise

herself. She didn't know how to cook. She didn't know how to keep the house clean. She didn't know how to do anything. She couldn't even remember the last time she had held a baby. Had she ever held a baby?

Somehow, she was supposed to now be responsible for her own child. She couldn't fathom how she was supposed to do that. Couldn't fathom how she had ever thought she could. She couldn't do this. She couldn't do it alone. She probably couldn't even do it with help.

Without thinking, she stood up, walking to the bedroom door and out toward the front of the house. She had left her shoes sitting by the door. She slipped them on her feet. She was still dressed from earlier, wearing a T-shirt and jeans and nothing more.

She opened the door, stepping out onto the porch. The air was thick, cold and heavy. Rain fell heavy past the small shelter of the porch, falling so hard onto the ground it felt like God was pelting the earth with a handful of rocks.

For some reason, she had the thought that she might as well go stand down there beneath the rain. She was already wet.

She walked slowly down the stairs, fat drops landing on her face, her chest, piercing the thin fabric of her T-shirt and leaving her cold, shivering. She kept walking, though she wasn't entirely sure where she was going. But she kept on down the path, no light guiding her, her hand stretched out in front of her to keep from running into the trees.

She continued until she came out to the clearing. Her hair was so wet it was sticking to her neck, her face. She pushed it away, ignoring the way the fabric of her clothing clung to her.

She looked toward Ace's house. It was dark. It was

probably really late, though she hadn't bothered to check the time. A clock was another thing she would have to get. Something for her bedside. A weird thought to have while she was standing out in the dark getting poured on. But she wasn't sure if there were any normal thoughts in this circumstance.

She started to walk away from the house, toward the barn. And she realized that she had been headed toward Lemon Drop this entire time. With her horse, there was at least some familiarity. Some chance of comfort.

She pushed open the doors to the barn, leaving them cracked a little bit, before making her way down to the end of the line of stalls. She unlatched the door, pulling it open before slipping inside.

Lemon Drop was lying down on the floor of the stall and Sierra stretched her hand out, placing her fingertips on the horse's forelock before sliding them down toward her nose. She inhaled deeply, taking in Sierra's scent. Otherwise, the sleepy animal didn't budge. But Sierra was fairly satisfied she wasn't going to panic her by sitting on the floor with her.

She sat down against the horse's side. It was her turn to inhale the familiar smell of horse and hay, letting the sweet, musky scent wash over her. There was something simple about this. Something perfect.

It made her wish she could go back in time. To when life was as simple as hoping she did well in her next barrel racing event. Planning the next moment she was going to go out and ride. Spending the day exhausting herself out in the stables before going up to her familiar room, the one she had spent her entire life in, and climbing into the same bed she had had since childhood, curling up on the familiar mattress and finding the same sort of sleep she always had. Her dreams full of fields and the pounding of horses' hooves.

Tonight, she hadn't dreamed at all. And she had woken up on a hard mattress to the sound of thunder. To the realization that there was a season of her life that had passed forever, one that would never come around again. And that she was in a new phase she couldn't predict or understand.

A tear rolled down her cheek, splashing down onto her hand. She did nothing to wipe it away. She took a deep, gulping breath, trying to get a hold of herself. But it was too late. Something in her chest was cracked, her emotions pouring through it, stinging her eyes, running down her cheeks.

She draped her arm over her horse's back, resting her face on the animal's body. She closed her eyes and gave in to her misery, crying until her throat hurt. She couldn't remember crying like this since she was a kid. Back when a scraped knee or the diner having the wrong flavor of ice cream was tantamount to the world ending.

But this couldn't be fixed with a Band-Aid, or by trying a new flavor and finding you actually liked it better. There was no easy fix to this.

Still, maybe she would get herself a Band-Aid and some Tillamook Mudslide ice cream anyway.

The thought made her laugh. And the motion of laughter dissolved into sobbing quickly. She was going crazy. It was entirely possible. She let out a low, miserable sound, rubbing her face against Lemon Drop's back.

The sound of the stall door sliding open jolted her out of her moment of misery.

"What are you doing in here?"

CHAPTER FIFTEEN

SHE LIFTED HER HEAD, turning to see Ace looming in the open door. "Having a nervous breakdown, can't you tell?"

"That is kind of what it looks like." She wiped her arm underneath her nose, then her fingers under her eyes, well aware that the action wasn't particularly sexy. Not really caring. He stepped into the stall, crouching down beside her, putting his hand on her cheek. "You're freezing cold."

Was she? Suddenly, now that he had said that, she realized that she was shivering. That her cheeks felt like they had been bitten by frost, and her lips were numb. "I walked out in the rain," she said.

"I see that," he said, his voice tense.

"I just... I woke up and..."

"I know. You set my alarm off. Because I don't really want people wandering around in my barn at two in the morning, so I have a system to notify me in case something is going on. But I don't think you're a burglar."

She shook her head. "No. I'm not burgling anything."

He leaned closer, wrapping her face with his hands, tilting her face upward, brushing the damp hair off of her forehead. "So what exactly are you doing?"

"I already told you."

"Nervous breakdown?"

She nodded, swallowing hard, trying to keep a fresh

batch of tears from running down her face. She shivered again.

He swore. "We should get you inside."

"I'm fine—"

Before she could finish the rest of her sentence she found herself being scooped up off the floor of the stall, and lifted up into his arms. He cradled her against his chest, holding her like she weighed nothing, and even in her distressed state she found that... Well, she didn't exactly know what. She only knew that it made her heart flutter a little bit.

He carried her out of the stall, then kept his hold on her as he reached out and slid the door closed behind them. Then he continued walking out of the barn, taking both of them back out into the rain. It was still pouring hard, each drop of rain splashing in the puddles around their feet. He continued on toward the house, holding her close as the rain pelted them both. She curled her fingers around his shirt, clinging to him, even though she knew he held her securely enough.

There was something comforting about being held like this. About him holding her up against his beating heart. It made her feel not so alone. Not quite so desolate.

Exhaustion flooded her, deep, down to her bones. And she sank into his hold, letting everything else melt away. Maybe she was going crazy, but at least Ace was here.

ACE BIT BACK a curse as he kicked open the front door of his house, keeping hold of Sierra as he maneuvered it back shut again. She was trembling, freezing and soaking wet in his arms, and about as substantial as a rag doll.

He should have known this was coming. That all of her determination, her spunk and her resilience were going to crumble eventually. It was one thing for him to deal with it. He wasn't the one facing down nine months of pregnancy. He was also thirty-five, not twenty-five. Had already experienced some of the ways that being a parent could change you. Enough that he knew he wanted to do it again.

Sierra didn't know any of that.

"I'm going to put you in the shower," he said, his voice gruffer than he intended it to be.

He felt her nod against his chest as he continued up the stairs toward the master bedroom. He carried her into the bathroom, then set her down gingerly as he turned the water on.

"You're going to have to get rid of these clothes," he said.

She just stood there, her arms wrapped around her midsection as she stared vacantly into the mirror above the sink.

"Or I can take care of it for you."

She nodded again. He moved forward, his own hands unsteady as he grabbed hold of the hem of her T-shirt and peeled it up over her head. She had a plain white bra on underneath, nothing that was designed to get a man's blood pumping hotter. And yet, his was.

Jerk. She's obviously going through something, and you are checking her out.

Well, sure. He was a man, after all. He wasn't a saint, and he had never claimed to be. Being gentlemanly in the situation was decidedly above his pay grade. But, while he might not be able to keep his thoughts pure, he was going to endeavor to be a little bit better with his actions.

He reached around behind her, unhooking her bra with one hand and letting it fall down her arms before he

pulled it off and cast it onto the floor. Then he made quick
work of her jeans, taking her panties down with them as
he struggled to get the wet denim off. Then, he waged
an even more intense struggle to keep his eyes off of her.

He put his hand beneath the spray and discovered it
was hot. "Okay, time to get in."

He led her gently into the shower, and she grabbed
hold of his shirt, pulling him inside, clothes and all.
Then she folded herself into his embrace, resting her
head against his chest, her naked body pressed against
his clothed one. He froze, keeping his hands down at his
sides, because he didn't trust himself to do the right thing
here. He didn't trust himself to do much of anything. So
he just stood there, and let her rest against him. Let her
take whatever it was she needed from this.

Finally, he lifted one hand, pressing it against the center of her back. Her skin was still chilly from those wet
clothes. He shifted their positions so that she was the one
getting most of the hot water. Then he took a bar of soap
from the ledge, suddenly very conscious of the fact that
he didn't have a loofah, or whatever other girlie nonsense
women liked to have in these situations.

He sent the soap down, turning her so that she was
facing the wall, away from him. Then he slid his hands
from her shoulders, down her back, to the curve of her
ass, stopping just short of anywhere too inappropriate.
She didn't tell him to stop, though. Instead, she made a
small, satisfied sound, and he closed his eyes, gritting
his teeth, trying to keep a handle on himself.

"Tell me to stop," he said, running his hands over the
bar of soap again.

She shook her head.

He put his hands on her shoulders again, this time running them down her arms. "Are you feeling warmer?"

Again, he got a silent nod.

He reached over and picked up a bottle of shampoo, squirting a small amount in his hand before placing it back on the shelf in the shower. Then he started to work his fingers through her hair, lathering it up as he did. He had never done anything like this in his life. Not even for his wife. He wasn't exactly sure why he was doing it now. He just wanted to fix whatever was happening with her. Wanted to heal the broken thing inside of her that he knew he was responsible for.

There were a lot of broken things left in his wake. No, he hadn't been the one to break his marriage or his family apart. But the rifts were still a part of his legacy. Then there was his biological family. His parents. His sister. Relationships that he couldn't handle because he had forgotten how to build bridges.

He only knew how to destroy them.

He needed to build a bridge between himself and Sierra. And if it had to start here—washing her hair, while he let water wash over his T-shirt and jeans—well, then he would damn well start here.

He worked his fingers slowly through her long hair, before adjusting her slightly and helping rinse all of the soap out. She made another satisfying noise, one that spurred him on. One that echoed deep inside of him, made his stomach tight, wrenched the growing desire inside of him higher, impossibly so.

Buried beneath everything that had happened in the past few days was the fact that he still wanted her more than he had wanted any other woman in recent memory. Maybe ever.

He wished they could go back to that. Just to the wanting. Rather than the result of the having.

He lathered up his hands again, sliding them down her rib cage, her narrow waist, then back around, moving over her breasts, the contact sending a jolt through him like a lightning bolt.

She leaned back against him, her head rested on his chest, her bottom fitted up against his hardening erection.

"You're upset," he said.

"Very," she murmured.

"I think you should just go to sleep. After you get warm, and dried off, of course."

"What if I don't want to sleep?"

"I'm not sure you should make a decision like that while you're upset."

She turned to face him. "I made a decision like this while I was drunk. I don't see why I shouldn't make it while I'm upset."

She looped her arms around his neck, pressing her breasts to his chest. "Don't test how nice of a guy I am. You're going to be disappointed by the results."

"I don't want you to be a nice guy. Not right now."

"You need a nice guy," he said, resting his hand on her ass, just resting it there. Not exploring any of her slick, plump flesh, not like he wanted to. "Right now, you could really use a nice guy who tucks you into bed and leaves you alone. Who reminds you that we're in this mess because of the attraction between us. Who reminds you that this isn't something you want."

She shook her head, and he couldn't tell if the drops on her face were from the shower or from tears. "I don't want to be alone."

He reached behind her, shutting the water off. Cursing himself while he did.

"That isn't a great reason for sex."

She got out of the shower by herself, taking a towel off of the rack and wrapping it around her curves before disappearing into the next room. He let out a harsh breath and stripped his clothes off in the shower, leaving them lying on the floor as he went after his own towel. He wrapped it around his waist and went into his bedroom, expecting to find it empty. Instead, she was there, sitting on the edge of the bed, the towel still covering her curves. She looked up, a determined expression in her blue eyes.

"That's not the only reason," she said, her voice soft.

"What's the other reason?"

She shook her head. "I just want you. No matter what, no matter what's going on, no matter how crazy it all is, I still want you. I was walking behind you earlier and had to remind myself of all the baggage that's between us now, because mainly, I just wanted to check you out."

He curled his fingers tightly around the towel, trying to fight the urge to drop it and go over to the bed, pull her into his arms and lay her flat across the mattress. "That isn't going to solve any of your problems."

"But it'll make me feel better for a while." She stood up, walking toward him, releasing her hold on the towel and letting it fall to the floor. "Make me feel better."

And with that, all of his good intentions were reduced to ash. He was a man, he wasn't made of stone.

He had told her they would find themselves here. And he was dimly aware that he should be rejoicing in his win. But he didn't feel like rejoicing. Instead, he felt humbled. And needy. Very, very needy. He couldn't crow about his victory, because his brain didn't even work right. He just wanted her.

And he wasn't strong enough to resist her wanting him back.

SIERRA KNEW THAT she was losing their wager. She didn't care. She couldn't bring herself to care at all. Not when she wanted him this badly. Not when she wanted nothing more than to lose herself completely in the heat and fire that built so easily between them. She was so cold. Cold from the inside out. Terrified about what the future might hold. But this thing between them, at least it made sense.

It was simple. It was need. In its purest, most undiluted form. She had never wanted a man the way that she wanted Ace. It had been that way from the first moment she'd seen him. And she knew it had been the same for him. No matter how irritating he found her, no matter how prickly he was to her, they wanted each other.

And now she was standing completely naked in front of him while he looked at her like she was the fulfillment of his every dirty wish.

This felt good. It felt right. She was going for it.

She curled her arm around his neck and rose up on her tiptoes, brushing his mouth with hers before settling more firmly against his lips, taking a slow, leisurely taste of him. He stiffened beneath her touch, but he didn't pull away. She sank more deeply into the kiss, his rough chest hair stimulating her sensitive nipples. He raised his hand, resting it gently on her hip as she continued to explore his mouth with her tongue.

She reached down between them, grabbing a hold of the towel that was resting precariously on his narrow hips, and she pulled it away, letting it drop to the floor.

He growled then, raising his other hand, planting both palms firmly on her ass cheeks, pulling her forward, rolling his pelvis against her, showing her the exact effect she was having on his body.

Yes. This was familiar at least. This didn't feel terrifying. This felt like coming home.

She broke the kiss, taking a step back, taking a moment to admire his body. She didn't feel like she had been able to do that their first time together. It had been too fraught, too quick. Everything had been fuzzy. Well, it wasn't now.

She was seeing sharp and clear. This moment was in brilliant Technicolor, moving in slow motion, allowing her to take it all in. He was gorgeous. From those dark, intense eyes, his straight nose and sharp jaw to his broad shoulders and chest. His masculine perfection, each muscle like a notch carved in stone, so purposeful, so finely honed.

He closed the distance between them, wrapping his arms around her, drawing her up against his body, his arms engulfing her completely, his palms pressed flat between her shoulder blades. The way he held her, he made her feel so small, so petite. Like he could hold every single one of her problems in those strong arms capably, easily.

And she wanted to let him. More than anything she wanted to let him.

He moved his hands down to her butt, then lower, to her thighs. He gripped her tight, lifting her up, wrapping her legs around his waist as he walked them both to the bed. He pressed her into the mattress, kissing her deeply as he did, his hands holding her tightly, blunt fingertips digging into her skin. She was sure he would leave a mark behind, and the thought secretly thrilled her.

He already left a mark, and there will be a very visible outward sign soon.

She pushed the thought away. Right now, all she wanted to think about was how much she wanted him. Not the consequences of that desire, not what it might mean tomorrow. Not what it would certainly mean in nine months. She just wanted to focus on him. On the moment.

She slid her hands down his chest, relishing the feel of his hard muscles beneath her fingertips. He was so perfectly masculine in every way, so very different from her. She loved touching every hard, well-defined inch of him.

Her major regret about their last time together was the fact that she hadn't gotten to taste enough of him.

She wasn't nervous this time. Not about her inability to have an orgasm. She didn't doubt that she would. How could she, after how good last time had been? Anyway, her own pleasure wasn't her top priority at the moment. Or, rather, that ultimate peak of pleasure wasn't her top concern. She had him now, and she was intent on getting what she wanted.

Though Ace seemed intent on driving.

She angled her head, nipping the side of his neck. That surprised him into loosening his grip on her. She slipped away from him, pressing his shoulder, encouraging him to roll onto his back. He didn't resist. She planted her hands on his chest, pressing a kiss between his pecs, then down to his abs. She was traveling a very similar path to the one he had taken their first time together.

She lowered her head again, trailing the tip of her tongue along the well-defined line that cut diagonally down toward the most male part of him. She shifted, curling her hand around his thick arousal, squeezing him gently as she pressed her lips to his shaft.

He jerked beneath her touch and she tightened her hold as she flicked her tongue over the head of his cock. Then she worked her hand down to the base of him as she took him into her mouth, savoring the flavor of him, the feel of him against her tongue.

He grabbed hold of her hair, sinking his fingers deep into the strands as he held on to her while she continued to pleasure him, while she continued to pleasure them both.

She loved this. Everything about it. The way that he shook because of what she was doing to him. He was so big, so strong. When he held her in his arms he felt like a mountain. Right now, she was making the mountain move.

"Baby," he said, his voice strained. "Sierra. Not like this."

She had to agree with him, only because she was desperate for some satisfaction. Still, she couldn't resist sliding her tongue along his length, teasing him just a little bit more. He tightened his hold on her hair, drawing her away from him. The pain sent a shock of electricity straight down her spine, arousal pooling between her thighs, an empty ache starting to grow there that she knew only he could satisfy.

He grabbed hold of her legs again, positioning her over him, before sliding his hands up to her hips, holding tightly on to her as he guided her over his arousal, teasing the entrance to her body.

She let her head fall back as she lowered herself onto him, just a little bit, teasing them both with the near penetration. She gasped as she gave herself an inch, then took it away. She could stay like this forever. Hovering on the knife edge between pleasure and pain, between satisfaction and desperation. Except she didn't have the restraint to hold that much longer.

Slowly, she took him inside, inch by agonizing inch. When she was fully seated on him, he tightened his hold, keeping her still for a moment. She looked down at his expression, at the intense concentration on his face.

She established a slow, steady rhythm, designed to torture them both. To hold them back from the edge of completion, to take them there, right there, and keep them from going over. She had never been able to tease herself like this before. Had never been poised on the brink in such a delicious, exceptional way. Before, it had always been a frustration to reach this point, because she had known she would never be able to go all the way. With Ace, it was a certainty. And knowing her destination, she was able to enjoy the journey that much more.

He slipped his hands around, holding on to her ass, guiding her movements as he thrust up inside of her, increasing the intensity, pushing them both closer. He wasn't going to allow a slow tease, not anymore. And, she wasn't going to fight it. Not when she wanted it so badly. Not when she wanted him so badly. Everything he wanted to give.

Suddenly, he reversed their positions, rising above her, thrusting hard inside of her. She gasped, lifting her hips from the bed, meeting his every movement with one of her own. He lowered his head, his lips crashing down on hers as he thrust into her one last time. He shattered, a deep growl rumbling in his chest. And then she broke in two, pleasure blossoming inside of her like a slow crack across ice, feathering outward until it shattered the entire surface, leaving nothing behind but glittering dust, so irrevocably destroyed it could never be put back together again. Not as it was.

He moved away from her, rolling onto his back, taking her with him. They were both breathing hard, aftershocks of pleasure moving through her. And left in its wake was an intense crash of emotion. Everything had seemed clear only a moment ago. And now she just felt tired. Of course, it was the wee hours of the morning, so that could explain it. Though she had kind of been operating on these hours for the last few weeks, so maybe the time had less to do with it than she might think.

"Get some sleep," he said, tightening his hold on her. "We'll talk in the morning."

CHAPTER SIXTEEN

THE NEXT MORNING'S conversation was served with coffee, and without clothes. Not exactly how Sierra had imagined planning her future, but, all things considered, she would take it.

Ace set a tray with coffee and pastries down in front of her, then slid into bed beside her, beneath the covers. It was early. Much too early for how late they had been up. But now that she was awake, she couldn't go back to sleep anyway.

Last night came and slapped her in the face almost as soon as she opened her eyes. She was *so* embarrassed. She had shown that kind of weakness, that kind of vulnerability in front of him. Embarrassed that she had experienced it at all. It wasn't like her. Usually, she was stronger than that. More resilient. But then, usually she wasn't pregnant and faced with the fact that she didn't know how to do anything. So, all things considered, she didn't really blame herself.

"We don't have to talk before you drink a cup, if you don't want," he said, keeping an eye on her as she raised the coffee mug to her lips.

"Well, with you staring at me like that, we might as well just go ahead and talk."

She shifted, moving up the headboard, trying to keep the blankets in place. There was really no point in being

modest in front of him, and she didn't have any issues
with her body, but it just seemed weird to have coffee
with your boobs out in front of a guy you'd only slept with
twice. Besides, it seemed like a burn hazard.

"I'm going to phrase this in a way that's potentially
ungentlemanly," he said.

She braced herself for commentary on the aforepon-
dered body part. "Okay."

"You lost the bet."

His words were a million times more galling than
commentary about her figure ever could be. "Oh."

"I told you, it's ungentlemanly. And I didn't want to
go there. But, the fact remains, you lost. I was right."

She worried her lower lip between her teeth. He was
right. She had lasted all of twelve hours at his place without jumping his bones. Of course, there had been extenuating circumstances. But it was very likely there would
always be some kind of circumstance. Something that
was distressing or upsetting. And what would she do
then? Would she always run to him? Seek shelter in his
arms?

"It was an anomaly," she lied.

"No," he said emphatically, "it's us. It's always going
to be messy, it's always going to be intense, but it's always going to be there between us. So, what's the down-
side to getting married?"

"Bitter unhappiness and a potential ugly divorce?"

"I guess those are possibilities. But those are always
possibilities when you jump into a relationship. I think
we're better off trying to make a family with each other
than we are trying to make one with someone else, don't
you?"

The logic in his statement shook something loose inside of her. Probably the newfound insecurity that she felt over every little thing that she suddenly realized she couldn't do. She had never noticed the dearth of skills in her possession because she had never been forced to confront them. But now, she was poised on the brink of being the responsible adult in the room, and she suddenly realized she didn't know how to be a responsible adult.

"Pregnancy is not the right reason to get married," she insisted.

"What are the right reasons to get married, then? Why did your parents get married?"

She shrugged. She honestly didn't have the answer to that question. "I don't really know."

"We have a lot more between us than a hell of a lot of people do. The kind of attraction we have… That's not normal. It's also the problem. It's why we can't pretend we're just going to be platonic parenting partners. Because you and I will get drunk one New Year's Eve and screw things up royally for whatever relationship we're actively trying to have. Give our child false hope of being together one Christmas when they catch us making out under the mistletoe. And they will. Because what we have is too strong to ignore. And it's as good a foundation as any in my opinion."

"Why did you marry your first wife? Because she was pregnant. *And* I assume you were attracted to her."

He shook his head. "Not like this. I married her because it was the right thing to do. When I say that, I mean morally. I felt really strongly about it at the time. I can't say that I don't now. It's pretty ingrained. In spite of the fact that I more or less walked away from what my father taught me, I still believe a lot of what the old man says. But it's more than that with us. It's common sense."

"To you." And to her. She didn't want to admit it. She didn't want to admit that she was starting to think he might not be as crazy as she had initially accused him of being.

He lifted up one of the plates that was sitting on the tray. "Croissants?"

She eyed the offered treat suspiciously. "Did you make these?"

"I did. I mean, they were frozen, and I set them out overnight to rise but I baked them."

"Wow." She picked one up off the plate and took a bite of it. It was flaky and perfect. And she hated him for being more proficient in the kitchen than she was.

"We have a lot more going for us than most people," he repeated. "Plus, I make coffee and croissants. I think we can make this work."

She looked around his bedroom, at the complete *matching* furniture set. It was sparse, sure. The navy blue curtains totally practical and nothing more. The bed-spread was the same flannel as the shirts that he wore, leading her to believe he'd gotten some kind of deal on the fabric and commissioned a seamstress to do the work for him.

The bed frame was large, made from natural wood, and the dresser and nightstands matched. It was very much a man's space, but it was definitely lived in. Much more than the bedroom in the little house she was currently inhabiting.

"If we get married you're going to have options," he continued. "You won't have to work. Especially if I get my brewery business off the ground. You can decide whether or not you want to be a stay-at-home mom. Or if you want to get a job. Start up a business. Go back to school for something else. If you have me to help support you, to help with the child, your options are a lot more open. I'll pay child support if you aren't with me, but that's different than being part of the same household. It's never going to be as much."

He was dangling a very impressive carrot in front of her nose. She wished that she were a little bit stronger. That it wasn't quite so appealing. That she wasn't quite so afraid.

He was the biggest enticement he was offering and he didn't even know it. She was afraid of being alone, and he was offering her someone to stand with. She didn't know she was strong enough to refuse.

At the moment, she didn't even know why she was trying to refuse. He was talking about giving her child a family. And, looking at the state of her own family, she didn't really have all that much to bring to the table.

"Do you see your parents?" she asked. Suddenly, the answer seemed imperative.

"Not as often as I should. But I'm speaking to them, if that's what you mean."

"Did you tell them about the baby?"

"No. I didn't. Because now, for the second time in my life, I have to make that phone call. And I can't say I'm especially looking forward to it."

"What was it like for them? When you came back. When you lost custody of Callie." She felt almost guilty bringing Callie up again. But Callie was the driving force behind Ace's actions and she wanted to fully understand all of it. Everything.

The far-reaching ramification it had on everyone she, and her own child, would eventually touch.

"They had come out to Texas to visit a couple of

times," he said. "They had only seen her twice. But that didn't matter. They couldn't have loved her more. And Hayley, my sister... She was a great aunt. Always so excited to hear about how Callie was growing. They're going to be... They're going to be thrilled. No matter what, trust me when I tell you they're going to be happy to have a grandbaby to spoil. Especially one here in town."

A sudden horrific thought occurred to her. "Oh my gosh. I'm pregnant with the pastor's son's baby out of wedlock." She looked up at him. "Your parents are going to think I'm a scarlet woman."

"My parents are under no illusions about my behavior. They know exactly who I am. They know exactly the kind of thing I do. To their credit, they don't say much about it. But I've never been under the impression they approve much of me."

She set her coffee on the nightstand and buried her face in her hands. "I'm sorry about all of this."

"Stop apologizing. I'm not sorry, Sierra. And I know that may not be something you're ready to hear right now. But I'm not. I was a good father. And I didn't think that I ever wanted to be a father again. Not after the way things ended last time. It hurt. Nobody wants to subject themselves to that kind of thing twice. But, now that it's happening, now that I have a chance again, I know that I want this. You're giving me a second chance, and I kind of hate saying that to you. I know you didn't ask to be my second chance."

His words made her made her heart freeze into a little block in her chest. "I... No, I didn't. But I don't suppose you can help but feel that way."

"I want this baby. I would like for us to be a family."

"And as far as us not…loving each other?"

He laughed, a hollow, bitter sound that ricocheted through her and hit her little frozen chunk of heart, making it hurt. "I've been in love. I married Denise because she was pregnant, but you have to understand that I *wanted* to marry her. I had been wanting to marry her, but I thought it was too soon. But then there was the baby and…I was thrilled when she said yes. I wanted to spend my life with her. I *chose* her. She was the first woman I'd ever been with."

"You mentioned that."

"I used to be a good boy, Sierra," he said, looking at her over his mug, looking like very much not-a-good boy. "I was a virgin until I was twenty-one."

"Holy crap."

"Yep."

"You were…you were a very good boy, weren't you?"

"I didn't even cuss above a whisper until I joined the circuit. And the first time I did that…I waited for a lightning bolt. If not from God, direct from my dad."

"You didn't *cuss*?"

"Shit, no," he said, his expression straight.

"I… You're different."

He grinned. "Well. Obviously my experience with love and marriage had a profound effect on me. In a few ways. I was naive then. I was blinded by the circumstances. I don't want love, not now. I want someone who is committed to building a family. Someone I'm happy enough to come home to. Someone I'm happy to go to bed with at night, and who's happy to go to bed with me. I think that sounds like a pretty damn good life, don't you?"

The picture that he painted wasn't the warmest one. It wasn't a perfect fairy tale full of hearts and roses. But she couldn't deny that it was warmer and rosier than the idea of her living across the property. Of their child having to choose between sleeping in the bigger, more beautiful house, or staying in the little one with her.

"I bought all that stuff for my house," she said.

"And we can use it when we have guests. If you like it better than you like my dishes, we can trade dishes. This is going to be your house too when you marry me, Sierra, and you're free to put your mark on it."

Tears started to spill from her eyes again, sudden, unexpected. "Why do you keep having to be so nice to me?"

"Why are you so upset about it?"

"Because you make it harder and harder to say no. You make me feel like it's stupid to say no."

"Because it is," he said, his tone unrepentant. "We're in this together. So, let's be in this together."

She took another sip of her coffee and adjusted the blankets again. Then she swallowed hard and looked up, meeting his gaze. "Okay, Ace. I'll marry you."

CHAPTER SEVENTEEN

ACE RARELY SHOWED UP at his parents' house without calling beforehand. In fact, he couldn't remember the last time he had done so in recent years. But he was here now, before heading over to the bar, feeling as nervous as a high school kid who had been caught misbehaving.

Or what he assumed a high school kid felt like when he'd been caught misbehaving. Ace had never misbehaved in high school.

It was a Monday, so the church was closed, and that meant he was pretty sure his father was at home. Unless they were out at some friends' house having an early dinner and playing cribbage. Which seemed like something like they might do.

He pulled into the driveway of the modest white house, and saw the same two old—but pristine—cars in the driveway. Which meant odds were both of his parents were home. He let out a heavy sigh and put his truck in Park.

He sat there a moment, then got out, making his way to the front door. He took his hat off and knocked. He heard footsteps, then the door opened. It was his mother. Her eyes—brown eyes that were exact mirrors of his own—rounded when she saw him.

She looked so small these days. So much older than when he pictured her in his mind. When he thought of his mom, he still thought of her as she'd looked about the time he'd graduated high school. It shocked him every time, how far removed from that she was. How many years had passed with him barely bothering to come by for a visit.

"Ace," she said. "What a nice surprise."

He cleared his throat. "Is Dad home?"

"No, he isn't. He went out fishing with Bud today. Do you want to come in?"

He shook his head. "No, I shouldn't. I just… I wanted to tell you both something. But I'll just tell you."

Her entire face fell. "You're leaving again, are you?" Her voice was tinged with a kind of fear he wouldn't have associated with her thinking he was leaving. He didn't see them often enough for it to make a real impact, in his mind. But she was…impacted by the thought.

"No," he said. "Not leaving. Actually, I'm opening up another business across town."

His mother's expression softened. "That's really nice. What is it going to be?"

"Well, a brewery. So, still alcohol. But a restaurant, too."

Her smile widened a little bit. "I imagine we'll be able to come to that."

Something shifted in his chest, cracking the wall of granite he kept built up nice and high. "I'd like that. Just let me know, anytime. You know I'll save your table."

"I know you will." She let silence linger for a moment. "What else did you come to talk to me about? I don't think it was the new business or you would have been by to tell me about it a lot earlier."

"Yeah," he said, rubbing the back of his neck. "I just wanted to let you know that I'm getting married."

A look of pure joy flashed across his mother's face and he felt lower than a bag of worms for not making it very clear right from the beginning exactly what kind of marriage it was. But why should he tell her? Why should any of them know? He and Sierra were going to make a relationship that lasted, based on their desire to do something good for their child. No one had to know the finer details about their feelings for each other. No one needed to know about the circumstances surrounding the conception of the baby.

"Yeah. I mean, there's something else, too, though. And you probably won't like it. She's... She's pregnant."

He really did feel like a naughty sixteen-year-old. Or, like the embarrassed twenty-two-year-old he'd been calling thirteen years ago to tell his parents he had gotten his girlfriend pregnant.

"Oh, well," she said, fighting a thread of disappointment in her voice. "It does seem to be the way people do things these days."

Or at least the way *he* did things.

His mother must have caught something in his face, because she continued, "That other woman you married... The baby wasn't even yours. So, don't think I'm judging it as the same thing."

"And you figure this time for sure it's mine?"

"I figure you're not the kind of man who makes mistakes twice," she said. "At least, not the exact same mistakes." She shook her head a little. "You do have your particular vices."

She meant women, he knew that.

"Yeah," he said. "Sierra is a good girl. A nice girl. You'll like her."

She frowned thoughtfully. "Sierra. Why do I know that name?"

"Sierra West. The West family."

Her eyebrows shot up. "Oh."

"Yes. Imagine how thrilled her parents are going to be that she's stuck with me."

Her expression turned fierce. "She could do a lot worse. And spare few people can do better."

The confidence in his mother's voice, the certainty with which she paid him that compliment, was a hell of a lot more than he deserved from anyone, really, but most of all from his mother, who had never really gotten anything special from him.

Nothing other than an adult son who could barely deal with his own issues well enough to engage with his family.

A son who was ashamed to go over for dinner because he smelled like whiskey. From pouring it all night and drinking it all night.

Somehow she still thought he was the best of something.

He wasn't sure he was the best of anything.

"I appreciate that," he said, the words coming out rough.

"It's the truth, Ace. Whether you think so or not."

"Well," he said, "it's your truth."

She smiled sadly at him, stepping to the side in the entry. "Are you sure you don't want to come in?"

He shook his head. "No. I have to get to work. The town won't send itself to hell in a handbasket. Someone has to give it a shove."

"I've never once thought anything bad about what you do for a living," she said, her tone soft.

For a second, her words struck him completely dumb. Made him question a whole lot of things. Question how much baggage he was bringing to their house every time he had dinner. How much of it he was unpacking and putting out on the table without even being asked to.

He cleared his throat. "I'll talk to you later, Mom. We'll have to do another dinner sometime soon."

"Do you want me to tell your father about your engagement?"

Ace nodded, taking a step back away from the door. "If you wouldn't mind."

"And Hayley?"

"I'll... I'll give her a call."

He turned away from the house and walked back to his truck, getting into the cab and slamming the door behind him. He watched as his mother closed the front door, and then he just stared at the house. At the familiar shape of it.

The small, rectangular lawn. The little brick pathway. The same faded curtains hanging in the windows that had always been there. It was like looking at a photograph he'd seen a million times before. But a photograph of a place he'd never been.

He felt so disconnected from this. So disconnected from the man he had been when he had first left this house in search of something bigger and better on the rodeo circuit. It didn't feel like home, because *he* didn't feel the same.

He damn well wished that it did. He wished that he could experience that rush of rightness, of homecoming, that he knew you were supposed to feel when you returned to your childhood house.

But he would have to get back to a person he'd been,

not just the place. And he figured that was an impossibility.

He didn't have any time to worry about it now. He had drinks to serve.

"WHAT DO YOU MEAN you're getting married?"

Sierra looked across the bar at her sister's wide eyes. Madison had come into Ace's tonight to check up on her, and her sister was clearly shocked to find out about her new status update.

"It makes the most sense," Sierra said. She wasn't exactly sure when she had started spouting Ace's party line as fact. But he had a point.

"It makes the most sense to marry a strange guy you slept with once?"

"Oh, I've slept with him more than once," she said, looking down at the bar top and tracing patterns over the wood grain with her fingertips.

"Did he…talk you into marrying him by using sex to muddle your brain?"

"His penis may or may not have been involved in the negotiation process."

"That penis must be some smooth talker."

"It's very…persuasive." She felt her cheeks getting hot. "I'm a little ashamed to admit how easy I made it for him."

"He *is* hot," Madison said. "And—as one who has not been totally immune to male charms in the past—I'm not judging you too harshly."

"But you *are* judging me."

Madison lifted her hand. "Yeah, a little. Also harshly. Just not *too* harshly. Just the right amount of harshly."

"I want my child to have a family. I don't want it to be

broken up. You can understand that, right? Look at all the drama that's happening with Jack, and Dad, and Mom, and the general drama surrounding the West/Monaghan debacle. I want to avoid anything like that."

"Well, Ace doesn't have a wife and other children. So I think you've pretty well avoided it."

"You know what I mean. If we don't get married, then we're going to have to contend with the fact that we'll have separate families to deal with. Separate lives."

"You say that like divorce isn't a thing. Because you know you might end up divorced."

Sierra let out a hard breath. "And then we'll be in the exact same place we're in now. But he… Well, he convinced me that things can never be strictly platonic between us. Our bond isn't exactly a lasting *friendship*. It's more based on a mutual need to screw each other's brains out whenever we're alone."

"That," Madison said, lifting her glass of chardonnay to her lips, "is too much information."

"Well, it's true. I just want you to understand. Don't you know what it's like to be so attracted to somebody you can't think straight?"

Madison tapped the counter. "Not really. I mean, it wasn't exactly like that with He-Who-Must-Not-Be-Named. I was *in love* with him. And because I loved him I let him talk me into a lot of things that I didn't really feel comfortable doing."

Sierra grimaced. "It isn't like that with Ace. He's… He's really not coercing me. I'm not clouded by emotion. But I *am* facing down the reality that he and I probably aren't going to have a very easy platonic relationship."

Madison fiddled with the coaster beneath her glass.

"I just can't believe you're going to be the first one to have kids."

A large roar went up in the crowd, the voices obscuring the country song on the radio, and both Madison and Sierra looked back into the dining room, just in time to watch someone tumble off of Ferdinand and onto the mats below.

Sierra felt a little sorry for the unknown, disgraced person, considering her own inglorious mechanical bull dismount only a few weeks earlier. Madison looked away from the spectacle and back to Sierra. Sierra cleared her throat. "Well, unless we plan this wedding at lightning speed Colton is still probably going to get married first."

"Yeah, unless a miracle happens," Madison said drily.

"I'm not holding my breath for miracles at this point."

Madison took another sip of wine. "You know, Gage could have kids. We don't know. He could be married for all we know."

"I guess so. I kind of still picture him as a teenage boy. But, I guess he's a man and everything now. I mean, I suppose he kept changing after he left."

"He got to escape the family early. There's no way he also found the fountain of youth. That just wouldn't be fair," Madison said.

"I don't want to escape the entire family. Just Mom and Dad for a little while. Actually, really just Dad."

"We both know Mom is pretty intense. I imagine getting away from her for a little while isn't the worst, either."

The door to the kitchen opened and Ace came out. Sierra's stomach turned over, her heart suddenly beating faster. Her entire body gearing up for... Well, the one thing that she wanted when he was around.

Madison's eyes narrowed, her focus now squarely on

Ace. "So," she said, her tone deceptively soft. "You're marrying my sister, I hear."

"That's true," he said.

"I was on board with you procuring her horse for her, but I was unaware you would be using said steed for manipulative purposes."

"I swear to you, the horse was a non-manipulative gesture."

"I don't believe you. Nothing personal. I'm predisposed to being suspicious of men." Madison tilted her head to the side and looked at him as though he were something potentially vile. "I just want you to know, Mr. Thompson, that while I might appear fragile, I grew up on a ranch. Yes, my family is well-to-do, but I made a point to educate myself on the finer workings of horsemanship. All of it. I am well familiar with the process that turns a stallion into a gelding. And I will not hesitate to use it on you if you hurt my baby sister in any way." She smiled then, the expression sweet, her blue eyes glittering. "I may be small, but I am fierce. And I will unleash my fierceness on you without mercy."

"I believe it," he said, his expression mildly amused and more than a little bit impressed.

"Well," Madison said, "now that we have that out of the way, congratulations."

Ace walked up beside Sierra, wrapping his arm around her waist and pulling her close. "Thank you."

It was strange, having him touch her like this in the bar, in full view of everybody. It wasn't as though the relationship was a secret, but they certainly hadn't made it public.

"Okay, you're going to start rumors now," she said, stepping away from him.

"There's nothing wrong with rumors. Anyway, they would be true," he said.

"I'm not sure I'm ready for the broader world to know the circumstances of our lives."

"By which she means Mom and Dad. Oh, and probably Jack."

Sierra groaned. "I forgot that I have another overprotective brother to explain this to. I already weathered talking to Colton."

"I haven't received a single death threat from him," he said. "After meeting your sister I have to say I'm almost disappointed by that."

"I can issue death threats for the both of us," Madison said.

"Clearly."

"So, when is the wedding?" Madison asked.

"As soon as possible," he said, at the same time Sierra said, "After the baby is born."

"You said you wanted to wait until you get a paternity test," Sierra said.

Madison's head whipped toward Ace. "You did *not* say that."

"To be fair, I had a bad experience," he said.

"Still," Madison scoffed. "That's asinine."

"No argument from me," Sierra said. "I don't really see the point of getting married until after," she said, directing that statement at Ace. "Anything can happen between now and then."

"Fine. I can see the point in waiting until after you're twelve weeks along, but after that, I think we should get married. Do you really want our baby *at* the wedding?"

"This isn't 1950. There's nothing wrong with that."

"That's really what you think? That's really what you want the whole town to see?"

She wanted to stomp her feet. "Madison, talk some sense into him."

"I don't have a lot of sense. Just physical threats. But, in this instance, I think he might have a point."

"That isn't fair," Sierra said. "You can't side with him."

"I'm not siding with anyone. I just think you might be happier ultimately if you do it sooner. That way you can prepare for the baby together."

"It isn't like I can't move in with him before we get married," she said.

"I'm just trying to consider the gossip," she said. "With what's happened…"

"I know. Jack. Dad." Sierra scowled, hating that both of them had a point. Hating that she cared. But if a few months made the difference between people viewing their child and marriage as the whoops that it was, and people seeing them as a normal couple… Well, she couldn't think of a good reason not to hurry up and get married.

She wasn't entirely certain that was a correct or stellar reason to go ahead with the marriage. Anyway she had… feelings for Ace. Sex feelings, mostly. But there were some heart feelings, as well. Not love, or anything crazy like that. He didn't believe in love, after all. And she had never been in love before, so she was hardly going to go fall in love with a man she had been involved with—in the loosest sense of the word—for just about a month.

"We'll cross that bridge when we come to it in a few weeks, how about that?" she said.

"Fine with me," he said.

"And you aren't invited to any more life planning sessions," she said, directing that comment at her sister. "Not if you are going to blindly side against me."

"I am on your side. The side of least resistance in terms of how your life will play out later. It's easy to give controversy the middle finger until you've actually experienced the toothy end of it." Madison tapped the counter, standing suddenly. "Well, I'm going to go. It was nice to officially meet you, Ace. I'm sure we'll be seeing a lot of each other."

Madison breezed out, leaving her barely touched glass of wine sitting on the counter.

"Well, she's a whole thing," Ace said.

"Yes, she is. A whole thing that is recently dead to me for taking an opposing stance."

Ace turned to face her, and she backed up against the bar. He moved toward her, gripping the side of the counter, his arms corralling her. "And why exactly is she presenting an opposing stance? I thought you were feeling a little friendlier toward the idea of marrying me."

She swallowed hard, trying to do her best to not get sucked into his dark gaze. He really was overly compelling. "Well, yes, but I thought I would have a little more time to adjust to the idea."

"Does the idea of marriage scare you?" he asked, raising his hand and brushing a strand of her hair out of her face.

"Well, I'm not feeling overly friendly toward the institution. All things considered."

She looked around, trying to gauge the reaction of her coworkers. A few of them had clearly noticed something was going on between Ace and herself, but everyone was going out of their way not to stare too obviously.

"What are you afraid will happen?"

I'm afraid it's just another thing I don't know how to do.

"I don't know. Affairs, secret babies."

He chuckled. "That's the last thing you have to worry about with me."

She bit her lip. "And why exactly should I believe that?"

He frowned. "Because I asked you to?"

"Right. The man who demanded that I get a paternity test thinks he can simply ask for trust and get it."

He sighed heavily, stepping away from her. "Okay, I was out of line. Except I don't really think I was."

"Right. Because you have to protect yourself. Well, I have to protect myself, too."

"My wife had an affair. Believe me when I tell you there aren't very many people on this earth who respect the sanctity of marriage more than I do. Because I've been kicked in the nads by people who didn't."

She gritted her teeth. "Okay, that's fair."

But she couldn't get rid of that nagging little voice that had spoken the truth immediately after he had asked the question. She didn't know how to be a wife. She was facing down the fact that she was about to be a mother, and she was expected to be a wife, too.

She knew how to be a girlfriend for a finite amount of time. She was pretty good at that. At least, she hadn't had any complaints. But she had a feeling that it was a far cry from engaging in a real, long-term relationship.

Being a wife meant that when things got difficult you had to stick it out. You didn't cut and run just because the guy said *anyways* instead of *anyway*, and after six months you wanted to shove the extra letter up his rear.

You had to stick it out. You had to stick it out even when things were hard.

Judging by the way she had handled the situation with her father, she was pretty sure she wasn't a shining example of how to do that.

"I should probably make a doctor's appointment," she said.

"I don't think they usually rush to get you in at this stage."

She shrugged. "Still, I would like to get confirmation."

"All right. I'll go with you."

"You don't have to do that."

"Sierra, you're going to get checked out because you're having my baby. Where else would I be?"

The strength in that statement, the certainty, struck her down deep. She wasn't used to men like this. Her father had barely bothered to show up to major life events after she was born. She couldn't imagine him being doting when she was in a prenatal state.

"I don't know," she said.

"Why don't you make an appointment and just let me know what time I should show up. Better still, I'll take you."

CHAPTER EIGHTEEN

THEY SPENT THE next few days settling in. Sierra had opted to spend the last couple of nights in the small house. And they hadn't had sex again. It had taken a lot more strength than Ace would like to admit not to press that issue.

She was pregnant; for all he knew she might not be feeling very well. Though she hadn't said anything about that.

He had a feeling it was all to do with accepting his proposal and dealing with the implications of it.

She had dinner with him every night, and they spent that time together trying to fill the enormous blank spaces in their knowledge of each other.

She told him about going to school in Eugene, and how waffles with bacon on them from hole-in-the-wall restaurants had been her guilty pleasure while studying. About how her first boyfriend had broken her heart. And how she'd never considered doing anything other than what her father had told her to do. Had never considered living anywhere other than Copper Ridge.

In return, he'd told her all about the rodeo while she'd looked at him with a wistful expression on her face, like the description of dust, hay and animal smells was her idea of heaven, too.

He was discovering she wasn't at all the woman he'd

first assumed she was. He was discovering she was a woman he liked quite a bit.

Still, he missed having her in his bed. He wasn't sure how a woman he'd only had twice had become an elemental kind of need that felt as necessary as breathing. He was going to have to get a handle on that.

Their relationship was going to be based on their desire to do what was right for their child. The passion was an added bonus. It had been instrumental in him convincing her to marry him. But it didn't mean he could just let it burn unchecked.

She had managed to get a doctor's appointment surprisingly quickly. Which was why he found himself up uncharacteristically early again, sitting in the waiting room at the office. That had been her request. He would've happily gone in so that he could be a part of it, but he could see that she needed her space.

She needed a lot of space.

That surprised him the most. She had her little freakout, and she ended that by clinging to him. Since then, he couldn't help but feel like she had been slowly backtracking.

He looked up at the clock. It felt like she had been in with the doctor forever. But it had only been about a half an hour.

He leaned back in the chair, letting out a long sigh.

The front door to the clinic opened, and in walked a mutinous-looking Kate Garrett, followed by her fiancé. Who also happened to be his reluctant fiancée's half brother. So that was great.

Damn small towns.

Kate locked gazes with him, her eyes very round. He

could tell she wanted to ask what he was doing here, but also that she knew it would earn a return question.

He had no idea how to handle this situation. Did you greet people you knew at the gynecologist? Just one of the many things he had never had to deal with before, since he hadn't ever been in a committed relationship while living in Copper Ridge.

"Howdy," Jack said finally, as he and Kate made their way up to the check-in desk.

Ace was suddenly hoping the clock worked in his favor and Sierra stayed back in the office until Kate was called back.

He imagined though, since he was sitting in the middle of the world's most obnoxious coincidence, that was a little bit too much to hope for.

Ace waved, and sat back in his seat, his eyes now firmly fixed on the door. Hoping against hope that a nurse would come out and call Kate, and quickly.

The door did open, but of course, it was Sierra who came out of it, carrying a stack of papers and looking like a particularly waxen ghost. Just about the time Jack and Kate made their way into the waiting area.

Kate and Sierra both froze. The look of abject horror on both of their faces would have been funny, had Ace's entire being not been echoing with the exact same horror.

"Well, isn't this a coincidence," Ace said, standing. He was ready to run for the door in case Jack came after him. Which was potentially not that gentlemanly. But he figured Jack would go after Sierra.

"What is going on?" Jack asked.

"Ace had to give me a ride to a doctor's appointment," Sierra said, edging toward Ace, or—probably more accurately—toward the door.

"If you're going to lie, tell a convincing lie."

"I filled in a whole bunch of forms before I went in here that says I'm entitled to confidentiality," Sierra said.

"Fine," Jack said, crossing his arms across his broad chest. "You're entitled to confidentiality but you have to understand that I'm going to draw my own conclusions. Especially if you're unwilling to share."

He was glaring at Ace now, and it looked like he had murder on his mind.

"I don't have to share," Sierra said, looking righteously indignant. "Come on, Ace." She started to make her way toward the door.

"We're early," Jack said, "actually. Let me walk you out."

Kate looked twitchy and more than a little bit nervous. "Jack…"

"Just five minutes, Katie." Jack made his way to the door and held it open. "After you."

Both Kate and Sierra lingered back in the office for a moment before both women went outside. Ace followed, fairly confident he was about to get punched in the face.

"Are you here for the reason I think you're here?" Jack asked.

"I could ask you the same question. Why are you here?" Sierra asked.

"Nobody knows we're here," Kate said. "So if we stand up here in the parking lot, we might be able to put on a show so grand it draws the attention of every busybody in the entire town."

"No one is going to notice," Jack said.

"If there's a giant fight in the middle of the ob/gyn parking lot you don't think anyone will notice?"

"Okay, maybe a few people would notice," Jack said.

"There isn't much point in keeping it a secret," Ace said, looking at Sierra. "Unless you didn't get good news."

Sierra shook her head. "It was…normal."

"Normal how?" Kate asked.

"I thought we were at least going to respect each other's privacy," Sierra said, giving her friend an accusatory glance.

"Well, we're both caught," Kate said. "It shouldn't be terribly surprising that I found myself in this situation. But…I'm a little confused about what's happening here."

"Ace and I are engaged," Sierra said. "Completely unrelated to anything else, obviously."

"You bastard," Jack said, his voice low. "I told you to give her a job. I told you to help her out. I did not tell you to take advantage of her."

Ace couldn't dig up any righteous indignation over that. Jack had a point.

"Oh, stop it," Sierra said. "I am a grown-ass lady. And not even my brother who was raised with me acted this crazy when he found out."

A muscle in Jack's jaw jumped, and Ace had a feeling it was only Kate's presence that was keeping his face unpunched. "Who else knows?"

"We barely know," Sierra said. "And as I can see, you're in a similar situation…"

Jack cleared his throat. "She is my fiancée."

"I'm *his* fiancée," Sierra said, pointing in his direction.

"That's different. I was engaged to Kate before…" He waved his hand. "Don't tell me you and Ace had a quickie engagement."

Ace exchanged a commiserating glance with Kate, who looked like she wanted to disappear beneath the asphalt. "Jack," Kate said. "As charming as it is to watch you standing here beating your chest, I'm pretty sure you don't get to pull this crap. Eli and Connor are your very best friends in the entire world. They put you in charge of protecting me. And what did you do? You deflowered me."

"Because I love you," Jack said.

"You didn't love me at the time. And you know it. Now I'm pregnant. And you are standing here casting accusatory glances at Ace. Pot, meet kettle."

"Congratulations?" Sierra said, her tone questioning.

Kate lifted a shoulder. "I'm in disbelief. That's why we're here. Blood test. Dates. You know, before I sue a condom company."

Jack cleared his throat. "I think you should probably sue Jim Beam because…"

"Enough!" Kate snapped. "This is ridiculous. Everyone is an adult here. Albeit awkward adults. I think you can settle down, Jack. And Ace…if you hurt my friend, I will—"

"You'll have to get in line to kill me," he said. "Madison has already issued threats."

"Threats for days," Sierra added.

Jack looked abashed. Slightly. "Well. I'm new to this," he said, directing his attention to Sierra. "I'm not used to the sibling thing. I knew about all of you but I never talked to you because of…stuff."

"I know," Sierra said, tucking her hair behind her ears and looking down.

Ace suddenly felt like an intruder. This was the kind of moment that Sierra deserved to have without him. There were probably a lot of those moments ahead. She had been at a point of transition in her life, and he'd swooped in and co-opted it.

Of course, being aware of how unfair that was didn't mean he was going to do anything differently.

He was going to keep her with him. He was going to marry her. If that made him a selfish bastard, it was hardly news to him.

"I have a feeling you two need to get to your appointment now," Ace said.

Kate nodded. "We do."

"Sierra," Jack said. "If you ever need anything… money, a place to stay, an alibi… I'm here for you."

"That's really…nice. And kind of intense. Thank you," she said.

"I mean it."

"I don't doubt it."

Ace would be offended about not getting the benefit of the doubt here, but he hadn't exactly earned the benefit of anyone's doubt in the past few years. He'd rolled back into town drunk and horny, and had hardly acted like the kind of guy who was ready to settle down and have kids.

Unless they knew his parents personally, people in Copper Ridge didn't really know about his years in Texas, his divorce or his daughter.

He and Jack might have crossed paths a few times when Ace was riding, but it had been before he'd married Denise, so Jack didn't know about any of that, either.

"I'll call you," Kate said, turning toward the building. "And…we can catch up on all the things."

Kate grabbed hold of Jack's arm and led him back into the building, leaving Sierra, himself and that stack of papers.

"Well, that was special," Ace said.

"I… I guess he cares," Sierra said, staring after Jack. "And also it looks like they're having a baby, too. Wow."

"I'm less interested in that than I am in what they told you in the office."

"December ninth," she said.

"What?"

"That's my due date according to…all the dates I gave them and stuff. Plus I knew the exact date that I…that we… You know."

"Yeah," he said.

She thrust the papers at him. "This is all the stuff. My graphs and crap."

He looked down at the paper that had results for various things like HCG levels and dates and… "The date of the last time you had intercourse," he said, reading the paper.

Dated too many damn days ago.

"They ask you that," she said, her cheeks turning red. "Who knew?"

He nodded. "Yeah. I guess so. December ninth, eh?"

"Yeah."

"Wow. Well, she gets under the wire to be a tax deduction."

"Yeah," she said. "We couldn't have planned that fornication better."

"The motto of my whole life." He reached toward her, taking hold her hand. She went stiff, freezing like he'd hit her with a bolt of lightning. "What?"

"We don't…hold hands. Do we?"

He laced his fingers through hers, never looking away from those sweet blue eyes of hers. "I think we should. Otherwise what the hell kind of marriage will we have?"

"The kind my parents had."

"Then we better hold hands as often as we can."

She didn't protest as he led her to the truck and opened her door for her. She didn't say anything as they pulled out of the parking lot and started down toward the main drag of town.

It was still early in the day and a few of the shops were just getting displays set out front. Cassie Caldwell was out in front of The Grind, wiping down tables that had already been well used, and getting ready for the lunch crowd.

Cassie provided the fuel for the poor hungover souls that rolled out of Ace's bar at night. Then tanked them up so they felt good enough to head out again that night.

The coffee shop and the bar had a funny, symbiotic relationship.

"Need any decaf?" he asked.

"No," Sierra said, her voice muted. "Why exactly are we in town?"

"To get some lace curtains," he said.

Her head whipped around, her expression suspicious. "Really?"

"Yes. I followed your advice about the brewery."

"Curtains," she said.

"Yes. And also we're going to stop by the Trading Post to get some things from Rebecca Bear. Art and some other decor. I asked her to help curate some things from local artists."

"Oh, wow."

"Yeah. I got some glass sculpture from Zack Camden. Some iron work from the McCormack brothers. Paintings from Rosie Dalton. And some crappy driftwood stuff, just because this is the coast and sometimes you need crappy driftwood stuff."

"I hope it has seagulls on it," she said, a reluctant smile tugging at the corners of her lips.

"Oh, hell yeah. Seagulls."

That earned him a laugh. And it felt like a badge of honor. One he was going to wear for a long damn time. "That's a little too emphatic for faux seagull art."

"Baby, if you can't get that excited about faux seagull art, what can you get that excited about?"

"I don't know, Ace."

"We can put some in the baby's room," he said. Sierra sniffed loudly. "Are you going to cry again?"

"I don't know," she said, her voice thick. "What the hell is wrong with me that you just forced me to picture the world's most ridiculous nursery, full of weird ocean decor, and it made me…misty?"

"Kids. It starts now. It never ends."

"Great," she said, laughing, the sound watery. "So I'm a mess from now to forever?"

"Possibly. But we'll be a mess together."

"Mutual messes," she muttered as he pulled the truck against the curb.

"Yeah. Sounds healthy. You want to come in?"

"Sure," she said, undoing her seat belt.

"Good." He let out a long, slow breath, trying to ease the tension in his stomach. They were picking up one more thing here, but he didn't want to tell her about it.

You're going to ambush her with it because you're a cowardly jackass.

Yeah, well. Guilty.

He was also getting married again when it was the last thing on earth he should want and he was dealing with the baby thing pretty damn well, so he was allowed his moment of cowardly behavior. At least, he felt he was.

And he wasn't asking anyone else's opinion.

He rounded to her side of the truck and opened the door for her, extending his hand. She didn't make any commentary this time as she accepted the assistance.

He wondered if he was making any inroads with her. He shouldn't care. She had agreed to marry him so how she felt didn't really matter beyond that.

Except you'd like to get laid again. Soon.

Well, yeah, there was that.

They walked down the sidewalk, a healthy distance between them. He wasn't going to press the hand-holding issue, not just now.

They continued down past the little shops—the secondhand clothing store, Alison's bakery and new hardware store owned by a local woman Ace didn't know all that well. Rebecca Bear's shop was on the end of a row, a dark, berry color, recently painted and restored to make the most of the influx of tourism coming into town.

An American flag hung out in front of the store and beneath it was a little flowerpot shaped like a frog, vines spilling out of its open mouth.

"This is certainly the place for eclectic items," Sierra said as they walked up the uneven stone steps and inside.

"It's Copper Ridge in a shop," he said, looking around at the small space, stacked high with wares from floor to ceiling. "We're the mountains and the ocean. Surf and turf."

Twining vines with glass berries were wound around antique, ornate cabinets, stuffed to the brim with plush toys, Copper Ridge mugs and seasonal decor. One corner of the store held Halloween, another Christmas. On some shelves were campy, homemade-looking items, while on others there were fancier, upscale souvenirs and old-fashioned kitchen utensils.

The air was heavy with the scent of potpourri, spicy and sweet, vanilla and pumpkin.

"I guess it is," Sierra said, wandering in and touching one of the fake vines curled around the lid of a large wooden chest on the floor.

"CAN I HELP YOU?"

Sierra looked up when she heard the woman's question. And felt a slight pang of jealousy when she saw the source of the voice.

The woman was petite, with long, straight brown hair and golden skin. Her dark eyes were fringed with generous lashes, her lips full, a natural, rosy color Sierra needed lipstick to achieve.

When she took a few steps toward them, Sierra noticed she had a slight limp. "Ace! I've been waiting for you," she said, tilting her head slightly to the side.

That was when Sierra noticed the scars on her neck, creeping up beneath her chin and extending down beneath her T-shirt.

Sierra didn't know her, but she seemed familiar. She remembered there had been a girl a couple of grades above her in school who'd been in an accident that had left her scarred and out of school for a while.

She didn't really frequent this part of town for anything beyond coffee, and she'd never been in this shop before so their paths hadn't intersected in the years since.

But she imagined this must be her.

"Good to see you, Rebecca," Ace said, holding out his hand and offering her a familiar, easy smile.

The little twinge of jealousy was back.

"Do you know Sierra West?" Ace said. "She's here assisting me."

Assisting him? Pffft. In the gestation of his child. But he hadn't said that. He hadn't even introduced her as his fiancée.

And why would he, cagey-pants? It's not like you've been acting like you want to shout it from the rooftops.

"The selection of lace curtains is a fraught business," Sierra said, her tone dry. "So he needed help."

"Well, for men I see how it might be. I know of you, but I don't think we've formally met. I'm Rebecca Bear." The expression on the other woman's face was closed off, inscrutable.

Sierra had no idea why she was feeling insecure. She didn't compare herself to other women, and she rarely felt threatened by them.

Because you've never felt desperate to hold on to a guy before.

That could be. She didn't particularly like that thought. That she was desperate to hang on to Ace. Even though she kind of was.

She had been spending nights in the little house, trying to cling to some independence. Then she'd decided to go into the doctor's appointment alone, hoping that she might find some… She didn't really know. Strength or something. But she'd just felt like half of her had been in there. Like it was wrong to do any of this, to find out information about their child without him standing next to her.

In spite of her moments of experimental resistance it was pretty clear that a good portion of her was well and truly acclimated to the idea of sharing this with him.

"If you're feeling sturdy, I've got some pretty big

sculptures set aside for you," Rebecca said, planting her hands on her hips.

"How big?" he asked.

"Well, big enough that I have a hand truck to put them on. But you're going to have to take it from here. Sam McCormack brought them in and he's…" She lifted her hand above her head. "You know, as big as a redwood."

Sierra could easily picture the man carrying wrought-iron statues in like they were made of papier-mâché. She didn't know him well, but she'd seen him around the ranch many times over the years, since he was the farrier for all the horses that stayed on the property.

He was—by all accounts—great at his work. But he seemed grumpy and more than a little antisocial. He made Madison downright feral.

She was always complaining about him whenever she'd been exposed to him.

"Right, well, if he can't lift it I'm not even going to try," Ace said.

That brought her thoughts squarely back to Ace's arms, and muscles, and general physicality. She had no trouble picturing him lifting heavy objects. His biceps shifting with the motion, his abs working to help support his back… Oh, his back muscles…

She blinked.

"I have the smaller things here up front," Rebecca was saying now. "The curtains, the little knickknacks, and… that other thing you asked for."

Immediately, Sierra's curiosity was piqued. "Other thing?"

Ace rubbed the back of his neck, which she was starting to notice he did when he was nervous or uncomfortable. "Yeah," he said. "The other…can I have it?" he asked Rebecca.

"Sure," she said, her expression questioning. She turned and wandered back behind the counter, returning a second later with a small white box.

Ace took it from her, then turned to look at Sierra, a strange light in his dark eyes. "Can you come outside with me for a second?"

"Um…"

"Come on," he said, his tone more insistent. Then he reached out and took her hand.

She really could get used to that.

They walked back out of the heavy, perfumed air and into the sharp coastal breeze, the air crisp and clear, hitting her with a greater impact after the sweet scent that had lingered in the store.

"This is for you," he said, holding the box out to her.

She looked up and down the street, then stretched her hand out to take it. But he held tightly to it. "I thought it was for me," she asked, holding on to one end while he held the other.

"It is. But I'm giving it to you."

"Okay."

"It's not fancy-ass. I can't afford a huge diamond. And I know this isn't a typical marriage or engagement, but I still thought you should have something."

Her heart was thundering in her ears, so hard she thought she might fall over. She was pretty sure she was getting an engagement ring on the main street of Copper Ridge, where even God paid closer attention to what was going on.

He opened the box and revealed a slim, rose-gold band with an iridescent, blush-colored round stone in the center. "It's a sunstone," he said. "Keeping with the way we're doing up the brewery. With the fact that we're making a life here in Copper Ridge. They pull these out of the dirt here. It's as local as we are. Roots and all that. I thought you might like it."

Sierra couldn't say anything. She could only stare at the offered ring, her heart pounding somewhere up inside of her head. She hadn't thought about this part. Hadn't really thought about him giving her something. Making it official.

Of course, it was the next step. And soon, she wasn't really sure how soon, they were going to stand in front of…people. She didn't know what people because she wasn't exactly on friendly terms with her mother and father at the moment, and they were going to make vows. And he was going to kiss her.

They were going to be together. When somebody mentioned his name, they would think of her. When somebody said her name, it wouldn't be her whole big West family that people thought of, not first. It would be her husband, Ace Thompson.

Did that mean she would be Sierra Thompson? She supposed only if she wanted to be. Did she? Did she want to take this chance to grab hold of a new name and associate herself completely with the new life she was choosing?

She didn't have an answer for that just now.

"Do you hate it?" he asked. "Are you going to just stand there and stare at it or…?"

"I don't hate it," she said, reaching out and taking hold of the box. "I… It just threw me into the deep end of the thinking pool, that's all."

"Well, that's a relief. I didn't think women usually

frowned that deeply when they were presented with jewelry."

"Well, you're not exactly just presenting me with jewelry. That would imply that the obligation ended with putting it on. The entire point of this is... Show people that we are together. To be together. And it's leading up to a wedding. So, I would say that it's about the world's most loaded piece of jewelry."

"Do you still want to take it?"

She nodded slowly. "Yes. I do."

Those words sent a shock of electricity down her spine. *I do.* They were the words she would be saying to him at the wedding. The words that would bind them together for life. Yes, divorce was a possibility. It was an option, but she wasn't marrying him with that as a goal. She made that promise to herself then and there. She was going to do her best to make this work. To commit to making this family, making this future.

She looked at his face. A face that had—over the past month—become so familiar to her, and yet had managed not to lose any of its impact.

Hard planes and angles, the dark shadow where he let his beard get a little too long sometimes. Bitter chocolate eyes. His mouth, which she had a feeling she could kiss every day and never, ever feel like it was enough.

She'd never felt this way about anyone before. Uncovering that pure, golden truth had been more difficult than it should have been. But, now that she had, now she had gotten past the baby, the antagonism, the blinding physical attraction, she could see that there was something else there. Something completely new to her. Something she had a feeling was more valuable than all the rest.

He took the ring out of the box and slipped it onto her finger. "Perfect," she said.

The word held a lot of weight, a lot of meaning that she couldn't even put words to in her brain. She only knew that something in this moment was changing her. Rearranging her insides.

"Ace," she said, looking down at the ring glittering on her finger.

"What?" he asked, his voice sounding thin.

"If you don't want this… If you're just doing it because you think it's the right thing… Take the ring back now. Please."

He shook his head. "There's no other reason to do things. You do them because they're right. Because they make the most sense. If you are doing that… I spent a lot of years doing things I knew were wrong. Behaving in a way that I knew I didn't have to. I've just been stuck. Sure, I opened the bar, I am opening the brewery, but those are just the kind of things you do to make yourself believe you're doing something. I was more of a man child at thirty-five than I ever was at twenty-five. This is the first real thing that's happened to me in a long time. I've been coasting, Sierra. It's easy to smile all the time, to be everybody's friend when nobody really knows you at all. When you aren't sharing anything. Do you know what I did the night of Connor Garrett's barn raising?"

She shook her head. "No."

"I went, I provided free alcohol. I danced with Liss, she rejected me. I went home alone and I got drunk out of my mind. Because if I don't have a woman to go home with, then I have to spend the night with a bottle, because there has to be something there to distract me and make sure I never think too deeply. Well, you're giving me something that I can think deeply about. Something that isn't all pain and destruction."

She realized, as he said that, it was the same for her. Sure, everything in front of them was huge, it was scary. But it was valuable. It was bigger than she was. Ever since the revelation about Jack she had been worried about herself. Worried about what all of that meant for her, what decisions she had to make to be a good person. What she would have to learn to survive away from the support—financially and otherwise—from her family.

And that mattered. It did. But it was also a lot like looking through a small hole in a wall and trying to see the broader world. It was all filtered through her needs, her concerns, herself.

Now she felt like she had stepped outside. But she was looking all around. At every possibility, at every angle. Ace had been brought into her concerns. Her baby had been brought into it. Their marriage. Their future.

She felt…swollen with those concerns. She should feel heavy. And yet, somehow she felt lighter. Maybe because as immense as all these responsibilities were, she was confident that Ace was carrying them with her.

"Thank you," she said, her words soft. "Thank you for giving me something so valuable."

"Sunstones are pretty common, actually," he said.

"Not the ring. Everything."

"Everything? That's a lot of things." He took a step back from her, stuffing his hands in his pockets.

"Well, okay, maybe not everything in the entire world. I assume you don't have a hand in quite that many things. But I think this is going to be okay. I think it might be better than okay."

"I'll take it."

She let out a long slow breath, looking down at the ring again. "I suppose we'd better go get the stuff and take it over to the brewery."

"I suppose we should."

Okay, maybe as official proposals went it wasn't the most romantic. But it had changed something for her. And that was all that mattered.

She was starting to look forward to the life she and Ace were going to have together. And from where she was standing, that was about all that mattered.

CHAPTER NINETEEN

"I CAN'T BELIEVE this all came together so quickly," Sierra said, taking a slow turn around the newly furnished dining room in Ace's brewery.

"Well, it wouldn't have happened if it weren't for you." Ace leaned up against the bar, gripping the edge of the counter, the muscles in his forearms flexing with the movement. And she couldn't help but take a good long moment to admire that.

The brewery was different than the bar. Much larger, much more upscale. And yet, it still looked like him. This sturdy, wooden furniture looked like the kind of thing he would put in his own house. And, the lace curtains weren't exactly him, but, she liked to think they represented her invasion in his life.

And she kind of liked that stamp being visible here for everyone to see.

That thought made her heart do a little stumble and fall. But, she felt possessive of him, and there really wasn't much point in denying that. Her reaction to Rebecca earlier was evidence of that. And, if that hadn't proven it, then her reaction to the curtains certainly did.

She wanted everyone to know that Ace was in a different place. That they were building something together. Which wasn't really fair, because like much of everything else in her life, Ace had built the brewery on his own, and she was getting a bit of undue ownership.

That made her frown.

"I didn't really do that much," she said.

"You did. I think I would have put uniform metal tables and chairs in here and not given any thought to what I can do to make it a bigger draw to the kind of people I want to bring in. But you had insight that I wouldn't have had. And, you helped me exploit all of my past good deeds. Really, what's the point of good deeds if you don't get to exploit them later?"

"I have no idea. I've never done any," she said, smiling broadly.

"That isn't true. Don't diminish yourself. There will always be people lining up ready to do it for you."

She shook her head. "That hasn't really been my experience. People have always been way nicer to me than I deserved. If you recall, you were the first person I ever apologized to. How on earth did I have friends?"

"You're a delight?"

"I had money. So, now I'm going to have to be a whole lot nicer to people."

He crossed the bar, moving toward her, reaching his hand out and brushing her cheekbone with his thumb. "You used to bounce a lot more, Sierra. Please tell me you didn't stop because of me."

She tried to force a smile. "What do you mean *bounce*?"

"From the moment I hired you, you were bouncing all over my bar. And I knew you were going to be a problem. Because I couldn't look away from you. You were…undeniable. You still are. But you aren't quite as bouncy."

That made her frown. "I spent a lot of time not having much to worry about. And when all of that stuff about my dad came out I just kind of kept moving forward. I thought that maybe I could change everything around me and not meaningfully change myself. And then all this other stuff happened. It kind of piled on. But I don't think it's a bad thing. I have to change. There's more weight to everything now, and I guess that makes it a little bit harder to bounce." She looked up, meeting his gaze. "I think maybe I'm finally seeing the world a little more clearly. Seeing myself a little more clearly."

"Do I make you unhappy?"

She shook her head. "I think in some ways I'm happier right now than I've ever been. But I'm sadder, too. A little more scared. But I'm not sure you can be certain that you're happy if you don't have anything to compare it with. I think… I think you need everything. I think you need your life to be full…to feel sad and bittersweet and scary to really understand happiness."

His gaze grew intense, his other hand sliding up to cup her face, holding her steady as he leaned in, kissing her slowly, softly. She parted her lips, sighing as his tongue slid against hers. His kiss was familiar and new at the same time. It had been too long. And they had never really kissed like this. With his hands on her face, a slow exploration.

The first time had been so desperate. The second… Well, they had started out naked. They didn't go slow. They didn't seem to know how.

And, even now, from the first touch of his lips to hers, she wanted him. Needed him.

She wanted to strip his clothes off. Wanted to take things to the next level. But, at the same time she wanted this to last forever. The simple moment where only their lips were touching. Where she wasn't so lost in what was happening between them that she couldn't think.

Right now she was thinking. Moving her hands over his chest, feeling his heart thundering there. His flannel shirt separated her skin from his, but she could remember what it was like to feel him with no barriers between them. Could remember what it was like to touch his naked body.

Being with him for the first time, discovering him for the first time, had been incredible. But knowing what was beneath those clothes? Being well aware of the reward she had coming? It was even better.

She'd never, ever, felt such intense things for a man's body before. She'd always liked men. Had been attracted to her previous boyfriends. But it wasn't like this.

She wanted to build a shrine to him. To worship at the temple of Ace and his incredible body. She had never, ever felt this way about a man before. She wondered if anyone had. Or if right here in an unopened brewery in the small town of Copper Ridge, Oregon, she had discovered something no other woman had ever known before.

She let her fingertips trail down, skimming the buttons on his shirt, down to his belt, then lower. She traced the line of his hard cock through his jeans, a sharp, shocking thrill assaulting her as she did.

So much for going slow.

He released his hold on her face, wrapping his arms around her and deepening the kiss, pulling her whole body flush against his.

She wrapped her arms around him, sliding them down his back, down to cup his ass. He growled, the sound rumbling through him, rumbling through her. She loved that she affected him. That in all his infinite experience, even though she wasn't the first woman to give him an orgasm, even though she wasn't the first woman he'd been engaged to, even though she wasn't even the woman he loved.

He had loved someone once. He didn't love her.

But right now, that didn't matter. Right now, he wanted her. She affected him. She'd made him shake back at his house, she'd made him lose his control in the bar. She was making him growl here.

She was more than just lace curtains hanging in the brewery. He had changed her, altered the course of her entire life, altered the reason behind her heartbeat. Surely she had changed him, too.

She squeezed her eyes shut and kissed him deeper, held that thought close.

"Are you all locked up?" she asked, wrenching her lips from his, kissing his neck. Her mouth was hot, swollen from desire. Every damn part of her was hot and swollen with desire for him.

"Me personally? Or the brewery?" he asked, his voice strained.

"The brewery. I hope you aren't locked up, I'm going to need to use you."

He chuckled. "The door is locked. I, on the other hand, am open for your business, and pleasure."

"Excellent." She found his mouth again, kissing him until neither of them could catch their breath.

He wrapped his arms more tightly around her, lifting her up off the ground.

"You pick me up a lot," she said, her voice hoarse.

"I can't help it. You're pickupable," he said, not sounding sorry in the least.

"What does that mean?"

"It means," he said, kissing the edge of her mouth, "that it takes a lot of restraint for me not to lift you into my arms at every opportunity."

He walked her backward, toward the bar. "Does it?" she asked, sliding her hands upward to the back of his head, forking her fingers through his hair.

She adjusted her positioning, wrapping her legs around his waist as he carried her.

"Yes. But it's a displacement activity," he said.

"For?"

"You're also very," he said, tilting his head and biting the side of her neck, the scrape of his teeth over her skin raw and hot, "very, fuckable."

It was a good thing he was holding on to her because if he hadn't been she would have turned into a melted puddle of Sierra.

"Oh," she said. "And you aren't even drunk."

He chuckled, and she pulled her head back to get a good look at his expression. A naughty smile curved his wicked lips and she felt heat pool between her thighs. "I don't need to be drunk to say things like that. I mean it. I don't see the point in holding it back."

"I'm not sure I can anymore," she said, gasping as he lifted her slightly before setting her down on the countertop, her legs still locked around him, but forced lower now, around his hips, bringing her into contact with the hardest, most masculine part of him.

"Good," he said. "Don't hold back."

"I think you're ruining me," she whispered.

"For other men?" he asked, his smile curving upward a little more.

For everything.

But she didn't say that last part out loud. She wasn't

sure she could talk now, even if she wanted to. Not when she was so empty and aching with need for him. Not when she thought she was going to die if she didn't have him *right now.*

Fortunately, they were on the same page.

He reached down, grabbing the hem of her top and tugging it over her head as she started to work the buttons on his shirt.

She didn't push it off his shoulders, she just left it open, running her hands over his skin, luxuriating in the feel of him beneath her fingertips.

She leaned back, looking at his perfectly cut body, at the lines those low-slung jeans put on display.

He leaned forward, unbuttoning her jeans and drawing the zipper down slowly. Then he pushed his hand down beneath the waistband of her panties, sliding his fingers over where she was wet and ready for him.

She clung to his shoulders, locking her heels more tightly around his back.

"Don't tease me," she said.

"Oh, baby, I'm going to tease you till you beg," he said, the coarse promise whispered over her lips.

He slipped his finger deep inside her, stroking her with his thumb. She arched her back, her eyes closed tight, her heart fluttering around in her chest like a caged bird as he pushed a second finger inside of her, working them in and out slowly.

She shuddered, pleasure coursing through her as each stroke of his thumb over her clit brought her closer and closer to the brink. Then, abruptly, he pulled away. She let out a harsh groan as he abandoned her pleasure, then a shocked squeak as he hooked his fingers into the waist-

band of her panties and jeans, pulling both down her legs
as he knelt in front of her, her thighs parted wide.

He pulled her forward, looping her legs over his shoulders as he leaned in, kissing her inner thigh, making eye
contact with her as he did.

"Ace..."

"You can still talk," he said, kissing her again, closer
to the source of her desire for him. "That's no good. I've
gotta make you a lot more mindless than that."

He leaned in, sliding his tongue over her sensitized
flesh before adding his fingers back into the mix, plea-
suring her with his hands and his tongue, pushing her
up over the edge. He had one hand planted firmly on her
lower back, holding her in place so that she couldn't escape, while the other toyed with her.

He drew it out for as long as possible, taking her just
to the edge before pulling her back and pushing her
there again. Finally, with one long stroke of his tongue
he sent her over. Wave after wave of pleasure claimed
her, wrapped its fingers around her throat and squeezed
tightly, leaving her gasping for air, leaving her spent and
utterly breathless.

Then he rose up on his feet, positioning himself between her legs as he undid his belt, then slowly unzipped
his jeans. She reached forward, tugging his underwear
down, freeing his erection, and locking her legs around
his back again, urging him inside her.

He didn't need a lot of encouragement.

He thrust home in one smooth motion. She should
be replete from the climax he'd already given her. But
still, she was ready for more. It didn't seem possible. She
shouldn't be ready for anything but sleep. But, with Ace,

it turned out she always wanted more. It turned out she was insatiable.

She clung to him, fingers curled into the fabric of his shirt, which was open and still mostly on. She liked that. Liked that he hadn't bothered to get undressed entirely. That he was still wearing his jeans. That there had been too much urgency for either of them to worry about ridding him of his clothes completely.

She looked up at him, pressing her hand to his cheek, tracing the square line of his jaw. She loved the expression he had on his face. One of absolute concentration. He looked like a conqueror and a supplicant, rolled into one.

She couldn't speak now if she wanted to. She was completely lost in this. Lost in him. She could do nothing but feel. Not just physically. Emotions invaded her, expanding in her chest, working their way deep into her soul. This was more than she had wanted it to be. From the beginning it had been more than she wanted.

She had wanted her job, not an attraction.

She had wanted sex, not a baby.

She had wanted help, not a husband.

She had wanted a connection, not love.

But no matter what she had started out wanting, it didn't matter in the end. Because she had everything that had *not* been on the list.

Baby. Future husband.

And as she watched his face, as she was filled by him, in every way, she had to admit to herself that she had fallen in love with him.

She didn't want it. Any more than she had wanted anything else. It was a recipe for nothing but pain. He had already told her he didn't want love. He was never going to give it. She imagined he didn't think he wanted to receive it. But she felt it. An overflowing well of it right now, joining the pleasure that was building inside of her, threatening to burst out of her whether she wanted it to or not.

She couldn't contain all of it. There was no way. It was too complete, too devastating.

He rolled his hips forward, making contact with that sensitive bundle of nerves at the apex of her thighs. And for a moment, the blinding, white-hot pleasure forced her mind blank. She couldn't worry about the future. Couldn't worry about her feelings. He increased his tempo, his own control starting to fray. She could feel it. In the trembling of his muscles, in the tight hold he had on her hips.

"Yes," she said, a whispered, urgent prayer for him to keep going. For him to lose himself as she was. For him to be as completely lost as she was. So she wouldn't be alone.

And he obeyed.

On a hoarse growl he gave in completely, his capitulation securing her own.

She clung to him as he shook, as his pleasure became her own, as their release poured through both of them. It didn't feel like it was coming inside of her. Instead, it felt like they were both standing in the middle of a storm, clinging to each other as they were battered from all sides.

And when it cleared, when everything around them was still again, she was left with a kind of sick, horrifying certainty.

She loved him. But no matter how deeply, no matter how strongly she loved him, he wouldn't love her back.

Along with that was another certainty. If she wanted

to keep him, she could never tell him. If she wanted this to last, she would have to keep her feelings to herself.

She looked up at him, the impact of his gaze hitting her like a blow.

"What?" he asked, his voice husky, his touch on her cheek gentle.

"Nothing," she said. "It's nothing."

CHAPTER TWENTY

OVER THE NEXT few weeks they settled into a routine. Something Ace would have said was impossible only a few months ago. That he would find himself happily co-existing with a woman. Headed toward holy matrimony and fatherhood and all those things he had been steadfastly avoiding for so many years.

He hadn't been with the same woman more than twice since his ex-wife, and here he was, having Sierra every night, multiple times a night, and not feeling like he would ever get enough of her.

But that wasn't it. It wasn't the only thing.

It was comfortable to have her around. To have her soft touches slowly invading his home.

She had brought a few of those *things* from her shopping spree over to his place, bringing some of her taste in and mingling it with his. Well, if you could call what he'd had in his house his taste. It really had been an outward symbol of the apathy and carelessness he'd treated his life with.

Much like his house, he'd been a functioning structure with not much more to it. Now, there was Sierra. And she had brought wall art, doilies and impending fatherhood in his life. She had brought some measure of happiness and comfort.

But those things had brought along something else.

With doilies came a strange sense of unease. The feeling that he was standing beneath a guillotine that could drop at any moment.

So, that was fun.

But he felt like he more or less had the guillotine propped up with a broom handle. Sure, it was there, but he and the madame had an agreement of some kind. Sierra was going to marry him. They had commitment. They did not have ridiculous things like emotions involved.

Right. You have no emotions about any of this.

Well, he did. But not unstable ones.

He and Sierra had an arrangement. A commitment. That was the broom handle. Potentially breakable, he was aware. But better than nothing.

Right now, he was outside working with the horses, getting prepared for work later. They would ride over together. That had become part of the routine. It was downright domestic, and he didn't even mind. If anything, he relished it.

That thought jolted him a little bit as he straightened, wiping his forehead and setting his pitchfork to the side. The stalls were clean now, and if he played his cards right he would have time for a shower and for some quality naked time with Sierra.

It was no mystery why he relished *that*.

He looked up, just in time to see Sierra walking toward the barn, a wide grin on her face and a basket in her hand. She was even bouncing a little bit.

"What brings you out here?"

"The horses," she said, winking at him.

"Right. I know I rate way down the list."

"Way down."

"What's in the basket?"

Her cheeks turned pink, her smile turning sheepish. "Food."

"Food?"

"Yes," she said, looking determined. "Food that I made."

"You make food?"

"I did! I mean, you can hold your praise in reserve. It's turkey and cheese sandwiches and a very basic pasta salad. But that is possibly the most food assembly I've ever done in my life."

"And you brought it out here?"

"Yes. I thought you might want to have a picnic."

For some reason, that very simple offer made his stomach wrench up tight. He didn't know why. Except that picnic lunches were a gesture that went somewhere beyond domesticity. There was sharing a practical meal together, and then there was... Well, he didn't even know what this was.

"I'm kind of sweaty," he said.

Her face fell a little. "Does that mean you can't eat a sandwich?"

He shook his head. "No, I can eat a sandwich."

He reached out and took hold of the basket, setting it on top of one of the work tables in the barn. He opened it up and examined the contents before taking out one of the sandwiches and unwrapping it.

"I thought we might actually sit down and eat them."

He looked at her, the sandwich poised in front of his mouth. "We can do that."

He didn't want to. And at the moment he couldn't exactly examine why. Except that he hadn't agreed to a picnic. They didn't really have time. He had some work to finish, and then there was that shower he wanted. And the sex.

He had a feeling that saying he didn't want to have a picnic because he wanted sex wouldn't go over well.

She shifted, and he noticed that she had a little checkered blanket under her arm. Red checkers. Like a component to a picnic that came straight out of a dream. And for some reason, that blanket felt like a threat. To what they were establishing. To what he had planned.

"Look, Sierra, I appreciate this, but I don't really have time. You know, for a full sit-down thing." *You asshole, what are you doing?*

Her face fell even more and his stomach twisted tighter.

"Oh. I didn't realize."

"There's just a lot going on out here. I'm thrilled about the sandwich. And thank you."

"Sure."

"Don't go acting upset," he said, ready to cut out his own tongue as soon as the words exited his mouth. He doubted there was anything worse he could possibly have said.

"Oh," she said, her tone dry. "Sorry. I guess even when I'm upset I shouldn't act upset?"

"Look, we can sit down and have a damn picnic if it means that much to you."

"It doesn't. Not anymore." She snatched the basket back and turned on her heel, walking quickly out of the barn.

Annoyance spiked and he walked after her. "Sierra," he said. "I told you we could have the picnic."

"But you don't want to!" she returned, her cheeks

flushed red. "And if you don't want to then there isn't any point."

"I can't read your mind," he said, exasperated. "I didn't realize it was going to be an issue."

"You didn't realize turning down my picnic lunch as I stood before you with a blanket and the only sandwiches I've ever made in my life would be an issue? How's the view right now?"

"What?"

"Your head is shoved so far up your ass I wondered if you could see anything."

He scowled. "I have a schedule. This didn't fit. I said I'd make it work and now you're making a federal issue out of it."

"Because you did! You're acting like I'm inconvenient." She started to storm away again and again he followed her.

"Sierra, you can't go acting like this all the time."

Her hands locked down at her sides, her shoulders shaking. "Gah!" She whirled around. "All the time? Are you kidding me? I asked you for a freaking picnic, not a…a…tour of Europe. Did you think I was just going to slip quietly into your life and not change anything?"

"Lace. Curtains," he said.

"Oh, woo. I got to put curtains in your living room. I'm not going to be your Stepford Wife, here to provide you with some *Leave it To Beaver* life plus blow jobs. I want things, too. And you said you wanted to share with me, but now I wonder if that was really true."

"Because I didn't immediately jump on board with having a picnic? That's a bit dramatic."

Dimly, he realized he'd been a jerk, and now it was

spiraling out of control. That he should back down and apologize. But he didn't want to.

Her eyes narrowed. "Did you just call me dramatic?"

"I don't think I stuttered."

"You're unbelievable."

She strode back toward the house, and he followed. She stomped angrily up the steps into the house, opening the door and slamming it behind her, and he followed her every movement, stomp for stomp.

When he went into the house, she was standing in the entry, her arms crossed over her chest, her glare evil. "Oh, so you decided to follow me?"

"Yeah, I had to make sure you didn't do anything crazy. Like take your lace curtains and run off."

"Where would I go? I don't have anywhere to run off to."

He advanced on her, wrapping his arms around her waist and pulling her up against his chest, taking her chin between his thumb and forefinger and forcing her to meet his gaze. "You don't need anywhere else to go."

He kissed her then. Hot and hard.

She tasted like anger and sadness, and he knew that he was responsible for both. He wasn't even her husband yet he was already messing things up.

She was right, maybe to a degree he had imagined she did just that in his life in all of the spaces that were empty, without rearranging any that already felt full.

But that was a damned selfish perspective on relationships.

Do you know how to have any other kind of perspective on a relationship?

Maybe not anymore. A long time ago. A lifetime ago. Before his first marriage, before his first child and the loss of that child, he cared about other people first. He had loved people more than he'd loved himself.

And look where that got you.

Well, his way of doing things now wasn't getting anywhere better. Except that she was kissing him back. Fiercely. Like she was all out of words and had to fight him with her body.

She pushed him backward, pressing him up against the wall, her breasts flush against his chest. She placed her fingers through his hair, tugging hard as she parted her lips and slid her tongue over his. Then she nipped his bottom lip, not gently at all.

He grabbed hold of her hair, taking her head back. "Are you trying to punish me?"

"Yes," she said, her voice low.

"I have to tell you, I don't feel very chastised."

She rolled her hips forward, sending a shot of lightning through his body. "You would if I walked away."

"But we both know you can't."

Something flashed through her eyes—fear, indecision. "I could," she said.

"You don't want to."

"Yeah, well, what I want doesn't always work out, does it?"

"Is this about the picnic again?"

"Everything," she said.

That word, so angry, so filled with pain, touched something wrong inside of him. He reversed their positions, pressing her against the wall, kissing her as he pushed the hem of her dress upward, but he never got over her hips. "Everything? Now you regret everything? Just the other day you were telling me how happy I make you," he said, the words biting.

"Well, it's a new day."

"Yeah, a new day where you decided you were going to be completely unreasonable," he said, putting his hand between her thighs and stroking her through the fabric of her panties.

"A new day where I made you turkey sandwiches and you rejected them," she said, her breath hissing through her teeth as he stroked her.

"I didn't reject your turkey sandwiches."

They were fighting for something right now, and he wasn't entirely sure what. It wasn't as simple as dominance or submission, it was something else entirely. Starting with the picnic and ending up here.

You know what you're fighting for.

Yeah, he did. And he had a feeling he was on the side of wrong here. But he wasn't entirely sure what he was supposed to do about it. Because he didn't see a life full of picnics for them. In fact, he didn't want that. He wanted stability, and she had something else in her picnic basket that went way beyond stability and into territory he wasn't comfortable with.

It became clear then why he had put his hand between her thighs. Because he was trying to prove to her that this was enough. That sex, sharing a life here in this house, filling the empty spaces was enough.

Not just for him, but for her.

He had a feeling that she was using sex for an entirely different reason. And he wasn't sure who would win.

"Do you want me, Sierra?"

She bit her lip, nodding.

"Even when you're mad at me," he said, marveling, not questioning.

"Sometimes especially then."

"Why?"

"Because it's the only way I feel like we aren't on a different planet."

"Definitely not on a different planet," he said, undoing his belt and drawing down the zipper of his jeans.

He moved into position, thrusting inside of her. His breath hissed through his teeth, his arousal climbing higher as he watched her eyes glaze over with pleasure, watched the flush deepen across her skin.

He could see how much she wanted him. Could see it clearly over every part of her.

After all that, he wasn't sure he deserved it. No, he was sure he didn't deserve it. But he would sure as hell take it.

"You feel that?" he asked, his cock pulsing deep inside of her. "We're here. We're together."

She nodded, looking away from him.

"Look at me," he said. Her eyes widened, her focus going to him. "Watch," he commanded. But he realized, even as he issued the command that it was mostly for himself. And, as soon as he became conscious of that fact he wanted to look away. He didn't want to meet her eyes. But the fact that he didn't want to made him more determined to maintain eye contact. There was nothing to be afraid of. Nothing there in Sierra West's clear blue gaze that he should have a problem with.

She was just one small, bouncy blonde. There was nothing to be scared of here.

She gripped his shoulders, her fingernails digging into him. But it felt like it went much deeper than that. Like it hooked all the way down into his insides. Somewhere much deeper than he wanted her to go.

That should be enough to get him to pull away. But he found he wanted to push it further. To dare himself.

To dare her to see how far he could go. To see how far they could go.

He felt the need to put distance between them when she had shown up with the picnic basket. And now, he was fighting against that. Trying to prove to himself he didn't need it. Because he knew that he couldn't have her like this and have his distance, too.

Intensity built inside of him, a fist tightening around his stomach, making it difficult for him to breathe. He closed his eyes.

"Look at me." Sierra's voice jolted him, and he obeyed.

He watched her the whole time, as he drove them both to completion. She cried out when she came, her eyes still on him, a tear rolling down her cheek.

"Oh," she said, her words registering dimly as his own orgasm took him over completely. "This would be so much easier if I didn't love you."

Those words echoed in his head, mixing with the pleasure that had grabbed him by the throat, shaking him like he was a rag doll. He was at the mercy of both. Of the bomb that Sierra had just dropped into his chest and of the release that had full and total control over every part of him.

And he knew for a fact that he would never be able to separate the two things again. Knew that never again would he experience sexual pleasure without those words ricocheting through him.

This would be so much easier if I didn't love you.

She wasn't supposed to love him at all. He had told her that it couldn't be like that. And now…

He moved away from her, his heart pounding. He rubbed the back of his neck, trying to figure out what to say next. Trying to figure out what to do next.

"I have to get showered," he said finally.

"Oh… Okay."

He turned away from her and started to walk toward the bathroom.

"No," she said, "wait."

SIERRA HAD NO IDEA what she was doing. All she knew was that her heart was pounding and her entire body was still humming with what had just happened between them. In the middle of all that, the words that she had just spoken were echoing in her mind. For a moment, she had been about to let him slink away. She had been on the brink of allowing him to just pretend like she had never said she loved him. Because she kind of wanted to pretend she hadn't said it.

That was the easy thing. But she was suddenly over-taken by the realization that she always did the easy thing.

It was easy to pretend that she didn't. That somehow she had been brave in running away from the issues with her family. That striking out on her own was the more noble thing, rather than what Colton and Madison were doing. Keeping with the status quo. Trying to keep the peace.

But it hit her then that she was avoiding dealing with the hard things. She was avoiding the opportunity to un-pack the messy things, to see what kind of relationship could be made now that she realized the father she had always looked up to was far from perfect. That her family life wasn't a fairy tale.

She had bailed on that life. The moment she had found out it might not be perfect.

"I told you I love you and you just want to go take a shower?"

He stopped, his posture going rigid. "I don't know what to say to that."

"Well, I know what people usually say. I'm not sure what you want to say."

"Why do you think you love me after we fought like that?"

"Because I realized that you not wanting to have a picnic with me upset me enough to have a fight like that. If I didn't love you why would I want to have a picnic with you?"

"I don't know. There are a lot of reasons to have a picnic that don't necessarily involve love."

She let out a long breath. "To be fair. I realized I love you couple of weeks ago."

"What?"

"At the brewery. You know, after that time."

A slash of dull red color bled across his cheek bones. "That was just…"

"If you say it was just the sex I'm going to throw something at your head."

"Sierra… You know what this is. You know what this was supposed to be."

"Yeah, and that's really actually very stupid, Ace. You think we're somehow going to make a marriage without love? We're going to make a family without love? Ace, people get a dog and love it. How did you think you are going to get a wife and never have to contend with loving her?"

"It's not like that. I mean, I expect that we should care about each other. I do care about you."

"You want us to not love each other. I don't even think that's possible. We're supposed to sleep together. In the same bed every night. Stay together forever and… On what foundation?"

"You didn't have a problem with this when you agreed to marry me."

"Well, I was afraid. And there were a lot of new things happening. And I... I was a different person. You know, I almost let you walk away. I almost didn't press the issue. I need to press it. Because I'm not just going to take it easy. Not anymore. That's what I do, Ace. I run away from home when I get angry at my parents. I don't apologize when I hurt people's feelings. I just let it kind of smooth over. I take the path of least resistance because the path of least resistance has always had pretty good results for me. Because my life has been easy. And I haven't known what to do when it got hard. Well, for the past couple of months it's been hard. But there's more to me than I thought. And I... I'm not going to be my father."

"Of course you aren't. I don't know what that has to do with anything."

The moment she said the words it was like a dam had burst open and everything, feelings, clarity, poured out like a rushing river. "I told you I like games," she said. "Light flirtation and happy smiles and nothing too real because it gets down to the bottom of things and makes you have to show who you are. Not just the name on your birth certificate, but who you really are and everything you can and can't be."

"What does that have to do with anything?"

"Everything! That's what he does—what he did. He preserved the mask so that no one would ever see what was under it, and I... That's why I was so angry at him. It's why I *am* so angry at him. It's why I've been so determined this whole time to do the right thing. When he told me why he didn't tell anyone about Jack. When he told me why he went to such great lengths to cover it up... It made sense to me. That was my first response. If I could make something that painful, that difficult go away... I would be tempted to. And that moment of identification horrified me. So I got angry. I yelled at him. I told him there was not any reason on earth for him to do something like that. I couldn't understand. When the truth is I can understand. Because it's me. I don't do the hard thing. I never have. Well, right now I'm going to do the hard thing. I'm going to be real. I don't… I don't know how to do anything. I don't know how to be a wife, or be a mom, or be a waitress, but I love you, Ace Thompson. And I'm standing here with no protection, not my name, not my money, not anything to fall back on, and I want you to see my heart. I want you to love me. I want this marriage to be real. Not just legal."

He was just staring at her, his expression blank, his eyes dark and haunted. She could already see this wasn't going her way. And still, she wouldn't take the words back. It was killing her by inches, tearing strips off of what remained of her pride. Killing each new surge of confidence the moment it rose to the surface. But still, she wouldn't take it back.

This, she realized, was the lesson. This was who she needed to be. To become the woman she wanted to be. To be the kind of mother she wanted her child to look up to.

She had to stand. She had to fight. She had to do the hard thing, she had to stop hiding.

But oh, as he kept on looking at her with those tortured eyes she wanted nothing more than to hide. To take it all back. To stuff the words down back inside of her and pretend this had never happened.

"I already told you. I can't do that."

They were the words she had expected, but still, they hit her with the force of the slap. So harsh, so painful that it took her breath away.

"I mean, I know you thought that we shouldn't. But it just seems like things have changed."

"Nothing has changed for me. I never promised you anything other than this. I will be faithful to you, Sierra. I'll be a good husband…"

"And freak out when I bring you picnics. Because, Ace, it isn't that you can't love me, it's that you don't want to. You're afraid to love me. That's why you wouldn't just eat a sandwich with me." She realized how true that was as the accusation came firing out of her mouth. He was afraid. That was why he was doing this. It explained the entire afternoon. "You had to put distance between us because you feel this, too. You feel it changing. You know you can love me, and that scares you a whole lot more than any inability to love. If you just couldn't love me it wouldn't matter if we had picnics, or if I was upset. You wouldn't feel desperate to break the bond between us, then immediately try to rebuild them again."

"You're attributing a whole lot more thought to the situation than I gave it. I was annoyed because I had a schedule planned for the day. It included getting some work done, going back to the house and taking a shower, then having sex with you. And I had to squeeze all that in before work, and I'm sorry, but a picnic ranks somewhere below sex as far as I'm concerned."

His words were designed to be as hurtful as possible. To reduce what they had to the physical, and physical only. She gritted her teeth. This was where it got harder. Not just that initial revelation, but sticking to it. Somehow, she was doing it. Somehow she was determined to go on. To continue what she had started. Stand firm in her desire.

"That's a really great narrative you have going there,"

she said. "But I don't think it's true. You told me that we were going to hold hands…" Her throat tightened. "You told me that we were going to make something happy. Build something together. For our child and for each other."

"And we can do that without love."

"Why does love bother you so much?"

"Because it doesn't mean anything! Nothing. I already made vows to one woman. I promised to love her until the day I died and she promised me the same. Knowing the entire time that she was deceiving me."

"Are you going to make me pay for her sins forever? Because I didn't commit them. It wasn't me. It was never me. I'm not the one who lied to you."

"You don't understand. If I can't… If the man I was then can't make that work, then the man I am now sure as hell can't."

A tear slid down her cheek.

"I didn't even know the man you were then. The man you are now… That's the man I love. That's the man I'm having a child with."

"This isn't going to work."

"Why?"

"We can't do this. You're right. It was never going to end any other way. It was never going to be okay. I was an idiot for thinking different."

"Are you… Are you breaking up with me?"

He looked at her, the expression on his face completely unreadable. A muscle in his jaw ticked, his mouth pressed into a firm line. "I don't think marriage is going to protect us. Not in the way that I hoped it would. Not in the way that we agreed."

"Because I love you?" she asked.

"Because it will end. Because you love me. Because you're going to want something that I can't give you. And I know where that ends. Trust me. I know a little bit too well."

"Stop acting like I'm your ex-wife. You're only doing it to protect yourself. You know I'm not her."

"Maybe not. But the problem is the same. Because I'm still me."

"You don't want to marry me," she said, her tone flat.

"I don't think it's going to solve anything."

She closed her eyes, a wave of misery washing over her. "Tell me that you don't love me. Tell me you never will."

"I don't love you. I'm never going to. I'm never going to love someone like that. I don't need it. I don't want it. I know people say that love is great and it changes you. But it didn't change me for the better. I'm nothing more than a drunk manwhore, Sierra. And I'm going to have my hands full figuring out how to be a good father the way I am now. Forget being a husband. So all this just confirms that marriage shouldn't be in play here. I've been having doubts for a while."

"No, you haven't," she said, the words desperate, torn from her. "I don't know about any of those other things you just called yourself, Ace Thompson. But you are a liar."

"I'm guilty of everything else. Why not that, too?"

She felt suddenly empty. Just as a wave of pain had threatened to buckle her knees, to send her straight to the ground, warm, tingling numbness overtook her from her head down to her toes.

She was grateful for it. Without it, she had a feeling she wouldn't make it through the next few minutes. She had a feeling she wouldn't make it through the next few days. Maybe weeks. One thing was for sure, the pain wasn't going to go away immediately. There was no easy fix to this. She had chosen to take the hard road, and she was going to pay for it during each agonizing step.

"I'm leaving," she said.

And she knew that if he didn't try and stop her, then there was no reason for her to stop.

"Okay."

She gritted her teeth, locking her jaw to keep herself from howling in pain. And then she turned away, straightening her dress and walking toward the door.

"I'll get my things later," she said.

"All right."

He sounded hollow. Far too casual and way too okay with the fact that she was about to walk out the door and out of his life. She wasn't okay with it.

But the fact that he was… That reinforced her decision to go.

So she did. She kept her head held high. And she didn't start crying until she got behind the wheel of her truck. Didn't start sobbing until she was out on the road, putting more and more distance between Ace and herself. It occurred to her then that she didn't tell him she wouldn't be coming in to work that night. But she figured he should pretty much guess that.

She didn't know where she was going. She didn't want to go back to Colton's because he would probably lead the townspeople to Ace's with pitchforks, which seemed fair enough at this point. But she wasn't ready to lead a ragey mob against him.

What was she doing? She was leaving behind the man she loved for what?

She pulled her truck over to the side of the road, breathing hard, shaking. She didn't have to leave. She could stay with him. She could go back and tell him that love didn't matter. She could love him, he didn't have to love her. It wouldn't be a problem.

Love could fit on the shelf in his living room and never get in the way. It could be the thing he ignored. The thing they pretended wasn't there. Only she would ever know.

She gripped the steering wheel tighter and she let herself imagine it. Let herself imagine turning the truck around and going back. Getting out and finding him and saying she was being an idiot. She didn't need love and picnics if she had him.

She thought back to him, standing there and looking like he'd been hollowed out. Telling her he didn't want love.

He was lying and she knew it. As well as she knew anything.

But she would have to be brave to test that theory. She would have to be willing to wait him out.

And she would have to hope that she was right.

That he was afraid. That he was lying—to himself and to her—about what he wanted. About what he needed.

She wouldn't let herself think of the road ahead. Of what would happen if he meant it. If he would really never love her.

He would love someone. That was the great and terrible truth. He might think he wouldn't. But he would. Someday his wounds would scar over. Someday he would decide it was worth the risk.

"I wish you would decide I was worth it," she whispered.

She felt around on the seat for her purse, then opened it up, pulling out her phone. She weighed it in her hand for a moment before going through her contacts.

"Maddy?" she asked, when her sister picked up the phone.

"What's wrong?"

"I just… Can I come and stay with you?"

"Of course! Is everything okay with you? Are you physically okay? Do I have to go and kill a bartender with my bare hands?"

"I'm physically okay," she said. "Save killing the bartender for later. I just… I don't want to deal with Colton right now. Or Mom and Dad. So I want to sneak into your place for a while and hide."

"What are big sisters for but to offer a place to burrow in a time of crisis? Come over and I'll make tea. And a voodoo doll."

"Thank you, Maddy," she said.

She hung up the phone and pulled her truck back onto the road, heading away from Ace, headed toward Madison.

She didn't have Ace right now, and she hated that.

But she didn't actually lack for love in her life, and right now, she was more grateful for that than anything else.

She would never truly be alone.

She would try to hold that close. Even though it still meant her bed would be empty. Even though she knew she would always have an empty space in her heart, too. Right where Ace's love should have been.

CHAPTER TWENTY-ONE

SHE WAS GONE. Just like that. She'd walked straight out of the house and gotten in her truck and driven away.

And he'd let her.

He had pushed her.

Because it was going to end that way someday, so it might as well end that way now. When a little less blood would be shed. Before their child had to live through a bitter divorce.

Before he forgot why he shouldn't love her.

It's not her. It was never her. It was you.

He knew that. Damned if he didn't know it well.

It was late. The bar was closed. Earlier he'd gone out riding. And he'd begged the universe for some sense of clarity. For that moment of total bliss he used to feel when he rode. When his muscles became one with the horse and everything around him became an indistinct blur, his mind wiped clean.

But his mind hadn't been clear. Not in the least. It had been full. Of Sierra.

After that he'd gone in to work at the bar, where he'd had no time for anyone's shit, and had in general been a terrible boss and an even worse bartender.

Then he'd gone to his office after everyone had left to pour himself a drink. And now he had no higher calling other than getting completely wasted.

This was his pattern, after all. When life got hard, he got drunk. He'd forgotten how to do feelings any other way.

He knocked back his first drink, letting the alcohol burn all the way down. Accepting it as his penance. This guy, this guy sitting here in his office drinking instead of dealing with himself, was the last thing a woman like Sierra needed. That was the honest truth.

He wasn't even sure if he was the kind of father a child needed.

That thought made him feel like he had been kicked in the gut. Because he wanted to be there for his child. He wanted his child more than anything.

That thought brought Sierra's face into his mind. Her clear blue eyes, the way she had looked at him the last time they made love. The way she had looked at him when she had walked out of his house for the last time.

He wanted *her*.

But he didn't know how to have her.

Loving her would mean trusting. It would mean opening himself up. Changing himself. It was exactly as she said. Being together, being a real couple, meant changing in a real way.

He had spent almost ten years changing into something he didn't recognize. It had been a slow process, one forged by grief and anguish and bitterness. But he didn't know how to make that change again just because he wanted to.

He didn't even know if he wanted to.

He poured himself another drink.

When Ace woke up a few hours later he realized that he was lying across his desk, his fingers still wrapped around a glass of scotch. He hadn't had a night like that in a long time.

The sky was just starting to fade into a dusky gray, edges of gold shimmering around the mountains. It was Sunday morning, he realized. Years ago, that would have been significant. Now, it was just a regular morning.

But for years upon years Sunday morning had meant getting up early and going to church.

He had traded that for staying up all night and getting drunk. The thought made him laugh. Not because it was funny, not really. Just because there was really nothing else.

He stood up from his position behind the desk, the world around him pitching slightly. His head was pounding, his throat dry. Everything hurt. His body, straight down to his soul.

The sun was rising, but Sierra was gone.

He dragged a hand down his face and started to walk out of the office. He wasn't sure where he was going. He still wasn't sure when he got behind the wheel of his truck. When he started to drive down the main road of Copper Ridge and back out of town. He wasn't really sure where he was going until he pulled into the parking lot of the little white church building that had been a second home to him for most of his life.

Of course, just like his family home, walking up to the doors of the place didn't really produce that feeling of homecoming he had imagined it might. He was a different man. It was a different time.

It was early, and the parking lot was empty, but back when Ace had been a kid his father had had a policy about keeping the sanctuary unlocked. In case anyone had a need to come and pray. He wondered if that was still the case.

He put his hand out and tested the handle of the door.
It opened.

That made him smile. Where else but Copper Ridge
could you keep the doors of the church unlocked?

He walked inside slowly, his feet echoing on the
wooden floors. He looked up the row of empty pews, to
the pulpit, to the cross that hung just behind where the
preacher normally stood. Then he looked up higher at
the wooden ceiling.

When he'd been a boy it had always made him think
of Noah's Ark for some reason. The shape of it looking
like the hull of the ship. It always made him feel small,
impossibly so. Like he was a pretty damn insignificant
piece of the universe.

He started to walk up the aisle, tapping the tops of the
pews with the tips of his fingers until he came to the third
row. He slipped into the seat there, leaning forward, his
forearms resting on the bench in front of him.

He took a deep breath, looking up at the cross. He
wasn't sure what he was expecting. Something. He was
back in church, after all. For the first time in a decade
and a half at least.

Back in church with a hangover and a piece of himself broken off inside.

He took a deep breath, lacing his fingers together and
bowing his head. Just waiting in the stillness. Being back
here made the years fade away. Made the time between
the last service he'd come to and this moment seem so
much shorter than they were.

He had been a boy here with his whole life stretching
in front of him. And now, here he was, a good portion
of that life lived, not a whole hell of a lot to be proud of.

He had a failed marriage behind him. Years of bad behavior. A brokenhearted woman who was pregnant with his child.

But on his list of sins, the one that stood out in red, the one that he couldn't reconcile, was the child he had failed.

Memory grabbed hold of him, wrapped its icy fingers around his throat. For a moment he could barely breathe. He was just sitting there, gasping in the dark, the sound echoing in the empty sanctuary.

He had failed her.

He hadn't fought hard enough. He had given up. He had left.

That child had loved him. The purest kind of love on earth. She had trusted him. And he had let himself be defeated. Had walked away because it was the only thing he could think to do. His strength had failed him. It had failed her.

How could he ever accept the kind of love Sierra was offering?

His heart clenched tight, his eyes stinging. She had told him that she loved him. He didn't deserve to have anyone love him. Couldn't accept it. How could he? His love had proven fallible.

He squeezed his eyes tight, trying to combat the anguish that was pouring through him. And he saw her. Not Sierra. Callie. Round-faced, two years old. Could hear clear as day her little voice calling him daddy.

He had failed her. He had left her.

He didn't deserve love from Sierra. Or anyone. He didn't even deserve to have a second chance with this child.

Sure. He was drowning. Drowning in alcohol and his own misery, but how could he accept a hand up when he knew that he deserved to be down here?

He opened his eyes and a tear rolled down his cheek. He wiped it away, looking up at the altar again.

He had imagined he'd hit rock bottom years ago. It turned out, he had farther to fall. It turned out, it hurt worse when you thought for a few minutes there was hope again.

"Ace?"

Ace looked to the left of the stage, to the sound of the familiar voice. "Dad?"

"Yes. I came here to prepare for the sermon. I thought I heard someone out here."

"I hope I didn't scare you."

"No. I am surprised, though."

Ace didn't know what to say. He didn't know if he could say anything. He was sure that he smelled like booze, like a night spent in a bar drinking and serving. He was sure he looked like the mess that he was. And here he was, darkening the doors of his father's church.

"Me, too," he said, the only words he could manage to squeeze out through his tightened throat.

His father walked down to the pews, then settled himself in the one across from Ace. He rested his forearms on his lap, leaning forward. "They say confession is good for the soul."

"This isn't a Catholic church."

"No, it isn't. I won't be taking your confession in an official capacity. But if there's something you want to talk about, it's quiet in here anyway."

"Unsurprisingly I screwed up my life again." He took a deep breath. "Found a woman who agreed to marry me. And now she says she's in love with me. But I can't…" He shook his head. "I can't accept it." He looked forward, fixing his eyes on the cross. "I feel like I had love.

Someone who trusted me. Callie…" He closed his eyes for a moment, trying to hold everything together. Difficult when he felt like he was cracking apart inside. "It's myself I don't trust. It isn't rich women or Sierra's love. It's my own. I don't deserve it. Maybe at one point in my life I might have. But not now. Not like this. This man I've become."

His father was quiet for a long moment. "While we were yet sinners, Ace."

"I'm not sure how that applies."

"The thing about love is you don't have to be worthy of it. That's why it's beautiful. It's a gift. It isn't something you can earn, it isn't something you can buy. It has to be given to you. And it will never be on your terms."

"That's a nice idea, but I think she deserves to love someone who's worthy of it."

"She chose you. There's no shame in being loved. In needing that love. The only shame I can think of is turning down such a beautiful gift because you're too afraid, too prideful, to accept it."

"I need to… I need to get it together. I need to be something else. Maybe even be someone else."

His father paused for a moment before he spoke again. "You don't change and then find yourself worthy of being loved. When you're loved, you find reasons to change. When you love someone you change for them because it's your great delight to become everything they could ever need. It isn't a burden. It's something you want. Something you desire with every part of yourself."

"I can't," he said, his throat raw.

"Why not?"

The words, so simple and quiet, pulled him up short. He didn't know what to say to that. Because he already said he didn't deserve it, and his father had an answer for that.

"It can't be that easy," he said finally.

"Love is the easiest and the hardest thing in the world. It's almost impossible to understand because it transcends so much pettiness. It transcends fairness. Love is patient, love is kind."

Ace could finish that verse, but possibly not the way his father knew it. Love, to him, was blonde. And bouncy. It was willing to call him out when he was being a jerk. Willing to stand its ground when it knew it needed to. Love wasn't proud, it reduced itself to nothing more than pure honesty even while he rejected it.

Love was Sierra West. And he had turned her away because he was afraid. Because he was afraid of failing again. Because he was afraid he wasn't enough.

"What do you do with the fear?" Ace asked.

"That's where trust comes in. Perfect love casts out all fear. But I don't think it's instantaneous. I think it's something that you have to deal with daily sometimes. But you hope, and you trust, and you talk to the woman that you love."

"What if I fail her?"

"You probably will. But you ask forgiveness, and you work toward doing better. You don't have to sit here with full confidence knowing you're going to be perfect forever just to love somebody. You just take that one step forward with faith, and then another. Just keep walking forward. You'll get there eventually."

"You say that from experience?"

"Forty years with your mother, and I'm still just walking forward. I make mistakes, I try to learn from them. And I know that, no matter what, she's the one that I want. So whatever changes I have to make, whatever mistakes I have to atone for, I do."

Ace stood, his heart pounding hard. "I know that I want to be with her. And I know that I love her."

"And that's enough. Love isn't a finish line. It's the first step on the journey. You don't decide you love someone, and everything is complete and finished. You're just committing to taking the first step. One step."

One step. That felt like something he could do. It was all possible. He looked around the empty sanctuary, something in his chest shifting, breaking open. "I'm sorry," he said.

"For what?"

"She isn't the only one I've shut out. I just haven't felt like I could accept you and Mom. Your support. Your love. I felt like I couldn't stand to disappoint you."

"You never had to question our love, either. And we never stopped."

He nodded, his throat tight. "I love you, too."

His father stood, taking a step forward and taking his son in his arms. He patted Ace once on the back before releasing him. "Be happy. Don't feel like you have to live the rest of your life atoning. No one wants that from you. We just want you. We just want you to live."

"I'm not sure if I'm going to make the service this morning," Ace said.

"I think we already had church."

Ace laughed. "I guess so."

"I hope you'll consider letting me officiate at the wedding."

"If there still is a wedding. If she'll have me."

"If she loves you, and I think she does, you don't have

anything to worry about. It wouldn't hurt you to look a little worried, though. She might make you work for it."

"She will."

"Then she's perfect for you."

SIERRA WALKED OUT of the familiar barn and toward the corral, propping her boot up on the bottom rung of the fence and resting her forearms on the top, leaning forward and looking out at the view that she knew from memory. She had looked upon it from the time she was a little girl, at the perfectly manicured patches of green field, partly enclosed by tall, imposing mountains. And beyond that, the smooth, tan stretch of coastline, white-capped waves spilling onto the shore.

The view from the West ranch was her comfort—at least, it had been for years. It had been when she was a child, and complications had yet to worm their way into her perfect life.

She laughed. She had nothing but complications now. She had nothing but heartbreak spread from here to Ace's. She wasn't sure if there was a view on the entire West Coast that could offer comfort at this point.

Still, being home was a little like being wrapped in a fuzzy blanket. Even if it wasn't entirely comforting, even if she did still feel her losses keenly, painfully, there was a buffer here.

She had been resistant to setting foot back on West property after what happened with her dad, but she was glad she was here now. Glad she had spent the night in Madison's little house. Glad she was wandering through the stables and visiting with the horses.

Well, maybe *glad* was too strong a word. Glad might be somewhere beyond her right now.

She curled her fingers around the top rung of the fence, leveraging herself into a standing position with her foot before bringing her other foot up to join the first. She released her hold, spreading her arms wide and letting the wind blow her hair backward. The sun shone on her face, but she didn't feel warm. The wind just felt cold.

She sighed heavily, stepping back down, turning away from the view and leaning back against the fence.

"I didn't expect to see you here."

She looked up, her heart slamming against her breastbone when she made eye contact with her father's icy blue gaze. "Well, I am," she said.

Her mind was racing and she tried to figure out what she was supposed to say. What she was supposed to feel. Like every feeling hidden here on the ranch, this one was complicated. She was angry. But she was happy to see him. She wished—not for the first time—that he was the kind of father she could run to. The kind of father who would take her into his arms and tell her everything would be okay, even if it might not be.

But he had never been that kind of father. And it was strange to be upset about it now. He hadn't reached out to her at all since she'd left; his pride wouldn't allow it. And even knowing that she was here, he wouldn't reach out.

"Are you through having your tantrum?" he asked.

His words touched already tender places inside of her, making her ache. "It was never a tantrum." Although she suspected part of it might've been at first. "Though I admit I didn't handle it very well. We are family and cutting you off was immature."

"Living without my money for a couple of months has been that difficult?"

She had to fight back a bubble of laughter that threatened to escape. The money? She hadn't missed the money once since she had met Ace. All of the strange, new, wonderful, terrible things she had experienced with him made money seem pretty small.

"No, it hasn't been. At least, things didn't feel all that difficult until yesterday."

Nathan West looked confused by that statement, but didn't ask for clarity. Of course not. "Are you staying?"

"I don't think so. I mean, I might for a while until I figure out a new place to stay. I really can't go back to Colton's with the wedding and everything so close. And I need to find a new job."

"You got fired?"

"So you knew I had a job?"

"Of course. I have kept up on your comings and goings by speaking to your brother."

"Not all of them, I bet. I'm having a baby."

That effectively shocked him. His face was almost comically frozen. "What?"

"Well, these things happen. As I'm sure you know."

"With who?"

"Ace Thompson. You know, he owns the bar. And a brewery." And her heart, and her soul. Nothing major.

"Sierra, this is unacceptable. Are you still in touch with that ex-boyfriend from school?"

"What?"

"He was from a good family, if I recall. And if he's doing well in business he might be looking to settle down."

Sierra put her hands up. "Wait a second, are you actually suggesting I find someone else to claim the baby?"

"Yes, I am suggesting that. I spent years doing what I could to protect our family reputation, and regardless of the fact that Monaghan is now doing his best to ruin it—"

"Jack isn't ruining anything. Jack is trying to live. He wants to have his life on his terms and not on yours. I refuse to be angry at him for that. I can't be. He's my half brother. That matters to me. It means something."

"Why should it? The fact that he's my son has never meant anything to me."

Sierra felt like all the wind had been stuck straight out of her. "How?"

"What I did, I did to protect our family. I did it to protect you, even though you weren't born yet. I did it to protect your brothers. Your birthright. An affair is one thing, Sierra, and I'm not going to judge you for your behavior on that score, but what you do afterward is important."

"So, Jack was collateral damage. The rest of us are supposed to be grateful because you preserved the appearance of our life?"

"That's all anyone is. Appearances. If you haven't realized that by now—"

"No, I did realize it. I realized that was my whole life, too. I can't live that way. I would rather have nothing, I would rather live in a small house alone than have a sham marriage." She thought not just of Mark and her father's edict that she track him down and marry him, but of Ace, and the loveless union he had proposed. "If there's one thing I've learned over the past couple of months it's that I would rather hurt honestly than be happy in a lie."

"I built a lot of years on a lie," he said, looking around them. "Most of a lifetime. All of yours. So you can say you would rather have honesty, but you've never lived with it. You don't know. If your mother had found out before you were born you might not even exist. She might have left. You don't know what it's like to grow up with honesty, so it's easy for you to stand there and talk about it."

That stabbed deep, in part because it was true. She couldn't prove different. She might not have been born had he not covered up his affair with Jack's mother. Or her mother might have left eventually under the strain of dealing with shared custody of a child who served as a reminder of her husband's faithlessness.

"It's too late to go back," she said. "I know that. But I can go forward. I can go forward having the kind of life I want, being the kind of person I want. I'm going to do that."

"I wish you would make a better choice for yourself than a bartender."

"I'm actually choosing to be single. Because he isn't in love with me. So I imagine you're really thrilled with that."

"I can find someone to marry you," her father said, his tone fierce. "I have a great many colleagues who would love to have their sons…"

"No. I'm not a horse. This isn't some kind of ideal match you can arrange. I don't think we're ever going to agree on this. I'm not sure how we're going to reconcile each other's decisions. You did what you did with Jack. It's over. It's too late to fix. And I'm making this decision. Either we accept each other and we move forward or I don't see us having a relationship."

"Of course we will keep the peace," her father said. his tone measured.

"For Colton's wedding?"

"For family gatherings, for the wedding. But I don't approve."

Sierra's heart felt like a brick. "I guess it's important to you that I understand that?"

"I want you to understand that you're making a decision here. One that has consequences."

"Yes, I am. And I'm grown up enough to accept them. I'm adult enough to know that I prefer the consequences. As hard as they are."

"If you end up needing work, you know you can get it here. I won't have the town saying I abandoned my pregnant daughter in her time of need."

"Wow, thank God for town gossip."

"Do you accept?"

She shook her head. "I'm going to have to look for something else. But I will see you again for Colton's wedding. Maybe it's best if we don't talk to Mom about any of this until it's finished. I don't want to upset her."

"I agree with that."

She started to walk away, then she stopped. She turned to face her father. "It isn't that I don't understand. I do understand. When you first explained to me about Jack I understood so well it almost scared me. I really valued my comfortable life. You have no idea how much. I suppose I should thank you for it. I do. I... I loved my life. And I could see how you would want to lie to protect it. Why you would want to cover up your mistakes so that the consequences didn't touch this little thing that you loved. So that it didn't rock your kingdom.

"But I fell in love with someone," she continued. "Really fell in love. And I knew that my life with him had to be built on honesty. I knew that we had to feel the same way about each other, that I couldn't walk around just pretending things were okay when they weren't. Because when you're in love it isn't the words that matter. It isn't the appearance that matters. It's the deeper things. The harder things. And I want that more. More than the comfort of a job at the ranch, or a nuclear family that looks good on the outside but is rotting at the core. I don't hate you. But I feel a little bit sorry for you."

"I have everything," he said. "Everything I ever wanted. There's nothing to feel sorry for me about."

She realized then that he didn't care if anyone loved him. As long as he had this place, his name…he didn't need it to be real. And she could never understand that.

"Be happy with it, then," she said. "And I'll go find my happiness."

Then Sierra turned away from her father, and started walking away. She closed her eyes and let the breeze clear her mind.

But she would come here still. She would see him, see her mother. She would make sure her child knew them both.

Her relationship with her father had changed forever, but she didn't have to let it turn into endless bitterness. She didn't have to hold on to the anger, just because she thought he was wrong.

And as she walked on, she felt a weight she didn't know she'd been carrying fall away.

It turned out that anger was heavy. And she was glad she wasn't carrying it anymore. Whatever Nathan West chose to cling to was his own sad story.

Sierra was going to cling to her child. Her family. To love.

She walked on ahead, into the sunlight. And then she smiled.

CHAPTER TWENTY-TWO

ACE GOT OUT of his truck and walked across the driveway, headed straight toward the barn. He was going to get Lemon Drop and load her up and take her to Colton's. Or to the West ranch. Or to the moon if that's where she was.

He had to find her.

He had to tell her.

He heard a truck engine and the sound of tires on gravel behind him and he turned, just in time to see Sierra's cherry-red truck pulling up to the front of his house. And he ran.

He ran like his life depended on it. He was pretty damn sure it did.

He didn't want her to take one more breath thinking he didn't love her. Didn't want her heart to beat one more time believing a lie.

Even if she said no now, he didn't want her thinking that. He didn't want those last words he'd said to her to be the ones she believed.

She got out of the truck and slammed the door, turning toward the house.

"Sierra!"

She stopped and turned, her eyes round. "Ace. If you came to—"

He didn't let her finish. He pulled her into his arms and kissed her with everything he had. With every bit of love he had inside of him. Because he had to come with something more than words. He had to erase the memory of everything hurtful he'd said, erase the truth he'd tried to put into them.

She clung to his shirt, holding on to him while she kissed him back. It wasn't a happy kiss. It was angry. But he was glad. Because it meant she still felt something. He would take anger over apathy any day of the week. From now until forever.

"I didn't come to…whatever you were about to say," he said, breaking the kiss, his heart thundering hard, his breath coming in harsh gasps.

"Why are you here?"

"Well, it's my house. Actually, you're the one who came here."

"All of my stuff is here. And my horse."

"I was going to bring you your horse. And your stuff. And me."

"That's a lot of things you were going to bring me," she said, sounding dazed. "It's not even my birthday."

"No. But it is 'I Was an Ass and I'm Sorry' day."

"I'm not sure sorry is enough."

"Well, that's not the only thing. I went to church this morning."

She blinked rapidly. "You did?"

"Yeah. Not for a service. Well, maybe for a private one." He cleared his throat. "This will come as no surprise to you, but I'm fucked up."

She laughed, a watery, shaky sound. "I do realize that."

"I can't promise that I'll just be fixed."

"I didn't ask you to be fixed."

His heart burned, his whole body shaking. "I know. I couldn't believe that. I couldn't accept it."

"I know," she said, sliding her hand along his jaw. "I had to believe that if I just stood my ground you would. But I was scared. I was scared you wouldn't see it."

"I don't deserve that, either. That faith you have in me. I didn't have it in myself, I have no idea how you held on to it for me."

"Someone had to."

"A lot more people were holding on than I realized. I pushed so many people away. My parents, you. I've been…coasting. I'm everyone's drinking buddy and nobody's friend. Because I never wanted to explain my past to anyone. I'm… I'm ashamed of it, Sierra. I feel like I let her down. Callie. I—"

She wrapped her arms around him, pressing her head against his chest. "You didn't. You did everything you could. You fought for her, Ace. You did."

"It wasn't good enough. My hardest fight wasn't enough."

"It was an impossible battle. One you fought anyway. One you kept fighting long after you lost." She took a deep breath. "When you first told me about Callie, I was so sorry for you. So sad. But so…satisfied for myself."

"What do you mean?"

"Because I looked at you, at that fierce protectiveness in your eyes, and I thought…that man is the father of my baby. I could see that you would die for your child, that you would move heaven and earth for him or her. That you love hard, even when it hurts. That you are as faithful as they come. Ace Thompson, you think you're unworthy for the very reason I think you are the only man on earth I could ever have children with. The only man I could ever think of marrying.

"You can't guarantee the outcome of a battle, Ace," she said, her voice soft, her fingertips tracing lines over his cheek. "But the fact that I know you'll fight? That means more than anything else."

"I didn't feel like I was good enough for you," he said, his words strangled. "I still don't. But you're right. I will fight for you. For us. For our baby. And I would… I would give anything to go back and never say some of the things I've said to you. To never say you were a silly rich girl. That I didn't trust you. That I didn't love you."

"I guess," she said, taking a slow breath, "all you can really do is apologize. That's something I learned from you."

"I'm sorry," he said, the words rough.

"Next time you say something stupid let's start here. I won't storm out. You won't try to keep pushing me away."

"I think that's a great idea. I will say more stupid things, you know."

"I know. And I'll be unreasonable. And too emotional about things. I'll take things personally that I shouldn't and hang on to being mad for too long because that's… what I do. But under all of that you can be sure that I love you. That I want this to work more than I want to prove I'm right. More than I want my way. More than I want to win a fight."

"And I love you," he said. "More than I want to be protected. More than anything. I'm not the man I used to be, I don't think I ever will be. I've been beaten pretty bad by life and I'm kind of jacked up as a result. I spent a long time just not dealing with it. And then you bounced in."

She made a face. "You keep saying that."

"You bounce," he said. "It's charming and irresistible."

"Am I charming and irresistible?" she asked.

"Yes."

"But more important…you *do* love me."

"I do," he said, brushing a kiss over her lips. "Sierra… I love you so much. You dragged me out of the darkness, baby. I didn't even realize I was there. I was so used to it. I had accepted it. But you showed me light. You made me want to walk in it again. You've given me…so much and I don't know if I've given you even one damn thing."

"You have," she said, taking his hands in hers. "Ace, you were the one who showed me what I wanted. Even when it ended up with me…leaving it was because of you. Because you made me realize that I had to stand and fight. That I couldn't run. That anything worth having was worth waging war over. Even if you might lose."

"I'm so glad you didn't lose."

"Me, too, Ace," she said, kissing him slowly, thoroughly. "Me, too."

Ace Thompson knew the secrets of nearly every person in Copper Ridge. He had listened to countless confessions from across the bar at Ace's. Had heard every trial, tribulation and sin the citizens of town had endured and committed.

But there was only one person on earth who made him want to share his own.

Sierra West was the one who knew him.

"You know, Sierra, a lot of people share secrets with me. That's part of being a bartender."

"I bet," she said.

"People tell me about their past. Their failures. Their fears. But I've never shared mine. For better or for worse,

I've shared all that with you. But I don't just want you to know my past, that's not enough."

"Is that right?" she asked, a tear sliding down her cheek.

He lifted his hand, wiped the tear away with the edge of his thumb. "Yeah. That's right. The past is full of pain, and I'm glad you know about it. I'm glad that you know where I came from. But that's all it is now. Where I came from. You're where I'm at, you're where I'm going. I will never allow the past to be bigger than that. Not anymore." He kissed her, just a brief brush of his lips against hers. "Remember when I said you were my second chance?"

"Yes."

"I don't think that's true. This isn't my second chance. This is my new beginning. The first step into the rest of my life. And there is no one I would rather walk on this road with than you."

He put his arm around her, and they turned, and started walking toward the house. Ace was struck with an intense wave of emotion that washed over him, expanded in his chest. That sense of deep belonging, of rightness he'd been searching for all this time, that had evaded him when he'd come back to town, back to his parents' house, back to the church.

Home.

For the first time in years, Ace Thompson felt like he was coming home. It wasn't the town that mattered, it wasn't the house that mattered.

Home was Sierra. Now, and forever.

EPILOGUE

It HAD BEEN a long nine months. But Ace was attentive, and generally perfect, and the best husband a woman could ask for, so Sierra supposed she shouldn't complain.

Of course, she had complained a little bit, but honestly, those complaints usually got her whatever food she was craving so sometimes being a squeaky wheel definitely meant getting grease. And she was fond of grease.

Especially when it came in the form of french fries.

She was currently eating a basket of sweet potato fries out on the deck of the brewery, overlooking the ocean. The sun was shining on her—not too hot. Which was good because almost everything made her too hot—a light breeze ruffled her hair, the scent from the sea pleasant now that she was so far along in her pregnancy. Early on it had been a little bit strong for her sensitive sense of smell.

"Daddy!"

Sierra looked away from the ocean, just in time to see her three-year-old daughter scramble down from her chair and run over to the doorway that led into the dining room. Straight into Ace's arms.

The smile that lit up his whole face warmed her from the inside out. He bent down and picked Lily up, holding her close and kissing her little round cheek. Sierra put her sweet potato fry down and wiped her hands on a napkin, blinking back the tears that had suddenly filled her eyes.

Darn pregnancy hormones.

"I thought I'd find you both out here."

"I can't stay away," she said, smiling up at him. "And I don't just mean I can't stay away from the fries."

"If you love fries more than you love me right now I understand," he said, walking over to the table and crouching down, Lily still on his hip. He reached out and put his hand on her stomach, his touch gentle and—frankly—electrifying. Always.

She kept waiting for their relationship to feel like comfortable clothes. For it to feel like everyday, routine, just-taking-another-breath stuff. It never did.

Touching him was electric. Talking to him. Fighting with him. Sleeping with him. Breathing next to him. Watching him with their daughter. It was remarkable every day. She loved it. She loved him.

Even more remarkable was how her family had changed. How grandchildren had brought her mother peace. How much healing—even if it was imperfect—had taken place between her father and everyone else.

How much healing had taken place in general.

"Never," she said. "I don't even love milk shakes more than I love you."

"Wow," he said, a lopsided grin on his handsome face. "That's pretty high praise at the moment."

"It's pretty high praise always, Ace, don't forget it."

"In a couple of days…there will be four of us," he said, looking pointedly at her stomach. "This is one of our last moments to just be three."

"And we never had very many moments to just be two."

"No. But I've never really been worried about it."

"Oh, really?"

"Nah," he said. "When you have this much love to give out, adding another person is just…adding more love, right?"

"I think so," she said. "More kids. More time. More steps with you. It all equals more love in the end."

He leaned in and kissed her, and she felt it all the way down to her toes. "That's true. My dad was right. He said love would change me. It did. You have. In the very best ways. I want to be the best man I can be for you, because of the way you love me."

Her heart expanded. "It's not hard to love you, you know."

Lily chose that moment to turn, grab Ace's face and plant a kiss on his cheek. "Love you," she said.

Ace closed his eyes, a muscle in his jaw moving. "I love you both." He opened his eyes, and looked at Sierra. "Thank you," he said. "Thank you for this life. Thank you for being my home."

* * * * *

*Ranching heir Colton West is getting ready to say
"I do," but when the wedding of the century
takes an unexpected turn, the golden boy of
Copper Ridge just might get a lesson in love
he'll never forget.*

*Look for
TOUGH LUCK HERO,
the next installment of Maisey Yates's
unforgettable Copper Ridge series.*

*And don't miss the other Copper Ridge novels,
available now from Maisey Yates and Harlequin:*

SHOULDA BEEN A COWBOY
(Jake and Cassie's novella)
PART TIME COWBOY
(Eli and Sadie's story)
BROKEDOWN COWBOY
(Connor and Liss's story)
BAD NEWS COWBOY
(Jack and Kate's story)
A COPPER RIDGE CHRISTMAS
(Ryan and Holly's novella)
TAKE ME, COWBOY
(Chase and Anna's story)

*Read on for a Copper Ridge novella,
HOMETOWN HEARTBREAKER,
in print for the first time...*

HOMETOWN
HEARTBREAKER

CHAPTER ONE

ACE WAS VERY PROUD of the microbrews they served at his bar. Casey James didn't see what was so special about them. Because at the end of the day after she'd been serving drinks over the course of a seven-hour shift, whether it was a lager brewed in a small quantity or a light beer brewed for the masses, it all smelled the same to her. By then it had woven its way around the fabric of her clothes and settled down beneath the surface of her skin.

Ace's was the primary hangout in Copper Ridge, Oregon, for anybody looking to unwind after a hard day's work. At least, that's what she'd absorbed over the past couple of weeks working there.

Along with alcohol fumes and more country music than she had even known existed before she'd walked into this place.

When she went home—such as her transient dwelling was—she did so smelling like beer and oil from the deep fryer and humming Garth Brooks. She felt invaded by the place. Still, she couldn't complain. She'd been broke when she'd driven into Copper Ridge about sixteen days ago. Not enough money for a hotel, or even a sketchy motel. Not enough money for food on the road. She'd gotten sick of hitchhiking somewhere back in the Midwest and had bought the cheapest car she could find, and it had let out its last gasp when she'd rolled over into Logan County.

Now the car was parked at Copper Campground, and her tent was pitched at the most convenient space in the park. Not that camping anywhere was very convenient right now, considering that nights here in the little coastal town were cold and heavy with mist, and she possessed very serious black-bear-related concerns. Solitude also provided some pretty heavy silences. Not her favorite on the best of days.

But God knew she'd slept in worse. And *with* worse.

When Ace had first hired her she had sort of imagined he might be expecting a different kind of arrangement. Why else would a guy agree to hire a woman on a very temporary basis so she could earn a little pocket change before moving on?

He was good-looking, so she hadn't really thought it would be too big of a deal. Plus, she thought it might get her out of her sleeping bag and into an actual bed. But, much to her surprise, Ace had never even given her an inappropriate side-eye since he'd hired her.

Yay for his scruples. Less *yay* for her chilly sleeping arrangement.

"Hey, baby." The words were slurred across the bar, and she wasn't even going to bother with telling the guy that that wasn't her name. If he was going to leave a tip, her name could be baby if he really wanted it to be. "Another drink."

She turned and faced the guy sitting down at the far end, clad in a flannel shirt and overalls. He had been running up his tab all night, and was definitely starting to look a little bit worse for wear.

"Sure thing." She was not a human Breathalyzer. It

wasn't her job to worry about whether or not someone should have another drink. She just wanted to get paid.

Once she'd collected enough cash to figure out what was going on with her car, plus enough extra to crash somewhere other than a campground for a while, she would move on.

You have to stop sometime.

No, she didn't. Anyway, if she was going to stop it would be somewhere warmer. Someplace near the ocean, but not the kind of ocean that felt like a melted glacier.

She poured another measure of bourbon for the evening's best customer—which, in her world, was a dubious honor—and slid down toward him. "Another one on your tab?"

He nodded, picking up the glass and raising it in mock salute. She raised her brows in return.

Just then, the door to the bar opened, and for some reason she felt compelled to look. People filed in and out all evening, so there was nothing particularly remarkable about another arrival. But somehow this one felt remarkable. It kept on feeling more and more so while she studied the new arrival.

He was notable in part because he was enraged—which was something she paid attention to, but wasn't unique. People got mad, and they tended to get mad even easier when alcohol was involved. So pissed-off dudes weren't remarkable in and of themselves, or something she got too worked up over. But there was something about him…his dark brows lowered, intense and angry, his chiseled jaw clenched—broad shoulders, a trim waist. Well, really he was hot. He had some very admirable forearms and hands that looked just the right size to hold on tight to her hips.

Behold the power of a pair of sexy, masculine hands.

The handsome stranger stood in the door for only a few moments before storming down into the dining area and making a beeline toward the bar. He didn't notice Casey, or anyone. At least, not anyone besides her best customer.

"What are you doing here, Dad?" The stranger's voice was uncompromising, deep and very, very angry.

The older man grunted. "Winding down after work. I didn't realize that was a problem."

"It is when you're a damn alcoholic."

Unexpectedly, Casey's heart clenched with sympathy. Addiction. If there was one thing she was more familiar with than she'd like to be, that was it. Actually, there were quite a few things she had more familiarity with than she would like, but addiction was the most insidious. Still, she didn't usually waste emotion on strangers. Typically, she didn't waste emotion on anyone but herself, and when it came to herself she was still pretty spare with it. She couldn't afford to wallow. If she did, she might never get back up.

"That's your word, boy," the older man said. "Not mine."

"A John Deere isn't a Ferrari just because you call it one. Doesn't matter what you want to call it, or *not* call it. Anyway, you promised." He said the last part in a hushed, sincere tone that left her in no doubt that Handsome Stranger had truly believed his father wasn't going to drink again, just because the old man had promised.

She wondered how in hell he'd gotten to his age—his late twenties, she guessed—still believing the promises of an addict.

"Let's go, Dad," he said again, uncompromising.

He didn't wait for the older man to comply, but grabbed

him by the back of the shirt and hauled him off the stool. It was easy enough to do, given the inebriated state of his father. He started to direct him out of the bar, and irritation started to build in Casey's chest. She had spent all evening letting that drunk-ass old guy call her baby. And if she wasn't going to get a tip, it had hardly been worth it.

"Hey!" she shouted.

Handsome Stranger paused, turning to face her, the expression he treated her to as stormy as the one he had been aiming at his dad. "You have a problem?"

"Yes." She planted her hands on her hips. "Your dad ran up a pretty serious tab tonight. And I've been serving him. If you think you're going to walk out of here without passing any cash my way you're very wrong."

He didn't address her; instead, he turned to his father. "Dad, give me your keys."

"The hell I—"

"You aren't driving." He stood there, angry, but with something deeper radiating from him, as well. A well-worn patience unlike anything she had ever witnessed before. "Give me your keys. Don't make me call Sheriff Garrett."

Much to Casey's surprise, the older man complied, pressing his keys into his son's hand. Then Handsome Stranger moved back toward the bar, toward her. She wasn't the kind of woman to get breathless over a man. In her experience, men were like cheap appliances. They might be shiny out of the box, but all too soon they shorted out and left you high and dry. Fine in many cases, since she wasn't exactly looking for a promise, but as this man approached her she had to confess to a little bit of breathlessness. She blamed the broad shoulders, which looked like they would be very nice to hold on to. And again, those large hands, which looked like they would be very good at holding on to her.

He reached out, one of the very hands she had just been weaving inappropriate thoughts about extending the keys toward her. "Keep his car. Consider it collateral. I'll be back for it as soon as I can make it down here tomorrow."

She curled her fingers around the keys, the sharp edges digging into her palm. "You realize I could just drive off into the sunset with this. Or into the dawn, as the case may be."

"Don't," he said, casual, unconcerned. As though he were confident that his calm, rational command would be met with obedience, because how could she refuse?

Prick.

She kind of liked it.

As if she needed any more proof that her issues had issues.

"Just so you know," she said, earning herself another backward glance, "I'm not very good at following instructions." She jingled the keys, arching her brow meaningfully.

"Just so *you* know, I'm good friends with the sheriff. See you tomorrow."

And with that, Handsome Stranger stormed back out of the bar, propelling his old man with him, along with what she had hoped would be her biggest tip of the evening.

"Hey, baby, can I get another drink?" She turned toward the source of the request—the man now vying for position as new best customer—and let out a heavy sigh.

"Of course, sugar," she said. And by sugar, she meant

asshole. But she wasn't in the mood to lose all of her tip money in one evening.

By last call she was exhausted, grumpy and in no mood to walk all the way from the bar back to the campground. This, in a nutshell, was why it was so much better to work out an *arrangement* with someone if it was possible.

This was why she almost wished her boss was the kind of person who liked to take a little bit of personal advantage of his employees. She would have somewhere warm to sleep if he did.

Self-preservation was an art form she had taken to a new level. But in her situation, it was necessary. Men made great allies because she had something they wanted. She was perfectly comfortable going it alone in the general sense. But she'd been through enough to realize that while she never wanted to depend on anyone emotionally, it was practical to have someone else by your side.

Two a.m., with no car, and three miles to walk until she could finally lie down and get some rest, was one of those times.

Of course, that acknowledgment went hand in hand with feeling like she might prefer death to actually asking for help. She preferred to find ways to engineer receiving help without actually admitting how much she might need it.

Finding yourself in dire straits was one thing. Acting helpless was quite another.

She pressed her hand to the pocket of the black apron she was wearing, felt the bulk of the keys beneath the fabric. Oh yeah, she had that car. Wherever it might be parked. Farm boy was going to be back tomorrow to pick it up, but she would be at the bar before he would, most likely.

She chewed the inside of her cheek, pretending for a second that she was weighing her options. Like there was another option. She had keys to a car that no one needed tonight. And the difference between an hour-long walk and a two-minute drive was pretty much a no-brainer.

She smiled to herself as she took a clean rag out of the bleach water bin and started to wipe down the top of the bar. As things worked out, she'd managed to get help from a guy, after all. And she'd gotten to keep her top on.

CHAPTER TWO

AIDEN CRAWFORD HAD half a mind to let his father's car rot in Ace's parking lot. After all, his father would rot on a bar stool inside of Ace's if left to his own devices, so it seemed a fitting fate for the car.

He wasn't in the mood to go all the way to town just to deal with it, and he really hadn't been in the mood to coordinate getting the car back to the family farm. He didn't want to have to tell his mother that he had caught her husband drinking again, even though she had to know someplace deep down inside, behind the boxes of denial and passivity that she kept stacked up tall in front of reality in order to keep from having to deal with it.

Unfortunately, he did have to drive to the Farm and Garden to get new feed for the chickens since the damn barn cat had chewed a hole in the edge of the bag and let moisture get in, leaving mold covering all the grains like a little gray pelt. And he would have to drive by the bar to get to the store. If he couldn't figure out whose help to enlist to get the car back, he could always tow it home. It was just a bigger pain in the ass than he cared to put up with right now. But then, what wasn't?

As he drew nearer to the bar, he thought about the waitress from last night. Slim, petite. Some people might think delicate, but he didn't. Her blue eyes were shot through with steel, and there was a slight quirk to one side of her mouth and to one eyebrow that spoke of hard-earned and well-worn cynicism. Funny, since she couldn't be much over the legal drinking age herself.

It was a whole lot of observations to make about one waitress he'd spoken to for about two minutes. But it wasn't all that surprising, considering her world-weariness wasn't the only thing he'd noticed. She was beautiful. And she caught hold of his body's interest in a way no one had for a very long time.

Just another thing he didn't have time for. Not now.

Damn Caroline finding herself a functional relationship. He cared about her. Cared deeply about her happiness. God knew he couldn't give her what she'd wanted, no matter how much he wished he could. She'd moved on, and with his blessing.

But after six months of celibacy he was smarting from being cut off from his only source of physical satisfaction. So yeah, he had given the waitress a little bit more attention than he might have on a typical night spent dragging his father out of a bar.

He rolled up to the parking lot of Ace's and turned in, stopping when he found the parking lot mostly empty. Not a huge surprise, since it was only two in the afternoon—a bit late for the lunch crowd and too early for the drinking crowd. Really, the only notable thing about it was the fact that the car he had left here last night wasn't there.

He swore, turning into a space and putting the truck in Park. It wasn't like Ace to have it towed. He knew full well whose car that was. And, in fact, had Ace been manning the bar last night, Aiden had serious doubts his father would have been served a drink at all.

Not that it was a random waitress's job to know that

his father was more or less Copper Ridge's worst drunk. Though he hadn't expected her to take off with the car. In hindsight, that was a mistake. A pretty stupid one. He'd handed his father's car keys over to a perfect stranger.

He would ask himself what he'd been thinking, but he knew all too well. He'd been antsy, feeling gnawing desperation to get out of the bar combined with a desire to linger and keep checking out the waitress. He should've had better control over himself.

He was only human. A human who had been denied physical contact with another human for a very long time.

Still, it didn't give him an excuse to be a dumbass.

As he was sitting there castigating himself, he saw his father's car turn into the driveway and pull up to one of the spaces by the front door. He killed the engine on his truck and opened the driver-side door, getting out and slamming it shut behind him as he walked over to the car. Very much *not* to his surprise, it was the pretty blonde from last night who climbed out of it, long legs first. Yes, he noticed, even though he was currently dealing with the world's sloppiest case of grand theft auto.

"Decided to help yourself to my old man's ride?"

She froze, her posture going board straight before she turned slowly to face him. Her expression was inscrutable, unreadable, but he could see something in those blue eyes he didn't like. Fear. She covered it quickly, planting one hand on her hip and popping it out to the side. "Oh, I'm sorry, did I inconvenience you terribly by not having it sit here all night?"

"I felt a little inconvenienced when I pulled in a few minutes ago and thought it had been stolen."

"Dear God. Minutes of inconvenience. We should start a GoFundMe to help you deal with your trauma." She turned away from him, facing the bar, her blond hair shimmering over her shoulder as she tightened her hold in her purse. "If you'll excuse me, I'm going to be late to work."

"My keys?"

"Right." She turned back, fishing in her bag and taking them out, jingling them slightly. A very broad, very fake smile stretched across her face. "See? Not keeping it." She tossed the keys toward him and he reacted quickly, catching them at the last moment. "Nice."

His patience was wearing thin, and along with it, his control. "Why did you take the car?"

"Because I don't have one," she said, speaking slowly in a monotone voice, as though she were talking to someone very young or very stupid. "And since I didn't get off until well past midnight and there was a car available, I thought that I would cut an hour or so off my commute in the dark, damp weather. Problem?"

He didn't know how she'd managed it. All he knew was that a second ago he'd been angry because she'd taken off with his car, and now he was the one who felt like an ass.

"You could have asked," he said.

"Yeah, well, you seemed like you were in a little bit of a hurry, so I thought maybe not. Actually, I thought you probably wouldn't know, since I didn't figure you would be back for it this early." She shrugged. "Calculated risk. It failed. That happens. But no harm, no foul. You got your car back, and I didn't get ax murdered on my way home from work. Everyone wins."

"Wait," he said as she started to turn away again.

She paused. "I have a bunch of extra tips to earn, seeing as you walked out with last night's tips when you took your dad. And I'm on the early shift, which means less money anyway. So, I better go."

"Don't I need to pay my tab?" He didn't know why in hell he was still talking to her. She was pushing against things best left un-pushed against, and he should get on with his day.

But he was still talking to her.

And anyway, he did have to pay.

"I suppose," she said. "But I figure you can take that up with Ace."

"I thought you were worried about your tips."

"I am. Was. At this point, I figure I'm not going to get them."

That was his cue to take off. But he didn't. "If I'm anything, it's a man of my word." Even when it came to making good on promises given to carjacking waitresses. He wasn't like his father. Not now, not ever. He didn't promise one thing and deliver another just because it was convenient.

"Cute. You and George Washington."

"What?" he asked, as he started to follow her into the bar. And, though he tried, he wasn't successful in keeping himself from letting his eyes drift down so that he could admire the curve of her butt. It was a very nice curve.

"You cannot tell a lie. Neither could he."

"Actually, that didn't really happen," he said.

"It totally did. They reenacted it on Sesame Street. Muppets don't lie."

She walked quickly through the mostly empty dining room, making her way to the bar, fishing around until she found a black apron beneath it and tying it on before she put her long blond hair up into a bun. He watched as he moved closer, completely drawn in by her movements.

He was seriously hard up, and in no position to do anything about it. He had to hope the damp weather wasn't making his hay a bigger mess than the chicken feed he was dealing with today. Had to get through baling. Had to get all the accounts in order, and hoped his dad hadn't alienated anyone else with his recent bout of drunkenness.

Yeah, he didn't have any time to deal with women or relationships.

That was why the arrangement with Caroline had been so perfect for so long. They had acted as official itch scratchers for each other for years. Both of them in too deep with family issues to ever want a relationship. Then he'd gotten it into his head that maybe he did want one. That he could change things. Could have a life that was separate from his parents and save the farm all at the same time.

Until he'd found out his dad was in serious debt and had fucked some important business relationships six different ways. Then all the money he'd been saving, his hope for a future, had been poured back into the barn.

He'd tried to explain things to Caroline. To say that things would just go on as they always had. But she hadn't wanted that anymore. So she'd gotten herself a real relationship, and now he was back to spending his romantic Friday nights with his right hand.

As soon as that thought filtered through his mind, she looked up, her blue eyes meeting his, her brow arched as though she had read his thoughts. He felt compelled to keep the conversation going. To keep the connection, because it had been a damn long time since he'd felt one with another person.

"Sometimes, Muppets lie," he said, because he couldn't think of anything else to say.

"Well, shit." She slapped her hands down on the bar top. "Now I'm going to have to rethink every bit of advice I ever internalized as a kid. You know, I didn't have the most attentive of parents, so I kinda depended on the wisdom dispensed by Fraggles. Did you want to give me a tip along with the existential crisis?"

"I said I would," he said, reaching into his back pocket for his wallet.

"So," she said, "Muppets are liars. What about anthropomorphic bears?"

"What?"

"The very foundation of my childhood depends on your answer."

He looked at her, not quite able to figure out whether or not she was serious. "I'm pretty sure they're trustworthy. Not real bears, though. Don't trust a real bear." He took a twenty-dollar bill out of his wallet and handed it to her. "This is the tip. I'll pay the tab with my card." Knowing his dad, he'd run up more in drink costs than the eighty in cash he was currently carrying.

"Good." She took the money and her eyes widened slightly when she looked at it closely. "Generous," she said.

"My dad has a tendency to be obnoxious."

"Honestly? Not any more than any of the other guys who sit around on these stools. I've only been here for a couple of weeks, but I already have some favorites. And by favorites, I mean guys I want to punch with a broken bottle."

He handed her his credit card and she took it, swiping

it on the machine that was sitting on the lower counter. "How much damage did he do?"

"A bit. You might actually be trading me that car." She looked up, smiling for a second, so quickly he thought he might have imagined it, before handing him back the card and the receipt. "Sorry. Addicts, right?"

He gritted his teeth, uncomfortable with her referring to his dad that way. Even if it was true. "You speaking from experience?" He signed the total slowly, trying not to do the mental math on how many drinks it broke down to.

"Um, hi. I work in a bar. I pretty much invariably work in bars. There's at least one of your dad in every town I've ever been through. Not too many of you, though."

"What do you mean?"

"Well," she said, looking down at his receipt and reading the name printed on the bottom, "Aiden, most people just leave them to drown in it."

He didn't like taking the compliment, even such as it was. He didn't feel like he was doing anything especially good. He was just doing what had to be done. Life wasn't about comfort or happiness. It was about control. Doing the right thing, not the easy thing.

Following your heart was bullshit. His dad's heart said *drink up and screw the waitress*. No. Deciding on the right path and sticking to it was all there was.

"I have a farm to run," he said. "And my dad's name is on the title. So I can't very well let him drown in a whiskey bath."

"Sure. That's as good a reason as any. But at least you have a reason. Whatever, I'm trying to say nice things, and my lips aren't used to making friendly sounds, so clearly I'm not doing a very good job."

"No, you did a good job. Thank you." Now he felt extra-guilty for earlier. For scaring her, when she'd been driving the car because she didn't have another way to get back to wherever it was she lived. After midnight. In the rain. This was his problem in a nutshell. He didn't leave his dad to drown in his drink, and he felt bad for this woman who had essentially stolen his car. "Hey, what time do you get off?"

She puckered her lips together, raising both brows. "Well, about eight. But, I have to say, I don't think you're *that* nice."

"I'm not hitting on you. When you get off, why don't you follow me back to my parents' place with the car, and then I'll drive you over to wherever it is you're staying. You don't have to walk, and I don't have to tow the thing. How does that work?"

She squinted. "Why?"

"It helps everybody."

"I guess it does." She frowned. "In a surprisingly no-strings-attached way."

"It helps you, it helps me. It's hardly charity." He didn't want to stand here and make conversation with her. He wanted to get away, get his head on straight.

She laughed. "Just waiting for the part where you tell me I can offer you further help by sucking your dick."

Her words hit him with all the force of a slap. Heat barreled through his veins like a bullet speeding out of a gun. He was angry. Angry, and turned on. Turned on, because what guy wouldn't be when the topic of blow jobs was introduced? Angry because it affected him so much.

Angry because she had felt like it needed to be said. Clearly people had taken advantage of her in the past, otherwise there would be no reason for her to bring it up.

Yeah, he was angry for a host of reasons.

"I'm not going to ask you to do that," he said, the words coming out harder than he'd intended. "And if that's your first assumption about what a guy is after, then I think maybe you've been associating with the wrong kind of guy."

She lifted a shoulder. "Well, that depends."

"Depends on what?"

"Depends on what you want from the guy. I was warned a lot about guys who only want one thing, but here's the deal. Guys who only want one thing are pretty easy to handle. They're honest, at least. It's the Dudley Do-Rights that concern me. You," she said, jabbing her index finger in his direction, "you concern me."

"I just said I want to help you out, no conditions."

She crossed her arms and treated him to a skeptical expression. "Everybody has conditions, hayseed. Even you."

He gritted teeth. He was still angry, but now he was pretty much just angry at her. "Do you want to use the car later or not? I can hitch it up to my truck and tow it home now. I'd rather not, because it's a pain in my ass. But so are you. Which means I'm kind of doing compare and contrast right now."

"Yes. The Good Deed Venn diagram. I'm familiar. FYI, in my life, the good deeds I've attempted never really balance out right. So I usually just forget them. I prefer to look out for me."

"Do you," he said again, slower, his tone more intense as he fought to keep his control, "want to use the car or not?"

She blinked a couple of times, clearly surprised that he hadn't withdrawn the offer. That he hadn't backed down. "Yeah. I can drive it home for you."

"Good. I'll be back here at eight. If you keep me waiting, I'm going to hitch it to my truck and tow it back. I will leave you standing out in the drizzle on your own, and I won't lose any sleep over it." Except he had a feeling he would lose sleep over her either way, for all the wrong reasons.

"You know, they say it's more blessed to give than receive. You don't seem very blessed."

"I don't feel it, either. Eight o'clock."

He turned away from her then, heading out of the bar and back into the damp outdoors. He stopped and looked at the rolling gray sea off in the distance, hoping the horizon line would help steady some of the recklessness currently rioting through him.

It didn't.

CHAPTER THREE

THE SHIFT PASSED quickly and by eight o'clock her feet ached, even though it seemed like she hadn't been on them for all that long. As these jobs went, Ace's wasn't the worst.

He was nice. The customers were—by and large—nice. She had definitely been in worse situations. The floor wasn't sticky, the bar itself clean, with wood-paneled walls and a mix of lodge and nautical details paying decent service to the little town that sat at the base of the mountains and on the edge of the open sea.

That was another bonus. A step out to the parking lot, and she had an ocean view. That was tough to beat. She loved the ocean. She hadn't seen one until she was nineteen years old, and ever since then she'd felt like she wanted one in sight at all times. That made this place nice for more than one reason. But she still couldn't imagine staying.

She wanted to get to a city. Somewhere a little bit more anonymous. Where she could blend in and not end up left with cars in her care by overly trusting country boys. Sure, the hospitality could be nice, but it was also very *personal*. She wasn't a huge fan of personal.

She took her apron off and stuffed it beneath the counter, rounding the bar and walking into the main dining room just as Aiden walked through the door. Right on time. Right like he said.

It figured. This guy probably wouldn't even drive across the street without his driver's license, much less renege on a scheduled time to meet someone. He was... *good.*

She was pretty confident about that. And there weren't a lot of people who she would label good. This guy was.

It almost made her feel guilty about what she'd said to him earlier regarding sucking certain appendages. In the spare few minutes they'd spoken, he'd never acted like he was only talking to her to curry sexual favor.

But sometimes she just liked to cut to the chase and accuse people of the things she was most afraid they would do. It minimized the pain when they inevitably disappointed her.

Still, so far it didn't seem like he was hiding a secret inner pervert waiting to take advantage. She could only hope that stayed true.

Even if he is? Does it matter?

Her stomach tightened as she looked at him, his handsome face and truly noteworthy physique.

Getting physical with him wouldn't be a hardship, that was for sure. But there was something about him that made her hope—deeply, *stupidly*—that he turned out to be what he seemed, and not something else. Some part of her was actually hopeful that this guy was good. That he wasn't like the rest.

Hell, *someone* had to be. If a strong, upstanding farm boy who dragged his father out of dens of sin and forgave down-and-out waitresses who borrowed cars—without asking—to get home wasn't salt of the earth, then who would be?

"You're here," she said.

"Just like I said."

She smiled. "Yes. Just like you said. So, how far out of town is your place?"

"About fifteen minutes. Going to have to drive back there, then down to…where you live?"

"I don't *live* there," she said. "I'm kind of passing through town. My car broke down and I needed to earn some extra money so that I can get it fixed."

She wasn't sure why she was explaining all of this to him. Not only had she confessed that she was basically homeless, but for some reason she also felt the need to justify it. Which was stupid. She'd gotten past feeling the need to justify her existence a long time ago. It was what it was. Sure, a lot of people thought that someone like her should be living in a different situation. That a girl who was young, reasonably attractive, clearly in possession of all her mental faculties, should have gone to college. That she should be starting her career. Basically that she should be anything other than a transient bar wench.

But those people didn't know her. So they didn't deserve her story. Yet here she was telling it for his benefit. And she couldn't stop herself. "I'm staying at a campground. Kind of over by the beach."

"Which one?" he asked.

"Copper Campground. Since this is Copper Ridge, it seemed like it was probably the main campground. The hub, so to speak. I like to be where the action is. I thought maybe the real up-and-coming squirrels hung out there."

"And?" he asked.

"They *are* pretty metropolitan for squirrels."

"I meant, and what's your situation? How is it you're

camping out for... How long did you say you've been here?"

"Two weeks. And the *situation* is that I don't have a car. Ace was willing to give me a job on the temporary basis that I needed."

"Are you headed home?"

"No. I'm headed to some places I've never been."

They walked through the parking lot and he opened the driver-side door to the car. "You don't have anyone waiting for you?"

She stared at the open door for a moment, torn between feeling something that was almost...good over the gesture and wanting to run the opposite direction. He was too good to be real.

"No." She sat down in the driver's seat and jammed the keys in the ignition. "Which is great, really. I'm kind of off grid."

He arched a dark brow. "So you're a drifter?"

"Yes, but in the romantically applied sense of the word, rather than the vaguely skeezy one. I'm kind of like a feather. I waft in the breeze," she said, offering him a smile that was pretty damn fake if she said so herself.

The truth was, there wasn't much that was romantic about her existence. But sometimes, when she told the story of how it all worked, she pretended that it was. She pretended that all the places she'd seen had possessed something magical about them, when in reality, it was usually just more of the same: sad small towns and crappy roadside motels.

But in memory, things could be different. A little bit brighter, a little more fun. When she thought back on the night she'd ended up wandering the streets of some tiny town in Kansas, getting rained on and ending up sleeping in some back alley covered by cardboard, she pretended it had been some kind of important formative experience. When in reality it had been the most miserable, traumatizing night of her life.

Yeah, memory changed things.

She didn't lie. At least, she didn't fashion lies out of nothing. She was a master of embellishing the truth. At adding jewels and glitter to her circumstances, so that no one would notice it was all plastered onto a cheap cardboard facade. But then, she did it for herself as much as anyone else.

"Okay. Well, as long as you don't intend to kill my entire family and steal their identities, you can follow me back to the homestead."

"In all my years of drifting I've never committed mass murder, so I don't see why I'd start now." She closed her eyes and took a deep breath of the damp ocean breeze. "Yeah, no. Not feeling homicidal today."

"Good to know." He slammed her door shut and walked back toward his truck, and she waited for him to get in and pull over to the driveway before she followed suit. She wasn't quite sure how she'd gotten roped into this, but it definitely beat walking home, even if it would take her a little bit out of her way. And he said it had helped him. It wasn't terrible to help somebody. It had just been so long since she'd done it she had kind of forgotten that it almost felt good.

It was difficult to worry about the circumstances of others when your own were so dire.

The drive on the gently winding rural road passed quickly, and before she knew it she was pulling into a dirt driveway that wound back into the trees.

Branches from the ragged pines reached into the driveway, scraping against the sides of the car as she drove on. She could only hope this wasn't some kind of elaborate scheme to collect insurance money from her or something, by blaming her for scratches on the car. In all honesty, that seemed a little more likely than him just "helping her out."

She pushed that thought to the back of her mind. It didn't matter either way, since she was the worst person on earth to try to commit insurance fraud with. She didn't have insurance. Though that could probably get her in trouble. She chewed her lip as she turned that thought over, her eyes glued to the taillights on Aiden's truck.

Maybe he was a member of a cult out here in the woods. A cult that frowned on drinking. Maybe she was being lured here to be sacrificed to the forest gods. Unfortunately for them, if they needed a virgin sacrifice, they were shit out of luck with her.

Actually, a cult kind of explained Aiden and his general nice-guy appearance better than anything else. Certainly better than genuine kindness.

They rounded the last curve in the driveway and a small, stereotypical vision of a farmhouse came into view, a single porch light shining brightly by the red front door. "You are now entering…the Twilight Zone," she said to herself.

She parked the car beside Aiden's truck and waited. She felt frozen for some reason, not really wanting to get out and deal with whatever was going to happen here. Not because she actually thought it was a cult that wanted to sacrifice her to a deity, but because she sensed that there might be cookies and kindness afoot. And both made her terribly nervous.

Well, cookies in isolation didn't make her nervous. But

382 HOMETOWN HEARTBREAKER

she was accustomed to the store-bought variety. Not any that were made with actual human hands and love and other things she generally avoided.

She heard Aiden shut his truck door and she let out a long sigh. She turned the engine off and got out, the gravel in the driveway crunching beneath her feet. "Okay," she said. "I'm ready to get back to my campground now. Tent sweet tent and all."

He nodded once. "Go ahead and get in the truck."

She turned, ready to do just that when the front door opened and a woman peered through the slim crack. "Aiden?"

He froze, his posture going stiff. The glow from the porch light outlining his physique, drawing her eyes to his broad shoulders. She had a sense, in that moment, that he carried quite a bit on them. "Yeah, Mom. It's me."

Oh. He lived with his parents. Interesting.

"You have a friend with you?" The older woman sounded hopeful.

"Just giving her a ride," Aiden said. "She helped me bring Dad's car in from town." She noticed he didn't offer any further explanation for that.

"Well, why doesn't she come in and have some tea?"

She had sensed it from the moment they pulled up. The warm country vibe was undeniable. The place reeked of hospitality. Which was strange, given what she already knew. That his father was an alcoholic, and that Aiden seemed to be taking care of everything.

"I shouldn't," Casey said. "I've been working, and I'm tired." Silence descended for a second before she realized that she had skipped pleasantries. "Thank you. I appreciate it." She didn't really.

"Have you eaten?"

She hadn't. And she was actually really hungry. But she had consigned herself to a growling stomach tonight. "I..."

"Let me make you a sandwich."

Aiden was stiff as a board beside her, clearly uncomfortable with the entire situation. Well, he could join the club. What was it with these people and their aggressive need to do nice things? Aiden didn't even *want* to do something nice for her, and yet he seemed powerless to do anything but. She did not understand compulsory niceness.

She also couldn't turn down a sandwich. "I... That would be nice."

"I thought you were in a hurry," Aiden said, obviously not feeling as obligated to be hospitable as he'd been earlier.

"I said I was tired. Not rushed. It turns out my sandwich needs outweigh my sleep needs."

"Well, come on in," his mother said, her tone cheery, as though it were the late afternoon and she was inviting them in for an after-school snack. At least, that's how she imagined something like that might go. She wasn't really familiar.

The older woman turned and walked back into the house and Casey gave Aiden a sidelong glance. Suddenly, she realized she had never formally introduced herself. Not that he was the first guy she had spent *time* with who had never bothered to ask for her name. But this wasn't exactly the same.

"I'm Casey," she said. "Since I'm about to take a sandwich from your mother, I figured you might want to know."

"I didn't really," he said.

"And why are you suddenly being a dick?"

"It isn't you. It's her."

But he didn't offer further explanation. He just headed toward the house, walking up the stairs with heavy steps. She followed him, not waiting for an invitation, because she had a feeling he wasn't going to give it.

He held open the front door for her and she stopped, looking at the wreath on the door. It was woven together with twigs and flowers. Fake of course, and a little worse for wear. Still, it was a nice effort to cheer up the space, and for some reason she was seized with the desire to touch it. It was such a strange, homey little thing. The kind of thing you would never find on the doors of the motels she typically stayed at. Certainly not on the tent flap she called an entryway.

"Are you going to go in?"

She looked up, her eyes clashing with his. "Yeah," she said, feeling stupid at having been caught in a feelsy moment.

The entryway was as well-worn as the wreath on the door. There was a threadbare rug placed over scuffed-up boards, accented by faded wallpaper and framed pictures that looked like they'd been cut out of a calendar sometime back in the 1980s.

Aiden's mother walked back in, her hands clasped in front of her. "Why don't you sit in the living room?"

She turned and went back into the kitchen and Aiden looked at her, then turned to the right, leading her into a small, square room next to the entryway.

She sat down in a floral armchair and Aiden took his seat on the sofa across from her.

"Well," she said, patting her thighs with her palms.

"This is...not what I expected, considering our introduction."

Aiden rubbed his hand over his forehead. "My dad is probably passed out in the bedroom. That's why she has us in here and not in the kitchen."

"Wow. Way to shatter the whole *Leave it to Beaver* thing I was building up in my head."

"Sorry to disappoint you. Imagine how I feel."

"Yeah, that brings me to my next observation and question. You live here? Why?" She looked him over, making a show of it. And taking her time because, hell, why not? He was hot and she wasn't blind. "I mean, you seem perfectly able to live on your own. To get a job and pay for a place to stay. You are...absolutely able-bodied." She made that last part sound as lecherous as possible. It wasn't hard to do.

"So are you. And yet, you're living in a tent in a campground."

"Touché. Extenuating circumstances." She waved her hand, as if pushing said circumstances out of the way. "I assume you have them, too. And I'm curious about them."

"Yeah," he said slowly, "I have them. Who doesn't?"

"Good question. But not the one I asked. Why exactly do you live at home?"

"For starters, I don't live in the house." He leaned back on the couch, pushing his hand back through his dark hair. It was a nice hand, as she'd already observed. Strong. Capable. *Unf.* "I live in a cabin on the property."

"Nice. Very nice."

"I work on the farm, because of course my dad's general state makes it difficult for him to do that with any consistency."

"Okay, I can see that."

"This place is my legacy. I've been working on it since I was fifteen years old. It's mine. But my name's not on the deed. Technically, it still belongs to my old man. So, if I want to work it, I have to work around him."

She nodded slowly, feeling a little bit guilty for giving him a hard time. It was easy for her to make light of other people's circumstances. She spent so much time doing it with her own it was second nature. Sincerity was a whole lot harder. "Okay, I get that." She leaned over, resting her forearms on her legs. "So, what about your mom? She seems nice."

"She is. Too nice. She always wants to help other people, but she doesn't realize how much of it we need. How much she needs."

"Because of your dad?"

"It takes most of our resources just to keep this place afloat. Plus, there's supporting his drinking habit. But she wants to give to all kinds of charities, and feed hungry-looking waitresses that show up at the door."

"Well, I do appreciate that. I was going to skip dinner tonight."

He looked slightly abashed when she said that. She hadn't intended to make him feel bad. If there was one thing she hated, it was pity.

"Sorry. I shouldn't begrudge you a sandwich."

"Begrudging or not, a sandwich is a sandwich. I don't particularly care if you're happy about me getting it."

"Sorry. I'm being a dick."

The apology was a shock, and she didn't really know how to take it. "I don't particularly care whether you're a dick or not. I was just curious *why*."

"Does it make a difference?"

"Not really."

They heard footsteps in the home, and their conversation stopped as his mother walked in with a plate that had two sandwiches sitting on it. "I thought you might like one, too, Aiden," she said, her voice soft, her smile kind.

Casey was frozen for a whole ten seconds, wondering what it must have been like to grow up with someone who made you sandwiches. She was very skilled at making her own. A lot less skilled at accepting things like this from people.

"Thanks," he said.

"Thank you," she mumbled.

"I'll leave you," she said, turning and walking back out of the room. Again, Casey had the feeling the older woman was treating this like an after-school playdate. But she had a hard time thinking anything negative about it because it was so necessary for her right in this moment.

"You can have both sandwiches," he said. "I ate."

"Thank you," she said again, because she wasn't in a position to reject charity. Not now.

She picked up the first sandwich and began to eat, suddenly realizing just how ravenous she was. Really, she was kind of a mess, and something about this shabby but well-ordered house, and the fact that she wanted to cry over a sandwich, brought that to light in an undeniable way. Not even she could ignore it now. He didn't say anything while she polished off both sandwiches, sighing heavily when she was done.

"Thank you," she said for the third time, really meaning it this time.

"I had better get you back to the campground," he said, standing, his broad frame filling up the room.

She felt a prickling on the back of her neck and turned

around and saw Aiden's mother standing in the doorway. "The campground?"

Casey looked at Aiden, who was standing there, immovable and silent. She cleared her throat. "That's where I'm staying."

"Oh, no," she said, her brow creasing deeply. "That's no good at all. You should stay here."

CHAPTER FOUR

CASEY BLINKED. "I... WHAT?" It sounded an awful lot like the other woman, a stranger, was asking her if she wanted to stay with them.

She was back to having cult concerns.

"You're camping?"

"Yes," Casey said, hesitant now.

The look on her face was...motherly. "Are you with anyone? Are you staying all by yourself?"

"I'm by myself. Really, I'm fine. I always travel alone."

"No," she said. Her blue eyes—identical to her son's, Casey couldn't help but notice—were soft and filled with concern. "You can't stay by yourself. It isn't safe. Plus, it's been such a chilly spring. You have to be freezing staying in a tent."

Yeah, she was. "It's really fine," she lied.

"We have a trailer here on the property," the older woman continued. "Just a little travel trailer, but it has heat. And it's dry."

She looked back at Aiden, who was looking tense but resigned. "Yeah, Mom, you have a point," he said, a slave to Good Samaritan urges that were entirely foreign to Casey.

Understanding slowly rolled over her and she shook her head. "No. I don't want to put anyone out."

"Nonsense," she said. "You won't be putting anyone

out. It has water, and it's hooked up so that the bathroom works. And no one is staying in it."

"No offense," Casey said, "but you don't even know my situation. I could be a criminal."

"Are you?" his mother asked.

"Well, no."

"Then I'm sure it will be fine for you to stay here until you're back on your feet."

"Really, I won't be here for long. I'm just working at Ace's and saving up money until I can afford to get my car fixed."

"See? No trouble at all. You can call me Josie," she said, extending her hand. "Josie Crawford."

Casey took hold of it. "Casey James," she said.

Inexplicably, emotion expanded in her throat, making it difficult to breathe. Difficult to speak. She could hear everything he had just told her echoing in her mind. About how his mother helped people even when she couldn't afford to offer help. She felt like knowing that made her somewhat obligated to turn all this down. But she just couldn't.

As cynical as she wanted to be about people's motives, she also needed help. How could she turn it down when it was offered? She couldn't. Even if she gave it the side-eye the whole time, she had to accept the handout.

"I suppose I'd better get the trailer unlocked and turn the heat on," Aiden said.

"Oh," Casey said. "I don't have any of my things."

"I'll go take care of the trailer," Josie said. "Aiden, why don't you take Casey back to her campsite to get her necessities?"

"Come on," Aiden said. "Let's go." She could tell that there was a heavy sigh building inside of Aiden that he was refusing to let out. It would have been amusing, except she was currently at sea, floating in emotions she had very little experience with. So, no laughing was happening.

"Thank you," she said, the words sounding so flat and inadequate. She'd said them four times in the past few minutes alone and she didn't know what else to say, didn't know what else to do. This was why she preferred those kinds of arrangements with men where they clearly wanted her body in return for anything nice they happened to do for her. At least then it was equitable. At least then she didn't feel so at a loss. She could cut ties with a clean conscience, owing nothing. This was... This was just a *gift*, and she had no clue what to do with that.

She followed Aiden back out to his truck, climbing into the passenger seat and folding her hands in her lap. She was acutely aware that he was irritated with her, and that as soon as they were out of earshot from his mother, he was going to let her know.

As soon as he started the truck engine, he proved her right. "Well, there's a prime example of my mother being my mother."

"If it's terrible of me to accept, just let me know," she said. Annoyance built inside her, canceling out the warm fuzzy feeling she'd had just a moment earlier.

"It's not a problem. She's right. We're not using the trailer, and there's no reason for you to freeze your ass off in a tent."

"Actually, my ass has managed to stay intact for the past couple of weeks. It's not like it's going to kill me to spend another couple sleeping on the ground."

He threw the truck in Reverse and she had to grip the

door handle to steady herself. "Just let us do something nice for you."

"Well, you seem so pissed about it that you don't really make a girl want to accept your charity."

"I'm not pissed."

"Yes, you are."

"It isn't personal. There's a lot going on here, and I have a lot on my plate already. Adding anything to it just seems..."

"Impossible?"

He paused for a second. "You know the feeling?"

"No," she said, realizing the truth of it even as she said it, "actually I don't. I pretty much never have anything on my plate. And I'm not being sarcastic. That's the benefit of not having very many personal connections in your life."

"I have too many. Maybe we need to trade some around."

"No, thanks. You're not exactly selling me on the institution of family."

Silence gathered between them, tightening like a fist, and she took a deep breath, trying to dispel some of it. It didn't ease up. "This isn't exactly what you bargained for when you left your keys with me, is it?"

He huffed out a laugh. "To say the least."

They completed the drive to the campground in relative silence. As soon as he put the truck in Park and killed the engine, she scrambled out, desperate to escape the tension between them. At least, there was tension on her end. As far as his side went, it could just be that he thought she was annoying.

She heard the driver-side door slam, and she kept her eyes fixed ahead on the trail that led to her campsite.

"It's just up here," she said, tucking a strand of hair behind her ear and squinting into the darkness. Small solar lamps lined the walk, casting a soft orange glow over the asphalt. Trees loomed on either side of the walk. Every night, walking through alone, she'd imagined they were like a wall, closed off completely. Nothing lurking in the space between.

But now she could hear his heavy footsteps behind her, and she found it to be strangely comforting. It was nice to have him here.

Nice.

There was that word again.

Time to say something irreverent to diffuse that bit of warm fuzzy. "Welcome to my home," she said as they approached the space. "You know, since you let me into yours, it only seems fair."

An unanticipated bit of shame crept through her, heat bleeding into her cheeks as she saw her living situation through his eyes. It was all right for her. She barely looked at it anymore. Came home in the dark, curled up in her sleeping bag and went to sleep.

But looking at it, *really* looking at it, like someone who was just seeing it for the first time, was a whole different thing. One small tent, a sad little fire ring and nothing else. It was modest at best, derelict at worst. It was... Well, it was her life.

"Why don't you go get your things, and I'll help you take the tent down," he said, his voice hard, unreadable.

"I have to say," she said, finding a snarky comment to help break up the heavy rock that had settled in her chest, "many a man has pitched a tent because of me, but you're the first to help me take one down."

He said nothing, didn't even laugh.

"That was a penis joke," she said.

"I got it," he said, his voice rough.

"You don't seem amused."

"I'm not." He moved ahead of her, making his way to the tent and unzipping the flap. "Go get your things. I don't intend to stand here all night."

She smiled as sweetly as possible. "You are the meanest guardian angel a girl could ever hope for." She swept past him, going into the tent and kneeling down. The chill from the ground beneath seeped up through her jeans. She was not going to miss sleeping on this.

She rolled the sleeping bag up quickly and zipped up her duffel bag. Then she took both things and chucked them out in front of the tent before following them back outside.

"That's it. That's my life. I can pack up and go in five minutes. Well, except for the tent." He didn't say anything. "You're a tough customer."

"Am I?"

She rolled her eyes and started detaching the tent poles from the pockets they were settled in. "You don't have much of a sense of humor."

He moved over to help, placing his hands dangerously close to where hers were. She could feel the warmth emanating from his body. From his skin. She wanted to touch him. Wanted to lean in close and rest her head on all that strength. She didn't know where that desire had come from, only that it was strong, and very real. She blinked, pulling away quickly.

"I just want to get the tent taken down," he said, shot. Clipped. "I'm sorry that I'm not humorous enough for you."

"It's not… It isn't…" What was wrong with her? Why was she stuttering? Men did not make her stutter. She made *them* stutter.

"My dad has alienated so many of our clients, I'm afraid that we're not going to break even this spring." He said the words in a hushed tone, all the while continuing to work on her tent. "I've just had a lot on my mind."

"Sounds pretty stressful."

She wondered why she had moved away from his touch. Why she hadn't leaned into it. Really, what would be the harm? She was going to be staying with him, after all. And she didn't like the idea of feeling in debt. Maybe they could blow off a little steam together, and she could feel a bit more like this was a fair exchange.

She looked up, rolling her shoulders back, even though she knew he couldn't see what that bit of enhanced posture did for her boobs, not in this light. Still, she felt sexier. And that was what counted.

"Maybe you need a little bit of stress relief." She took a step toward the tent, and placed her hand very purposefully over the top of his. He froze, looking up, his eyes meeting hers in the darkness, illuminated by the little solar lights.

"What?"

"I was saying that maybe you and I could relieve a little stress together. Trust me, staying in a campground for the past couple weeks hasn't exactly been a picnic for me. Hell, the past few months haven't exactly been a picnic." In all honesty, the past life hadn't been much of a picnic.

"Do you feel obligated to make a pass at me because I'm letting you stay with my family?"

Heat stung her face, her cheeks. A sense of crawling

shame—foreign and completely unwelcome—assaulted her. "I don't… No." *Except, yes.*

"You keep making comments about it. The first time we had a conversation you basically accused me of angling to blackmail you into giving me a blow job. I don't know what you think this is, but if I want to get laid, I can damn well do it and I don't need you to offer me your body as a trade."

The way that he said it…as though she were dirty. As though suggesting it at all had impugned his character.

Didn't it?

Sure. Maybe in *this* world. Where people could afford morals and shit. Where they had a bed to go to every night no matter what and could always eat dinner when they were hungry.

But that wasn't her world. In hers, this was just the cost of doing business, and no guy that she'd ever come across would have batted an eye over it.

Maybe this one doesn't want you.

Now, there was something that hadn't occurred to her. Until now.

Now she felt guilty, ashamed *and* horrified. This was new.

Anger emerged from the center of her discomfort and she embraced it. "I'm sorry, okay? I just thought you might want to have a little fun. Sex isn't that big of a deal. Don't act like I asked you to kick a puppy."

"Sex is kind of a big deal," he said.

Why did that make her feel things? What the hell was wrong with her? That made her even angrier. "Oh, is it? I'm sorry, I missed that memo. No, maybe I *didn't*. Maybe one of my foster parents gave me the chastity talk. But I was only with them for a couple of months, so it didn't really stick."

She hated the way that she sounded now. Harsh, defensive. It was way too betraying of how she felt. About all of this. About herself. About the past. He didn't deserve that. He did not deserve to know her for five minutes, offer her a place to sleep, and pass judgment on the way she'd survived for the past twenty-two years. "I don't owe you an explanation of myself."

"I didn't say you did."

She gritted her teeth, curling her hands into fists. "If you want to call me a slut, just do it."

He paused, the tent still halfway intact. "I wasn't going to."

"You were thinking it." Had he been? Maybe not. But she felt like one. She felt dirty and it was his fault. "So, are you a virgin, Aiden?"

"No," he said through gritted teeth, his voice low, dangerous.

"Right. So, don't go standing there acting like you can lecture me on purity or some shit."

"I wasn't lecturing you on purity. I was lecturing you on acting like you have to trade sex for a place to sleep."

"Maybe I just want to do you. You're kind of hot. Well, cancel that. I thought you were hot until this. *This* is ridiculous."

"It's not how I do things."

"What? You only bang your girlfriends?"

"I'm not having this discussion with you. Do you want to sleep out here? Or do you want to spend the night in the trailer?"

"Neither. Not right this second."

"I don't recall presenting you with a third option."

Anger, and most of all embarrassment, made her reckless. "Right now? I just want to knock you off your high horse."

And with that, she closed the distance between them, wrapped her arms around his neck and pressed her lips to his.

CHAPTER FIVE

AIDEN WASN'T SURE how he'd gone from being yelled at to being kissed in the space of only a few seconds. He'd seen it happen in movies before, but it had never happened to him.

She'd asked if he was a virgin, and the answer was—of course—no. But he wasn't as far away from one as he'd like to be.

One woman. He'd only ever slept with one woman.

Their attraction had been companionable, but not connected to love. It had been about convenience. And when he'd imagined a future with Caroline, it had been about comfort. Stability. Logic.

Caroline had been easy. Caroline had been fun. *This* was neither.

Casey was tough. She was intense. Casey was angry—he could taste it on her lips. On her tongue. She pressed herself against him, her breasts crushed against his chest as she slid her tongue across the seam to his mouth, delving deeper, kissing him harder.

He should stop it. Should push her away. But he found he wasn't very motivated to do that. Heat roared through his veins like a beast, tearing at him, a new, unfamiliar sensation that had nothing to do with the kind of kisses he'd had before.

The sex with Caroline had all been carefully planned.

Carefully agreed upon. He had known her as well as he knew anyone. This… This was not that.

An angry, deep, passionate kiss from a stranger was about as far as you could get from a cautious, careful kiss from a friend.

He raised his hands, planting them on her hips, getting ready to push her away from him, but instead he found himself hanging on. Clinging to her, the blunt tips of his fingers digging into her soft body. She shifted, tilting her head, nipping his lower lip slightly before she soothed away the sting with her tongue. This woman knew what she was doing, no mistaking that.

And judgmental was not how he was feeling. No. He was in awe, grateful and so damn horny he could barely see straight.

She pulled her mouth away from his, kissing the line of his jaw, down his neck, tracing a path with the tip of her tongue.

Fire exploded in his midsection, his cock so hard it was painful. And he decided he was done letting her have the control. He growled, pulling her in tightly, letting her feel the effect she had on him as he claimed her mouth with his, tasting her as deep as he could.

She whimpered, her arms going tighter around his neck as she surrendered completely to the kiss. To letting him lead. Letting him have control.

He didn't possess the skills she did, but what he had was six months' worth of pent-up celibacy and raw, untried lust built up to the point of bursting.

He'd never felt anything like this before, and he was lost in it, only able to be carried out by the strength of the tide. Helpless against the current of need that had overtaken him completely.

She whimpered. A sound of feminine urgency unlike anything he had ever heard before. She was different than Caroline. It was impossible not to compare. Not
because he had cared especially for her, but because she
was the only woman he had ever touched like this until
now. Until Casey.

Casey. This woman whose name he'd only learned
twenty minutes ago. A woman he'd first laid eyes on
last night.

He couldn't think, couldn't breathe, couldn't do anything but bury his fingers even more deeply in Casey's
hair. She was so soft. Everything about her. More than
that, she was like a shot of alcohol to his system. Every
damn shot of whiskey he had denied himself for the past
twenty-six years.

Suddenly, he keenly felt the years of denial. The abstinence. From sex. From alcohol. From pleasure in all its
forms. Because it canceled out his control, and he knew
it. He knew that he had to do better than that, knew that
he had to guard against it. But not now. He couldn't do
it now.

She traced his bottom lip with the tip of her tongue
and a deep, intense shudder racked his body.

She slid her hand down his back, then around, placing
her palm over the hardened length of his cock, squeezing him as she deepened their kiss. A rough, harsh growl
rumbled in his chest. A hard, feral sound unlike any he'd
ever heard come from his body before.

She laughed, the sound tasting sweet on his lips as
she tightened her hold on his length, curling her other
arm around his neck and holding him tightly against her.
Not that he was tempted to pull away. Never in his life
had he been past the point of no return. He was a man

who prized his control above everything else. But now? Now there was nothing else but this. This campground, this tent, this woman.

With the darkness closing in tightly around them, it was easy to believe that.

She wrenched her mouth away from his, pressing a kiss to his neck before angling her face up, her lips brushing against his ear. "How about you take me inside the tent and fuck me?"

Never in his life had a woman uttered those words to him. He'd never even fantasized about such a thing. So he was completely unprepared for the effect that it had on him. He wrapped his arms around her, curving one tightly around her waist, sliding his other hand down over her ass before reaching lower, curling his fingers around her thigh and tugging her up, wrapping her legs around his waist as he held her tightly and took them both to the front of the tent.

She planted her feet back on the ground as he bent to haul them both inside, never breaking the kiss as he settled over her. She parted her thighs, arching against him, pressing herself hard against his arousal. She reached between them, flicking open the snap on his jeans and drawing the zipper down before reaching inside and gripping him tight. He hissed as her soft skin made contact with his own bare flesh as she squeezed and stroked him, while continuing to kiss him deep.

Without thinking, he put his hand on her stomach, pushed his fingertips up beneath the edge of her shirt, over her flat stomach, moving up to cup one perfect breast. Her bra was thin, lacy and insubstantial, and he could feel her nipple, tight and hard, through the fabric. He moved his thumb over the tightened bud and she gasped, tugging her mouth away from his as she did, panting and clearly as affected by all of this as he was.

She let go of him, wrenching her shirt up over her head and contorting so she could reach behind her back and unhook her bra, leaving her completely topless. It was too dark in the tent for him to see much beyond the pale shape of her body. He slid his hands down her sides, then covered both of her breasts with his palms.

"Oh, yes," she said, the words a sigh on her soft lips.

A shot of straight adrenaline to his system.

He traced the elegant curve of her body, down beneath the waistband of her jeans, beneath the flimsy fabric of her lace panties, until he made contact with her hot, wet center. She bucked against him and he kissed her as he stroked her, teased her.

"You like that?" he asked, his lips still pressed against hers.

"Yes."

Satisfaction roared through him like a beast and he shifted, sliding one finger inside of her as he continued to stroke her clit.

He couldn't believe he was doing such an intimate thing with a woman he'd barely had two conversations with. He didn't know how old she was, where she was from, whether or not she liked chocolate or George Strait. Real, important questions that a man should know the answers to before he put his hand between a woman's thighs.

But as she moaned and moved against his touch, he couldn't imagine doing this with someone who knew him. Because the stranger-thing cut both ways.

She didn't know he was doing his best to be responsible. Didn't know he'd only slept with one woman. Didn't know he'd never picked up a stranger or done a reckless thing in his whole life.

He could be anyone with her. Do anything.

He slipped a second finger inside her she moaned, flexing her hips against his hand, rubbing harder against him as she chased her release.

He wanted her to have it, before things went any further, needed her to have it. To defy the years spent not doing things like this because control had been so much more important.

"Come for me," he said, the words rough, unrecognizable.

She let out a hard, shuddering breath as she rocked against him, her internal muscles clenching around his fingers as she climaxed almost on command.

"Oh," she said, throwing her arm over her eyes, breathing hard. "That was…unexpected."

He nuzzled her neck, kissing her there. "Was it?"

"Unnh."

"Is that a good sound?" he asked, pushing her jeans down her thighs, taking her panties with them.

"I'm killed," she said, sliding her hands along his spine, gripping the hem of his shirt and pulling upward. "Now get naked."

A sudden thought struck him like a blow to the head. "I don't have condoms."

"Oh!" She scrambled from beneath him and hung halfway out the tent, reaching for something outside. She was bent at the waist, the display completely immodest and giving him a prime view of her ass. Or it would have been a prime view if it weren't so damned dark. "I have condoms," she called back over her shoulder. "Somewhere in my bag." She flattened herself in the doorway of the tent, reaching as far as she could. "Here!"

She moved back in, kissing him as she flashed the plastic packet. She opened it quickly, then placed the protection over the head of his cock, rolling it down over him quickly. Her breath hissed through her teeth and she swore.

"What?" he asked.

"Damn, you're hot," she said, wrapping her arms around his neck and pressing her breasts against his chest, pushing him back so that he was lying down and she was on top of him, her thighs draped over his.

"Am I?" he asked, unable to resist moving his hands over her back, her ass, and up again.

"This is already a lot better than it usually is. And you aren't even inside me. Yet." She shifted, lifting her hips and positioning herself over his length before lowering her hips down slowly, taking him inside her tight, wet heat inch by agonizing inch. She let out a shuddering breath, a whimper on her lips as she seated herself fully onto him, her fingernails digging into his skin.

She pushed herself up as she shifted her hips and he raised his hand to cup her breasts, heat washing through him as she established a rhythm that set him on fire. He lowered his hands, gripped her hips tight, bracing himself as she rode him.

He was lost in this, in her. In the way she felt, the way she smelled, the sounds she made. It didn't matter that he could feel every rock beneath the floor of the tent, didn't matter that the cold was seeping up through the thin fabric. Hell, the cold was welcome. Because he was on fire.

She was heat personified, a living flame dancing and shimmering in his hands, consuming them both. She rocked against him, her thigh muscles quivering. He could tell she was on the edge again. And so was he.

He held her tightly and reversed their position, settling between her legs and thrusting deep inside. She gasped, arching her back before wrapping her legs around his waist and taking him deeper.

"So good," she said, kissing his shoulder, the contact searing his skin like a brand.

And then he lost himself. His control, his every thought. His ability to breathe. He growled, lowering his head and scraping his teeth over her collarbone as he curved his hand around her back, slid it down to her ass and pulled her up against him. Hard.

A sharp sound escaped her lips as a shiver wound through her, her internal muscles tightening around his cock as she came again.

White-hot pleasure exploded behind his eyelids, release roaring through his veins like a beast as he let go completely, his mind washed blank of anything but her. Of being inside her, pressed against her, his lips on her skin, her flavor on his tongue.

For a moment, there was no past, no future.

There was only Casey. His entire universe made up of a stranger who might not even like chocolate.

And for the first time in recent memory, he was happy.

CHAPTER SIX

WHEN AIDEN SAT UP, moving away from her, Casey had to fight the inexplicable urge to cover herself. She didn't know why she was suddenly so conscious of the fact that she was naked. It was dark. And he was far from the first man to see her naked. But he was perhaps the first man that didn't just expect that he was going to see her naked, to not *require* it in order for him to hand out help. And what had happened between them was somehow beyond her experience.

Her response to it had been… Unexpected.

Her response to him was unexpected.

Normally, she was more calculating and all that. More skilled, more in control. But she had forgotten to put on her favorite persona when she'd taken off her clothes, and that just left her naked. So, no wonder she was so conscious of it now.

She swallowed hard, feeling around the tent for her clothes as he did the same.

She wondered if she should say something. Or if he was going to say something. Then she just felt irritated because normally she didn't think things through quite as deeply. It was sex, not calculus. It wasn't all that difficult. Everything had gone exactly as it should. Better, actually. She should be luxuriating in the aftereffects of not one, but two orgasms. Seriously, that *never* happened. She had become completely certain that the multi-orgasmic female was a myth. Well, Aiden had just busted that.

It was just difficult to luxuriate when you felt so damn self-conscious.

She pulled her shirt over her head, then wiggled back into her jeans. She snagged her bra and panties and crawled out of the tent to stuff them into her bag. There would be no brassiere left behind, because it wasn't like she had a surplus of them. But she couldn't really justify taking the time to put everything on. She just wanted to get her skin covered up and her head on straight.

She picked up her bag and slung it over her shoulder. Then she heard Aiden get out of the tent. She very purposefully didn't turn to look at him. The tent fabric rustled as he finished deconstructing the scene of their downfall.

"Are you ready to head back?" he asked, his voice sounding like it was scraping his throat raw.

"Yeah," she said.

The alternative was, after all, standing out here freezing her ass off.

Getting back into an enclosed space with him beat that out by a narrow margin.

"I've got your sleeping bag."

"Thank you," she said.

She had no idea where her wit had gone. Where her fantastically distancing one-liners had scampered off to. Little cowards. Fleeing at the first sign of difficulty.

"You're welcome."

Of course he was polite after sex.

They walked back to his truck in silence, and he continued with the old-school-gentleman routine by opening the passenger-side door for her. "I didn't realize all I had to do was flash my tits to get you to play the part of gentleman. Usually, it kind of works in reverse. But good to know that a little sex puts you on your best behavior."

Oh, there were the snarky one-liners.

He said nothing, only rounded to the other side of the truck to get in and start the ignition. She scrambled into the cab, shutting the door and buckling up, letting out a heavy breath as they pulled away from the scene of the crime.

The silence was too heavy. Like being wrapped in a blanket in a room that was already too hot. So she decided to throw it off. "You don't have anything to say?"

"Not really," he said.

She looked over, clearly able to see the tension in his muscular frame in spite of the darkness in the cab. "If you clench your jaw any tighter your teeth are going to explode. And I will not be paying your dental bill."

"I'm sorry. I don't know how to react casually to things like this."

His words made her stomach sink down low, that unfamiliar creeping shame spidering up her arms and neck. "I do. You just do, because it isn't that big of a deal." She despised the defensiveness in her tone. But she couldn't do anything to get rid of it, either.

"Maybe not to you."

"Oh, yes. Not to me. Because I'm obviously the one at fault here even though you were totally on board."

"I didn't say that."

"You didn't have to. So what, now you're just going to sit over there bemoaning the fact that I sullied your good little farm-boy member with my filthy body?"

"Hey, these are your issues, not mine. I was there in that tent with you. I don't absolve myself."

410 HOMETOWN HEARTBREAKER

She snorted. "You *do* think there needs to be some absolution."

"It's not the way I do things."

"Yeah, I'm going to go ahead and let you know I don't think there's a way for us to have this conversation where you don't come across as an insulting prick."

"I'm not trying to be. I'm just…trying to let you know that this isn't something I would normally ever do. I don't sleep with people I don't know."

"I'm Casey James. I'm a waitress at Ace's Bar. I won't be in town very long. I like cheeseburgers and long walks on the beach."

"Chocolate?" he asked.

"What?"

"Do you like chocolate?"

"Random. But okay. I do. I like chocolate a lot. I don't eat it half as often as I would like to."

"Why?"

She rolled her eyes and let out an exasperated breath. "You always interrogate your lovers?"

"No. But we already established that this is unusual for me, so indulge me."

"Chocolate is a luxury. One I'm not always able to afford. When I first ended up out on my own I bought all kinds of crap, just because I could. But you figure out pretty quickly that man can't live on Lucky Charms alone."

"Yeah," he said, "I can see that."

Now he sounded…vaguely pitying. Which was worse than judgmental. Or maybe she was just hard to please.

Well, that wasn't true, she thought smugly. She had just been pleased twice, very thoroughly. Of course, that was just physically.

"Yes, my sob story is one filled with boring nutritional decisions. Being an adult is not as advertised, at least in my experience."

"Mine, too."

"Do tell. Tit for tat." She watched his muscles tense again when she said the word *tit*. Funny. He was kind of adorable.

"More responsibility, less doing whatever you want."

"And I don't even have responsibility, beyond keeping my own self alive. But let me tell you, it can be a full-time job when you don't have any real place to stay."

"Yeah, why don't you have a place to stay?"

"Wow, really? You're going to ask someone why they're homeless?"

"Yes, I am. Because you have a job, and you seem to do it pretty well. So, I assume you could get a job anywhere you wanted to. And even if you couldn't get a great place to live, you could get a place to live. It seems to me that moving from place to place is part of what keeps you from having that. So, why do you do it?"

She realized then that they were on that long driveway that led back to his place. She'd been completely lost in conversation for the entire trip back and hadn't noticed just how much ground they'd covered. "I don't know. It seems to me you'd have a lot less responsibility if you didn't cling so tightly to one place. So, if you don't like it, why do you do it?"

Silence settled between them, and she had a feeling she'd crossed the line. It wasn't even an invisible line, the one that tried to ward off commentary about his living situation, about his parents. It was bold, black and plain as day. She'd never been one for minding the rules.

"Aren't you obligated to anybody?" he asked, his voice

raw. "Is there any one person you feel like you have to serve before you can serve yourself?"

She swallowed, her throat dry. "No. Nobody took care of me, Aiden. I had to take care of myself. So, I'm my highest priority. I can't afford to be a martyr."

"Just trust me, I can't afford to leave my family."

"Trust isn't really something I'm big on. But if you say so."

"The trailer is going to be cold," he said, the abrupt subject change nearly giving her whiplash.

"Fantastic. Any other selling features you want to throw out there? Black mold? A vole in the plumbing?"

"Maybe you should stay with me."

"I…" Her stomach twisted, and she couldn't decide whether she was excited by the proposition or slightly disappointed that he was basically the same as every other guy. "Because you want to have more sex?"

He cleared his throat, his obvious discomfort with his proposition proving that while he might have definite standard male tendencies, he wasn't exactly the kind of guy she was used to dealing with. "Yes," he said, the word bearing such weight that she could tell he hadn't arrived at it easily.

"So this is the payment, huh?"

He shifted in his seat, turning to face her. "No. If you want to go to the trailer, you're welcome to go to the trailer. I don't… This isn't a trade. Either you want to be with me again, or you don't. And the decision is yours."

She laughed, feeling nervous and more than a little bit unsettled. "You say that. But is it true?"

"I don't lie."

"I do," she said, her voice hushed. "All the time. Sometimes lying is the only option. The truth is so limiting.

Very often gets you into more trouble than it gets you out of."

"Well," he said, "I don't."

"So I can say no and I'll still have a place to sleep?"

"Yes, you can say no."

"I don't want to." She was surprised by that. Even more surprised that it had nothing to do with evening the score, or paying him back for any favors he'd done for her. Mainly, it wasn't even about her desire to avoid spending more nights alone, with nothing but her thoughts to keep her company. *Mainly*, it wasn't that. Mostly, she had just enjoy being with him. And, like chocolate, enjoyment like that was pretty rare in her world.

He was nice. He cared about her pleasure. She wanted him.

That seemed like more than enough reason to tell him yes.

"Okay. Let's go to your place, then."

CHAPTER SEVEN

IT WAS LATE. The sun was already washing through the trees, casting golden light into the darkened bedroom. He never woke up this late. Ever. But then, he never brought strangers back home with him only to spend all night engaged in every man's favorite type of cardio.

Heat spread through his veins as he thought about everything that had gone on in that bed. About Casey. About how many times he had reached for her at night, finding her there, warm and willing and so incredibly beautiful he didn't see any point in resisting.

He reached over to her side of the bed again and found nothing but a broad expanse of cold sheets. He sat upright, the blankets falling down around his waist as he looked around the room for any sign that she was still here. Her clothes were still there, in a little heap on the floor by the bed. And her bag was still sitting on top of his dresser.

He looked out the window, out to the deck that was attached to the back of the cabin. And there he saw her. Blond hair tumbled down her bare back, her soft, pale skin on display for him and the rest of the great outdoors. Her slim waist curved into perfect hips and a butt that was shaped like a heart. He'd never had that thought about a woman's butt before. But hers was most definitely shaped like a heart.

She tilted her head back, shook her hair out, releasing her hold on the deck railing and spreading her arms wide, as though she was greeting the sun.

She wasn't really a stranger anymore. Not after all that. Plus, now he knew she liked chocolate.

But she didn't get it as often as she would like. She also liked the sun, apparently. Just another good reason for her to move on from Copper Ridge when the time came. It was beautiful here, but the Oregon coast wasn't exactly known for its sun. It was an ideal environment if you liked mist or wanted to run into a sparkling vampire, but the weather wasn't to everyone's taste.

He was hesitant to interrupt her. She looked beautiful. Serene. And even though he didn't know Casey all that well, he got the feeling that she wasn't serene very often. Just looking at her made him feel calm. Settled. It was a deep, strange sense of stillness unlike any he could recall feeling before. He wasn't sure why looking at this sexy little drifter made him feel that way, only that it did.

Probably the sex.

They'd had a lot of sex.

It kind of made a mockery of all of his deeply held beliefs about his control. About what kind of man he was. It turned out he was just as susceptible to temptations of the flesh as anyone else. He'd just figured that living with one of the world's biggest cautionary tales had given him an edge in terms of keeping control of that susceptibility.

Only to a point, he'd discovered. *Casey* was that point.

But she was leaving. Her being here was temporary, so it seemed like there wasn't really any harm. He would waste a lot more energy trying to resist her while she was staying here on the property then he would by just giving in.

Potentially shaky logic, but he would take it.

Without thinking, he swung his legs over the side of the bed and dropped the blankets as he stood, walking toward the door that led to the deck. He grabbed hold of the doorknob, turning it slowly, because he didn't want to scare her. Of course, he realized as he took a step out onto the deck, walking up silently behind her probably wasn't less scary.

"Hey," he said, keeping his voice soft.

She turned around and his breath caught hard in his throat. He gave in to the intense desire to look down at her breasts, and he was not disappointed by the indulgence. Her nipples were tight from the frigid air, and so tempting he could barely keep his hands to himself. But he would. If he was going to cede one large victory to indulgence, then he would win small skirmishes for control.

"Hi," she said, a small, funny smile curving her lips. "I couldn't resist the view." She waved her hand back behind them, indicating the thick grove of pine trees.

"It's nice. And private, if you were wondering."

"I figured. You know, just now, since you came out here like this." Her cheeks turned pink when her eyes dropped down to where he was revealing everything.

He hadn't taken her for the kind of girl who blushed about things.

"Are you blushing?"

"No," she said. "It's cold outside. Maybe I have a rash? But I don't blush. Especially not over a naked dude. Not that you aren't an exceptional naked dude. You are. Completely a cut above." Her eyes dropped meaningfully again. "I want to make some kind of a joke about you being grade-A prime beef or something, because it seems like the kind of joke a farmer would get."

He nodded once. "Got it."

"But I don't blush."

"I believe you."

"No, you don't," she said, squinting her eyes and tilting her head. "Why don't you?"

"Because I saw you blush."

"But don't I come across as superjaded and stuff? The cold is a way more logical explanation."

For just one moment he turned over the words that had entered his mind, turned them over, examined them, asked himself why he was even thinking about saying them. Because he didn't say words like this. He didn't talk to women like this. But he didn't bring strangers home, either. So, screw it. "It would have to have been a big coincidence. A gust of cold air across your skin the second you looked at my cock."

Her mouth dropped open, her blue eyes widening.

"What? You're the only one allowed to be a little bit shocking?" he asked.

"Yes. Shocking is my territory. You're a very nice guy. Salt of the earth. Rarely shocking. Aggressively appropriate."

He reached out, wrapping his arm around her waist and tugging her up against him. She was soft, cold from standing outside and absolutely perfect. "Appropriate?"

"I might have to revise that opinion."

"Yeah, you might." He sighed heavily and released his hold on her reluctantly. "I have to go work."

"Oh," she said, wrinkling her nose. "There's that responsibility."

"You have to work today?"

"Not until later."

"Well, when it's time I'll give you a ride down there."

"You don't have to do that," she said, grimacing. "Because now I feel like you're paying me back."

"It's not an exchange." Frustration gnawed at him, because he wasn't quite sure what it was, only that this wasn't some kind of sexual-favors currency exchange.

"I'm sorry, I just don't understand that." She wrapped her arms around herself, shivering slightly as though she were suddenly feeling the cold. "We should go inside."

She brushed past him, her hard footsteps putting a little jiggle in the heart shape of her rear. And he watched, even though he shouldn't. Even though he should be more concerned with her emotional well-being than the shape of her ass. He was concerned. Just with both things.

He followed her back into the cabin. It was a small place. One bedroom, a bathroom and a living room—kitchen combo. It definitely wasn't where he wanted to be. Definitely wasn't where he saw himself being at twenty-six. But all of the money he'd saved to buy his own house had gone back into the farm. So here he was.

He knew all about paying into things and getting nothing in return. Knew all about uneven exchanges. Pouring into something hoping that it would be a long-term investment that panned out. In his experience, all of his investments had just required more investing. It was like rolling a boulder uphill, making a little bit of progress, then losing it again. Then hitting a slick patch and getting sent all the way back down to the bottom.

She was rummaging around in her things, pulling clothes on, obviously irritated with him. And for some reason it bothered him.

"I think that we need to outline some rules here," he said.

She looked at him as she pulled her shirt over her

head, shook her hair out and raised a brow. "You want to lay down ground rules? What, like don't fall in love with you?"

"I don't think you're in any danger of falling in love with me. I'm kind of an ass."

She snorted. "Somehow, you manage to be both the nicest guy I've ever met and kind of an ass. So, I won't argue."

"Right. Anyway, this thing between us. The attraction stuff…"

"The screwing," she said.

"If that's what makes you happy. What we're doing, it's completely separate from you having a place to stay. Separate from the rides to work and all of that. I would do that anyway."

"Your mom is the one who said I could stay."

"Yes. She does that. And when she does it, I'm the person who ends up taking care of her strays. She likes the idea of helping people, but the fact of the matter is she can barely help herself. So when she has someone staying on the property I end up driving them places when they need it. I end up taking care of any issues they're having with the trailer. I get them to job interviews, or whatever else they might need. Her heart is in the right place. Her life is in just about the worst place. Makes things difficult."

"Okay, so if your goal is to make me feel like an even bigger burden, you've accomplished it."

She started to walk out of the bedroom and he reached out and grabbed her arm, tugging her back to him. "No. My goal is to make you understand that this isn't me asking you for payment. Or giving you any favors because you're sleeping with me. I could go out and sleep with someone else. I'm damn sure you could, too. But I don't want to. Because I want you. That has nothing to do with debt."

She blinked, swallowing visibly. "You want me?"

"Yes."

"Say it," she said.

"I want you, Casey. That's the only reason I want you in my bed. Not because I deserve it. I don't."

"I don't know if I'd say that." She closed the space between them, curving her hand around his neck and drawing up on her toes to kiss him. "If anyone deserves a little bit of fun it's you."

He didn't know why, but he didn't especially like her characterizing what passed between them as *fun*. Yeah, it was kind of fun. But that was too simple. There was more to it. It was fun, but it was torture. It was easy, but it was also a bit like lighting yourself on fire. Desperate, hot, all-consuming.

Maybe it wasn't that for her. He didn't exactly want to get into the experience conversation, but he would guess that she had a lot more than he did.

But the fact remained that he had made her blush.

"I'll take your word for it," he said, instead of giving voice to any of the things he was thinking.

"I think I deserve some fun, too. Show me your tractor."

"Is that a euphemism?" he asked.

"No, your euphemistic tractor is out and proud. I want to see a literal tractor. And it better be green, just like on TV. It had better fulfill all of my farm fantasies."

"I hate to break it to you, but if you have farm fantasies you might also have some psychological issues."

"I have farm fantasies, but *you* have a farm." She

smiled. "I think that goes to show that your insanity is greater."

"Sure. Why don't you come with me to have a look at my insanity?"

JUST A COUPLE of days ago Casey could not have imagined that she would be taking a tour of farmland in a tractor. But she was. She had a strong feeling that he was only indulging her by letting her ride in it, because his truck would be the more practical way to get around. The tractor was, in fact, green. That pleased her.

Pretty much everything about the day had pleased her, and she wasn't sure what to do with that.

The property was beautiful. Acres of green fields, hedged in by mountains that stood tall and blue like centurions keeping guard over the kingdom. You couldn't see the ocean from here, but it didn't make it less beautiful. She had the thought not too long ago that she wanted to go to the city. Somewhere anonymous. Somewhere she could get lost. She could get lost here. Lost in the silence. In the wide-open spaces, and the tight knots of trees.

But the idea of being alone like that, of finding peace in the solitude, was scary.

Cities were busy. She could walk down the street and never have a thought in her mind that didn't pertain to what was happening around her. To the people walking past, traveling in tight groups like schools of fish, to the cars going by in a never-ending current, horns blaring, exhaust hanging in the air, advertisements flashing all around in neon. It occupied her every cell, every space inside of her, until she was filled with her surroundings.

But this place hollowed her out. Left her with empty chasms and so much quiet that her brain rebelled, sending thoughts and memories to the surface that had been resting on the bottom for years.

This wasn't the kind of solitude she wanted. It was all a little bit too much. Too intense.

But right now, she was riding on a tractor, so that helped keep the internal monologue at a minimum. Especially since she was riding next to Aiden. There was something perversely enjoyable about it. Sitting next to him as they bumped along on the dirt roads, their shoulders touching, as if they were some Amish couple on a date. Though she supposed that Amish people didn't drive tractors. But whatever.

It was sweet. And old-fashioned. And about a hundred other things that she'd never had before. Okay, so the fact that she'd had sex with him at least three times last night—and was seriously thinking that they needed to do it again soon—wasn't particularly old-fashioned. But that was fine by her. He was…*everything*.

She'd had no idea it could be like that.

He was enthusiastic, and he cared about her. About what she felt. About her enjoying herself. He didn't sit back like a king demanding service.

He was telling the truth. It wasn't payment. And he had never treated it like that.

"I'm sorry," she said, shouting over the tractor engine.

"About?" He looked toward her, one dark brow raised before he turned his focus back to the dirt road in front of them. She studied his profile. His strong nose, his square jaw. Those lips. Very, very talented lips.

"Accusing you of asking for payment, giving payment, whatever. I don't even remember all the lame stuff I said. I know that isn't what this is. And you've never acted like it was. Sure, you've been grumpy, a little bit judgmental—both of me and of yourself—but you've never treated me like a whore."

He frowned, his dark brows drawing together. "No. And I don't like you using those words when you talk about yourself."

She lifted her shoulder. "Why not? Plenty of other people have said it."

"So? You can't let other people decide what you think about yourself. All those people… Do they even know you?"

She snorted, laughing to try to get rid of the pressure in her chest. "You don't know me."

"Maybe not. But you know yourself, right?"

She lifted a shoulder. "Sometimes."

"Casey," he said, stopping the tractor and killing the engine, "tell me."

Her heart stopped beating. "Tell you what?"

"Whatever you need to. Everything."

"Why?"

"It's on the tip of your tongue all the time. You insult yourself. You put yourself down, and you make it sound like you don't care. But you keep bringing it up, so I imagine that you do care. It just seems to me that you're carrying something pretty heavy and are asking for help even though you don't realize it."

"Wow, I didn't realize that you offered psychoanalysis with your orgasms and tractor rides."

"You're pretty transparent. You deflect when I get close."

"News flash, jackass. You're not close. Physically, sure, you're close. But join the club. That's what people do. It's what lonely people do. It doesn't mean we're connected. It just means we were both alone and we didn't want to be."

"No. That's not it. Not for me. I've been alone for six months and didn't need to find anyone else. Not until you. So it can't just be that."

"Maybe it is for me." She tucked her hair behind her ear, her heart sinking because she felt bad saying that to him when it wasn't true.

It *wasn't* true. She didn't like the truth any more than she liked the lie. She wished that what she felt for him— the attraction, the other stuff—was about loneliness. Was about wanting to keep warm. But it wasn't. There was something else with him, something deeper. Stupid.

She'd known him for a couple of days. She had known guys for months and felt nothing beyond vague annoyance and shallow desire. So why did she feel like there was something wrapping around her throat every time she looked at him? Binding her to him in the most uncomfortable, dangerous way she could think of.

"Okay, then. Say I'm not special. And that this isn't different. Why not tell me anyway? You're leaving. You're leaving, so none of this really matters. It's kind of a time-out, right? From the real world and consequences."

His words were even more upsetting than her thoughts. And that was stupid. What he was saying was true. It was necessary. She was never going to stay with him. She didn't do permanent. Not with locations, not with men. She just didn't. Someday, perhaps. But until then, she was not in the market for actual relationships. Actual friends or companions.

But talking to somebody…

She was struck then by the realization that she had never had an honest conversation with another person.

The closest thing she could think of was that moment her mother had told her there was simply no place for Casey in her life. When Casey had walked away from that home she had spent years yo-yoing back and forth from for the final time without looking back.

But she had never shared her feelings. Never shared her story. Had never sat down and talked to someone with honesty. She kept a wall up. It was necessary. It was the thing that had helped her survive. The thing that had kept her from crumbling into a puddle of misery when everything around her was just too damn hard.

Maybe this was part of it. Part of heading toward finding a place to put down roots. Maybe she had to cast off some of the burden here in Copper Ridge, so that when she traveled on the load would be lighter.

"I was in foster care almost from the time I was born. My mom was an addict. *Is* an addict, in all likelihood. But we're not in touch. She failed a drug test and I was taken from her. Put in foster homes. And maybe it would be six months, maybe even a year, but then I would go back to her. And she would try for a while, but inevitably she would fail another test, or the social worker would come and find she had been neglecting me, and I would get sent to a different home. That was how I learned to pack light and be ready to pick up and move when I had to." She leaned back against the seat, resting her head against the metal behind her.

It was almost funny that she was sitting here spilling her guts out in the middle of this beautiful scenery, sitting on a tractor with a farmer. Almost funny because for once she couldn't dredge up a fake laugh to help put distance between herself and the feelings that were clawing at her chest.

"Everything in my life was temporary. All of it. And I… I don't even think it's weird, because it's the only thing I know," she continued.

"Did you ever settle anywhere?"

"No. I stayed in one foster home for two years, and that was the longest I was ever anywhere. If you don't count my mother's house, which I was in and out of over the years. You just kind of pack everything up in a trash bag," she said, not really sure why she was telling him any of this, or why she was thinking of those big black bags filled with all of her earthly possessions. Garbage bags. Because that's what those few possessions she owned, those few things that rooted her to those years, might as well have been to everyone involved in shuffling her around. "And you go to the next place." She swallowed hard, not really wanting to think about the next piece of the story. The next thing she was going to tell him. "The place I was at for the longest time… I got sent away from there. Because I ended up getting involved with their son. I was fifteen, and he was seventeen. I didn't feel like I could say no. I didn't really *want* to, because I did like him. He was nice to me."

Aiden swore, but she didn't stop. But the more words that spilled out, the dirtier she felt. Like she was getting it all over herself. All over him. What did he know about things like this? Why should he have to know about it? Why was she telling him this? He would never look at her right again. He would know exactly what she was.

But still, she couldn't stop. Like the stitches had been ripped open on a wound and all the blood and everything else was just pouring out.

"Anyway, we got caught." Tears stung her eyes, and she hated herself for it. She wasn't fifteen anymore. She knew that she and Dylan hadn't been Romeo and Juliet. She doubted he had even really cared for her at all. But he had kept her warm. And he'd made her feel safe. And his mother had called her a whore. "And I got sent to a new place. Someplace that didn't have teenage boys. But I was just pissed then. So I found teenage boys at school. It's kind of nice to have somebody to protect you, you know?"

"I bet," he said, his voice blank. There was nothing. No pity. No judgment.

"And when I ended up on my own, I just kind of kept going the same way. I don't like being alone."

"Nobody does," he said. "I mean, sure, some people like being by themselves but there's usually someone behind them that anchors them, right? Even if that person isn't there they have a connection. Someone that exists out there in the world that they care about. That makes you feel like you aren't really alone."

She nodded. "Yes. Except, I don't. So, there's nothing, even in my memory, that makes me feel connected to anything. Sometimes I think that if I wandered off into the wilderness I might just disappear. I mean, if no one could see me… If there was nothing tying me here, I might just float away." She smiled, trying to feel it inside as well as out, because all of this intense feeling business was starting to get old. "But then, I guess that's kind of what I already do. Like a feather. A drifter."

"I bet more people think of you than you realize."

She looked at him, at his earnest expression radiating with more sincerity than she possessed in her entire body. She had no idea what she'd done to deserve this little moment out of time, with this man who was so unlike anyone she had ever known. But she'd had very little beyond survival for the past too many years to count to deny herself this. "I'm not sure they think of me favorably."

She thought of her foster families. Of the way Dylan's mom had looked when she'd found them together.

Whore. Slut. Ruined.

Damage done. Irrevocable changes made. Complete with a new identity. One that she had worn when it suited.

But Aiden didn't see that. He knew the whole story, and still he didn't see her as some filthy, wrecked *thing*.

"I suppose there's a lot I could say here," he said, his words coming slowly. "But they would be the right things to say, not the true things. Because the fact of the matter is I don't know anything about the other people who have been in your life. I can't tell you for sure what they think of you, because I don't know what kind of people they are. All I can tell you is that you have to live the life you want. Don't let other people tell you what you can have. Don't let them decide which pieces of your past define you and which don't."

His words hit her hard in the chest, resonated. They were painful, because they came with a stark, harsh realization. "I haven't talked to any of those people in seven years. I'm the one who decided that they were right. I'm the one who decided to go ahead and make it true. I'm not just talking about what I've done, but how I felt about it." She blinked, staring up toward the sun, closing her eyes, seeing red spots behind her lids. "Why am I letting them decide? Why did I decide they were right?"

"That stuff… You don't decide what to keep. There are certain words that get under your skin and stay, and words that you can't even remember the next day. Hell if I know what separates one from the other."

"Great, so what do I do about it?"

"I don't have any answers for you. Have you *seen* my life?"

"Well, you have the coolest tractor I've ever ridden on. Not a euphemism. You have a nice cabin. You have a family. You have a hell of a lot of things that I don't have, Aiden."

"I guess those things are like the words, then. Some of it feels heavy, some of it you really feel. And some of it you just take for granted. But you're right. There are good things here."

"Okay, we did show-and-tell with me. But why do you stay? Give me an answer this time."

"It's all I have. If I leave now, then what did any of it mean?"

She could sense the helplessness, the frustration in his words. And she was struck then by the strange dichotomy of their lives. She went from place to place, and invested in nothing, and she always felt like the void was just one step behind her. As if everything would be revealed for the vapor that it was if she quit moving. He had invested everything into *one* thing, and if he lost it, he would be staring into the exact same void.

The realization took her breath away. Made it feel like both of them were parked right against the edge of a precipice. And dammit all, if Aiden wasn't secure, who could be? Maybe there was nothing but emptiness beneath everything.

She didn't want to think about it anymore. And he knew everything about her and still looked at her like she mattered. She would think about that.

She leaned in, pressing her palm to his face and kissing him slowly, much more tentatively than she would ever normally kiss anyone. He reached up, wrapping his fingers around her wrist, holding her hand to his cheek as he returned the kiss. He parted his lips, sliding his tongue against hers, but didn't make a move to touch her body. Didn't try to take it anywhere past this. There was something intensely erotic about it, something achingly sweet and sexy that she'd never imagined she might find in a kiss.

Honest words followed by the kind of touching that was meant to forge a connection, not just find pleasure. The kind of touching she had very little experience with.

She was no virgin. She was no innocent. But this felt new.

They parted, and she was breathing heavily, and she wanted more. She swore. "I have to go to work."

"You sound like you don't want to."

"No guesses for what I would rather do. But Ace has been really nice to me and I don't want to take advantage of that. So, I guess I have to show up for shift on time."

"I'll drive you. Because I want to," he added quickly.

"And I believe you."

As she said it, she felt it. And along with that, she felt a kind of happiness that was foreign to her. She wouldn't have long with this. Wouldn't have long with him. But she would take it for as long as it lasted. And maybe, when it was over, she would feel like there was something tying her to the earth. A connection back in Copper Ridge with a farm boy that she knew she would never forget.

CHAPTER EIGHT

CASEY HAD BEEN staying at the farm for one week. If his mother had noticed the sleeping arrangements, she had said nothing. More likely than not she hadn't noticed. Josie Crawford had a way of ignoring all manner of things she didn't want to see. Like the state of the farmhouse she lived in, the financial state of the farm they operated, and the state of her marriage. As far as Aiden's mother was concerned, her husband was not a cheating alcoholic. He drank a little bit too much and sometimes he stayed out all night, but that was what men did.

She didn't see things clearly, because she didn't want to. As a result, Aiden had never had the luxury of burying his head in the sand.

Someone had to look around. Someone had to see things for what they were.

He closed his eyes, thinking back to last night. To *every* night spent with Casey since she'd come to stay. He wasn't sure he was exactly living in reality at the moment. But didn't he deserve a break? A little bit of release before he went right back to the grind. He had given up everything to save this place. And he was no closer to saving it. Not really.

Instead he had destroyed a friendship, the only real relationship he'd ever had, and lost the down payment he'd saved to get his own place. No wonder he was a lot happier retreating into the fantasy of Casey every night than he was facing the actual situation.

She had the day off work, and had told him she was going to spend that time exploring the farmland. Part of him was afraid she was just going to take off.

She will eventually. You need her to. This is a vacation, but that's all it is.

He finished shoveling out the stall he was cleaning and wiped his forearm over his brow. It wasn't an exceptionally hot day, but it was sunny out and the work was warm. There was more to do, but he had his mind on Casey, and that meant until he got a glimpse of her he wouldn't think of anything else.

He did his best not to ponder the implications of that as he leaned his pitchfork up against the wall and headed out of the barn. Casey didn't have a cell phone or anything like that. No way to text her and say that he wanted to know where she was. No way to let her know that he needed to see her so that he could be sure she wasn't gone.

He walked down the dirt road that led back to the cabin, thinking back on the conversation they'd had in the tractor a week ago. The story of her past made him hurt. But not for the reasons she seemed to think. Someone should have been there for her. Not some prick teenage boy who treated her like a convenience when she was in desperate need of someone to care for her. Not the foster mom who had blamed her because it had been easier.

He couldn't fathom how she had walked through so many lives, so many homes, without someone feeling connected with her. Without her feeling connected to someone. From the moment he'd first seen her in the bar he had felt something burn into his soul. No, he knew she

couldn't stay. Knew that there was no kind of future between the two of them, two people who were so messed
up they didn't know from functional. But maybe he could
just give her something without expecting anything back.

Superman complex?

Maybe. But if he wasn't saving people, then how
would he keep from focusing on himself?

He walked through the front door of the cabin and
noticed a small, square piece of white paper sitting on
the counter.

"Went swimming."

He frowned, grabbed the note and walked back out
the door. A river ran through the property, but he hadn't
taken her down there. But she very often worked evenings so she spent a good portion of the day by herself.
She probably knew more about the property than he did.
He had a trail worn from his house to his parents' and
the various barns and fields. He didn't just explore anymore. Not like he'd done when he was a little boy and
the farm seemed to run itself, and his dad seemed to be
able to do anything.

The path to the river was overgrown, weeds curving
in over the trail that had been so well traversed by him
as a child. He could dimly remember them going on picnics as a family. But that was before. His dad had always
liked to drink. And they would go down with cases of
beer. But it hadn't stolen who he'd been yet.

He pushed away the memories—they were as useless as his old man. Casey didn't have roots, but he did.
Deep underneath this earth, so enmeshed with the farm
that he wondered if he could ever escape. And he wondered if being a drifter might actually be the better op-

tion. What did roots matter when the ground they were planted in was poison?

He pushed through a knot of pine trees at the end of the path and walked across rocks that had been rounded when the river had been higher and the current stronger. The air smelled like wood and water, that cold, fresh smell that was unlike anything else. Not even the ocean.

The water was still and dark in this section, and in the center of it he could see a bright blond head and pale shoulders sticking up above the surface.

"Casey?"

She ducked beneath the water, and he could make out her pale form swimming toward the shore. She resurfaced, extending her legs out in front of her, and rolled to her back. She was naked, a smile on her face. She seemed perfectly at ease in her skin, never ashamed of her body. And yet, she seemed so ashamed of everything inside. He wished that she could see that her beauty radiated from in there. Sure, her skin was beautiful, and he liked it a whole lot, but it was what was underneath that captivated him.

"You're lucky I'm the one who came down here looking for you," he said, shamelessly taking in the scenery. By which he did not mean trees and mountains.

"Am I?" She readjusted herself so that she was treading water again. "I just would've stayed out there. You're the only one worth swimming ashore for."

She wore that flirtatious, sassy persona that came so easily to her. But even though he knew it was kind of a put-on, it affected him. He was never quite sure what he was going to get when it came to Casey. The vulnerable woman who was desperately seeking a connection, or the sassy bar waitress. He honestly liked them both.

"Well, that's nice."

"Are you going to join me?"

"I have work to do," he said.

"Swim with me," she said, smiling such a beautiful smile that it wasn't any trouble to look up at her face rather than down at her body.

"You're crazy."

She moved a little nearer to the shore where she could touch instead, water sluicing down her bare skin, the drops rolling over her bare breasts, down her slender waist. "Yes. I am a little bit crazy. But don't tell me you don't want a piece of this crazy."

"You're going to start something we can't finish."

"Who says we can't finish? I came prepared."

"Oh, really?"

"Of course. I left you a note, didn't I? I knew you would come down here. I knew you would come find me."

Her words settled between them, heavier on impact than she had likely intended for them to be. "Of course." His answer landed heavily, too. But whatever meaning was woven deep into the fabric of it, it was the truth. If she needed him to, he would come find her. For all the good it would do her to have some burned-out farmer's son come for her. But it was all he had to offer, so he would offer it.

"Big talk for someone who's kind of leaving me hanging right now."

Without thinking he stripped his shirt over his head, then made quick work of the snap and zipper on his pants and tugged them down his legs, along with his underwear. He kicked his shoes off, too, looking behind him just to make sure no one was coming. Casey might be comfortable with outdoor nudity. He was not.

"Now, that's the best view I've seen all day," Casey said, a smile curving her lips.

"Are you going to admit that I make you blush yet?"

Telltale color flooded her cheeks and she sank back down beneath the water, paddling away from the shore. "No," she said.

"Why not?" He stepped into the water, getting in as quickly as possible, breath hissing through his teeth as the cold hit him with the force of a tractor-trailer. "Damn."

"I didn't even think about all of the man problems this could present."

"Such as?" he asked, making his way deeper in, the water going up over his chest now. He was afraid it might stop his heart. If she didn't stop it first.

"Shrinkage is a thing."

"Nothing is shrinking over here, babe."

She laughed. The minx laughed at him after implying his dick was going to shrink. And it made him smile. "I like it when you talk dirty to me, hayseed."

"Well, I've never done it before, so I'm glad it works for you."

"How is that possible?"

"How is what possible?" He dipped forward, swimming toward her, wrapping his arm around her waist and tugging her against him, making the most of their height difference, since he could still touch the slightly slick bottom and she couldn't.

"How is it you haven't dirty-talked your way into a hundred beds? I've been a lot of places. Met a lot of guys. Let me tell you…you're the only one who's ever tempted me."

"How is that possible?" he asked, echoing her question.

"I've never been with a man just because I wanted him," she said, wrapping her arms around his neck, her legs tangling with his. "I always wanted a bed. Or a ride. Or just to not feel so alone for a month or two. But you… I just wanted you. There was nothing but want. You were like chocolate." She leaned in then, kissed him gently. "Something I can't usually afford," she said, her mouth still pressed to his. "But you've been so worth it."

He didn't feel worthy of that compliment. Didn't feel like he'd risked a damn thing to be with her when he could feel that this was costing her. And what the hell was he giving her?

He got to hold this wild, spectacular creature, if only for a moment, and she just got him.

"I think we should get to shore, don't you?" he asked.

She nodded. He kept his hold on her, drawing her tightly to his chest, gathering her in his arms and walking them both toward the shore. "Towel," she said, pointing feebly toward a sandy patch off to the left.

He walked in that direction and laid her down on the towel, positioning himself over her. He looked to the left and saw the brightly colored packet partially hidden in a patch of grass. "Well," he said, "you did come prepared."

"I told you I did." She smiled, completely pleased with herself. There was something joyful about it, different than the types of smiles he was used to seeing from her.

"Yes, you did."

"Wait just a second," she said, wiggling herself into a sitting position. She kissed his neck, his chest, lower. He knew exactly what she was going to do. She was pretty generous when it came to handing out pleasure, and he never refused.

But now, it didn't seem right. Not when she was so beautiful and perfect, a gift that he didn't deserve. She should have torrents of praise lavished on her. Should be worshipped like the goddess she was. Her life had been void of indulgence, and all he wanted to do now was indulge her. If this was their time-out from the harsh reality of life, then he was going to make it the best damn time-out anyone had ever had.

"No," he said, capturing her chin in his hand, "you wait."

She slipped her tongue between her lips, slipped it over the edge of his thumb and a lightning bolt of pleasure shot straight to his cock. Testing his resolve. Testing his control. But no, here in this perfect storm of recklessness, he would act with intention. Even though pleasure raged inside him, even though he felt like he was caught in the middle of a hurricane, he would hold steady. He would give her everything.

"Lie down," he said, his words a command, leaving no room for argument.

She obeyed, lying back on the towel, lifting her arms up over her head, crossing her wrists and lacing her fingers together. It was a pose of complete submission, one of supplication. She took in a deep breath, her breasts rising with the motion as she let her thighs fall open. He put his hand on her stomach, then slowly slid it down lower, between her legs, testing her readiness. Her skin was cold from the river, but her center was molten hot. Ready for him.

She gasped, moving restlessly beneath his touch. "You tease," she said as he flicked his thumb over her clit.

"A little bit," he said, "but I think this hurts me more than it hurts you.

"I doubt it."

"Be good," he said, lowering his head and kissing the soft skin just beneath her belly button, "or I won't give you what you want."

She shuddered beneath his lips. "Is that a threat? I didn't think nice boys made threats."

"When I'm with you I don't feel very much like a nice boy."

"Oh, really?" she asked, gasping as he began to trace the trail down with the tip of his tongue. "What do you feel like?"

"Just a man. A very, very hungry one."

He turned his head, kissing her inner thigh and earning himself a harsh moan, and a short curse. He had never behaved this way with a woman before. Had never teased, had never said things like this. Things had never been this light, or this heavy, with Caroline. He wasn't sure how that was possible. That being with Casey could make him laugh *and* make him shake. That he could feel relieved, perfectly at peace, while feeling like everything inside of him was being torn apart.

He shifted his position, wrapping his hands around her thighs and drawing her down toward his mouth, tasting her deeply. She gasped, rolling her hips up toward him, and he held her tighter, keeping her still to tease her with his lips and tongue. She was shaking, sobbing beneath him, begging him for release. And he lost track of everything. That they were outside. That anyone could walk up on them at any time. That this was temporary.

All that mattered was this. This moment. There was no reason to look beyond it. No reason to look behind it. He was filled with Casey. Her scent, her flavor, the sound of her pleasure. And he didn't want anything else.

She grabbed hold of his shoulders, her fingernails digging into his skin, and he had a feeling that she would leave marks behind. But that seemed about right. She was leaving marks everywhere in his life. She might as well brand his skin right along with it.

She gasped his name, shuddering against him as she reached her peak. And that was about it for his control. He reached over, grabbing hold of the condom that she'd stashed in the grass. He took care of the necessities, then positioned himself above her, kissing her deeply as he slid deep inside. It was like coming home. Cheesy as hell, but no less true because of it. She felt right. She felt like his.

The farm wasn't his, no matter how much he wanted it to be. The cabin that he slept in every night didn't have his name on it, and it probably never would. At least not for years.

But Casey was his. And right now, that felt sufficient. It felt like everything.

He buried his face in her neck, pressing himself as tightly against her as he could, relishing the feel of being so close to her, so connected to her. "What are you doing?" she asked, her voice a whisper.

"Just being with you."

He felt the flutter of her fingertips next to his face, then she slowly pressed her palm against his cheek. "I like it," she said, her voice strangled, soft. "I like it very much."

"Me, too," he said, not quite sure how he managed to force the words through the lump in his throat.

A shiver of pleasure worked its way down his spine, and he couldn't hold still for another moment. He flexed his hips, pushing in deeper before retreating slightly, establishing a steady rhythm that drove the need between them to a fever pitch. Pushing them both harder, higher than he would've imagined possible. Sure, this wasn't the first time for either of them. Not with other people, not with each other. But it felt like it. It felt like the only time. The only thing that mattered.

"Aiden," she said, his name a prayer on her lips as she trailed her fingertips down his back.

And he lost hold of everything. Of his control. Of the earth. And he gave himself over to his pleasure. Dimly, he could feel her shuddering out her release beneath him, but he was barely even aware of that. Shamefully, all he could do was focus on the need roaring in his own veins. It consumed him, took him over completely, a living, breathing dragon that grabbed him by the throat and shook him, left him limp and utterly spent.

She curved her hand around his neck, stroking her hand over his hair. They lay like that for a long time, nothing but the sound of the wind in the trees and the slow rush of the current filling the silence.

He didn't want to move. Didn't want to speak. Didn't want to do anything to interrupt the moment. Because the more time passed, the closer they got to the end of this. To the end of them.

"Tell me about them."

"Who?"

"The women you didn't talk dirty to." She wiggled beneath him, scooting to the side, and he followed her lead, readjusting so that they were lying next to each other.

"It's a short story."

"Perfect. I have a limited attention span."

"Why do you want to know?"

She lifted a shoulder. "Because I told you about me.

I kind of bared my soul to you. Seems like maybe you should tell me about your past experiences."

"There was just one woman," he said, speaking slowly. She was right. She *had* told him about her past. And it had left him with a strong desire to destroy everyone in it. He wondered what she would think of his. Such as it was. "My friend. Caroline."

"Oh. Caroline," she said, her voice sounding funny.

"What? You wanted to hear about it."

"I didn't know there was only one. I didn't know she had a name."

He frowned. "What do you mean?"

"I didn't tell you the name of the guy I lost it to."

"No," he said, "you didn't." He hadn't really seen it as significant.

"Because it didn't matter."

"Well, Caroline is a friend. She was before we were together." She wasn't really now.

"I see."

"You sound…jealous."

"I'm not jealous. I never get jealous." She sniffed. "That is not how I roll."

"You're upset."

She let out an exasperated sigh. "I'm not. Finish telling me about Caroline." She said her name like it was an illness and not a person.

"She kind of had it tough at home, too. Her dad used to help out on the farm. I've known her for a long time. Neither of us really wanted a relationship, but we both wanted… Well, you know how that is."

"Yes," she bit out, "I do know how that is."

"We started sleeping together sometimes. And after a few years I started saving for a house. I started wondering why I couldn't have something else. Something other than this. And I thought… I thought maybe we could have a future together."

"You were in love with her?"

"No," he said, knowing that for a fact. "I wasn't. But I wanted a normal life, and I know she wanted one, too. We cared for each other. We had chemistry—" He faltered on that, because now that he had discovered chemistry with Casey, he doubted if Caroline and him had ever had anything all that exceptional. "I thought it would be enough."

"Okay. So why aren't you with Little Miss Convenience with a picket fence and a kid on the way?"

She was being prickly. Defensive. Because she was jealous, whatever she said.

"Debt collectors started calling. And I realized just how bad things were here. That my dad had lost a bunch of accounts. That we were behind on things. And the roof needed replacing, and all number of things just went to hell, right at the same time."

"You gave them your money, didn't you?"

"Yes, I did. I'm their son. I'm all they have. It's not my mom's fault that my dad ended up being worse than a child. I'm young. I have time to rebuild. I don't think they do."

"Still, that was your money, Aiden. It was supposed to be for your life."

"I'm well aware of that. But I made a choice. And I told Caroline that things had to go back to how they'd started. No more planning for the future."

"Great. So, you told her that she was being put back into the booty-call category. That didn't go well, I take it?"

"Understatement. She was mad. She left. I didn't hear

from her for about two weeks. Next time we talked, she told me she'd met someone."

"And that was it?" she asked.

"Yes, that was it. We aren't really even friends anymore."

"No matter whether you loved her or not, I think she must have loved you."

Her words made his heart clench tight. "I hope not. I'm not worth that."

She frowned. "Why would you say that? Of course you're worth it. You gave up your future for your parents. You give up everything to keep working this hunk of dirt for them. To spend your nights dragging your dad's ass back from the bar. Feeding your mom's strays and taking care of them, so she can feel like she's doing good deeds instead of wallowing in her life as it falls apart around her. That's who you are. It's what you do. How is that man not worthy of love?"

"Because. I might just grow from this into the same kind of drunk as my father. There are no guarantees, after all."

"You don't honestly think that could happen, do you?"

"My dad used to be a really great guy. I know you didn't know your mom before she was an addict. I remember my dad before he was one. He laughed a lot. He took care of the farm. He took care of Mom, and me. And then it was like he just let his control slip. Stopped caring about how much he drank. And then he stopped caring so much about what he did when he drank. You break your wedding vows once, it's not so bad to break them again. And eventually, he didn't even try to keep them. There was a whole lot of life to your mother before she started using. I know you never saw it, but there was. I've never taken for granted that I could turn into that."

"It's easy. You just don't start."

He laughed. "If it was that easy, no one ever would."

"I hate her."

"Who?"

"Caroline," she said, rolling onto her back and looking up at the sky. "And it's not fair. Because I'm not a virgin. Not even close. But I hate her for touching you before me."

"That's a little bit possessive."

"Well, I don't have a lot of possessions. So, just for a little while, can you be mine?"

His chest tightened and he studied her face. Open, beautiful, none of that hard cynicism that he was so used to seeing present. "Sure, Casey. I would like that."

CHAPTER NINE

BY THE TIME they headed back from the river, the sun was starting to dip low in the sky. It had been like a vacation from life. The kind that Aiden had rarely taken. Being with Casey was a high all on its own. It wasn't comparable to anything else, to anyone else.

He should feel claustrophobic when she said possessive things like she had down on the shore. There were already two people in his life who needed him. Who tore him in every direction and used up his every resource. He couldn't afford one more. But she wasn't staying. She wasn't staying.

That thought caused a hollow pit to settle deep and low in his stomach. He ignored it. Because there was nothing else to do. He looked over at Casey, who was walking along beside him, turning her head every which way, taking in the scenery around them. He envied her. For her ability to see all of this like it was new. He barely saw it anymore. It was a blur of hard work, sweat and blood poured into dirt that didn't belong to him.

He felt delicate fingers touch his, and he looked down to where Casey was closing the distance between them. He should've pulled away, because there was no reason to walk through this property holding her hand like they were together. Like they were living some kind of fantasy where this belonged to them and the mountains in the future stretched long and tall in front of them with nothing but possibilities and ever after.

They moved farther down the dirt road, and Aiden heard the sound of men's voices. "I wonder what's going on."

"Visitors?" Casey asked.

"Who's going to visit us? My mom is out of touch with reality, my dad is a drunk and I'm an asshole."

"Well," she said, "sure."

They kept walking up the road and as they drew closer, he moved away from Casey. There was no reason to announce that their involvement went beyond casual acquaintance. Just another of his mother's strays.

Asshole.

Yeah, well, he'd said he was.

"Except," she added, even as he put more distance between them, "you aren't. You're a good man, Aiden. Even if you don't always feel like one. It's what you do that matters. Trust me. I've heard so many promises that they just kind of wash over me like rainwater. You are what you do. Not what you say."

She was trying to help, he knew that, but it made him ask himself what the hell he'd done lately to prove he was anything but a man stuck in one place.

When the house came into view, his pulsed raced ahead of him, blood pumping hard through his veins. "What the hell?"

He walked ahead faster, not waiting for Casey as he approached the scene before him. There were two men, and a large tow truck with his dad's pickup hitched to it. The old man wasn't saying much, just standing there looking resigned.

His mom wasn't out there.

She'd probably gone back inside. All the better to not hear any of what was happening. She could just pretend they weren't losing one of their most valuable assets as long as she didn't see it happen.

She would probably emerge with PB&J and a smile in thirty minutes like things weren't falling apart around them.

"What the hell is this?" Aiden asked, storming into the driveway.

"Sorry, Aiden," one of the men said. Aiden recognized the guy from around town, but didn't know his name, or care to. "Just following orders, you know?"

"You're repossessing my dad's truck," he said, his tone flat.

"Yeah," the guy said, almost apologetically. "No payments made for more than six months."

Aiden swore low and harsh, rounding on his dad. "Dad, come on. Why didn't you say anything?"

"Say what? That there was more trouble? That I spent all the money and I don't know where the hell it all went? Yeah, I could have told you that, I suppose. What's the point? You're worse than a cranky old man about things like that."

Aiden thought his head was going to explode. "Oh, you mean about things like keeping a farm going? Preserving our livelihood? Our legacy?"

"It ain't your legacy, boy. It's mine."

"The hell it is. Without me, there wouldn't be anything here. You wouldn't be here."

"No, you're thinking of yourself," his dad said. "Without me, *you* wouldn't exist. Get off your high horse and stop acting like you've never made a mistake."

Aiden gritted his teeth, rage pouring through him now.

"No. I never have. I've been too busy cleaning up after yours."

"Well, why don't you go make some of your own? Leave me to mine."

Sure, it was easy for his father to be belligerent and angry now. Easy for him to say that he didn't want or need Aiden's help. But if the time came when the bank decided to foreclose on the farm, Aiden knew he'd feel differently. Even if the old man didn't know it.

"Sure, Dad. But if I'd left you to it you wouldn't have the farm anymore. You know I invested more than twenty thousand of my own dollars into this place just this year. I was going to buy myself a house. But I'm here instead, giving everything to you so you don't end up out on your ass."

"I didn't ask you to do that," his dad said, not backing down, not having the decency to be shamed.

"No. But you benefited from it all the same." He turned around and walked away, briefly stopping in front of the tow truck. "Just take it," he said, continuing on away from the house. Back toward his cabin.

He could hear soft footsteps behind him, evidence that Casey was following him. Casey, who had been silent through this entire exchange. Casey, who had kept him away from work and the house for most of the afternoon, had him indulging in things that could never be part of his real life. Could never be part of *him*.

This was what happened when he looked away. This was what happened when he took time-outs, even for a little while.

And suddenly, it was all just too much. It wasn't her fault, dammit. He knew that. But he couldn't deal with it. Not all of this. It was like the whole world was caving in on top of him, and swallowing him whole. His dad, the repo men, the fallout his mother would feel…

And then there was Casey.

"Aiden," she started, her voice soft.

"What?" he asked.

"I'm sorry," she said.

"This is why staying is hard," he said, turning all of his anger on to her, even though it wasn't fair. "Because you just see how little things change. Year in year out. I stay and I stay, and this is how it is. Nothing changes. He won't change…"

"And neither will you," she said.

"What the hell is that supposed to mean?"

"You think you can put a Band-Aid on a mortal wound, and you just can't. But that doesn't stop you from trying. Year in. Year out. That's on you."

"Right, so I should run away like you do?"

She flung her hands wide, her cheeks pink, clearly telegraphing her frustration. "I don't know. But you sure as hell shouldn't invest your entire life in someone who doesn't even want you to."

"He says that, but he doesn't mean it. He doesn't actually want to lose his house. His livelihood."

"Well, he isn't a man who's earned the right to it."

"My mother…"

"Is a grown-ass woman. Aiden, at least I *know* I made my own bed. It sucks. But I have to lie in it. I mean, sure, I didn't have the best start in life, but blaming other people for my life now doesn't get me all that far."

"Casey, it isn't your fault—"

"Bullshit. Plenty of this is my fault. You're right. I'm a completely capable person. I can hold down a job anywhere. I could be midway up the ladder at…well, a semi-non-horrible job. I could be doing better than minimum wage by now. I could at least be renting an apartment. You know what costs a lot of money? Running. Living the way that I do. And nobody forces me to do this." Her eyes widened, her breasts rising and falling with the force of her breath. "Nobody forces me to do this," she repeated. "I do it. It's me. I do this to myself."

His throat tightened, and his spine went stiff. He was witnessing something he had no right to. A revelation about her life that belonged to her, or someone who meant to share the future with her. Not him.

He gritted his teeth.

"Well, fine for you. You're welcome to your little personal revelation. But I have a crisis to deal with. In case you didn't notice, we lost my dad's truck. And I don't necessarily think I have the six months of payments to deal with it, not on top of all the other expenses."

She spread her hands. "So don't. What happens if you don't?"

He laughed, forking his fingers through his hair before he turned away from her, shaking his head. "The whole world goes to hell."

"No. Your dad's world goes to hell. A hell of his own making. Your world would be opened up."

Aiden couldn't process what she was saying. Couldn't deal with those words, because they worked in direct opposition to what he'd been doing for the past ten years. He had given up everything for his parents. Repeatedly. To have her talk like that, to have her say that walking away was just that easy... It wasn't. It couldn't be. He was linked to this place. He was. He had poured so much work into it that now walking away and leaving it to fall apart was impossible.

"I didn't ask you to psychoanalyze me."

"No," she said, "you didn't. But I'm doing it anyway. Because you've given me a lot over the past week, Aiden, whether you realize it or not. You have. You look at me like I matter. I travel light when it comes to belongings, but I've been carrying a lot of weight inside. But you... you make it seem like I don't need to bring all that with me. I want to do the same thing for you. I know you worked hard to keep this place running. But at what point is it just a millstone? I know you see it as an investment, but I see it dragging you down to the bottom of the ocean and drowning you. You can't save what doesn't want to be saved."

He turned back to her, his heart pounding hard. "And neither can you."

CHAPTER TEN

CASEY LOOKED AT AIDEN, her heart breaking for him. She had no idea what it was like to be in a situation like this. To feel yourself being torn up by the roots.

Because she had none.

But she knew full well what it was like to have a parent looking at you like you didn't belong. To have them choose the addiction over you, over everything good in their life. She had allowed that rejection to become a part of who she was. She didn't want him to do the same.

"He's wrong," she said. "It isn't you. He just can't see it. They—they love the substance too much. They love it more than the people around them. And you can't make the choice for them. You can't choose to give it up on their behalf. It doesn't work." She swallowed hard, instantly back at the door of that small house in Kansas, the hot, damp air coating her skin, fear tightening her throat. "I stood on my mother's doorstep, with my one pair of shoes, two sizes too small, and my garbage bag that contained everything I owned in the entire world, and I told her that I was out of the system. She invited me in. Gave me some iced tea. We visited and then she… Then she said she had some errands to run so it was about time I moved on. She never asked… She never said I could stay. No one has ever asked me to stay. And here you are, staying and staying, and he *lets* you. But he's just bleeding you dry. It's what they do."

"My dad isn't the same as your mom," he said through gritted teeth. "He *raised* me."

"Right. He did. Do you really think that version of your dad would want you to be this way? Do you think this is the life that he wanted for you? He didn't build the farm to trap you. He built it to give you a life. He's lost sight of that now. Because addiction is a fierce and evil beast. But if it didn't have him by the throat... Aiden, he would want you to have a life."

"You don't know that."

"No, maybe I don't. But if what you're saying is true, if you feel like you owe him because you had good years with him, then I have to believe that there was a time when he was different. And that father... If he's worth any kind of loyalty, then this isn't what he wanted for you. It isn't your job to save him. Right now, the house is burning down and you have to save yourself."

He clenched his hands into fists at his sides. "Why? There's nothing else for me. This is what I have."

"You have *me*."

Saying those words was like tearing a strip of her own skin away, exposing herself. Exposing everything inside of her. She had been telling the truth when she'd said no one had ever asked her to stay. And she had never asked anyone to come with her. Right now, she knew there was nothing else she could do.

"Come with me."

He only glared at her, his eyes hard. "You're being crazy."

"Maybe. Maybe I'm crazy. But I can't stand the thought of you being here forever. I can't stand the thought of that man hurting you while he steals everything good from you. Come with me. And we'll… I don't even know what we'll do. But we'll be together."

"I can't do that."

"Then let me stay." The words broke her. Her pride was on the floor now, in pieces, completely irreparable. But she didn't care. She had to do this. "If this is what you need, then let me stay with you. Let me share it with you."

"I can't do that, Casey. I can't afford to be distracted. I have to get to where everything is sorted out here."

"What if it never is? What if it's never fixed? What then, Aiden? Are you just going to keep living like this? For the rest of your life? Why? To keep an old drunk in a comfortable lifestyle?"

"For my mother. Because she lets her love for this guy take everything from her. She stays when she should leave."

"Listen to yourself," she exploded. "You can see it when it's her. Because she's his wife. Because you think she should just be able to walk away. But look at yourself. You're staying. You're staying because you don't know what else to do. You're staying when you should have left years ago. No, you're not looking away and pretending everything is fine like she is. You're being stubborn because you want to save him and he won't let you do it."

"I don't know what else I would do," he said, his voice raw.

"I know. That's the problem, isn't it?" she asked, stopping in the path. "This is who you are. This struggle has become your entire life and you don't know what else to do without it. You're afraid of who you'd be without this."

She knew, because she'd done the same thing. Let her past define her. All the way up until this moment. This moment where she was standing in front of this man who made her want to stop protecting herself. Who made her want to stop hiding behind all of the trauma, all of the pain. Yes, her life had been hard. There was no denying that. No erasing it. It was part of who she was. And it always would be.

But it wasn't *who* she was.

"I'm not a whore," she said, her voice trembling. "I'm not useless, or stupid. I can be more than that. More than those things other people said I was. I want more than that. I want… I love you," she said. "I do. I love you. Aiden, I've never said that to anyone before in my life."

He looked as though she had slapped him in the face. It wasn't the most flattering expression to see someone wear when you'd just confessed your love for them.

"You've only known me for a week."

"It doesn't matter. I've known people for less time, and I've known them for a whole lot more, and I've still never wanted to say it. Ever. I know I felt it for my mom, because that's what you do, but I was never able to say it. I knew she wouldn't be able to say it back. Otherwise? I've never even been tempted. When I say that I love you, it's not because the sex is good. I've had sex with other men. When I say that I love you it isn't because I want a warm bed to stay in for the foreseeable future. It's not even because I'm afraid to be alone. It's not because I want some kind of an easy dream life. I see your struggles. I'm willing to inherit those. To share them with you. I'm willing to make your pain mine. I'm willing to drop the load that I've been carrying for years so that I can pick up some of yours."

"No," he said, his voice raw, a note of pure horror running through it. As though she'd just asked if she could cut him open and live in his chest cavity, not professed her love.

"I know I'm not much of anything," she said. "I do. I want to be more. I want my life to be more. I'm tired of everything I own being able to fit into a trash bag. And I don't just mean my things. I'm tired of not having ties. You. You're my roots, Aiden. And where you go…I want to go. And where you stay, I'm willing to stay."

"No, Casey, it just can't… You can't be saying that."

She frowned, tucking her hair behind her ear and giving him her fiercest glare. "I am."

"*Dammit*, woman, you're supposed to be my vacation. You're supposed to be a moment for me to step away from my control and have some release. You're not supposed to be… You weren't supposed to be another complication."

"Oh," she said, a sound more than a word, filled with pain and shock. She hadn't known what he would say when she confessed her love. How could she have? She hadn't even known what she was going to say until the moment the words left her mouth. She could never have anticipated something like this. Or the pain that the words had brought. She had been rejected countless times, in thousands of different ways, but nothing had ever hurt so badly as this. She was worn-out, she was jaded. She had learned to hold pieces of herself back in her every interaction with people. But she hadn't done that with him. She had *believed* in him. Believed in this. Believed in his ability to be more. To be everything that he seemed.

But, of course, he couldn't be. She'd thought of him as good the first time she'd seen him, and she still thought he was good. Better than anyone she'd ever known. But he was afraid. Afraid of letting go. Afraid of losing what rooted him to the earth. She had spent so much of her life living in fear that someday everything would fall away and reveal that there was nothing. But it was the same for him.

Family, a home—neither was magic. He didn't draw strength from them any more than she drew strength from her isolation while moving from place to place. Neither of them was immune. Neither of them was protected. And she was left to wonder what could change it. What could anchor you if none of that did.

I would. I would anchor him. If he would let me.

She knew that. Trusted in it. More than anything in her whole life. But looking at him, standing there with his jaw clenched tight, his expression uncompromising, she could see that he wouldn't let her.

That made her angry. Made her heart beat faster and her palms sweat. No one had ever offered her help. No one. And here she was, offering what little she had. Everything she had, and he was rejecting it.

"I don't think that love has to be such a terrible thing," she said. "Love doesn't have to be a burden."

"How would you know?"

His words ran her through like a sword, deflating her lungs, making it so she couldn't breathe. "I guess you have a point there," she said, the words coming out strangled.

She turned and started to walk back toward the cabin and he reached out and grabbed her arm, pulling her back.

"Casey, wait…"

"No. Don't ask me to wait. You can ask me to *stay*, Aiden. But don't ask me to wait if in the end you're just going to let me go."

He fell silent, the space stretching between them saying more than words ever could.

"Don't say you didn't mean it, either," she continued. "Because you did. You meant it. You don't think I know what love is because I didn't have a family to love me. But sometimes the absence of something, the need for it, teaches you a whole lot more than having it. I'm not used to love. I don't take it for granted. There is no way for it to be there and for me not to notice. I'm…changed by it. Completely. The way I think. The way I feel. The way I breathe. Don't ever tell me I don't know. I know better than you."

She walked quickly, then broke into a run, up the steps and into the cabin, gathering her things as quickly as possible. There were perks to having all the pieces of your life compacted down so small that they fit into one bag. It didn't take long to leave. And right now? She desperately needed to leave.

"So, that's it?" She heard his voice coming from behind her, and she forced herself to keep from turning. "You're just going to go?"

"Yeah. It's kind of what I do." She stuffed a pair of underwear into her bag. Then looked at the bed they had been sharing for the past week. She had been happy here. Happy with him. And it wasn't because the cabin was amazing. Wasn't because she wanted to live here the rest of her life. It was because this was where he had held her in his arms. It was because for just a little while they had belonged to each other when she'd never belonged to anyone before.

She'd never had anything that had felt too good to last before. She'd just had a lot of shit that had lasted however long it had lasted and then gone away. So she hadn't been prepared for what it would feel like when this was over. It was horrible. It was violent and shocking, tearing at her insides like a savage beast.

You always knew it would end this way.

Yes, she had. Except in the days since she had come here, during the nights when she had fallen asleep in his arms, she had begun to entertain a strange, warm glow in the center of her chest. One that she now recognized was hope. Hope unlike any she'd ever had before. Hope like she imagined she would never have again.

"I'm leaving."

"Leaving town?"

"Don't know." She shrugged one of her shoulders. In reality, she was no closer to having her car fixed. It was parked over at Jake's garage now, but it still wasn't running, and she still didn't have much in the way of funds.

"You're not going to tell me."

"What do you care?"

"Dammit, Casey, you know I care."

"Yeah, but you care about your drunk of a father. You care about this farm. You care about your mother. You care about a lot of things in an angry, protective way. But do you *love* any of it? Do you have any love left inside of you at all? Or is it all just grim, forced duty?"

"It doesn't matter. It's not about how I feel. My dad follows his feelings. Follows them right down into the bottom of a bottle. And I'll never be that."

"No. You won't. I believe that. But you know who you've become? Your mother. You were so busy keeping yourself from becoming your old man that you became her. You think you can fix it for him. You think you can want it enough. But you can't. *He* has to want it, Aiden, and the simple truth is that he doesn't. You don't know what to do with that. So you push everyone else away to try to heal this one broken person who doesn't even want it. This is why Caroline left you. Because she could see that you would never open yourself up to her. She could see that this was never going to end. And I see it now, too."

"Great. Maybe you can go find some other guy to give you what you want. That's what she did."

She shook her head, gritting her teeth against the anger and sadness that were fighting for dominance in her chest. "I won't. I'm not going to find anyone else." She laughed and shook her head. "I mean, there might be some someone elses. In the biblical sense. But…it was never like this before you. It sure as hell won't be like this after you." She flung her backpack over her shoulder and breezed past him, walking out of the house and starting down the road. Part of her hoped the whole way that he would ask her to stop. That he would be the first one to ask her to stay. She hoped, and she hoped, until she went around the first bend in the drive. And then she hoped some more. Until she was back at the campsite. Until darkness had fallen around her with finality, smothering the light, smothering her last bit of optimism. He wasn't going to come after her. And at this point, she wasn't even certain if the sun would rise.

CHAPTER ELEVEN

AIDEN KNEW THERE were no answers in the bottom of a glassful of whiskey. His father had tried to find them for years. He had never been tempted to do the same. But he was now.

It was such a dark, damp night, and he didn't know anything. Didn't know what he was going to do tomorrow. Didn't know how he was going to fix all of the shit that had just gone down. Didn't know what he was going to do with every day of his life that didn't have Casey in it.

It didn't make sense. He'd only known her for a week. She was a drifter who knew even less about love than he did. She'd also been the only bright spot in a world of darkness for longer than he could remember. What he found with her wasn't simply physical release. He wanted to share with her. Wanted to open himself up to her and give her pieces of himself. Wanted to take pieces of her back into him so that they carried enough of each other around that they became inseparable. Now she was just gone. And he felt empty.

It was nothing like when he'd lost Caroline. That had felt like an inconvenience. An annoyance, because he was a man and he didn't like the idea of his one source of sexual release being taken away. This wasn't about the sex.

He could live with Casey for the next hundred years

and never touch her as long as he got to wake up and see her face in the morning. As long as he got to go to bed next to her every night. It would be torture, but not like this.

She gave him more than sex. She made him feel like life wasn't an endless bid for control and nothing more.

She loved him.

The realization made his heart seize up tight.

She loved him, and it'd been so easy for him to turn her down because of the farm. Because he was too busy with it. Because his father required his care.

She was right, but she was also wrong. He hadn't become his mother, not really. But he'd been afraid of it. Deep down, more than he'd ever been afraid of becoming his father. And staying here, doing this, was easy in comparison. Easier than opening himself up again and hoping again. Because she was wrong about that, too. He didn't really hope his father would change. He knew he wouldn't. Aiden wasn't a fool. But he was a coward.

There was nothing to hope for here. Nothing ever changed. Casey… She was soft, alive, dynamic. She would change all the time. Would ask things of him, real things, that he'd have to dig deep for. Not just hard work and sacrifice.

All those were easy. They didn't cost anything but money. Didn't cost anything but sweat.

Love…love cost more. You had to open yourself up, show all of your ugly places and ask for someone else to give you theirs.

He would have to care for someone who wanted him, and keep her wanting him.

That was terrifying. Not a life spent on this farm, but a life spent away from it.

His chest tightened and anguish rocked him. He could see her face, the way she looked when she said that she loved him and he'd told her no.

This woman who had spent so much of her life being turned away by people, and he had just become one more in a long line of them. He was a bastard.

She didn't deserve a bastard. She didn't deserve one more guy using her for his own selfish desires. She deserved someone who would give her a home. Who would keep her forever. Who would give her all the chocolate that she wanted. Who would call her beautiful names, give her enough kind words to erase the ugliness she'd been forced to endure for all those years.

And if he was going to be that man he would have to leave for it. He would have to open himself up. He would have to release his hold on all this anger. He couldn't love her while he was angry. Couldn't give her everything she wanted.

Anger made such a wonderful shield, but it kept everything away. Everything bad. Everything good.

There could be no Casey as long as anger and fear controlled him.

He dropped down onto his knees at the foot of his bed, bone cracking hard against the floor. He didn't know what he wanted. He only knew it wasn't this.

That's a lie. You know what you want. You're too afraid to take it.

Yes, he was. He was too afraid to be the man she needed. Didn't know what the hell he would do if he didn't have all of this to hide behind.

You won't know unless you stop fighting. Stop blaming other people.

It was easy to blame his father for the situation he

was in. But they were *his* choices. His. She was right. He couldn't continue laying blame in his father's door. Not for decisions he'd made. He was nothing more than what he decided to be. And now he would be alone because of his decisions, too.

"No," he said out loud, rising to his feet. "No."

He had given up a future once. One that he didn't see the use in fighting for. But he was not giving Casey up.

CHAPTER TWELVE

SHE WAS DYING. Okay. She probably wasn't dying. But she kind of wished she were dead. And if someone called her baby one more time tonight she was going to shank them with the wrong end of a busted ketchup bottle.

Heartbreak made her mean.

Casey sighed and walked back behind the bar. She pulled out a towel and wrung it out into the bucket of water before setting it on the countertop to wipe at imaginary dirt. Anything to keep her hands busy. So she didn't, like, strangle someone. Or pull out her own hair. Or rend her garments in some biblical expression of grief she hadn't even known she was capable of feeling. Damn Aiden.

He was a damn ruiner. Worse, he was a fixer who ruined what he fixed because he was an assbutt who couldn't handle anything real.

She should know.

She'd been the same until a week ago.

And now she was...devastated. Stripped completely of all of her pride. Still waiting tables in a bar, alone as always, and hating it.

So, great. That had really worked out.

Except in some ways she felt lighter than she had in years. In some ways, she felt completely different even though the circumstances around her remained the same.

She was back to sleeping in a tent, but that tent had felt different ever since Aiden had made love to her in it. She felt different. She *was* different.

Too bad he was choosing to stay the same.

He was stubborn. He was scared. It was pretty sad when a maladjusted foster child was able to sort out her own shit faster than a guy like him. She grimaced as she continued to scrub at the already clean counter.

The door opened and she looked up, her heart rolling over when she saw the striking figure standing in the door, backlit by the sun. Without seeing his face, she knew who it was. She had to do a quick sweep around the bar to see if his father was in here. He wasn't. Which meant that Aiden was here to talk to her.

He walked deeper into the dining room, a white-and-red shopping bag clutched tightly in his hand. His jaw was clenched tight, his expression as stormy as the first night she'd seen him walk into the bar. He was here, but he wasn't happy to be here.

Then his eyes met hers, and she revised her opinion. He wasn't angry. He was scared.

Which, on Aiden, she had discovered looked about the same.

"What are you doing here?" she asked.

Out of breath and dizzy, she didn't have it in her to wait to hear what he had to say. If he was going to be awful, he could hurry up and get it over with. If he had come here to grovel, he could hurry up and get that over with, too. She'd suffered for long enough.

"I came to give you this," he said, thrusting the plastic bag toward her.

"Are you, like…giving me another piece to my luggage set for the trip out of town? Because that's fucked up."

"No," he said, his expression horrified as he drew the bag back toward his chest, opening the top of it and pulling out a bag of chocolate. "This." He thrust it back toward her. She could only stare.

"Is this...candy?"

Which was a stupid question to ask, because obviously it was. But she wasn't entirely sure why he was handing it to her in an empty bar in the middle of the day. Especially after he had just broken her heart.

"It's chocolate. You should have all of the chocolate that you want. Which is why I bought you a bunch of chocolate. It was supposed to be symbolic. Not offensive. But I'm bad at this. I'm bad at feelings. But I'm stepping outside my comfort zone. My very uncomfortable comfort zone."

"Which is?"

He took a heavy breath. "The farm. It's easy to stay disconnected from everything when you're throwing yourself into something that's so all-consuming. Even easier when you've convinced yourself it's the moral high ground."

"Right," she said, pulling the bag of chocolate into her chest and holding it tight.

"I was using it as a shield. You're right, I was afraid of becoming my mother. But not with my father. Not with the farm. I was afraid of what it would mean to love someone so much that I would overlook anything they did. That I would even enable their self-destruction because I didn't have it in me to speak up. Because I wanted to keep the peace more than I wanted to fix their problems."

"People like that... You can't fix their problems."

"I know. But I watched my father hurt her with his drinking and infidelity, with every broken promise, with no end in sight. I watched her retreat deeper and deeper into this fake idea of a perfect life. Love is… The love that I saw was toxic. It did nothing but destroy. At least in choosing to tie myself to the farm, it was something I could control. It was something that would never devastate me.

"I never thought I could save him. Not really. I was just trying to save myself." He rubbed his hand over his forehead. "I thought that I was doing it right. That sacrificing myself on the altar of the farm was somehow noble. But it was just a shield. It allowed me to keep everyone at a distance. And when you told me you loved me… It was easier to choose the farm. Because I would rather work hard for no return than make myself vulnerable."

"So, did you just come here to give me the chocolate and leave?"

He closed his eyes, swallowing hard. "No. I came here to tell you that I'm done hiding. I'm done dealing with other people's mistakes. I'm finished pouring myself out into something that can never be filled. I want more than that. I want you more than that. And it scares the hell out of me. To want something. To invest in something that can actually succeed. But being without you scares me even more. I love you, Casey. One week, one month, one year, one lifetime, it won't make a difference. I'll love you just the same."

She looked down at the bag of chocolate and flung it back on the bar top. "Then I don't really need this chocolate." She took a step forward, flinging her arms around his neck and kissing his cheek. "The only thing I really need is you."

"But you don't have to choose. You can have chocolate and me."

"That seems… That seems too good to be true. Like a whole lot more than I can fit in one trash bag."

"I'm a little bit heavy for a trash bag. I'll tear the bottom out."

"Then I guess I'm going to have to stop moving." She looked at his face, and his serious blue eyes. "Unless you want to. If you want to run, say the word. We don't even have to wait for my car. We can get in your truck and drive away."

"Actually, I was thinking that you should stay. We should stay. Together."

She smiled, her heart expanding until she thought it might explode. "I would like that."

EPILOGUE

STARTING FROM SCRATCH was never easy. Casey knew that better than most. She had been starting over every few months for most of her life. But this was different. This wasn't a temporary fix, short-term plan or a Band-Aid on a life-threatening injury.

She and Aiden were planting roots deep, and it would take time. But it was worth it.

"What do you think?" he asked, walking up beside her and taking her hand.

She looked out across the flat expanse of land, at the mountains behind it, then looked back behind them, at the view of the ocean. "I think it's perfect. Do you want me to start pitching the tent?"

He smiled at her. "You're ridiculous. We'll keep the rental until we can get the house built. And you can choose whatever style you want. It will be your house from the ground up."

Two years in Copper Ridge, two years with Aiden, and she still didn't know quite what to do when he said things like that. He had given her so much, and now he was giving her more. Her first home. Her first real home.

"I might be a real diva about this."

"You can be if you want. You can call me at work and harass me about light fixtures."

She laughed. "I might."

For the past couple years she had continued to work at Ace's. Aiden had taken a job on the Garrett ranch, owned and operated by Connor Garrett and his brother, Sheriff Eli Garrett, saving as much money as he could to put toward a down payment on their land. Their farm.

He had convinced his parents to sell theirs. It hadn't been easy. Emotionally or otherwise. But they were in a more manageable place, living much more within their means. Not all of their problems were solved, but they weren't poised on the brink of disaster, either.

Most important, Aiden was free to see to his own life, rather than obsessing over theirs.

"I'm adding a few new words to the list of things I use to define myself."

He arched a brow. "Are you?"

"Yes. Oregonian. Homeowner. Loved."

"That last one is the most important." He dipped his head, kissing her lips. "You are so very loved."

"So are you."

"Do you think you have room for one more word on that list?"

"Sure. What word? If it's *ferret*, I'm out."

"You don't want me to call you my little ferret?"

"Not especially. Anything rodent-related just isn't all that romantic."

"Well, good thing it's not ferret." He reached into his coat pocket and pulled out a black velvet box. "I was kind of thinking that maybe you wouldn't mind being called wife."

There was a time in Casey James's life when she'd felt like she hadn't had a connection to anything or anyone. When she'd thought needing that, needing anyone, would be a weakness.

But loving this man for the past two years had taught her the truth was just the opposite. It took so much strength to need. To allow yourself to be needed. To stay in one place and fix your life, instead of leaving discarded, broken pieces behind.

Here, with him, she wasn't broken anymore. She was finally whole. Finally home.

Tears filled her eyes, love filling her heart so full she thought it might burst. "I wouldn't mind. I wouldn't mind at all."

* * * * *

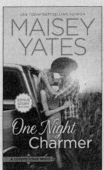